PRAISE FOR PJ PARRISH

"The past and the present come into stunning focus in this brilliantly crafted thriller. You'll love every fast-paced minute spent with Michigan cold case detective Louis Kincaid as he lifts the lid off a series of horrific unsolved murders and finds himself forced to confront their present-day legacies. Relentlessly plotted, yet filled with poignant family emotion, *The Damage Done* will grip you from start to finish."
—Jeffery Deaver, *New York Times* bestselling author

"Welcome to the Michigan State Police Special Investigations Unit, where cold cases turn red hot and Louis Kincaid finds a disturbing new home for his skills, his compassion, and his relentless obsession with rendering justice . . . *The Damage Done* is a gritty thriller with a high-octane pace and a beautifully-evoked sense of place."
—C.J. Box, *New York Times* bestselling author

"For the last decade and a half, PJ Parrish has delivered one fine thriller after another featuring the complex and compelling Louis Kincaid. *The Damage Done* is no exception. With a pace that never flags, dialogue that pops like a string of firecrackers, and a cast of characters so intriguing you can't look away, this newest Kincaid novel highlights the mastery of a writing team at the top of their game."
—William Kent Krueger, *New York Times* bestselling author

THE
DAMAGE DONE

BOOKS BY PJ PARRISH

Louis Kincaid Series

DARK OF THE MOON
DEAD OF WINTER
PAINT IT BLACK
THICKER THAN WATER
ISLAND OF BONES
A KILLING RAIN
THE UNQUIET GRAVE
A THOUSAND BONES
SOUTH OF HELL
THE LITTLE DEATH
CLAW BACK
HEART OF ICE

Other Novels

SHE'S NOT THERE
THE KILLING SONG

THE
DAMAGE DONE

BY PJ PARRISH

Clay
Stafford
Books

Published by Clay Stafford Books, Nashville
www.ClayStaffordBooks.com

ISBN: 978-0-9788427-0-3

Front cover design by Clay Stafford Books
Book design by Clay Stafford Books.

Printed in the United States of America.

To all our friends in the Mitten

I came to explore the wreck.
The words are purposes.
The words are maps.
I came to see the damage that was done
and the treasures that prevail.

—Adrienne Rich
"Diving Into the Wreck"

CHAPTER ONE

Something was wrong. This wasn't where he was supposed to be.
Louis Kincaid leaned forward and peered out the windshield. The gray stone building in front of him went in and out of focus with each sweep of the wipers, appearing and disappearing in the rain like a medieval castle on some lost Scottish moor.

But it was just an abandoned church, sitting in a weedy lot in a run-down neighborhood in Lansing, Michigan. Louis picked up the piece of paper on which he had scribbled the directions. It was the right address, but this couldn't be the place where he had come to start his life over again.

He rested his hands on the steering wheel and stared at the church. A car went by slowly and pulled up to the curb, parking in front of him, maybe fifteen feet away. Louis sat up, alert. It was a black Crown Vic with tinted windows and a small antenna mounted on the trunk. But it was the plate that gave it away—three letters and three numbers, just like all Michigan plates, but this one had an X in the middle.

An unmarked cop car. The driver didn't get out. But he didn't have to. Louis knew who it was.

The devil. It was the fucking devil himself.

As Louis waited for the man to emerge, all the doubts that had chewed on him for the last three days, piling up during the thirteen-hundred-mile drive up from Florida, were now pushing to the front of his brain, coalescing into one big question: Was this a mistake?

He had a sure thing going back in Florida, a new start wearing a deputy's badge again. But this . . . this was the promise of something so much grander, to be on the ground floor of an elite new homicide task force. And to be back in Michigan near his daughter Lily and his lover Joe.

But at what price?

The door of the Crown Vic opened and the man got out. He pulled up the collar of his windbreaker and reached in the back for a small cardboard box. Louis sat forward to get a good look at his face. He hadn't seen the man since that day back in 1985 when he had vowed that Louis would never work as a cop again in Michigan.

Six years had gone by since. Six long years spent in exile.

But now Louis was back. And the same man who had taken his life away was now offering him a chance at a new one.

Mark Steele hurried up the walk and unlocked the church's front door. It wasn't until Steele disappeared inside that Louis sat back in the seat. For a long time he sat there, then he finally pulled the keys from the ignition.

There was no point in sitting here any longer. The bargain had been made. It was time to face him. Louis got out of the Mustang, jogged through the rain to the wooden doors of the church and slipped quietly inside.

The church was empty, emptied of almost everything that told of its true function. The pews were stacked like old cordwood in a corner. There was a shadow on the floor where the stone baptismal fountain once stood. The faint outline of a large crucifix was visible above the altar. A cold wind swirled around him but he couldn't tell where it was coming from. Then he looked up and saw a broken pane in the large stained glass window behind the altar.

But he didn't see Mark Steele.

Louis moved slowly through the nave, his eyes wandering up over the dark wood beams, the ornate pendant lamps, and finally down to the dark carved paneling scarred with graffiti.

What had happened to this place? How had it come to be left to ruin? Why had they given him the address of an old church instead of the task force's new headquarters? And what was Steele doing here?

Whooooooo . . . ahhhh.

His eyes shot upward. *What the hell?*

The sound came again, deep and mournful, floating on the cold air from somewhere on high.

He saw the source. Up in the choir balcony above the entrance. Just the wind moving through the old pipes of the organ.

Louis scanned the shadowed corners but there was no sign of Steele. Louis decided to wait and looked around for somewhere to sit, but the only thing he saw was an old low-slung slat-backed chair up on the altar. He mounted the four carpeted steps, unzipped his parka and sat down, rubbing his eyes. He had driven almost straight through from Fort Myers, the backseat of his Mustang packed with his suitcases, boxes and Issy wailing in a cat carrier. A driving April rain had found him in Ohio and had stayed with him all the way here to the state capital.

Louis leaned his head back and closed his eyes. The soft wail of the wind in the organ came and went, lulling him. He wasn't sure how long he stayed like that, but suddenly the air around him changed—the cold displaced with something warmer. He opened his eyes.

Mark Steele was standing at the foot of the altar.

"You're supposed to kneel," Steele said.

"Excuse me?" Louis said.

Steele nodded at the wooden chair Louis was sitting in. "That's not a chair, it's a *prie dieu*. You're supposed to kneel on it, not sit."

Louis rose, his eyes locked on Steele.

The man hadn't changed in six years. Except for the clothes. The last time Louis had seen Steele, he had been all starched white shirt, black suit and clean iron jaw. Now he was wearing jeans, a blue state police windbreaker and a day's growth of whiskers.

It struck him again how odd it was that Steele had offered him this job without even one in-person interview. The first phone call had come out of the blue on a breezy Florida day a few months ago, from a woman with a velvety voice. She identified herself only as Camille Gaudaire, Mark

Steele's personal aide, and said Steele was offering him the chance to be part of a five-man elite homicide squad working for the state of Michigan.

He had one day to decide.

Louis had spent the next few hours walking on the beach, trying to work past his shock, telling himself that this must be some kind of joke or worse, some kind of weird Karmic trap. His gut still churned with anger at Mark Steele, but his heart ached for a chance to be closer to the woman he loved and the daughter he needed to know—and to wear the badge he so desperately missed. In the end, he knew this was his best chance to get back to Michigan, and by sundown, he had called Camille back to accept.

Louis came down the steps. There were a dozen things he wanted to ask Steele, hard questions about their volatile past and what appeared to be a chancy future, but instead he found himself extending his hand.

"Thank you for this opportunity," Louis said.

Steele held Louis's eyes for a second then shook his hand. "Don't thank me yet," he said. "This type of unit is new to the state. Things are still in flux. There's a chance this job may not turn out to be what you hope it is."

Louis stared at him.

"It may not turn out to be what *I* hope it is," Steele added. He moved away, his eyes wandering up over the beams and down to the scarred paneling. He turned back to Louis.

"What do you think?" he asked.

"About what, sir?"

"Our new home."

For a second, Louis thought it was a joke, but Steele's expression was deadpan. This was going to be the task force's permanent headquarters?

"It's . . . unusual," Louis said.

"You don't like churches?"

How to answer that one? His experience with churches was limited to snapshot memories of sitting on a hard bench in a hot clapboard building in Blackpool, Mississippi trying to catch the air from the women's fans. Or those cold Sundays sitting next to his foster mother Frances in the drafty

Presbyterian Church in Plymouth, so very aware of being the only black face in a field of white.

Steele was looking up to the choir balcony. "Lansing has quite a few abandoned churches, so I got a good break on the rent," he said. He looked back to Louis. "I'd rather spend the money on other things."

"I thought we'd be working out of the state police headquarters," Louis said.

"When you work in a glass cubicle you get a glass cubicle mind. You get cautious. You get limited. You worry about impressing the wrong people. I don't want people like that working for me. We need to be independent."

Steele went to a bank of doors, opened one of the confessional booths and peered inside. "We'll set the desks up here in the nave. There's also a kitchen and bunkrooms in the basement," he said. "We'll need them."

Louis looked around, envisioning long hours and living on coffee and takeout. Camille Gaudaire hadn't told him much, only that he would be one of five members of a special squad assembled to work on unsolved homicides, cases that had been long ago abandoned by local police. Lots of travel and long hours. And, given the fact this squad was Steele's baby, probably a lot of pressure to not screw up.

Steele's voice broke into his thoughts. "I imagine you have a few more questions for me, but put them on hold for now. I don't want to have to repeat myself five times so we'll clear things up at our first meeting."

Louis doubted that his particular questions could be cleared up at a staff meeting. They were too personal, still too raw, the experience in Loon Lake too vivid, even after six years.

"You find a place to live yet?" Steele asked.

Louis shook his head. "I just got in."

Steele nodded. "Check the *State Journal* classifieds. There are decent rentals near campus. We start back here Monday morning."

Two days? No way would this place be ready in two days. Again the question was there. What the hell had he gotten himself into? He knew what cops were like, how they protected their turfs. What kind of politics and shit went into building an investigative unit that operated separate from the usual lines of authority and webs of bureaucracy?

And again, stuck inside him like a hard-driven nail, the question: How in the hell could he trust this man? If something went wrong, if he screwed up just once, Louis had no doubt he'd be out, with no chance of ever wearing a badge again anywhere. There were no guarantees, no protection.

Steele headed toward the door. Louis followed slowly, feeling an urge to linger just a bit longer in his new home. When Steele pulled open the door, he paused and looked back at the empty nave, like a man surveying a newly purchased fixer-upper.

For some reason Louis felt compelled to fill the silence. "There's nothing here," he said.

"I have everything I need," Steele said. "I have the right people."

Steele pushed through the door and Louis followed him out. The rain had stopped but late afternoon fog was like being wrapped in gray felt. Louis watched as Steele locked the door, then went down the steps, over to the squat stone pillar on the lawn and removed the FOR LEASE sign. He went to the Crown Vic, popped the trunk and tossed in the sign. He turned back to Louis, still standing on the steps.

"Monday morning," Steele said. "Nine o'clock."

Then he was gone.

Louis zipped up his parka and looked back at the church. The stone pillar where the FOR LEASE sign had been now was bare except for the Bible verse on it. Some of the letters were missing but Louis could still read it.

The new creation has come. The old has gone, the new is here! – 2 Corinthians

Louis's eyes went to the name of the church on the top of the sign. It hadn't registered the first time he saw it but it did now. SAINT MICHAEL'S CATHOLIC CHURCH.

Michael . . . the patron saint of cops.

CHAPTER TWO

When Louis walked into St. Michael's on Monday morning he didn't recognize the place. The old stone floor had the gleaming look of a pressure-cleaned patio and the graffiti had been scoured off the confessionals. The stack of pews had been removed and the flaking walls had been re-plastered.

The sides of the nave had been outfitted with five plain metal desks, each topped with a computer monitor. There was a long table in the middle of the nave, a gleaming mahogany monstrosity that looked like it had come from a corporate boardroom. Four black telephones were clustered in the middle of the table.

Louis glanced at his watch. Twenty to nine. Apparently, he was the first one to arrive. His decision to get here early wasn't an attempt to suck up to Steele. It was more because Louis had barely slept since his arrival Friday, his usual insomnia made worse by the *rumble-blat* of I-96 outside his Super 8 room, and the rattle of the ice machine in the hall. Two days of searching and he hadn't been able to find an apartment. Stupid to think he would, given that spring semester was just starting up again at Michigan State. He just prayed he could find a place tonight before some maid discovered Issy cowering under the bed.

He looked at his watch again. Where were the other squad members? He was anxious to meet them to assess who he was working with.

He moved toward the altar. The beautiful stonework and murals were now hidden by three bulletin boards and a large green chalkboard, the kind that could be wheeled around and flipped. He felt a stream of cold air and looked up. The stained glass window was still missing its pane.

As he took a step back to get a better look at the window, Louis saw that it depicted Jesus surrounded by a cluster of men in robes and beards. The apostles, he guessed. The cold breeze was coming from the man kneeling at Jesus's feet—it was the missing pane. The guy had no face.

A door banged shut and Louis turned to the front door, expecting Steele or one of the other unit members. But it was a workman carrying a power tool. Two other workers drifted in, carrying boxes emblazoned with the word DELL. They gave Louis a quick glance before splitting off and disappearing beneath the desks.

Louis moved to a desk to look at one of the computers. They were alien to him. He realized that being out of law enforcement for so long, he was already miles behind whatever technology the state of Michigan was probably using. Hell, he wasn't even sure he could figure out how to run his own wants and warrants checks. His best friend back in Florida, Mel Landeta, had something called a MacIntosh, and Louis had meant to ask for a tutorial. But after that first phone call from Steele's aide, Camille Gaudaire, there had been no time.

Camille had told him that there would be some follow-up interviews and paperwork, then she gave him some concise marching orders: he had to get in top physical shape. He had to qualify on handgun, long rifle, assault rifle and shotgun. He had to familiarize himself with Michigan's most infamous unsolved homicides. Then Camille laid out the kicker.

You must attain a rudimentary knowledge of a foreign language. The captain knows you took French in college. He expects you to become fluent as quickly as possible.

Louis didn't ask why. He just got to work. For the next three months, he worked his ass off. Pumped iron in Fort Myers gyms until he couldn't make a fist. Tried to memorize the Michigan State Police policy and procedures manual. Faxed Camille the results of his physical and his firing range scores. Took a French adult ed course and fell asleep each night to the singsong sound of a strange woman conjugating verbs. He also read every book and article he could find on Michigan homicides, never sure he had the right ones, or if he was learning from them what Steele expected him to learn. And he turned down the offer he had with the Lee County Sheriff's Office, giving up a sure thing for this flyer of a job, so he could be just hours away from Lily and Joe.

Ils aiment. Nous aimons. Vous aimes. J'aime.

They love. We love. You love.

I love . . .

A sharp whirring noise made Louis start. The guy with the power tool was crouched atop the conference table and was drilling holes in the center. When he paused to adjust his safety glasses, he saw Louis and gave him a twisted smile.

"Never had to run phone lines in a church before," he said. He made the sign of the cross over his sweatshirt and went back to his drilling.

From somewhere deep in the bowels of the church came the sound of hammering. Every time it stopped, Louis could hear the wheeze of the wind through the pipe organ up in the choir loft.

The banging of the front door closing made Louis turn.

The man standing at the entrance was big—at least six-foot-seven. He had a bald bullet head that stuck out of his worn, black-leather bomber jacket, and meaty, bowed legs that were encased in faded, black jeans. As he came forward, the man took off his mirrored sunglasses, revealing two white raccoon patches pinpricked with small, bloodshot, blue eyes.

The guy had to be a member of the unit, but he looked like he had just gotten off a three-day bender at Daytona Bike Week.

He came forward and gave Louis a once over, and for a second Louis saw himself in the man's eyes—new blue blazer, slacks, tie, and white shirt so fresh from the dry cleaners it still had creases down the front.

The guy took an unlit cigarillo stub from his mouth and smiled, revealing big movie-star teeth. "You with the task force?" he asked.

Yeah," Louis answered. He stuck out his hand. "Louis Kincaid."

"Cam Bragin."

The guy had a vice-grip. When he let go, Louis resisted the urge to shake the blood back into his hand. But he did take a step back to distance himself from the burnt-cherry smell of the cigarillo.

The front doors banged open again. A large woman with wild gray hair, carrying a briefcase and wearing a bright red cape, paused just inside, her eyes wandering up over the beams and windows. With a flourish, she flung off her cape.

A man appeared behind her, as if by the magic of her cape's movement—short, wiry, dark floppy hair, and black-rimmed glasses. He wore baggy khakis and a green windbreaker. There was a huge mail pouch slung over his concave chest.

Before either of them could say hello, Louis heard the echo of footsteps somewhere high above and looked up to the choir loft.

Mark Steele was leaning on the railing, gazing down at them. Then he disappeared from view and reappeared on the spiral staircase that curled down to the nave. Steele was dressed all in black—open-collar shirt, trousers. All eyes were on Steele as he came up to the conference table. Even the guy running the phone lines had stopped his drilling to stare.

"Can you work somewhere else for a while?" Steele asked the man.

"It's your dime. I'm on triple overtime and need a smoke," the phone man said as he headed toward the door. As if by heavenly decree, all other banging and clanging in the church stopped.

Steele was holding a small cardboard box, the same one he had brought in the first time Louis had seen him. He set it down on the conference table. "Please, all of you take a seat," he said.

Louis took the chair closest to Steele. Cam sat down next to him and the two others grabbed chairs on the far side. The woman had a difficult time arranging her cape and briefcase in her chair and Steele waited, but not without a glimmer of annoyance.

"We have two people who have not arrived," Steele began. "Our fifth team member will be coming to us from the FBI, area of expertise: psychology and profiling."

A sharp clang made Steele stop. His eyes shot to a worker who was picking a wrench off the stone floor. Steele waited until the man had disappeared before he went on.

"The second person you have all talked to by phone," Steele said. "She is Camille Gaudaire, my *sénéchal*." He surveyed the blank faces before he looked at Louis. "Translation?"

He didn't know the word *sénéchal*, so he decided to guess. "Assistant?"

"Close but not quite right. She is my consigliere and will be your coordinator and chief contact."

Steele turned to his left. "First, let me introduce you to each other. This is Cameron Bragin. After serving his country, Cam went into police work in Chicago, distinguishing himself in undercover work. He's been ass-deep in narcotics, gun trafficking, prostitution, organized crime—everything on the criminal menu—but has never once been made. So, if you need undercover infiltration, male or female, he's your man. Or woman, if you will."

Louis couldn't help but think that any perp who took Cam Bragin for a woman had to be blind.

Steele said something to Cam in what sounded like Russian or Polish. Cam replied with a chuckle.

"Next up is Junia Cruz," Steele said, turning to the other side of the table. "Junia's from the City of Angels, where she has discovered there are few. She's an expert in cutting edge crime scene investigations, forensics, blood spatter, and bullet trajectory. She has significant contacts in the most advanced labs and universities in the country, so use her."

Steele paused for a second, as if trying to remember something, then spoke to Junia in Spanish. "*Los muertos siempre dicen la verdad, no?*"

"Si," Junia said with a smile.

Steele gave a nod to the small, dark-haired man. "Sanjay Thukkiandi. He likes to be called Tooki. He brings with him six years as an investigator in Madras, India, and three years as the FBI's leading computer tech expert. But maybe the best way to introduce Tooki is to quote something he told Camille during his interview. 'Like my computers, I am a complex machine, built of spare parts from the Madras gutters, the bowels of the FBI and the trash cans of Microsoft.'"

Tooki's cheeks reddened and he lowered his head.

Steele went on. "Tooki is not only an investigator in his own right, he is our technology expert. If the information you need is on a database somewhere in this country, he can find it for you. He'll also be working on linking us up to NCIC, VICAP, the new AFIS network, and as they go live, other databases that will allow us to search shoe and tire tread prints. I would welcome Tooki in what I have been told is Bashai, but that is one language I am still learning."

"It is not a real language, Captain," Tooki said softly. "Bashai is a loose polyglot of Indian English, Telugu and Hindustani. Impossible for an American to pick up. Plain English is fine with me."

Steele gave him a smile. Louis suspected Steele would try to learn the language anyway, just to prove he could.

Steele's eyes moved to Louis. "Louis Kincaid," he said. "Criminology degree from University of Michigan, ex-patrolman, ex-detective, lionized in multiple law publications as Florida's premier private eye and the captor of Florida's Paint it Black serial killer."

Louis wondered if the edge he heard in Steele's voice was ridicule or respect for the tabloid notoriety Louis had gained.

"Louis has been studying to become our in-house expert on unsolved Michigan homicides," Steele said. He paused with the barest of smiles and added, "Louis has exceptional instincts and a special feel for unsolved cases that you will all come to appreciate."

Louis held Steele's hard brown eyes, not happy with the description of his resume. It made his past sound sensational and his investigative skills almost paranormal. That's the last thing he needed with this group—to be tagged as some sort of celebrity mystic who dug through dusty folders.

"Louis," Steele said, *"bienvenue chez vous."*

Welcome home? Louis was so surprised it took him a moment to answer. "It's good to be back," he said.

"Now, as I told all of you, this task force will be focusing on Michigan's unsolved homicide cases," Steele said. "I have loosely modeled it after one of the first squads of this type, a three-man team formed in Miami eight years ago to solve the old murder of a young girl. A local reporter dubbed them the Cold Case Squad and the name stuck."

Louis had a vague memory of hearing about this squad at one point. His lover, Joe, had worked for Miami PD—had she mentioned it?

"As you may have guessed, I have a special affection for unsolved cases," Steele said. "I fought hard not only to establish this unit, but to get the funding and equipment we will need to be successful."

Steele's eyes moved around the faces at the table, holding the moment on edge as skillfully as anyone Louis had ever met. Even the wind was still.

"I am a believer in the power of justice," Steele continued. "Not because it brings closure to the families, because it can't. And not because it allows us, as a society, to get revenge by incarcerating the offender for the rest of his life because, as we all know, for many prison is not the hell we wish it was."

Steele took a deep breath.

"I believe in justice because it restores a balance," he said. "Not only in the broad philosophical sense of the way our world is supposed to work, but more importantly, in each of you. And you, above all others, need that balance. Do you all understand?"

Someone murmured a yes. Louis looked down at his leather folder, his thoughts drawn back to a PI case he worked in Florida, where the need to catch a killer had a compelled him to not only beat the shit out of the man, but to bury a piece of evidence in order to send him off to jail.

"To paraphrase Malcom X," Steele said, "our mission first is truth, no matter what it is, and then justice, no matter who it is for or against."

Louis was still back in Florida, remembering. Although he hadn't recognized it at the time, he had sought this balance Steele talked about because he had thought seeing the killer in jail would bring him that. But it had brought him nothing because in what he had done, there had been no truth. In the end, he had returned the evidence anonymously to the local PD.

"Now that we have all that out of the way, let's get down to basics," Steele said. "You will all be issued a new Michigan-blue Ford Explorer, equipped with video cameras, shotguns, rifles and a long-range state of the art radio that will allow you to communicate with the *sénéchal* from almost anywhere in the lower peninsula. The radio will also come with pre-set frequencies that will allow you to communicate with most major agencies in the state."

"Sweet," Cam said softly.

"In order to travel as cases dictate, you will all have a go-bag with you at all times," Steele went on. "You will also each receive a pager and a cellular telephone. These phones are high-tech experimental models designed to work with radio frequencies and should give you service anywhere your radio works. But they are not a hundred percent reliable, so please keep that in mind when you are working in a desolate area."

Louis saw Tooki nodding.

"They're also expensive to operate," Steele said. "Excessive charges will be taken out of your paycheck. And don't lose them. That cost, too, will be deducted from your check."

Louis lowered his head to hide his smile. For the first time in years, he was going to have a regular paycheck and it was going to be big. If he decided to impress his daughter Lily by calling her on the damn phone at least now he could afford it.

"In general, your schedule will be dictated by your work load," Steele said. "Even though you are all salaried, you will log your hours and travel expenses with the *sénéchal*. I expect a six-day workweek, no less than ten hours a day. We are converting the basement here to bunk rooms and there is a full kitchen, so when the work dictates that I need you here together, at least you will be comfortable."

Steele reached into his box and retrieved a thick blue binder Louis recognized as the procedure manual.

"You've all read this by now, I'm sure," Steele said. "Make sure you know the rules but keep in mind, in the end, at any given moment, you will be the one who makes those instant decisions we all face from time to time. Exigent circumstances, use of force, how far and how hard to push a suspect."

The room was quiet, except for the whistle of the wind through the broken pane in the stained glass window.

"Be aggressive but be smart," Steele said, "because the first time your reckless decision costs us an innocent life, gets a case thrown out of court, or brings unnecessary shit raining down, you're finished. Not just with me, but in the entire state. Are we clear?"

Louis looked away. In other words, exile.

When no one said anything, Steele went on. "One more thing before you get your first assignments."

Steele opened the cardboard box and withdrew a handful of black leather wallets. "Your credentials," he said.

One by one, he checked the name on the inside then slid the wallet across the table to its owner.

Louis opened his wallet. On one side was his ID card, the photo taken a few weeks ago on one of his trips up from Florida for new-hire processing. His eyes moved down the type. Louis W. Kincaid, Detective, State of Michigan.

On the other side of the fold was a gold shield cushioned in black leather. An embossed eagle sat atop the MSP emblem of two elk on their hind legs, bookending a man holding a flag. Under that were the words: *si quaeris peninsulam amoenam circumspice.*

He could still remember the translation of the state motto from his police academy days: *If you seek a beautiful peninsula, look about you.*

There was a lone word in the middle of the badge —*TUEBOR.*

I will defend.

"When you're all done admiring your gold, I'll ask you all to stand up and raise your right hand."

The sound of chairs scraping across the stone floor filled the nave.

Steele opened a small black notebook. "Repeat after me. I . . . do solemnly swear . . ."

Louis' face grew warm as the murmur of voices echoed softly through the church. For a split second, it almost seemed a dream—but he knew it wasn't. He was back. He was finally back.

"That I will faithfully discharge the duties of an officer of the Michigan State police . . ."

Louis looked around the table. Everyone had the same expression—restrained excitement and pride.

"With the authority invested in me," Steele said, "I appoint you detectives of the department of Michigan State Police. Congratulations."

Louis sat down, his eyes moving back to his open badge. Then he closed the wallet and looked back at Steele.

"Our first couple cases will come directly from the state's attorney general and his office is currently reviewing requests from local agencies," Steele said. "So, to keep you busy, I have selected unsolved cases for you to work on. Consider these cases a getting-your-feet-wet process. You're not being tested, but you will be studied. What I want is to see is how your mind works, how you utilize your tools, your skills and those of your partners. This process will help solidify you as a team."

Steele went up to the altar, dragged the large, green chalkboard to the center and flipped the board over. On the other side were five large photographs. Above each was a case number and a brief description written in chalk.

The Dumpster Hookers 1988.

CMU Death Ring. Suicides/homicides? 1990.

Palmer Park Wolf Pack murders 1985.

The Bay City Black Widow. 1989.

Boys in the Box. Copper Harbor. Found 1979. Died?

Junia was the first to get up and go up to the altar for a closer look. Cam and Tooki followed. Louis joined them, standing at the bottom of the stairs, eyeing the photos.

They were grainy blow-ups, obviously taken from case files. The bloodied nude body of a woman lying next to a garbage bin. A young man hanging in a shower stall. A battered body sprawled in a field of wild flowers. A whale-like bloated body on a rocky beach.

When Louis got to the last photograph, he took a step closer.

It was a color picture but faded to orange, as photographs from the seventies often were. It showed two small skulls lying on their right sides inches apart on a wooden surface.

"Louis."

It took him a moment to realize Steele was talking to him.

"Your pick."

"Excuse me, sir?"

"Cam has chosen the hookers, Junia the black widow. Your turn."

Louis glanced at Steele then looked back at the photograph of the skulls. It was the oldest case and he suspected it would be the toughest. He also knew he had to take it.

"The boys in the box," he said.

CHAPTER THREE

He wanted to start on the case immediately. Not just on the research, the digging through the old files. He wanted to see the place where the boys had disappeared. But it was way up in the Upper Peninsula, almost a nine-hour drive north from Lansing. There was also some more new-hire paperwork, dress uniforms to pick up, and tutorials on the computers and communications. And he still had nowhere to live.

At four, Louis headed out, want ads in hand, determined to find an apartment by nightfall.

He checked out more run-down apartments, most with empty beer kegs on the porch and loud music booming behind closed doors. He was about resign himself to living in one those sprawling modern complexes out near the interstate—places with fake fireplaces, community Jacuzzis, and lots of rules—when he took a wrong turn and found himself on Elizabeth Street in front of a large Victorian house with an APT FOR RENT sign in the window.

Louis checked his watch. Almost six. No time to hunt down a pay phone. He dipped out of the Mustang into a misty rain and jogged up to the porch. He knocked hard and, after a minute, the door opened and a teenage girl peered out. Thin, with straight hair dyed as a black as oil and wary, blue eyes outlined in blue, sparkly shading.

"Yeah?"

"My name is Louis Kincaid," he said. "I'm here about the apartment."

"My grandpa's at work. You'll have to come back." She started to close the door.

"When?"

"Tomorrow."

"Could I come back when he gets home this evening?" Louis asked.

"No way," she said. "He gets off at midnight."

"Look, I really need to find a place to live tonight."

When she drew back slightly behind the door, Louis gestured to his car. "I'm desperate. I have a cat and I can't find a hotel that will take her."

The girl's eyes slipped by him to the Mustang, and Louis knew she could see Issy's cat carrier atop the boxes in the back seat.

"Have you been living in your car with your cat?"

"No, I drove straight up from Florida and just got kicked out of the Super 8. My cat is old and she's had a rough few days."

The girl brushed aside a hank of hair. She wore five rings of different designs, one on each finger. "You got a job or are you going to school?" she asked.

"Job. I'm a police officer."

The girl's eyes clouded and for a moment she seemed to go somewhere else. "You got something to prove you're a real cop and not a serial killer or something?"

Louis dug under his jacket for his new wallet and held it open so she could see the gold badge.

"State police," she said softly. The blue eyes came up to meet his. "Okay, the apartment is three hundred a month and includes lights and stuff. You got to take your trash out every night to the alley, smoke outside, and keep your music down. There's a phone in the hall for local calls. You okay with all that?"

"Can I see it?" Louis asked.

She waved for Louis to follow her into a narrow, oak-paneled foyer. He got a glimpse of a living room with the TV tuned to MTV. A Michigan State Spartans tapestry hung over the fireplace mantle.

The steep wooden staircase creaked under his weight as they went up to the third floor. Before the girl even opened the door, Louis knew that, barring a colony of roaches or black mold, he was going to take the apartment.

It was roomy inside, taking up the entire third floor, with a bay window that overlooked the street and a kitchenette tucked behind louvered doors. The furnishings were spare—a lumpy burgundy sofa and matching chair, a double bed with a white chenille spread, an old oak dresser, a desk with a goose-neck lamp, a bookcase, and a scarred yellow Formica dinette set positioned in front of the bay window.

Louis turned to the girl. "I'll take it."

"Good," the girl said. "Now maybe you should go get your cat out of the car."

An hour later, he was sitting at the Formica table, sucking down the last of the Chow Mein he had gotten at Wong-Fu's down the street. It was lousy stuff, but he had been too hungry to care after unloading the boxes and suitcases from the Mustang.

He looked to the bed. Issy had still not emerged, even after he set out her water and Tender Vittles.

Louis pushed the food container away. He should have asked the girl—Nina was her name, he had discovered—where the nearest grocery or party store was because he really wanted a beer right now, and maybe something sweet.

Fortune cookie . . .

Sure enough, there was one in the takeout bag.

Louis broke open the cookie, and as he chewed it, he unfolded the little piece of paper. Though he had his share of strange experiences and had once met a girl who had convinced experts she was reincarnated from the Civil War, he still couldn't fully embrace anything he couldn't see for himself or prove. But tonight, after his first day working for a man who once hated him, he decided it couldn't hurt to take a look at what might come. *There are some people who must* break before becoming whole.

Some fortune. He tossed the paper into a container and put the food container in the trash. He stood, looking around the room. No TV, no radio. Just the steady drum of rain on the bay window.

He had already called Camille to alert her to his new address and a backup home phone. Steele had told them he never wanted them completely out of touch at any time.

Now, he thought about calling Joe. But when he tried to reach her at the station this afternoon from the church, the dispatcher told him she was going to be tied up all evening with a political reception. And Lily was at another ballet recital. Nothing left to do but unpack.

He dispensed with his clothes quickly, except for the newly pressed blue uniforms which he hung carefully, leaving them in the cleaners' bags until he would be required to wear one—for a ceremony, or God forbid, a funeral.

Then he turned to the boxes. His sparse collection of books—investigative manuals, a couple John D. MacDonald paperbacks, FBI agent Robert Ressler's *Whoever Fights Monsters*, and a first edition of Eudora Welty's *The Golden Apples*—took up only one shelf of the bookcase.

Louis opened the last box, in which he had packed the things that had he kept on his mantel back in his Florida cottage. It struck him that not so long ago he didn't have anything—except Issy—that he would have considered precious enough to cart from state to state. But now he did.

They weren't souvenirs or even keepsakes. He had gathered them from the people whose lives had touched his, however briefly. He had come to think of them as markers in both his work and his life.

He first pulled out a red wool hat with braids, then a black silk Brioni bow tie. Next came a baby skull he'd found on Captiva Beach after a hurricane. He took out a postcard from Lily, her first attempt to reach out to him after she learned he was her real father. On the front was a picture of

Greenfield Village and on the back one word: HI. They had traded many postcards since, Louis sending her cards from wherever his cases had taken him, hoping to connect with her, Lily always sending some version of a horse picture as her messages became ever less cautious.

Next, he took out a small, framed photograph. It showed him and Lily posed in a carriage in front of the Grand Hotel on Mackinac Island. It was taken last October, on their first trip together, the only time so far that her mother Kyla had trusted him to be alone with Lily. It was two weeks later that Lily's newest postcard came. It was the first time she signed it LOVE LILY.

Louis set the frame carefully in the middle of the mantel then reached back in the box. He pulled out a larger frame. It was a picture of him and Joe, standing in front of a frozen Lake Michigan, taken the day four months ago when he had first told her that he loved her.

He set the frame next to Lily's and reached down for the last item, an old silver frame. It held a photograph of a beautiful black woman. His late mother, when she was just eighteen. Before she met his bastard father. Before she began to drown in booze. Before she gave her seven-year-old son away to the state foster care system. That was the part of her he had not yet forgiven.

He kept her picture not out of sentimentality. He had barely known his mother. He kept it because it was all of he had of where he had come from. And maybe to remind himself that no matter what happened to people, no matter how deep into the gutter they crawled, there was always a "before."

Louis started to set the box aside when he saw a small object under a flap. He dug it out.

It was a snowflake Obsidian stone, a gift from a fellow cop named Ollie. It was meant to bring its owner balance, serenity and protection, Ollie had told him when he gave it to him. A few days later, Ollie was shot in the neck by a sniper and had died in Louis's arms.

Loon Lake. It was only a ninety-minute drive due north of where he now was. But what had happened there six years ago still felt so very close. Tonight, even closer still.

It was all still there, frozen in his memory.

A bronze, flag-draped casket below a cold, cobalt-blue sky surrounded by hundreds of officers standing at attention. One man standing apart, a tall man in black overcoat—Mark Steele.

Steele wasn't there to mourn. He was there to watch. Steele was from the state's internal affairs division and that's what those assholes did: watched and waited for cops to screw up. And the cops in Loon Lake had screwed up big time. So had Louis.

Things had gone mad, a chief had gone mad, and by the time it was over, three cops were dead, and Louis had taken his first life—his own commanding officer.

The actions of Louis Kincaid, while technically legal, were unethical. I intend to make sure Kincaid will never work as a police officer in the state of Michigan again.

Four days after Mark Steele went on TV and said those words, Louis's name was red-flagged by the state police as a trouble-maker, a man not be considered for any law enforcement position. Two months later, Louis moved to Florida and began to scrape out work as a private investigator.

Louis's hand went to the back pocket of his jeans, but it wasn't there. His eyes scanned the room. Where was it?

Then he spotted the black wallet on the dresser and went to it. He opened the wallet and stared at the gold badge and the two words STATE DETECTIVE.

There was a soft knock on the door.

He put the wallet on the dresser and opened the door. Nina stood there, headphones around her neck.

"You got a woman downstairs."

"Who?"

Nina shrugged.

"Did she say what she wanted?"

"She said she works with you."

"Tell her I'll be right down. Thanks, Nina."

He shut the bedroom door. What was Junia Cruz doing here? One day into a new job and already there was intrigue in the ranks. He threw off the old sweatshirt and pulled on a sweater and a pair of worn Topsiders.

Downstairs, he stopped short at the entrance of the living room. A small woman in a bright yellow rain slicker and matching hat was standing in front of the fireplace, her back to Louis. She seemed to be staring up at the Spartans tapestry hanging over the mantel.

She turned and smiled. "Hey, Kincaid."

"Hey," he said.

He had no idea who she was.

His brain did a quick scan of the faces of all the women he had ever known but nothing came up. Her smile spread. She was enjoying this.

She took off the yellow hat and shook her head, letting loose a curtain of curly hair the color of a new penny.

"Emily Farentino," he said.

"You dog," she said. "You didn't know who I was at first. Some impression I must've made."

He hadn't seen her in five years, hadn't talked to her or contacted her once, even though they had worked Florida's most notorious serial killer cases together. When the Paint It Black case had ended, he had gone back to trying to survive as a PI in Fort Myers and she had gone back to the FBI field office in Miami.

Then it clicked. Emily Farentino was the missing link in their team.

"Your hair used to be short," he said. "And you wore black horn-rimmed glasses." He smiled. "You look good."

"You always were slick with a compliment," she said.

He started to hold out a hand then drew her into a hug. When he pulled back to look at her again, he realized it wasn't just the hair and lack of glasses. Something else had changed. She had changed. Her eyes were a shade more knowing. She had seen things, experienced things, and it had turned her darker, like one of those old master paintings that took on a patina after being exposed to the years and the elements.

"You just get in?" he asked.

"Yeah, delayed by a storm," she said.

"How did you get on Steele's team?" Louis asked.

She arched a brow. "For that, you have to buy me a drink."

CHAPTER FOUR

Louis didn't want to end up in some frat-filled bar on campus, so he asked Nina where they could go for a beer. She recommended Dagwood's on Kalamazoo Street. "Get the fried pickles," she said.

It was a classic neighborhood bar, crowded for a rainy Monday night. A quartet of guys in Spartan sweatshirts. Two sketchy old men who looked like they had drifted in from the nearby freeway underpass. A gaunt man in a tweed jacket reading Stendahl's *The Red and the Black*. Two tired waitresses still in their Big Boy uniforms snarfing down Reubens.

They took the only empty booth and Emily ordered a bowl of chili and a Bud Light. Louis asked for a Heineken and added an order of fried pickles.

As they waited for the food, they caught up on where they had both been in the last five years. Emily seemed surprised Louis had still been working as a PI. Louis wasn't surprised she was still with the FBI. He was surprised, though, when she told him she had been teaching at the FBI academy's behavioral science unit.

Back in Fort Myers, when they had worked together, she had been adamant about wanting to be out in the field, wanting to prove herself as a special agent. This despite the fact she was a rookie, despite the fact she was maybe five-three and ninety pounds soaking wet.

"How'd you end up teaching?" he asked.

"It wasn't my first choice," she said. "But I was one of the first special agents with profiling experience and had the master's in psychology. When they were looking around to expand the forensics teaching unit they asked me to come up to Quantico."

"Did you like it?"

"I liked working with the students. But I ended up traveling a lot because they sent me out to field offices to train agents."

"I remember you telling me once you wanted to travel," Louis said.

"Oh yeah," she said. "Omaha, Jackson, Newark, all the world glamour spots. You haven't lived until you've seen Buffalo in January or El Paso in August."

Louis laughed.

"I don't think I unpacked for three straight years," she said. "It got old."

The waitresses brought their beers and a basket of fried pickles. They both stared at it.

"Your funeral," Emily said.

Louis took one of the greasy breaded spears and bit into it. "This could be one of the best bad things I've ever tasted," he said.

He slid the basket over to Emily but she shook her head and took a drink of beer.

"So how'd you end up on Steele's team?" Louis asked.

"It was perfect timing," Emily said. "I wanted back in the field but it wasn't going to happen. I'd gotten too good at what I did. But when Steele called my boss and asked for me, I jumped."

"You've left the FBI?"

She shook her head. "I'm on loan."

The waitress brought the chili. Emily ate like a starved kid, half emptying the bowl before she came up for air. She sat back in the booth and gave Louis a sheepish smile. "Sorry, I've been living on plane pretzels and 7-Eleven burritos."

"Did you get to meet the others yet?" Louis asked.

She smiled. "In a sense."

27

When Louis gave her a quizzical look she reached into her purse and pulled out a yellow legal pad.

"Cameron Bragin," she read. "Vietnam vet, Marines. Five years Chicago PD. Brief detour as stunt stand-in for Stallone on *First Blood*. Fluent in Russian and Vietnamese. Goes by the nickname Chameleon."

She looked up at Louis. "What, he has scales?"

"Bald as a baby," Louis said. "The nickname must refer to his under-cover work."

Emily looked back at her paper. "Junia Cruz. First job was as a dis-patcher with Inglewood PD, despite the fact her immigrant father made a fortune building a chain of laundromats. She worked as a crime scene cleaner and eventually became a crime scene expert with LAPD. Has been there ten years total. Fluent in Spanish. Nickname Cruz Control."

"How do you know this stuff?" Louis asked.

"The Feebies have files on everyone. I just went in and had a look."

He shook his head, smiling.

Emily took a drink before going on. "Sanjay Thukkiandi. Graduated University of Delhi at age fifteen. Busted at sixteen for hacking into Air India to score tickets, but not before he traveled the world free for six months. After two months in jail, he emigrated to London and ended up doing free-lance computer investigation for Scotland Yard. Landed a job at Microsoft in California at twenty-five and has been working there since. Fluent in Mandarin and proficient Bashai and seven other dialects. Nickname Tooki."

Louis thought about what Tooki had said about coming from the streets of Madras. Louis knew little about India, but he did know that it operated on a strict caste system, with a society of very rich and very poor.

"Louis Kincaid," Emily said.

He looked back at her. She wasn't reading from the paper now. "Dissatisfied PI, loner, wanders the earth like Caine in *Kung Fu*, looking for wrongs to right and women to love." She smiled. "And he's fluent in French."

"Not yet." He took a drink of beer, debating whether to tell her about Joe and Lily. He wanted to tell someone about the good in his life, but that part of him that couldn't share personal stuff put on the brakes, and he decided it could wait.

"What about you?" he asked. "What do you speak?"

She gave him a withering look. "Hello . . . *Farentino*?"

The waitress appeared, asking if they wanted anything else. Louis looked at Emily, nodded at their empty beer bottles and ordered two more.

"You know, the others all have nicknames," Emily said.

"Then we need nicknames."

Emily glanced at the professor reading his Stendhal. "The Red and the Black?"

"Too literal. Rocky and Bullwinkle?"

"Now you're making short jokes?"

The new round of beers appeared. They both took drinks and then Emily leaned her head back on the booth and closed her eyes.

"What about Steele?" Louis asked. "Did you look him up?"Emily opened her eyes. "I get hired sight unseen with a phone call from a mystery woman? You bet I looked him up."

She sat up and looked at her legal pad. "Michigan man all the way," she said. "Born and raised in near Mt. Pleasant, undergrad degree from Central, master's from MSU."

"In what?" Louis asked.

"Double major in psychology and legal studies, minor in art."

"Art?"

Emily shrugged. "I knew a cop once who glued rhinestones to her handcuffs."

"What was the master's in?"

"Psychology."

Louis took a drink of beer. "Any family?

"He's never been married. He has no living relatives, in fact," Emily went on. "He's an only child, and his father died of a heart attack when Steele was young. For some reason, Steele went to live with his aunt and uncle not long after the father died, even though his mother was still alive."

"Was his father a cop?"

"No, but his uncle was Mecosta County Sheriff."

"Where's Mecosta County?"

"West of Mt. Pleasant. Pretty rural. Biggest place to work is the shoe factory."

Louis took a drink. Maybe Steele's grieving mother thought her son needed a firm hand after losing his dad. And ending up a state police captain was a helluva lot better than stuffing boots in boxes. But just the idea of a parent dumping their kid on someone else because things got a little too tough hit a sore spot with him.

"So Steele followed in his uncle's footsteps?" Louis asked.

"Yeah, he started as a state trooper right out of college. It looks like his degree did him some good because he moved up fast and ended up in the recruitment department, doing background investigation and psych interviews for new candidates."

Louis nodded. "I remember that from my first job in Ann Arbor, the fit-for-duty shit."

"That led to a job with the Office of Professional Responsibility."

"Ah, yes, internal affairs, the assholes who bust other cops."

Louis realized Emily was staring at him oddly. He had heard the bitterness in his own voice and so had she. But he wasn't about to spill his guts to her about what happened in Loon Lake. But then, given her access to FBI files, maybe she already knew.

He took a big swig of beer. "Any personal stuff on Steele?"

"Well, he doesn't seem to have a nickname, if that's what you mean."

"What does he do, when he's not being king?" Louis said.

"He goes skiing, takes trips all over the world to the most dangerous slopes. Went to New Zealand last year to ski down some volcano there."

Louis nodded. "Expensive hobby. Maybe that's why he wears the same black suit every day."

"He also collects antique death masks."

"What?"

"Death masks," Emily said. She must have seen something on his face because she laughed softly. "It's not as gruesome as it sounds. In Victorian times, it was popular to make a cast of the corpse's face for identification. Turns out, folks liked to keep them and they eventually became collector's items."

"Still sounds macabre," Louis said.

"It's not much different than forensic sculpting." Emily punctuated this with a huge yawn.

Louis realized she looked exhausted. "Maybe we should get going," he said.

She sat up straighter. "No, I'm okay."

"I should warn you," Louis said, "Steele wants us to hit the road running. We've already gotten our first cases."

She raised an eyebrow, and he gave her a quick summary of Steele's approach.

"You all got to choose your cases," she said. "Which one is left?"

Cam had taken the hookers, Junia took the black widow and Tooki got the Palmer Park wolf pack.

"Three hanged students at Central. Apparent suicides but too many questions. Maybe a cult thing," Louis said.

Emily stared at him for a long time then looked away. He had the weird feeling she had gone somewhere else. The *swoosh* of the dishwasher started up and Louis looked around. The place was almost empty.

"Where are you staying?" Louis asked.

"A friend of a friend got me a townhouse out near Patriarche Park. Cute place but a little big for one person."

It didn't surprise him that Emily Farentino was still alone in the world. She was certainly attractive, but there had always been something about her that was all business, all career. Like a lot of women cops he knew. Hell, like all cops he knew.

"Those files you have on us," Louis said.

"Junia, Cam, and Tooki. Any of them married?"

She rifled back through her notes, then looked up. "None of us is married. None of us has children."

Steele had put together a team of loners. People without family or spouses. It had to have been deliberate because a man like Steele didn't leave anything to chance. He wanted the team to be their sole focus, the only thing they thought about, maybe the only thing in life that gave them purpose.

It was possible that Steele knew about Joe and didn't care. But Louis was sure Steele didn't know about Lily. If he did, there was no way Louis would have gotten this job. A cop desperate to reconnect with a ten-year-old daughter didn't fit Steele's mold.

"Louis?"

He looked over at Emily.

"Something wrong?" Again, the temptation was strong to tell her about Lily. But he knew he couldn't take the chance. He had taken this job partly because it had given him the chance to come back to Michigan to be close to Lily. He didn't want anything to screw that up.

"No," he said, "Everything's fine. Let's get going. We've got a big day tomorrow."

CHAPTER FIVE

The church was quiet. The only sounds came from the *click-click* of Tooki pecking away at his computer and the sigh of the wind through the broken window pane.

Louis had gotten to work at eight, but was the last one to arrive. It didn't surprise him. The team was primed and eager to move forward. Since the moment when Steele had handed out their gold shields, there had been an undercurrent among them, like they all understood they were connected to Steele in some unique way and that now their powers came from him.

The first business of the day was a private meeting with Steele. Junia Cruz had been the first to meet with Steele and had left quickly after, heading up to Bay City, the site of the black widow case. Tooki had finished his meeting as well and was now hunched over his computer, tethered by earphones to a CD player on his desk, almost hidden from view by a white case file box. Emily had been third up, and had said nothing to Louis when she returned. She went immediately to her desk and began to read the thick case file on the college suicides.

As he waited to be summoned to the choir loft, Louis concentrated on his own task—learning to navigate the computer.

The access the computer provided was mind-boggling. He was used to a dispatcher or admin person doing all the work, or wearing down his own shoe leather in search for information. Now, here at his fingertips was a new world of databases. Michigan BOLOS, warrants, rap sheets, driver licenses, inmate populations, vehicle info and anything else anyone had ever typed into state's computers. Even better was being able to tap into Lexis Nexis, a powerful search engine, and Westlaw, a new database of all trials.

Within weeks, Tooki had told him, they would also have access to VICAP, a FBI database that categorized crimes of a similar nature, an invaluable tool to catch serial offenders who crossed state lines.

Footsteps thumped from the spiral staircase and Louis glanced up to see Cam coming down from the choir loft. He looked different today— cleaner. Same leather jacket but new jeans and a pale yellow dress shirt. He carried a large, white storage box to his desk.

"You're up, Lou," Cam said looking to Louis.

Louis headed upstairs. He hadn't slept well. Too much beer with Emily and too much thinking afterwards. He had finally drifted off about three a.m.

At the top of the stairs, Louis paused. The choir loft was filed with gray shadows, silhouetting Steele and his desk in front of a peaked window. Louis hadn't heard music when he was downstairs but now he could—a whisper of a piano coming from the CD player on the otherwise empty bookshelf. Behind the desk was a credenza that held a neat stack of folders, a long wood plaque engraved with the words The Truth Takes Time, and a miniature wood staircase that spiraled up and stopped in midair. Something an architect might create as a model, Louis guessed—a staircase to nowhere.

"Louis, come in."

Steele stood up and gestured to a chair in front of his desk. Today he wore a crisp white shirt with a burgundy tie, the only color to break up the black vest and slacks. A matching suit coat was draped the back of his chair.

Louis saw the jewel case for the CD sitting on Steele's desk and could read the title—George Winston's *Winter into Spring*.

"Sit down, please."

Louis took the chair and waited as Steele reached back to pick up a thin manila folder from the credenza. He handed it to Louis then sat down.

"I was finally able to get the case file on the boys in the box," he said.

Louis opened the folder. Inside was the same photo of the skulls that had been tacked to the board yesterday. Clipped to the picture was a Xerox of an article from the *Daily Mining Gazette*, the northwest UP's newspaper. The headline read: BONES FOUND IN MINE. The date was October, 1979.

Louis scanned the short article, which revealed little more than the fact that the bones were found in a wooden box by two teenagers trespassing in an old copper mine.

There was a second shorter article about how the community was organizing a memorial service and burial for the boys, whose remains had never been claimed.

Louis looked up at Steele. "Where's the rest?"

"There is nothing else."

"There has to be more," Louis said. "The ME's report, witness statements, interviews, forensic tests on the bones. Where is the real file?"

"I imagine it's locked away in some dusty store room in the Keweenaw County Sheriff's Office."

For a second or two, Louis could only stare at Steele. "I don't understand, sir," he said finally. "If the sheriff's office up there asked the state to come in this why didn't they provide you with what they had?"

"They never asked us in," Steele said. "You're going to have to persuade them to extend an invitation."

Louis was quiet, remembering his last case here in Michigan back in December, up on Mackinac Island. State investigator Norm Rafsky had treated the local police chief like he was a dog catcher. In the end, Rafsky turned out to be a decent guy—in fact Rafsky's recommendation was one of the reasons Louis had gotten this job—but in the early days of the investigation Rafsky's hubris and condescension had won him no friends and no cooperation.

Louis remembered what Steele had said the first day, that the real work would come later, that these cases were only to see how they handled themselves. But Emily had been given a thick case file and both Cam and Tooki had full evidence boxes. Was this some kind of special test?

Louis set the folder on the desk. "With all due respect, sir," he said, "I don't like the idea of muscling my way into a small agency's investigation when they haven't asked for help."

"I don't expect you to muscle anyone," Steele said. "I expect you to use persuasion."

The music was there again, a slow, solemn trill of piano chords. Steele reached back and turned the music down. It seemed a long time before he spoke again.

"Listen to me, Louis," Steele said. "Most of the time we're invited in. But there have been times in my career when I have felt compelled to pursue jurisdiction. In all but one case we were successful in bringing a killer to justice and saving lives."

And the one time you failed?

The question was there but Louis didn't ask it. He already knew the answer. The failure had been the Loon Lake cop killings.

"We are justice seekers, Louis," Steele said. "That's what we do and who we are. And we do not let small town sheriffs, politics, lack of evidence, or even time get in our way."

Steele picked up the thin file, and for a second tine, held it out to Louis. "Until we get other cases, this is your focus. Make something happen."

Louis took the folder. "Yes, sir."

Steele picked up a second folder from his credenza. "Here is some background on Keweenaw County Sheriff, Reuben Nurmi. It will help you figure out how best to approach him."

Of course, Louis thought, wasn't that the nut truth behind psychology? Know the man's mind and you have his heart. Louis accepted the second folder.

"I want you up there by tonight," Steele said. "Check in with Camille after you talk to the sheriff."

Louis stood up and left the loft. He could hear the piano music again as he went down the spiral staircase. Everyone was gone but Cam, who was at his desk, sipping a Mountain Dew as he read his hooker files.

Louis went to his desk and put the folders in his new briefcase. When he grabbed his jacket off the chair, Cam looked up.

"Where you off to?" he asked.

"Keweenaw Peninsula."

Cam swung his chair around. "Keweenaw," he said. "My grandfather used to talk about that place all the time."

"He from there?" Louis asked.

"Nah, just made a few trips up to hunt until diabetes took his feet. But he absolutely fucking loved it up there. Called it God's Country."

Louis snapped his briefcase shut. "I have to get going. Catch you in a few days."

"Yeah, sure," Cam said as he turned back to his files.

"Stay safe, my friend, and watch out for the wolves."

CHAPTER SIX

It was almost a nine-hour drive to Keweenaw but, five hours in, he was stiff and had a hunger-headache from the Ho Hos and coffee he had grabbed back at the Marathon station before leaving Lansing.

He had been to the Upper Peninsula before, but he had forgotten how long the distances were between towns and how desolate it could be—especially now in early April when the tourists hadn't yet returned and there was nothing to relieve the eye except spindly pines and heaps of dirty snow bordering the blacktop.

The road was deserted. He hadn't seen a town of any size since crossing the Mackinac Bridge hours ago. He needed a hamburger, a Dr Pepper and a bathroom.

Hell with this.

Louis slapped the button on the dash to start the gumball light and floored it. The Explorer shot ahead, the red needle creeping up toward ninety.

He didn't let off the gas until he hit Munising. In a log cabin restaurant called The Dogpatch, he wolfed down a steak sandwich, fries and a Dr Pepper, grabbed a postcard for Lily from the cash register, and was back on the road by three.

Just after Marquette, Louis picked up US-41 and he had the crazy thought that if he turned around right now he could take the road all the way back down to Fort Myers.

It was another monotonous two-hour drive through pine forests before he hit Houghton, a hilly college town of red brick buildings. Across a suspension bridge, through Hancock and Calumet, and he was back out in the trees again. He was in the Keweenaw Peninsula, the huge expanse of empty land that extended like a crooked finger out into Lake Superior, pointing the way toward the Canadian wilderness beyond.

Every ten miles or so, he would pass through a knot of weathered buildings. But he didn't take notice of the names of the little towns on the small state-issue green signs. There were no stores that he could see, no businesses of any kind except one boarded-up motel and an abandoned building bearing the letters THE LAST PLACE ON EARTH.

What the hell did people up here do for a living?

He knew the area had once been a big mining center—copper, iron, silver, even some gold. But all of that had closed down decades ago. The harsh winters probably ruled out any kind of farming, so that left logging and tourism.

His thoughts turned to Reuben Nurmi. Back in Munising, as he ate his lunch, Louis had read Steele's file on the sheriff. Nurmi was fifty-two, a born-and-raised Yooper, working for a logging company in L'Ance before he joined the Keweenaw County Sheriff's Department. He had just been elected to his second term as sheriff.

Louis knew what his reception in Eagle River would be like. The sheriff had no college degree and was probably a little defensive about it. Entrenched in his small town and protective of its people and its past. And like all cops everywhere, suspicious and probably resentful of any state interference.

Louis had called Nurmi's office before he left Munising and reached a woman named Monica. When he told her he was coming to talk about the old case of the boys in the box, her response had polite but clipped. She had told him she would advise the sheriff he was coming.

Eagle River was a small collection of well-tended homes with no business center that he could see. His directions said to turn at the "big, white community center" and the sheriff's office, housed behind the county courthouse, would be just beyond that. He slowed as he came up on the courthouse. It was an imposing building for a town this size, a big, white-pillared building that reminded him of the courthouses back in Mississippi. He parked next to a low brick wall and found the sheriff's office in the rear.

Inside, everything was modern and cut into clean cubicles with all the new computers and radios a good force might need. Beneath it all was a pleasing smell of old wood and fireplace ash. The wood wall clock was in the shape of the Michigan mitten. It was almost six. He was a little early.

"Sheriff Nurmi is expecting me," he said, flipping open his state police wallet to the pretty, plump brunette woman manning the reception desk. The nameplate read MONICA. She was wearing a pink sweatshirt, the front emblazoned with the initials from some college called SISU.

"You made good time," she said with a gap-toothed smile.

"The roads were empty."

"They always are." She punched a phone button. "He's here, Sheriff."

She motioned to her left and Louis saw a man waving him toward the glass office in back. There was no one else in the small office, no chatter coming from the dispatch radio. Louis wondered how many officers the department had.

The man sitting behind the desk wore a crisp, dark-brown uniform shirt and a tan tie. He had a pleasant, pink face, sparse hair, and warm, blue eyes that reminded Louis of the Florida Gulf. He reached across his neat desk and extended a hand.

"Reuben Nurmi. Good to meet ya," he said in a voice that sounded like it belonged on some late-night jazz station. Except for the distinctive Yooper twang. Louis had always liked the accent, which fell somewhere between the hard nasal vowels of Detroit and the odd lilt of Canada.

"Louis Kincaid. Thanks for seeing me, Sheriff."

Nurmi motioned to a chair and Louis sat down. "No problem. I'm happy to help the state out on this. Though I really don't know what I can offer."

The guy was actually smiling. Cam's words came back to Louis in that moment. *Watch out for wolves.*

"So, where do we start?"

"A few questions maybe?" Louis said.

Nurmi nodded. "Shoot."

"You weren't here twelve years ago when the remains were found in '79?"

"That's right. I'm not from Eagle River. I lived most my life down in L'Ance. Sheriff Tom Halko was here then. He passed on almost four years ago now. Found him dead in his bed, right on Christmas morning. Heart attack."

"What do you know about the case?" Louis asked.

Nurmi shook his head slowly. "Not much. Just talk around town but that's not worth much, eh? But I had one of my men give 'er tarpaper for you."

"Pardon?"

Nurmi smiled. "I've had one of my deputies working hard since your call earlier. He pulled everything he could find on the case for you. Wasn't easy. Things were sort of disorganized before I took over." He pushed the folder across the desk. "Go ahead, take look."

There was a touch of pride in the sheriff's voice. Louis patted his jacket pocket, found his reading glasses and slipped them on. He opened the file and did a quick scan of the tabs—police reports, autopsy results, witness statements, and photographs. He pulled out the autopsy report. The first thing he noticed was that the report wasn't from a state lab, but from a place called Blue Water Laboratories out of Houghton.

"What's this lab, Blue Water?"

"Bunch of quacks who decided to start their own forensic lab back in the late seventies," Nurmi said. "Half the cases they worked on were thrown out and they finally lost their accreditation due to corruption. They're long gone."

Louis wondered why any sheriff would entrust the remains of two children to a disreputable lab when the state facility was just a few hours down the road in Marquette. Probably trying to save money.

Blue Water Labs had placed the year of death somewhere between 1965 and 1975. That seemed an intentionally vague span and Louis knew— *hoped*—that now the Marquette lab could be more precise. He would have the bones exhumed and take them there.

He pulled out the stack of photographs and sifted through them quickly—exteriors of a mine entrance and interiors of the mine shaft, many shots of the grounds. He stopped briefly at the photograph showing just the skulls in the wooden box, the same photo from his own thin file, but then he moved on to others that showed the whole skeletons laid out on stainless steel tables.

There were many photos of the empty wooden box. He paused at one, a close-up of the side on which lettering was clearly visible—GOODWIN M'F'G COMPANY MINING CANDLES ST. LOUIS MO. U.S.A.

"Candles?" Louis said, turning the photo toward Nurmi.

The sheriff glanced at it and nodded. "The mines were all lit by candles in the old days. They were lighter to carry than lanterns and put out more light."

"Are these boxes rare?"

"They are now. Twenty years ago you could still find them if you went deep enough into the old mines. Folks were always going in there looking for junk they could sell to tourists. But things are picked pretty clean now. And you can't really get inside the mines anymore. Only place you find a candle box these days is in some fancy antique store."

Louis slid the photographs back in the folder to go over later. "Hard to believe no one ever came forward to claim these boys," he said.

Nurmi just nodded.

"Where are their remains?" Louis asked.

"Well, you know, I couldn't find any internment notice, but I'm think-ing they would be at Evergreen Cemetery. You passed it coming in."

"And what about the candle box?" Louis asked.

"It's down in the courthouse basement with all the other physical evidence."

"Can I see it?"

The sheriff looked out over Louis's shoulder toward the window. Louis turned and saw the brunette woman pointing her pencil up at the wall clock.

"Well, it'll have to wait until tomorrow. My wife says our time is up," Nurmi said with a small smile. "Come on, I'll walk you out."

Louis rose, gathering up the file, trying to hide his disappointment, wondering how much to push this man who, so far, had been unexpectedly cordial. When he looked up, he was shocked to see the sheriff scooting around the desk in a compact lightweight wheelchair. Louis tried hard to recover but Nurmi saw his expression.

"Car accident four years ago," he said.

Nurmi wheeled out to the front office. A young uniformed officer had come in and was taking over the reception desk.

"What's for dinner?" Nurmi asked Monica, who was pulling on a parka.

"Pot roast," she said. "If it's not all shrunk up to nothing by now."

Nurmi looked up at Louis. "You want to come over for dinner, Detective Kincaid? Our place is just next door."

When Louis hesitated, Nurmi smiled and held up a hand. "You're too polite to say it so I'll say it for you. You'd rather be down in the basement, eh?"

"Yes sir, I would, to be honest," Louis said.

"Okay then," Nurmi said. "All my men are out on the road right now and the courthouse is closed. But the fellow who cleans up should be there. Monica will get you the keys to the cage."

"Thanks, Sheriff," Louis said.

PJ PARRISH

• • • • • • • • •

"Call me Reuben." He looked up at his wife. "Let's get rolling, Monica."

There was a man in a red plaid shirt, jeans and ball cap waiting for him under the white columns of the courthouse. Louis noticed he was staring at the blue state police car parked out by the wall, and when the man's eyes shifted to Louis, they held the same suspicion he had seen from others who lived in small towns and didn't like outsiders. It was especially true here in the U.P., a place where signs announced drivers had come to THE END OF THE EARTH.

"Thanks for letting me in," Louis said as he followed the man into the deserted lobby.

"No problem," the man said. "Basement's this way."

The man slapped the wall switch and, down below, the fluorescent lights buzzed to life. They reached another door, which the man unlocked. Inside, Louis found himself looking at a chain-link partition with a padlocked gate. Beyond were rows of metal shelves filled with white file boxes.

Louis had been anticipating a couple hours in a dank cave rummaging through mildewed liquor boxes. But this place was as neat and organized as an operating room.

"You gonna be down here long?" the man asked.

Louis knew the guy probably wanted to go home to his dinner and didn't want to leave a stranger in the courthouse. He realized suddenly he hadn't seen a hotel or even a restaurant in Eagle River. The last motel he had passed was that boarded up dump on US-41. Because of his stupidity, he would probably have to backtrack to Calumet, if not further.

He noticed the emblem on the man's ball cap—EAGLE RIVER INN. "Is that inn here in town?" he asked, nodding to the cap.

The man hesitated then nodded. "Right down the hill. If you end up in the lake, you've gone too far."

44

"Thanks." Louis used the key Monica had given him and unlocked the gate. Inside, he began to scan the dates on the nearest boxes. It took him a moment to realize the man was still standing by the door, waiting.

"I can lock up when I leave," Louis offered. "No need for you to wait."

The man's gray eyes narrowed. "You from downstate, eh?" he asked in the flat nasally Yooper accent.

"Yes," Louis said.

"What you looking for?" the man said. "Maybe I can help."

No matter how small the town or how suspicious its people, they were always curious about police work and often wanted to help.

"Just some evidence," Louis said. "And an old candle box."

"Candle box," the man said softly. "Well, okay, then. I'll leave you to it. Just pull the front door closed and it'll lock behind you."

The man left and Louis turned his attention back to the shelves. Because it was not known what year the boys were killed, the evidence was probably filed under 1979, the year the bones were found. That's where Louis found the white evidence box. It was neatly labeled JOHNNY DOES (2) GRAY WOLF MINE 79-0250.

Louis pulled it from the shelf, surprised it was so light, and set it on a table under one of the fluorescents. Inside the box, he found two small brown paper bags. The evidence tape on each was brittle and the writing smeared. Snapping on latex gloves, Louis used his pocket knife to carefully slice the tape and opened the first bag.

Inside was a small piece of cloth that was maybe once white but had yellowed with age. He opened the second paper bag, which held a duplicate piece of cloth. Louis carefully laid the two pieces on the table.

It took him a moment to understand what he was looking at and he didn't want to believe it. But then he saw the faded manufacturer's tag on the elastic waistband—JOCKEY JUNIOR.

With a slow exhale, he arranged the two pieces of fabric on the table until each vaguely resembled its original shape.

Two pairs of small, white briefs. He looked back in the evidence box. No other clothing or shoes.

He repackaged the underwear, put the bags back in the evidence box, then went in search of the wooden candle box. He found it in the darkest corner of the basement, identified by a tag thumbtacked to the lid. It was smaller than the picture showed, but heavy, about the weight of an old tool chest. He carried it into the light and set it on the table.

The lid was nailed shut but, using his pocketknife, he was able to pry it off. He set the lid aside and moved the empty box under the fluorescent lights.

The wood was naturally the color of red oak, but the inside bottom was dark with stains that Louis could only guess were a mixture of decomposing flesh and blood, maybe some water seepage. He picked up the lid to put it back on but then caught a glimpse of the underside. He froze.

There were small gouges in the wood on the inside of the lid, like someone had raked at it with a dull blade. But he knew the marks had not been made by any instrument.

They had been made by the boys' fingernails.

CHAPTER SEVEN

He found the Eagle River Inn at the bottom of Pine Street, just where the man said it would be. It was a sprawling dark-green building sitting alone on the deserted two-lane blacktop road. When Louis got out of the Explorer, it was too dark to see Lake Superior but he could hear its crash on the shore and feel its bite in the air.

There was no one manning the desk in the empty lobby so Louis headed toward the restaurant. The place was empty. A bearded man hauling a beer case emerged from the back. He seemed surprised to see someone in his restaurant.

"Sorry, the restaurant's not open tonight," he said, setting down the case.

"Can I get a beer?" Louis asked.

The man smiled. "That we have. Whatcha drinking?"

"Heineken?"

"That's one I'm out of. Delivery truck broke down." The man slid a menu across the bar. "I don't think you'll have a problem finding something else you like."

Louis pulled out his glasses and scanned the long list. It started with Bell's Amber Ale and ended with Weihenstephanar Dunklewiessbier. He estimated there were at least a hundred beers listed, foreign and domestic, most he had never heard of.

"You're that state cop from downstate, right?" the man asked.

Louis looked up. "Yeah."

The man wiped a hand on his jeans and thrust it out. "Sheriff called and said you'd probably be coming by. I got your room ready. The name's Paul Sternhagen."

Louis shook the man's hand, surprised again at the friendliness of these folks toward a state cop, let alone a "troll" from under the Mackinac Bridge.

"Thanks."

"Let me choose a beer for you," Paul said. "And I'll scrounge up something from the kitchen, too. Whitefish okay?"

"I'd eat anything right now."

Paul moved away and Louis dropped onto one of the wood stools. The long day and the hard drive were still there in the cramp between his shoulder blades. He shut his eyes.

When he opened them the image of the scratched candle box lid was gone and there was a tall sweating glass in front of him, something dark red with a lace collar of foam. He took a sip. It was vinegar and caramels, probably the best beer he had ever tasted.

By the time the fried whitefish had arrived, Louis had moved on to Pick Axe Blonde and then a bottle of Aged Pale Ale. After Louis had finished the hot apple pie a la mode, Paul brought him a room key and a snifter of Sazerac 18 Year Old Rye.

"You're here in town for that thing with those little boys, eh?" Paul asked.

Louis looked at him. "You know anything about that case?"

Paul shrugged and wiped the counter. "I was too young to remember much. Most folks figured they were somehow killed by some family on a hunting trip and put in that mine because they couldn't bury them in frozen ground."

Louis nodded. "You're probably right," he said, making a mental note to check into Paul's background. "What do I owe you?"

"It's on the house," Paul said. "I've got about a hundred other whiskies if you don't like this one."

"Thanks. This is enough for tonight," Louis said.

By the time he had pulled his go-bag and Nurmi's case file from the Explorer and headed to his room, Louis was feeling the booze. In his early twenties, he had veered too close to chronic drinking and figured he probably had his mother's alcoholic gene. And ever since Lily had entered his life, he had cut back to almost nothing. But tonight, for some reason, he had tiptoed up to that edge again.

The room was too warm. He went to the window and yanked it open. The cold air poured over him. From somewhere out in the blackness but very close it seemed, came the crash of the lake.

For a second, he thought of the Gulf coast at night, with its sweet salty breezes, whispering palms and its constant seagull caw. And for another second—only a second—he missed it.

Bienvenue chez vous.

Welcome home.

With a deep breath of cold fresh air, he turned from the window and spotted a clock on the nightstand. Eleven fifteen.

Shit.

He'd forgotten to call Camille and give her a rundown of his meeting with the sheriff for Steele. It reminded him that he still had some things to get used to. Like having a boss to report to. It would have to wait until morning.

He took some reports out of the accordion file and sat down on the bed. He kicked off his shoes and settled up against the headboard to start reading.

Dammit. His glasses were in his jacket pocket, hung on the chair across the room.

For a long moment, he stared at the jacket, not being able to find the will to get up. Reviewing the file could wait until morning, too. Even if he did read it tonight, he knew he wouldn't remember anything.

He fell asleep sitting up.

He awoke in a panic, disorientated enough to throw his arms out for balance. Something crashed nearby and the darkness came down around him a black blanket of ice.

Fuck . . . fuck! What the hell?

He put a hand to his chest, his mind struggling for stability. Slowly it came to him. He was in the lodge, on a bed and it was dark because he knocked the lamp to the floor. Holding his breath, he waited—but he heard nothing but the waves below the open window.

He slid from the bed, spilling the papers from the accordion file to the floor. Following the rush of cold air, he made his way to the window and slammed it shut. Then he found the bathroom light and turned it on.

His heart was pounding as he moved unsteadily back to the bed. He gathered up the papers and stuffed them in the accordion folder. For a moment, he just stood there, his breath slowing, but something hard and sharp—something he had never felt before—was still knotted in his gut.

He had to get out of here.

He rummaged in his duffel for a sweatshirt, pulled on his sneakers and was quickly out the front entrance of the lodge. He followed the sound of the waves down to the lake.

A half-moon had snuck out from behind a cluster of clouds, casting the shoreline in a misty white aura. It was enough for him to see where the white sand met the black water.

He started to run.

His body grew hot, his lungs grew cold. But still he ran, like a maniac across the soft sand, toward the glow of the moon, toward the barely visible jagged rise of rocks far ahead.

The unknown terror that had awakened him was finally easing but still he ran on. Finally, he stopped, bent over, hands on his knees, and gulped in the icy air.

As his muscles cooled and heart slowed, he started to regain some balance, but he knew *it* was still there, this thing he could feel but not describe. This hard, painful thing that was vaguely familiar but incredibly distant.

THE DAMAGE DONE

He straightened and looked around. The moon had slipped away and he stood in total darkness, except for the tiny amber light of the inn far away along the water's edge.

He turned and started toward it, the wet sand pulling at his shoes, the cold air biting at his face.

It was a long and dark walk back.

CHAPTER EIGHT

S leep hadn't come easy after his run on the beach, and for hours he had laid awake in the dark of his room. Finally, just after seven, he found his way back to the bar, taking the accordion file with him. Louis took a table near the window and ordered an omelet. A young woman set a mug of coffee at his elbow. It was probably the best coffee he'd had in years. Or maybe it was just the troubled night. Or the chilly air of Lake Superior that seemed to permeate everything up here.

He moved aside the condiments and opened the accordion file. He started with the responding officers' reports. The first deputy had described the location of the mine, the size and color of the box, and had taken measurements that placed the candle box at a junction about fifty yards inside the entrance. An analysis of the candle box showed it had been constructed around the turn of the century, that it was not unique to the area, and not traceable beyond its company logo. Someone had noted the candle company shut down around the time the mine closed in the 1920s.

The second deputy had interviewed the downstate hikers who had found the bones. Louis wondered if there was anything to gain from talking to them again, but their contact information was twelve years old. It might take a while to find them.

The preliminary medical examiner's report, written by a man who had come to the mine to arrange transport of the bones and he box to the Blue Water lab in Houghton, contained nothing of interest.

Louis turned to the autopsy report from Blue Water. It was long with attachments and diagrams. The boys had been found as they probably died, forming two intact skeletons lying in the candle box. A couple chemical tests appeared to have been administered with no conclusive results. No one could state an exact cause of death, as there was no soft tissue to examine and no sign of blunt force trauma to the skulls.

There was one interesting detail. Based on bone size and maturation, the examiner had determined the height of both boys at approximately three-foot-nine inches. But based on dental examinations, they were not the same age. On Johnny Doe #1, the permanent incisor teeth and molars had already erupted, along with the first molars, which set the boy's age as between seven and eight. On Johnny Doe #2, the front baby teeth were still intact, which set his age at about five.

"Your breakfast, officer."

When he looked up at the young waitress, her brown eyes slipped to the dental chart on the autopsy page. She stared at it like most folks stare at an accident scene—uncomfortable but riveted. He turned the paper face down.

"Can I get a coffee refill, please?" he asked.

After she left, Louis arranged his food and the reports on the table so he could read and eat at the same time. It appeared that Nurmi's predecessor Halko had conducted most of the investigation himself. He canvassed the few residents who lived within twenty miles of the Gray Wolf mine and interviewed other hikers. He had put out missing persons alerts to Michigan, Minnesota, and Wisconsin, and had also made a note indicating he contacted the Royal Canadian Mounted Police, but there was no follow-up report.

It didn't take long for the dates on Halko's report to grow farther apart and by early 1981, except for the occasional noting of a dead-end phone tip, it appeared that Halko had given up.

Louis finished his toast and set his plate on the adjoining table. As he began to put away the reports, Mark Steele's words came back to him.

No one has ever been charged or convicted for this crime. You're going to change that.

He *was* going to change that.

Twelve years ago, no one knew what DNA was. Blood could only be typed, or hairs could only be categorized by race. In today's forensic lab, the stained box could be treasure chest of evidence. All he had to do was get the bones and the box back to the state lab and under the eyes of a forensic anthropologist.

He gathered up his papers, laid some money on the table, and went back to his room. He wasn't sure he would head back to Lansing today, but he packed his duffle anyway and loaded the Explorer. As he climbed in, he remembered he owed Camille a check-in phone call.

He picked up the cellular phone from its cradle between the seats, studied it for a second then hit the ON button. He got a connection and dialed. When Camille answered, it took him a moment to get past the soft huskiness because although the words were sheer business, it sounded just like how Joe talked to him in the darkness of her bedroom.

"Good morning, Louis. It's nice to hear your voice again. Captain Steele has been waiting for you to check in."

"Please give him my apologies. I got in to Eagle River late and went to sleep early and—"

"Well, I will give him your apologies but not your excuses. Now, what's your status?"

Louis felt reprimanded but let it go. The woman was absolutely right. "I plan to make arrangements to have the bones exhumed and transferred to Marquette for examination. Can you tell me who has the authority to—"

"You have the authority to do anything you wish with the remains, Louis," Camille said. "I'll start the paperwork for exhumation and fax it to the SO up there for your signature and get the ball rolling."

"Thank you. I'll have to get you Sheriff Nurmi's fax—"

"Already have it. Anything else you need, Louis?"

It felt good to have someone at your fingertips who could tear through the red tape. "Nothing else right now, but I owe you one, Camille," he said.

"Bring me a cinnamon sweet roll from the Hilltop Restaurant in L'Anse instead. You have to go right through there on your way home."

His mind conjured up images of a curvy woman sitting under silk sheets, smoking a cigarette and nibbling on a frosted cinnamon bun.

"You got it."

Louis hung up and went back inside to get a coffee to go, leaving a thank-you note scrawled on a napkin for Paul. He headed out of town to the cemetery he had seen on his drive in. Evergreen Cemetery was small, but he suspected it had a children's section. He found it in a pine-sheltered corner called God's Cradle.

Slowly, he moved along the row of small headstones. A few were as old as the late 1800s, one as new as this year, 1991. He counted twenty-seven, but none was unmarked or bore the names of Johnny or Jimmy Doe.

He wondered if the bones had been buried in the pauper's section, but a quick walk through the entire cemetery showed what he suspected—that, in a town as small as Eagle River, people would show the same respect to a poor dead man as one with means.

Back in the Explorer, Louis checked the case file again. The only note about the bones disposition was an entry on the autopsy report that the remains had been returned to the sheriff's office. But a check of Sheriff Halko's paperwork showed that no one had accepted the bones back into the county's possession or that the county, state, or anyone had paid for a burial. Louis closed the file and stared out the windshield at the headstones. This was not good. He had to have the remains examined. But where the hell were they?

Sheriff Nurmi was eating pancakes and reading the newspaper when Louis walked in his office at nine.

"Your office faxed me a request to transfer the boys' remains to the custody of the state," Nurmi said. "I'll call the crew down in Hancock to come up and—"

"The remains aren't in Evergreen Cemetery," Louis said.

Nurmi set his fork down. "You check every grave? They'd be in with the babies, you know, in the back."

"I found that section, but they aren't there. I checked every headstone. No Jimmy or Johnny Does."

"You look back through the file?"

"Yes, sir."

"Damn Halko anyway," Nurmi said. "He was as useless as they come when it came to organizing things."

"Is there anyone here who might remember? Another deputy? A lab tech?" Louis asked.

"Doubtful. I had to clean house after Halko died, so all my officers have only been here a few years. But I'll do some asking around."

"We'll have to search burial records," Louis said. "How many cemeteries are there in your county?"

"Twelve, counting the one over on Isle Royale," Nurmi said. "I'll get a man over to the courthouse today. If we draw a blank, we can expand the search to the whole peninsula."

They were both quiet for a moment. Louis knew Nurmi was thinking the same thing he was—that the bones could be lost forever, either in some distant cemetery, in the basement of a municipal building, or in a storage locker abandoned by Blue Water labs.

Monica poked her head in the door. "You done with that?" she asked Nurmi, nodding to the tray.

"Sheriff, I remember there was a newspaper article about the community holding a memorial service," Louis said. "Maybe someone remembers something about that."

Nurmi nodded. "I can get the word out to the local churches."

"You might want to talk to Reverend Grascoeur, too," Monica said as she picked up the tray.

"That old guy up in Copper Harbor?" Nurmi asked.

"Ya, I remember talking about him coming down here to do a special service around that time."

Nurmi waved a hand. "He's into that new age junk. Last time I saw him, he was holding a service under the northern lights at twenty below. Harmonica something, it was called."

"Harmonic Convergence," Louis said.

"Ya, that's it. Crazy stuff from a crazy man."

Louis didn't tell Nurmi that some of his best leads had come from people who weren't considered normal. Like Danny Dancer, the savant on Mackinac Island who had held a dead girl's image in his memory for twenty years. Or Amy Brandt, the girl from Hell, Michigan, who claimed to have lived a past life as a slave.

"I'd like to talk to Grascoeur," Louis said.

"Suit yourself," Nurmi said. "Give the reverend a ring, Monica, and see if he's still around."

"Will do," Monica said and left.

Louis glanced up at the wall clock. It was almost ten, not enough time to see this minister and make the long drive back to Lansing. And there was no way he was going back to Steele and tell him the bones were missing. He made a mental note to call Camille and alert her he was staying another night. Which would give him time to check out one more thing.

"Sheriff, the mine where the remains were found," Louis said. "What can you tell me about it?"

"Gray Wolf? Well, the mining operation closed down back in the twenties," Nurmi said. "The shafts were all grated off and the main entrance is boarded up."

"Is it far from here? I'd like to see it."

Nurmi gave Louis a dubious look then leaned over his desk toward the open door. "Monica, is there a county map somewhere out there?"

"You got one on the wall behind you."

"I mean one of those gas station fold-up kinds." He looked back at Louis. "It's not far off the highway on your way up to Copper Harbor."

Monica came in, handed Nurmi a map, and gave Louis a piece of paper. "There's no answer at Reverend Grascoeur's church but here's the number and address."

Louis took the paper and Monica left. Nurmi spread the map out on his desk, turning it so Louis could see. He gave him directions and made a large X on a spot on the shore of a place called Bete Grise Bay.

"Are there any signs for it?" Louis asked.

"Nope, just some rocks and old ruins and not even much of that anymore."

"How do I find the entrance then?"

"Stop in at the Bear Belly Bar and ask for Dave. He'll show you where the mine is. I'll call him and tell him you're coming."

Louis leaned on the desk and stared down at the map. No towns, no landmarks. Nothing but green denoting empty land and, below that, the yawning, blue expanse of Lake Superior.

"The killer knew the old mine was there," Louis said. "Which means he was probably from around here."

"But I don't think the boys were."

Louis was about to ask Nurmi why when it hit him. Everyone up here knew everyone else. News of two local boys going missing would have spread like wildfire. There would have been a report from distraught parents, names in the local paper, mention of it in the police files. Yet there was nothing.

Nurmi folded the map and handed it to Louis. "The grounds are pocked with old shafts that have caved in. Most have been secured with grates or boards but some haven't. You watch your step down there."

CHAPTER NINE

Dave from the Bear Belly Bar didn't seem to have any trouble steering his beat-up Dodge Ram Truck down the rutted road tunneled with thick trees. But following him in his Explorer, Louis had to work to keep up.

Dave left him at a dead-end with directions to hike about a quarter mile south and watch for a large rock outcropping shaped like a hawk's beak. Dave gave him a final *you-crazy-fuck* shake of the head then disappeared back down the road in a spray of mud.

Louis grabbed his Maglite and headed into the dense brush. If there was a path, he couldn't see it, so he took it slow, picking his way over fallen trees and pushing through birch saplings. Twenty minutes in, he was breathing hard and stopped, sure he was lost. He looked up at the sun to get his bearings. That's when he felt it—a rush of air on his neck, as if someone had exhaled too close behind him. Except there was no wind stirring the trees and this air was ice cold.

It had to be the mine entrance. He turned in a tight circle, then felt the cold air again, stronger, coming from his left. He pushed through the trees then stopped abruptly.

At his feet was a metal grate, almost hidden in the dead leaves. It was maybe four feet across and rusted through in the middle. If he had taken two more steps, he would have fallen in.

Letting out a hard breath, he moved carefully around the grating, following the stream of cold air.

He pushed through some brush and stopped.

It wasn't what he had expected. But then maybe he had seen too many westerns. Hollywood's idea of mines were dusty tunnels with railroad tracks leading in, flanked by villages of tin shacks. This was a fifty-foot canyon of high jagged rock, the ground strewn with boulders the size of Volkswagen Beetles. There was a giant maw in the rock, crisscrossed with one X of weathered boards.

As Louis went closer to the entrance, he saw a tin sign nailed on one board. It was so crusted with rust he could barely make out the words.

DANGER OPEN MINE SHAFT
UNSTABLE ROCK FORMATION
TRESPASSERS WILL BE PROSECUTED
BY OWNER GRAY WOLF MINE COMPANY

He switched on the Maglite and shined it into the entrance. The beam picked up rough rock walls, a copper-dusted floor, and then disappeared into the darkness of the tunnel.

Louis leaned in to get a better look. There was a sudden crack and the board under his arm gave way. He drew back quickly. The board was hanging by one rusted nail. The other board, he realized, was just as flimsy. He could get in.

If he wanted to.

He took his radio from his belt. He knew he couldn't reach Camille, but it was just as well. He didn't really want to alert her and Steele to what he was about to do. He changed frequencies to the Keweenaw SO and Monica answered.

"The sheriff just left for a doctor's appointment, Louis," she said. "He'll be back in an hour."

"Okay, just alert him that I'm at Gray Wolf and I'm just going in a few feet and take a look."

"He's not going to like that."

"I know." He paused. "I'll radio again when I come out. If you don't hear from me, well, send someone out here."

As he replaced his radio, it occurred to him that a few years ago, he would not have thought to advise anyone that he was about to do something risky, like enter an abandoned copper mine. But he had Lily and Joe now, and that had changed a lot of things in his life.

He pulled off the broken boards and stepped into the mine. The cold air flowed over him and copper-colored dust motes swam in the Maglite beam. The shaft was domed, maybe ten feet across and eight feet high. The walls looked like they had been gouged with a giant claw. The ground was solid rock so he was able to move with more assurance than he had outside.

From the police reports, he knew the candle box had been found about fifty feet in, just past a fork. He decided to go that far and then get out.

He shined the beam ahead into the darkness and moved on. Two black holes appeared ahead—a fork in the tunnel. He took the left side, but ten feet in it dead-ended in a pile of rock so he backtracked out. The right tunnel was lower, and he had to stoop slightly to keep going. The ground began to slope and the air grew frigid.

He stopped. His breath was shallow and he felt a tightening in his gut.

For a second, he flashed back to another dark place, another time he had left the sunlight behind and gone underground. It had been the tunnels under an abandoned insane asylum and he had been lost down there for hours, chasing a mad killer.

He pulled in a deep calming breath. He was alone here, yet it felt as if he wasn't. It was just a feeling, another one of those odd vibrations he got when he was in a place where someone had died. In his early years as an investigator, he used to dismiss them. But over time, he had learned to respect them.

He ran the flashlight beam slowly over the walls and ceiling, not sure what he expected to find. Maybe carved initials or graffiti the police had missed in 1979 when the box had been found. Maybe even a message or memento that would tell him the killer had returned to emotionally relive his crime.

There was nothing.

Louis started to turn back. But something pulled at him and he shined the beam downward, sweeping it slowly across the floor. He knelt and carefully sifted through the cold coppery dust. It was littered with pebbles and splinters of rock. Then he touched something that didn't feel like a rock. It was flat and perfectly round. He held it up in the flashlight beam.

It was metal, the surface covered in a black film and a crust of green oxidation. He weighed it in his palm. It was too light for a half-dollar, too small for a silver dollar. What the hell was it? And why hadn't cops hadn't found it in 1979? Given what Nurmi had told him about sheriff Halko, such an oversight could be chalked up to incompetence, though Louis knew any CSI tech would have found this. It was more likely this thing, whatever it was, had been placed here after the candle box had been removed. By why? And by who?

He rummaged for a Kleenex in his jeans, wrapped up the piece of metal and put it in his jacket pocket. For twenty more minutes, he scoured the dirt for more pieces of metal, but finally, finding nothing else and frozen to the bone, he stuck a pencil in the ground to mark the spot.

When he shined the flashlight on his watch, he saw he had been in the mine almost an hour. If he didn't call Monica soon, she'd send out a rescue team. Besides, he still had to get to Copper Harbor and see Grascoeur.

He rose and started back toward the mouth of the mine, walking quickly toward the light.

CHAPTER TEN

The first thing he did when he got back in the Explorer was radio Monica. Then he started the engine, turned the heat on high, holding his cold hands up to the vent.

When the feeling had returned to his fingers, he reached over to the passenger seat for the accordion file and pulled out the photographs. After being inside the mine, he had an itch in his brain that he had overlooked something.

He sifted through the photographs taken in 1979, starting with the exteriors of the mine. It had been early October when the hikers had found the candle box and the photos showed the rocky canyon around the mine's entrance softened by yellowing trees, lush ferns and grass, and a riot of purple and orange wild flowers. Whoever had taken the photographs seemed to dwell on the flowers, making the place look almost as pretty as one of those postcards he sent to Lily.

In stark contrast, the photos of the mine's interior looked exactly like the shaft looked now—cold and dead—with eerie shadows on the rock walls created by camera flash. There were several photos of the closed candle box, copper-dusted against the rock wall, and one taken outside in the sunlight of the empty box sitting in the grass, lid open, after the bones had been removed.

Louis moved on to the second set of photographs, the ones taken in the Blue Water lab. There was the same close-up photo of the two skulls that had been tacked to the board in Lansing, others of the full skeletons arranged on a stainless steel table, and two photos of the long leg bones on a measuring board.

But there was nothing new here that he could see.

He started to put the photographs back in the accordion file then paused, his eyes fixed on the top photo of the candle box sitting in the grass. The *empty* candle box.

That's when he saw it—saw what was *not* there. There wasn't one photograph of the candle box with the skeletons still inside it.

He went back through the photos to make sure he hadn't missed it. It wasn't there, and it should have been. A full-sized photograph of the bones in the box would have been vital to legally document how the boys had been positioned when they died.

He flipped over the top photo. The stamp on the back read PHOTOS PROPERTY OF KEWEENAW COUNTY SO. There was a faded inked-in signature: J. Halko.

The dead sheriff's name was Tom. This J. Halko had to be a relative, which wasn't surprising given that small town departments were often deep in cronyism. He keyed the radio and reached Monica.

"I was just getting ready to call you," Monica said. "We got a lake-effect snow warning."

He peered up through the windshield. The sky was gray but didn't look threatening. "Consider me warned," he said. "Monica, do you know who J. Halko is?"

"That would be Jennifer, Tom's daughter."

"Do you have an address for her?"

"Sure. She lives in her dad's old house out on Wyoming Road, not far from where you are now. She's a strange bird, so you might need to tread gentle about her old man."

"Will do."

Monica gave him directions and he thanked her and signed off. He put the Explorer in gear and started away from the mine. It was a long shot, but he was hoping that the woman who had taken all those pretty pictures of the wild flowers had kept her negatives.

• • • • • • • • •

He was just opening the Explorer door when he heard the roar of an ATV. Across the field, a three-wheeler was rumbling his way, kicking up mud in its wake.

The rider, dressed in a mud-splattered camouflage jumpsuit and black helmet, skidded the ATV to a stop a few feet from the Explorer and dismounted. A shotgun was secured to the side of the ATV and a pistol hung on the driver's leather belt. When she pulled off the helmet, a nest of dark hair sprung free.

She was in her mid-forties, almost as tall as he was. Her eyes were tiny green ponds in her dirty face, her lips flat pink lines in a puppet chin.

"Detective Kincaid, state police," Louis said.

"JennyHalko."

She had a strong grip and a stronger Yooper accent. When she released his hand, she just stood there, staring at him.

"I have some questions about a case your father worked," he said.

"The boys in the box," she said. "I heard there was a statie in town sniffing around. What do you think I can tell ya?"

"My questions concern the crime scene photos," Louis said. "You took them?"

Jennifer nodded. "I took them all right."

"Did you keep your negatives?"

She cuddled the helmet to her chest, taking her time to thaw out towards him. "No, afterwards I turned everything in to my father's office. I didn't need any photographs to remind me what I saw that day." She paused. "That was a long time ago. Why are you asking about my pictures?"

"I think some photographs might be missing from the case file," Louis said.

She was silent, staring at him hard.

Louis reached in the open door of the Explorer and pulled out the photographs. "This is all there is," he said, holding the stack out.

She took the photographs and sifted through them, rapidly at first then more slowly. "I took a lot more than this," she said, looking up.

It was there in her voice, confusion and something Louis couldn't quite decipher—pride?

"Do you have any idea where they might be? Did your father keep files here at home?"

Her look was as if he had asked to search through her bedroom drawers, but when she spoke her voice had softened. "I don't know. I boxed everything up after he died," she said.

"Do you still have his things?"

She was silent.

"Miss Halko, I'm not suggesting your father did anything wrong," Louis said. "If there are more photographs, I just need to see them."

She stared at him for a long moment, then held out the photographs. Louis took them and set them back on the Explorer's passenger seat.

"I put all his stuff in the barn," Jennifer said. She hesitated then gave him a short nod. "Okay, follow me."

At the barn, she unlocked the door and waved him to follow her inside. Louis expected the place to smell of animals and hay but there was nothing in the air but dust. Two snowmobiles sat in the horse stalls. A pair of skis was propped against the wall, near a snow blower.

Jennifer pointed to a ladder that led up to the loft. It was a high climb, twenty feet easy. "Go ahead and look all you want," she said. "It's mainly just boxes, his tool chest, and an old Army footlocker. The locker's padlocked."

"Do you have a key?"

"Nope. If you can get it open you're free to look. Just stop by the house and let me know if you're taking anything."

"Thanks. Will do."

Jennifer left and Louis climbed the ladder. The loft was full of junk—broken furniture, boxes, plastic bins, bowling trophies, green rubber fishing waders, rusty fans, a stuffed elk head, and old plaid coats strewn over a trunk.

Louis started with the boxes, figuring that was the logical place to store old office files. But a quick look told him all the papers appeared to be personal—tax returns, old newspapers, some letters and military records. The second box held Louis L'Amour paperbacks and soggy magazines, mainly copies of *Argosy* and *Penthouse*.

The tool chest yielded rusted saws, hammers, wrenches and a tangle of fishing lines, lures and hooks. The plastic bins were filled with old clothes.

He blew on his cold fingers and searched the shadows for the foot-locker. He found it in the corner, buried under a pile of plaid wool coats. It was the standard khaki-green wood chest, scarred and stenciled on the side: L.T. T.M. HALKO 0-456029.

Louis looked around the loft for something he could use to pry off the padlock and spotted a spud bar, a metal tool used in ice fishing. It took him four tries but he finally popped the lock.

When he opened the locker, the strong odor of must drifted out. The tray on top held yellowed wool socks, old, green boxer shorts, and a pair of scuffed, black boots.

Louis removed the tray. He jumped back at what he saw beneath—a clump of brown fur.

It took him a second to realize he was looking at a coat and not a dead animal. When he shook out the fur, he saw a faded orange tag pinned to the sleeve. He had left his glasses in the Explorer and had to squint to read it.

EVIDENCE
DESCRIPTION: mink coat size 12
VICTIM: Gloria Halloway
RECOVERED: KCSO

Louis set the coat aside, shaking his head. Halko had recovered the coat from a burglary and for some reason never returned it to the owner. He probably planned to sell it. It wasn't the worst thing a cop could do, pinch something from a crime scene, but it definitely told him what kind of man he was looking at here.

The next item he pulled from the locker was a small box with a .22 Colt revolver inside. The serial number was scraped off. No evidence tag.

Then came a rhinestone necklace, a pair of women's pink panties, both items still bearing evidence tags from a 1982 rape case in Alpena.

There was more.

A bloody blouse in a plastic bag, sealed with evidence tape from the Ypsilanti police department, packaged with a certificate of authenticity and stickered with a label: Alfred Yules, $150.00.

A child's white sock in a Ziploc labeled Lori Butts, 1984, $400. A lock of blonde hair in a bag sealed by the Muskegon police. Holly Cardrone, 1986, $200.

Louis realized he was holding his breath and when he exhaled, it came out in one long stream in the cold air. He *knew* these cases—they had all been part of his homework in getting familiar with Michigan's most infamous crimes. Yules was a serial killer who had worked the I-94 corridor. Lori Butts was a seven-year-old who disappeared from her Flint home. Holly Cardone was a suburban mother of three whose body had been ground up in a wood chipper by her husband.

Halko wasn't just an evidence thief. He was a dealer in crime memorabilia, the kind you could auction off only in a very special black market.

What a sicko.

But it gave Louis hope that somewhere in this footlocker were the photos he was looking for. He just hoped Halko hadn't sold them before he croaked.

Finally, near the bottom of the locker, he found a stack of manila envelopes. Each envelope contained photographs from different crime scenes—eight-by-tens of bloodied and decomposing bodies. Each picture had a price tag.

Then there it was—an envelope marked GRAY WOLF BONES. Sitting back on his heels, Louis pulled the color photos from the envelope.

There were twelve, each taken by Jennifer Halko from slightly different angles but all showing the same thing: the bones of the boys lying inside the candle box, just as they had looked when the top of the box was pried off.

He knew they were the same skeletons he had seen in the lab photos, but here, in their makeshift coffin, they looked so different. The skeletons were lying on their sides, kept intact by strings of mummified cartilage, the pelvises encased in the yellowed Jockey Junior briefs. One skeleton was cradling the other in a position lovers would call spooning. The right arm bones of one boy were draped across the shoulder of the smaller boy.

For a long time, Louis just sat there, staring at the photograph.

• • • • • • • • •

The boys might have clawed for a while at the underside of the wooden lid, but it was clear to anyone who saw this photo that in the end, they had turned to hold onto each other.He slipped the pictures back into the envelope and rose. The barn was ice cold, the air thick with dust. He was hit with the same feeling he had last night—the need to get out—to run blindly and quickly away from this place with its macabre souvenirs. But first he had to face Jennifer Halko.

He knocked on the door of the farmhouse and waited, a cold wind blowing at his back. He had managed to get the footlocker down from the loft by lowering it by rope. It was locked in the Explorer.

Everything Tom Halko had collected was the property of various law enforcement agencies, and he would have to take the footlocker with him so it could be sorted out. Jennifer Halko might understand that part. He didn't know if she would understand what a disgusting man her father had been.

The door opened and Jennifer stood there, arms folded over her chest.

"Can I talk to you for a moment?" he asked.

She stepped aside and he came in. A skinny hound dog rose to its feet from its place by the roaring fireplace and started a throaty growl.

"Sit, Ansel!" Jennifer snapped.

The dog obediently sat, but the look on its face told him it would get back up if it had to.

"I saw you moving my father's footlocker," Jennifer said. "I take it you found my photos in it?"

Louis looked back at her. "That and more."

Jennifer sighed, like she knew this would be a longer conversation that she had expected. "Would you like some coffee?"

"No, thanks."

"I need some if you don't mind," she said.

Jennifer led him into a family room. When she stepped away to the adjoining kitchen, Louis looked around. Braided scatter rugs lay over scarred wood floors, and a sagging sofa covered in a Northern Michigan University blanket sat near a picture window that overlooked the empty fields. But folks invited in probably never noticed any of that because their eyes would have been drawn immediately to the photographs on the walls.

Evocative landscapes of bright colors. Streaks of midnight-blue, flamingo-pink, and cherry-red that captured Lake Superior at sunset. Splashes of tangerine, russet, dove-gray, and foamy-white that brought Tahquamenon Falls alive.

He moved to the wall, drawn to a photograph with an almost solid white background. In the center, at the end of a snow -covered breakwater, stood a small lighthouse, shrouded in icicles, freezing it—and the Michigan winter—in time.

Suddenly the dog's name clicked: Ansel Adams, the famous landscape photographer.

Jennifer came back into the room, blowing softly into her coffee cup.

"You took these?" he asked.

"Yes."

"They're beautiful," he said.

"Thank you."

He looked back at her. "Quite a contrast to crime scene photos."

Jennifer hesitated then nodded. "When the boys were found, I had just returned home here from Cheboygan, broke and divorced. My grandfather talked my father into paying me for taking the department photographs so I could get on my feet. That case was my first assignment." She paused. "It was also my last."

"This might not mean much to you," Louis said, "but you should know you did a good job. The photos I found in the barn will help us. I'm sure of it."

Jennifer sipped on her coffee, quiet, her eyes drifting to the still alert Ansel.

"You need to know something else," Louis said. "There were other things in the trunk besides the missing photos."

"Other things? Like what?"

"Souvenirs and photos from other crimes," Louis said. "Jewelry and bloody clothing that your father took, not only from his own department, but from other police departments."

"Why would—" Jennifer dropped her voice to a whisper. "Why would he have stolen evidence?"

"To sell."

Jennifer looked confused then her eyes narrowed. "Like murder memorabilia?"

"Yes."

She turned away and set down her cup. Louis realized she was looking at something on a shelf, a framed photograph of a white-haired man in a Keweenaw County Sheriff's uniform. He had a feeling it was her grandfather.

"Did he sell any of *my* photos?" Jennifer asked without turning around.

"There were twelve in the envelope. Does that sound right?"

Jennifer gave a small nod but still didn't face him.

"I have to take the footlocker back to Lansing," Louis said. "The items need to be returned to their agencies. And I'm sorry, but the state will also be coming by to do a more thorough search to make sure there isn't anything else."

When Jennifer turned around, her face was like her photograph of the lighthouse in winter—desolate and lonely.

"This was my grand-parents' home," she said softly. "And I sort of grew up here. This is where my better memories are. So this stuff you talked about, I don't want it here. Take it. Take it all."

Louis gave her a moment, his eyes still wandering. There were other pictures of the grandfather and two of women of different generations—maybe a younger Jennifer with her mother—but no father memorialized. And what little she did have left of him, she wanted gone.

Louis wanted to say something, but no words came. But he did understand. He knew about the holes that could be left by a lousy father. Or in his case, an absent father. The wounds never healed, no matter whether you threw the photo of the man in the trash or kept it in the bottom of a drawer you never opened.

CHAPTER ELEVEN

He was back on US-41, driving through the thick pines to Copper Harbor to see Reverend Grascoeur. Snow flittered against the windshield and again he looked up to the sky. He hadn't told Monica he wasn't exactly sure what lake-effect snow was, though he knew it had something to do with the water churning up snow and the lake being warmer—or maybe it was colder—than the land. Downstate, they just had regular snow that came straight down and stayed there. This lake-effect stuff, how bad it could be?

Finally, he saw the sign for Copper Harbor and slowed down. Monica's directions placed the church down by the ferry docks on Brockway Avenue. Louis passed a sign with arrows pointing north to Eagle Harbor, west to Hancock and east to Isle Royale Ferry. Some wag had added a second official looking sign below that read MIAMI FL 1990 MILES.

Copper Harbor was just a larger version of all the other little frontier-like towns up here: a log-cabin bar, mom-and-pop motels, and gray, weathered homes. The mud-caked cars were armed with giant, nubby tires and the trucks were built for survival—not pleasure. An old man coming out of the post office was carrying his mail and a rifle.

Louis spotted the ferry docks and slowed. There was no way to miss the Church of the Northern Lights.

It stood out like a rainbow in a gray sky. Each log of the cabin was painted a different candy color and a bright-yellow cross made of two-by-fours graced the peaked roof. There was a sign on the snowy lawn, one of those metal portable jobs with an arrow pointing toward the front door. The letters on it spelled out: KEEP USING MY NAME IN VAIN AND I'LL MAKE WINTER LONGER — GOD.

Louis got out of the Explorer, ducked his head against the stinging wind and walked to the door. As he reached for the handle, he saw a note tacked to the wood, dated that day.

WENT TO VISIT MY SISTER IN HARVEY.
MIGHT BE 2 DAYS MIGHT BE 6.
IF YOU NEED GUIDANCE, PRAY.
—REV GRASCOEUR

Dammit.

What now? There were no witnesses to hunt down and who knew when Nurmi's guys could locate any new records on the disposition of the remains? Louis got back in the Explorer, staring out at Grascoeur's note flapping in the wind.

Well, that left Harvey.

He pulled out the map Nurmi had given him, thinking that, with his luck so far on this case, Harvey was probably in Wisconsin. He scoured the little dots of the Keweenaw Peninsula and finally spotted HARVEY, a speck near Marquette.

He glanced up at the sky. The clouds were getting lower and closer, like a dust storm moving in across the plains. Only this dust was coming across the churning gunmetal lake and it was white.

The best thing to do would be to swing by Nurmi's office and drop off Halko's footlocker, pick up the candle box and the other evidence and take them to the Marquette lab himself. Then he'd head to Harvey to find Grascoeur, and if the guy told him anything useful, he'd stick around. If not, there was no sense in staying up here right now. Until the lab results came back or Nurmi's men found the boys' remains, he could get more done on the case sitting in front of a computer in Lansing.

He hit the accelerator. He'd have to kick it hard to Marquette if he was going to stay ahead of the snow.

It was near five by the time he pulled into the lot of the state forensics lab in Marquette. When he killed the engine, snow began to pile up on windshield. It had started about thirty miles out of Copper Harbor, forcing him to turn on the bubble and grill lights so the Explorer could be seen more clearly. The drive had been a nerve-cramping crawl.

Louis slowly took his hands off the steering wheel and flexed his aching fingers.

Man, he needed a drink.

But there was no time. He pushed from the truck and went around back to open the rear door. Nurmi had re-sealed the box and wrapped the candle box in plastic, sealing it with evidence tape to protect the chain of custody.

Inside the lab, the woman at the front desk directed him to a small room and left him a stack of forms and a roll of orange evidence lapels. Louis filled out the form for the candle box and underwear. As he rose and started gathering everything up, he remembered the metal object he had found in the mine and retrieved the piece of Kleenex from his jeans, unfolding it.

Even here, under the glare of the fluorescent lights, he couldn't tell if it was a foreign coin, a medal, jewelry or something else entirely. On the form, under EXAM REQUESTED, he wrote one sentence: "Tell me what this is."

A young lab tech came in with a large plastic bin stenciled MICH STATE POLICE. He didn't seem fazed at the sight of underwear but scrutinized the candle box.

"Man, this is an oldie," he said, as he pressed the lid down tighter through its plastic wrap.

"Careful with that, please," he said.

The tech gave Louis a tired smile. "I always am," he said. He set the candle box carefully in the plastic bin and snapped the lid on.

"Where you from?" the tech asked.

"Lansing," Louis said. "Got a long drive home."

"Not tonight," the tech said. "They just closed the bridge because of high winds."

Louis let out a long sigh.

"There's a Ramada down the block," the tech said. "They've got a decent bar and grill."

A new plan formed in Louis's head. Grab a steak and beer at the Ramada tonight and check in with Grascoeur in the morning on his way back to Lansing. Louis thanked the tech and left.

By the time he checked into the hotel, the wind-whipped snow was coming down like razors. After a quick dinner, he went back to his room and called Camille to give her a progress report. He then called Joe, but she was out of her office and he got her machine at home. When he tried to reach Lily, her mother Kyla told him Lily was at sleepover at a friend's house. Finally, Louis called information and got a phone number for an Evelyn Grascoeur in Harvey. When he called it, he got an answering machine, so he left a message identifying himself, saying he was trying to reach the Reverend Grascoeur about the boys found in the Gray Wolf mine.

After he hung up, he crawled into bed with the TV remote. But after a half-hour watching *Night Court,* he clicked off the TV and rolled to his side. His body was exhausted, but his brain was on overdrive, moving puzzle pieces that didn't seem to fit.

He closed his eyes. It felt like he had been asleep only minutes when he was jarred awake by the ringing phone. He groped for the receiver.

"Yeah, Kincaid."

"It's Camille."

He struggled to sit up. In the window across the room, he could see a swathe of pink on the horizon. The snow had stopped. It was dawn.

"Captain Steele is calling everyone back," she said. "You're going to Grand Rapids ASAP."

"Grand Rapids?" He looked at his watch. "It'll take me—"

"Three hours by jet," she said. "You need to be at the Marquette airport in forty-five minutes. Gate 12. Leave the Explorer there."

He pushed back the blanket and looked around for his pants. "What do we have in Grand Rapids? What kind of—"

"You'll see the scene yourself when you arrive," Camille said.

CHAPTER TWELVE

He couldn't believe what he was looking at. A church . . . he was standing in front of another church. It wasn't anything like the task force's old stone home in Lansing. And it sure as hell looked nothing like Reverend Grascoeur's hippie retreat up in Copper Harbor.

But it was definitely a church. A very big church.

It was sleek and modern, all white stone and sharp angles, a huge main building with tentacles radiating out to smaller buildings and chapels, set down over what looked to be about two acres of grounds bordered by woods. It could have the corporate headquarters of some high tech firm.

Except for the steeple.

Louis's eyes traveled upward, up to where the steeple, soaring at least fifty feet upward, pierced the gray sky like a giant white stiletto.

"Sir?"

He looked back at the Grand Rapid's Sheriff Department cruiser. The officer leaned across the seat to look at him.

"Don't forget your bags, sir."

Louis reached back into the cruiser and retrieved his duffel and briefcase. Tossing a thanks to the officer, he headed toward the church's entrance. The Grand Rapids deputy hadn't been able to pull very far into the church's long circular drive because it was blocked with cruisers, the medical examiner's car, and a white Kent County Crime Scene Unit van. The prime spots up near the entrance were taken by four dark-blue state police Explorers, just like the one Louis had left at the airport back in Marquette.

Two CSU techs, standing outside their van, eyed Louis as he passed. It had been three hours since he had gotten the call from Camille summoning here. Why weren't the techs inside processing the scene? But then again, Louis had no idea what was even in the church. Camille had told him nothing other than the other members of the team would meet him.

Louis zipped up his parka and cut across the icy lawn. He passed a large stone sign emblazoned with BEACON LIGHT CATHEDRAL and the announcement of worship at nine thirty and eleven a.m. on Sundays and six p.m. Wednesday evenings with Rev. Jonas Prince. Below that was a Bible verse: *Let brotherly love continue—Proverbs*

The Kent County sheriff's deputy guarding the door stepped forward to stop Louis but drew back with a brisk nod when Louis flashed his badge. He held the door open and Louis caught a glimpse of the words carved in the stone header above the double doors: COME UNTO ME.

Inside, the first thing that hit him was a faint smell of wood polish. Then came the sensation of cold. After the chill wind outside, he had been expecting the comfort of heat. But it was as cold in here as it was outside.

Another Kent County deputy was standing guard in the wide circular foyer and stepped forward.

"Can I take that for you, sir?" he asked, nodding to Louis's duffel.

"Yeah, thanks." Louis said. He handed over the duffel but kept his briefcase. The foyer was white marble with two hallways leading off to the right and left. There were two benches covered in red leather, and some metal chairs stacked in a corner near two folded wheelchairs.

As he stepped between the white pillars that led to the sanctuary, Louis paused to take a look.

Three long, red-carpeted aisles led up to a wide, elevated white marble altar. The other team members were gathered up on the altar. He started in, but the deputy touched his arm.

"Sir, you'll need these," he said, holding out a pair of latex gloves and blue shoe covers.

Louis took them and slid the covers over his shoes. He started down the middle aisle, snapping on the gloves as he walked.

The sanctuary was cavernous, three stories tall, the white marble walls broken by soaring panels of stained glass that forced the eyes ever upward. Two levels of balconies rimmed the wood pews of the main floor and Louis estimated the place seated a couple thousand people. It looked like a huge modern theater.

Except, Louis noted as he approached the stage-like altar, this theater had a thirty-foot, carved-wood pulpit off to the one side and a fifteen-foot, gleaming, silver crucifix in the middle of the altar. And behind the cross, thrusting upward like space-age metal stalagmites, were the pipes of a mammoth organ.

Emily Farentino's red hair gleamed in the spotlights on the altar. She saw him coming and said something to the others. They turned in unison— Cam in his black leather jacket, Junia in a cape as red as the carpet. Steele was nowhere to be seen.

When they parted, Louis saw the body.

It was lying in front of the crucifix, and as Louis climbed the six steps, he could see it was a man—elderly, with wispy, white hair and a long, concave face, tinged blue. He was wearing a royal-blue robe with a flat, gold scarf laid over his chest, the collar of a white dress shirt just visible beneath the robe.

"We've been freezing our asses off here," Cam said, his voice low. "What took you so long to get here, man?"

"High winds up in Marquette," Louis said. "We had a delay in taking off."

Cam let out a sigh that emerged as vapor in the cold air.

"What are we doing here?" Louis asked.

"Not sure. Steele hasn't told us yet," Emily said. "Just that this guy was found dead here on the altar this morning."

Louis decided not to ask the obvious. The task force was charged with cold cases. This guy looked like he hadn't even turned stiff yet.

"What's been done so far?" Louis asked Emily.

"Nothing," she said. "No one's been let in except the ME. Steele said he wanted us to get a feel for things first."

That was why the heat was off, Louis realized. Steele had probably ordered it turned off to preserve the body and the scene until the team was in place. That also explained why the CSU guys were still outside cooling their heels.

"Get a feel," Louis said. "Did he say for what?"

"You tell me. You're supposed to be the psychic one," Cam said.

Louis thought back to the first meeting of the task force, how Steele had hinted at Louis's "special feel" for homicides. As a PI who handled a fair amount of cold cases, his impressionistic walk-throughs of crime scenes often came ten or more years after the body and blood—and those weird intangibles his friend Mel once called *restless energies*—were gone.

But this scene was fresh.

"Where's Steele?" Louis asked Emily.

"Not sure. He disappeared about ten minutes ago."

Louis realized someone else was missing. "Where's Tooki?"

"In the church office, getting a phone line to connect his portable computer to his never-never land of databases," Junia said.

Louis glanced around and finally spotted Steele off in a far corner, talking to a man in a green parka. The man had blueprints in his hands and Louis guessed that Steele was getting a layout of the place.

Louis turned back to the body. The hands were covered in brown paper bags, the fingernails protected for evidence. It didn't look as if the ME had disturbed any of the clothing, and Louis couldn't help but wonder if—once the man had been declared dead—Steele had ordered the ME out for a while.

"Do we have an ID?" Louis asked.

"The Right Reverend Jonas Prince," Cam said.

"It's just 'The Reverend,'" Junia said.

"What's the difference?" Cam said.

"This is a Methodist Church," Junia said. "American Methodists don't use the term 'right.'"

PJ PARRISH

Cam let out a sigh and moved away.

Louis squatted next to the body. The eyes were open—pale-gray with tiny, red dots in the whites. He heard sniffling and looked up into Junia's face. She was holding a Kleenex to her red nose.

"Capillary rupture in the sclera," she said. "Result of a struggle and asphyxiation."

"Asphyxiation with this sash thing?" Louis asked.

"It's called a stole," Junia said, kneeling next to him. "And no, asphyxiation by hand. I'm guessing the killer put the stole on after death. Ease it down and look at the skin on the neck."

Louis pulled gently at the stole until he could see the man's neck. There were two thumb-sized bruises on both sides of the windpipe, which meant the man was strangled from the front. It was an unusual way to strangle someone because it allowed the victim to fight back. It was a helluva lot easier to come in from behind and use a garrote or chokehold.

"Make sure the stole is back where it was," Junia said softly. "Captain's got his own photographer coming and he wants it exactly as it was."

As Louis tucked the stole back in place, he noticed a design embroidered on one flap. The design looked like a house with three circles hovering above it, but the threads were so worn, it was hard to tell.

"Any idea what this means, if anything?" he asked Junia.

She peered at the design then shook her head. "I don't know," she said. "Catholic priests wear stoles, or cinctures, and I know they have different stoles for different occasions. It could just be personal."

Louis smoothed the stole over the reverend's chest. "Did the ME estimate the time of death?" he asked.

"Between seven and midnight last night."

Louis lifted the man's wrist. He was still in partial rigor and cold to the touch. "It must have been closer to eight," he said. "They had a service last night. He didn't have time to change out of his robe afterward."

He looked around at the sanctuary. This seemed an odd place to confront a man and kill him. The location presented a high risk of being interrupted, especially in the early evening.

82

"What time was the service over?" Louis asked.

Emily stepped forward. "Seven. Afterwards, the janitorial crew did its usual cleanup in the sanctuary, the back offices, halls, and restrooms, and they were gone by two a.m. The reverend was found by the janitor who came in this morning at six."

Louis nodded and rose. If the cleaners had been in the church until two a.m., and the reverend was already dead about six hours earlier, that meant his body had to have been hidden somewhere else, somewhere the cleaners didn't routinely go. He had been moved out here after two a.m.

Louis turned in a half-circle, looking down the three aisles that led off like arteries from the heart of the huge church. There were many rooms to examine to find the primary crime scene. And then there were the pivotal questions. Who had access to the church after two a.m.? And why move the body out here for display?

"How much do you think he weighs?" Louis asked.

Junia looked up. "Well, I'd guess around one-eighty alive."

"Alive?"

She gave him a wry smile. "The soul weighs twenty-one grams so do the math."

Louis heard Cam chuckling but ignored him, looking back at the body. Even without his soul, Jonas Prince would have been hard to maneuver, even harder once rigor started to set in. Most likely, he had been dragged here.

Louis looked down the center aisle to the nearest rear door, then across the floor. Except for the long runners of red carpet in the aisles and a few other patches of carpet near the steps to the altar, the floor was all white marble.

He moved to the reverend's feet. His shoes, beneath the cuffs of his blue, pinstriped dress trousers, were plain black leather lace-ups with solid-black heels. They were well cared for—the soles pristine and the heels still sharp—which meant the shoes were probably worn only here in church.

Louis scanned the white marble nearby but saw no scuffmarks to indicate the body had been dragged. Maybe the killer had used a cart or one of those wheelchairs out in the foyer to transport him. Or maybe he was just strong enough to carry him.

Louis pushed to his feet and again his eyes were drawn to the soaring windows then down to the crucifix.

Again, the question was there. Why had the killer left the body here at the foot of the cross? It prompted questions Louis couldn't begin to answer. His own exposure to churches had been too sporadic, and religion-driven killers were a breed he knew nothing about.

He realized Emily was gone and, finally, he spotted her standing at the back of the altar, dwarfed by the wall of massive organ pipes. She was making notes in a binder. He picked up his briefcase and went to her.

There was a soft slump to her posture that gave him the impression she would rather be anywhere but here. Maybe her mind was back with her cold case, the university suicides. He understood that. He wanted to be in Copper Harbor looking for the boys.

"First impressions of the scene?" he asked.

She looked back to the corpse. "I hate to even begin a profile without seeing where he was actually killed."

Louis wasn't surprised that she had picked up on the same thing he had—that the body had been moved.

"The body was obviously positioned here, but the unsub didn't feel the need for ritual," she said. "No candles, symbols, blood, or bizarre messages left near the body. No defilement of the body or church."

"Any messages in leaving him here in the sanctuary?"

Emily nodded. "Understanding the importance of the dump site to the killer is one of keys to understanding him. He left him in full sermon regalia, which he took the time to smooth and straighten after he laid him out here."

Louis thought back to the time of death. His first assumption had been that Jonas Prince had been murdered closer to eight because he was still dressed for his sermon. But what if the time of death had been later and the killer had felt compelled to redress him in his robe and stole?

"So he did this so the reverend would be dignified?" Louis asked.

Emily nodded. "Even in death."

"Do you think the killer was religious?"

"That's not the right word," she said. "More like reverential."

"That sounds like someone with a personal relationship," Louis said.

"Not necessarily. A stranger, a parishioner, could have done this. We have no idea about motive here."

"But asphyxiation is a personal way to kill."

Emily nodded. "I know. But that's not enough for me to settle in on a family member or someone close just yet. Homicides like this . . ."

She paused as if she had lost her thought. Louis gave her a moment and when she didn't respond, he prompted her.

"Are you okay?" Louis asked.

"Yes . . . no. I don't know. It's just these kinds of murders—ones with religious undertones—they have a pathology all their own. And it's always complicated and messy and hard to wrap your head around."

"Any other impressions?" he asked.

She forced a small smile. "I *can* tell you this. Whoever killed Jonas Prince really, really wanted him dead."

"And you know that how?"

"It takes a long time to strangle someone, up to four minutes. Four minutes when you have to keep your hands around someone's neck, looking into their eyes. The unsub had all that time to think about what he was doing, and he didn't stop."

"Sounds like a man with a purpose," Louis said.

Emily glanced over Louis's shoulder. "Yes, and here comes another one."

Louis turned. Steele was heading their way, carrying his leather binder and the rolled blueprints. He stopped in front of Cam, handed him the blue prints, said something, then continued toward Louis and Emily.

Louis knew Steele had been up since before dawn but everything—his trench coat, suit, hair, and even his step—was crisp. His brown eyes snapped with a wire-tight kind of excitement that Louis knew came from the moment. This wasn't some old stale cold case. This was fresh and, given the victim, high profile. Steele's baby was taking its first steps, and it would be in front of the attorney general, the TV cameras and—in this case, Louis thought—maybe even God.

What wasn't clear was why this case had landed on Steele's cold case desk.

The other team members gathered around.

"This will be the interview process," Steele said. "Six employees made it in this morning before we were able to shut down entry. They are secured in separate rooms and Cam and Junia will be conducting those interviews."

Steele opened his binder. "Reverend Jonas Prince, age eighty, was a widower," he said. "His wife, Reeta, died in 1961. He has one son, Anthony, aged forty-five. He's the general manager of the church. He's in his office on the second floor waiting for you."

"Me or Louis, sir?" Emily asked.

"Both of you," Steele said. "I like double-team interviews. What one misses, the other should pick up on. One antagonizes, the other connects and so forth."

Steele started to walk away then stopped. When he turned back to them, it was as if something in Steele had slipped away for a second, leaving him exposed and without the armor of command. It was so completely out of character, Louis wasn't sure what he was seeing.

"I know in our business, we look first to family members," Steele said. "But don't get tunnel vision. Anthony Prince is not a man we can afford to be wrong about."

Steele slapped his binder closed and walked away. Louis watched him as he made his rounds, stopping to talk to a newly arrived police photographer and a uniformed cop whom he directed to the front doors.

Finally, Steele stopped about halfway down the middle aisle and turned back toward the altar. Then, in a barely discernable movement of his hand, he crossed himself.

CHAPTER THIRTEEN

The executive offices were on the second floor. The corridor was long, carpeted in royal blue and adorned with framed photographs that ran the length of the hall.

Emily headed straight to Anthony Prince's office at the far end, but Louis walked slowly, taking in the photographs. He expected to see a gallery of images honoring the ministers who had come and gone over the years. But apparently, the Beacon Light Cathedral had always been a one-man show, starring the Reverend Jonas Prince.

The photographs included Jonas Prince on the steps of the state capitol with former governors George Romney and William Milliken. Others showed Prince in a lavish garden with William Clay Ford and posed on the veranda of the Grand Hotel on Mackinac Island with Bob Dole and Pat Robertson.

As Louis continued down the hall, the portraits of Jonas Prince continued, but the reverend grew younger and the faces of the men posing with him grew less familiar. And while Jonas Prince was always in a robe and stole, giving him a sense of timelessness, the wide lapel suits and long sideburns on the other men offered a journey back in time through the seventies and eighties.

Then came a photograph unlike the others, and it stopped Louis in his tracks.

Sepia-toned and still bearing the cracks and imperfections of the original, it was of Jonas Prince with a woman, probably his wife Reeta. She was seated at an organ, her hands clasped in the folds of a long skirt, her dark hair drawn into a severe bun. Jonas Prince stood behind his wife, hand on her shoulder. He appeared to be in his late forties, dressed in a simple, dark suit and stiff-collared shirt. Behind them, Louis could make out the edge of a scarred wooden pew and the corner of a small, stained-glass window.

The humble beginnings, Louis thought. From chapel to cathedral in thirty years.

"Louis!" Emily called.

Louis looked down the hall. Emily was standing at an open door about twenty feet down the hall. He followed her in to Anthony Prince's office. An empty secretary's desk sat in a reception area. The door to Anthony Prince's office was open.

The inner office was also empty, but then Louis heard the flush of a toilet behind a closed door. Emily wandered over to the bookshelves, and Louis suspected she was profiling Anthony Prince's reading tastes and what the large montage of plaques and awards might reveal.

Louis looked around the office. The walls and plush carpet were beige. There was a huge floor-to-ceiling window, framed by beige sheers that overlooked distant, black trees. The furnishings were sleek, all chrome and glass with black leather chairs. Anthony Prince's glass desk was neat—not one smudge mark that Louis could see—with a black leather blotter, a Rolodex, an in-box with papers, and telephone. To the left of the blotter sat a small silver tray, holding a carafe, a silver creamer and sugar set, a teaspoon, and one white coffee cup rimmed in gold. To the right of the blotter was a carefully-folded copy of that morning's *Grand Rapid's Press*. The only other things on the desk were three gold pens positioned above the blotter and perfectly spaced.

"You're detectives, I presume."

Louis turned toward the voice. Anthony Prince was standing at the door to the bathroom, holding a white towel. He was about five-ten and stocky, but not in a sloppy, gone-to-pot way. He stood stiffly, almost like a fighter waiting for the first punch. He wore a white dress shirt, sleeves rolled and open at the collar with his striped tie hanging loose. His face was doughy, and Louis had the thought that the son had inherited Reeta's round-ness rather than Jonas's sharp angles. His hair was wispy light-brown. The only memorable thing about Anthony Prince was his gray eyes—narrow and deeply hooded. Eyes that seemed to say *I am in control.* Or would have, if they weren't bloodshot from crying.

"Detective Louis Kincaid," Louis said. "This is Detective Farentino."

She gave a nod from her position by the bookshelf.

Anthony ignored her. He set the towel on the desk and started to roll his shirt sleeves down.

"Sir, before you do that, can you show me your arms, please?" Louis said.

Anthony stared at him. "Why?"

Normally this would be done later, but Anthony had forced the issue. "I have to examine you for scratches, scrapes or bruises."

"You think I murdered my father?" he asked softly.

"It's just routine, sir."

Anthony thrust out his arms, turning them over and back, revealing nothing but smooth pale, almost hairless skin.

Anthony jerked down his sleeves. "This is unbearable," he said. "I have been locked up like a prisoner since I arrived this morning. No one has told me anything except my father has been murdered. I haven't even been allowed in the sanctuary to see him."

"We're sorry for the inconvenience," Emily said.

Anthony looked at her. "Inconvenience? I just lost my father."

Louis knew he couldn't piss Anthony off or they would get nothing from him.

"My apologies for the lack of communication, Mr. Prince," he said.

Anthony stared at him. "It's *Reverend* Prince." He started to his black leather chair but decided to stay standing. "All right," he said, his voice more conciliatory. "I am aware that, as a family member, you must look at me as a suspect. So, can we please get on with your questions? I have parishioners who need consoling and media people to talk to."

"And a father to see downstairs," Emily added.

Anthony blinked rapidly. "Of course," he said softly.

Louis opened his binder and drew a pen from his pocket. "Where were you last night from the time the service ended until let's say, two a.m.?"

"I left almost immediately and went to dinner downtown at the Chop House. After dinner, I went home."

"Was anyone with you at dinner?"

"No. I went alone."

"What time did you get home?" Louis asked.

"Ten thirty-five."

"Can anyone verify that?"

"My wife. Her name is Violet. She's at home now. I called her to tell her what happened, and as you can imagine she's very upset. So please be considerate when you talk to her."

"Was she at the service last night?" Louis asked.

"No, she never attends the Wednesday service."

"Why not?"

"Violet comes on Sunday. To both services."

Anthony's eyes shifted and Louis realized he was now watching Emily, who was wandering around the office. She picked up a crystal obelisk from a credenza, peering at the engraved plate.

"Would you put that down, please?" Anthony said.

Emily looked at him, then set the crystal down.

"Why didn't your wife go to dinner with you?" Louis asked.

"She never comes to dinner with me. I use the time to think and meditate."

"Is there anything going on right now in your life that needs meditating over?" Louis asked.

Anthony was still watching Emily closely. She came back to the desk, picked up one of the gold pens and began to examine it closely. Louis wondered what she was doing but then he noticed Anthony's expression. It had gone stony.

"Reverend Prince?" Louis prodded.

Anthony couldn't take his eyes off Emily. She looked up at him, gave the pen a twirl between her fingers and set it back on the desk. Anthony reached down and realigned it with the other two pens.

"Reverend Prince, is there anything in your life that needs mediating over?" Louis asked again.

"One does not need a crisis in order to meditate."

Anthony moved to the credenza and picked up a water pitcher. As he poured himself a glass, his hand shook. He set the glass down and looked back at Louis.

"I'm sorry," he said quietly. "This whole thing with my father . . ." His eyes welled with tears and he looked around the office, finally settling on the towel on his desk. He picked it up and dabbed at his eyes. "I suppose you'll find this out when you talk to the church council," he said. "My father and I were at slight odds about whether to accept a television offer to broadcast our services."

"Aren't you already on TV?" Emily asked.

Anthony turned back, wiping his eyes. "Yes, but right now we broadcast only on Sundays and only here in the Grand Rapids market. Recently, we were offered a contract by Glory Days Broadcasting to take our services nationwide on Wednesday nights."

"You wanted to accept and your father didn't?" Louis asked.

"That's correct."

"How much money was the deal worth?" Louis asked.

"It wasn't about the money."

"Humor me," Louis said. "How much?"

"Six million."

"Why didn't your father want to accept the offer?" Emily asked.

"He felt we were losing touch with our congregation," Anthony said. "He was already distressed at the amount of time it took to prepare for the local broadcasts. My father was a simple man. He didn't like dealing with the production people, the noise, all the activity. He used to say it was like turning the word of God into a game show."

"Then why go on TV at all?" Emily asked.

"My father's mission was always to reach as many people as possible with God's message," Anthony said. "When we were originally asked to broadcast locally, I was able to convince him that it was a way to reach thousands of new people, people who were ill or confined to their homes. I also told him that we could use the money to support our charitable causes. Eventually, he saw the benefit and agreed. But he didn't want to expand. He thought we were already successful."

"Seems so," Emily said.

Anthony's red-rimmed eyes shot to her, but he said nothing.

"But you were still pushing him?" Louis asked.

"I was trying to persuade, not push," Anthony said. "I assure you that, in the end, I would have accepted whatever his final decision may have been."

"But now the decision is yours," Louis said.

Anthony stared at Louis, clear indignation in his eyes. "My father was the soul and heart of our church," he said softly. "I gain nothing by killing him, not even the six million dollars. The television people wanted the Reverend Jonas Prince. I don't think they will want me."

"You're not so silver-throated, I take it," Emily said.

There was an odd mixture of anger and embarrassment in Anthony's eyes. He was still holding the white towel and he began to carefully fold it.

"No one could match my father's charisma and innate divinity," he said. "But I will pray for the strength and ability now to step into his shoes and fulfill his mission. I have no doubt, with God's help, that I will succeed. Maybe not on television, but I will continue to lead the congregation."

"There's no one else?" Emily asked. "No other family?"

"No," he said. "My mother passed when I was very young and my younger brother, Nathan, died in a boating accident when he was twelve. For most of my life, it's been only my father and me. I was always the heir to his mission. I've accepted that."

"Accepted?" Emily asked.

Anthony was quiet. He seemed to be staring at something on the far wall but there was nothing there that Louis could see.

"Sometimes a child can feel pressure to follow in a father's footsteps," Emily said. "Especially a powerful father."

"I knew from a very early age that helping to spread God's word would be my purpose in life," Anthony said. "But it wasn't just my father. It was the Holy Father who compelled me."

Anthony set the towel on the desk, folded in a perfect square. "Are we finished? I would really like to go see my father now," he said.

"Just a few more questions," Louis said. "Do you know anyone who would want to kill your father?"

"Of course not, I—" Anthony stopped himself.

Louis waited, pen poised over his binder.

"There is one man," Anthony said slowly. "His name is Walter Bushman. He's an atheist activist in Detroit."

"Your father had trouble with him?" Louis asked.

"Yes. Three months ago, he started a harassment campaign against my father. I'm sure it was to boost the ratings of his radio show. He demanded my father debate him on the air about the existence of God. My father, of course, refused to even be in the same room with the man, but Bushman just wouldn't stop. He wrote articles and took out newspaper ads calling my father a coward. We tried to ignore him, but eventually our own council began pressuring my father to respond to Bushman. My father's response came in the form of a sermon, on live TV on a Sunday morning. He called out Bushman by name."

Anthony smiled slightly at the memory.

"It was the Reverend Jonas Prince at his best," he said. "He called Bushman a soulless philistine whose inflated sense of self simply would not allow him to accept the idea of anything or anyone greater than he. I believe the sermon was what prompted Glory Days to want to take us nationwide."

"And it put Mr. Bushman in his place?" Louis asked.

"I assume so," Anthony said. "We never heard from him again."

Louis wrote Bushman's name in his binder. It seemed a long shot that Jonas Prince was the victim of a religious feud, but anything was possible. As Emily had said, religious fanatics had no patent on crazy.

"May I please go see my father now?"

Pained impatience edged Anthony's voice and Louis didn't blame him. Steele was simply doing his job, trying to keep his crime scene as sterile as possible. But to prevent the man's only son—an ordained minister—to see his dead father and say whatever he needed to say over the body seemed unusually cold hearted.

"I'll check for you," Emily said. She pulled her radio from her belt and moved away from the desk. Louis looked back at Anthony. He was drinking water again.

"One more question, Reverend Prince," Louis said. "Your father was dressed in robe and stole."

"Yes. He always wears a robe and stole for services."

"Don't most Methodist ministers wear suits?" Louis asked.

"My father wasn't like most ministers," Anthony said. "He felt God should be exalted in every way humanly possible, that there should be a grandiosity in worship. His vestments, as old-fashioned as some think they were, were his way of glorifying his message."

"And the stole," Louis said. "Is there a significance to the embroidered design on the front?"

Anthony was quiet but Louis saw something pass quickly across his eyes. Surprise? Or was he just trying to remember something?

"No, it was just an old design," Anthony said. "It has no significance."

Emily had stepped forward, stuffing the radio back in her belt. "I can take you downstairs now," she said.

Anthony quickly moved to a closet, got out his suit jacket and slipped it on. He was knotting his tie as he followed Emily out of the office.

When Louis heard their footsteps fade, he moved closer to the desk. He didn't have a warrant to search, which meant he couldn't open drawers or closets, only observe whatever was in plain view.

A stack of letters lay in the in-box. Like everything in the office, the letters were in a neat pile, so Louis could read only the top letterhead—Ministries of Light. It was a letter about a lecture Anthony was scheduled to give next month.

He hesitated, but the PI in him couldn't resist.

He used his pen to nudge the top letter so the next two letterheads were visible. Michigan Conference 1991 of the Methodist Church, and something called the Fresh Start.

Emily's voice came from Louis's radio, almost a whisper. "Prince wants you out of his office, now."

Louis acknowledged her with a 10-4 and went to the door. He stopped to close the door behind him and that's when he saw it.

A faint shadow on the far wall, a rectangle about three-by-four-feet, just a shade darker than the beige wall. Louis moved closer. There was a picture hanger above it.

Someone had taken down a picture. A pretty good-sized one that had hung there long enough for the sun to have bleached the wall around it.

The closet door was still ajar. Louis went to it and moved it open with his shoulder. There it was, a framed portrait of Jonas Prince. Anthony must have taken it down.

The question was—had it been removed out of grief or something else?

CHAPTER FOURTEEN

Back downstairs, Louis took his time returning to the sanctuary. He walked slowly, wandering down hallways, taking time to look for any strange marks on the walls, floors or doors. He was searching for the place where Jonas Prince had been murdered, knowing it probably wasn't far from the sanctuary, but all the surfaces looked pristine, doors were locked, and there was no evidence of struggle. His breath rose in a steady stream of cold vapor as he walked, a sign that Steele still hadn't ordered the heat turned back on.

His radio crackled. "Louis?"

He jerked it from his belt to answer Emily. "Yeah?"

"Where are you? Steele wants us back at the altar."

"I'm on my way. Where's Anthony?"

"I brought him down to view his father. He broke down pretty bad when he saw him, and Cam had to almost carry him out to the lobby. Then he got ahold of himself and asked how long we were going to leave him like that. I told him it was going to be a while. Then he said he was going home."

"And you said?"

"Like hell you are." Emily chuckled. "No, I told him we'd appreciate it if he stayed in case we had more questions. He said he would wait up in his office, that he had calls to make."

"I haven't seen him up here," Louis said, starting down the stairs. "Tell a uniform to watch his car. I just want to know if he leaves and where he goes."

"Will do. Anything else?"

"Any word on a search warrant yet?"

"Yeah, Steele just got it."

"Good." Louis clicked off and stuffed the radio back in his belt. He decided to take a different hallway back to the sanctuary, but a walk down yet another long white hall yielded nothing but locked doors. As he neared the sanctuary, he saw a door that stood ajar. There was a small sign on it: DRESSING ROOM. PRIVATE.

Louis pushed the door open and went in. It was a small room, maybe ten-by-ten, with a stained-glass window and wall of wood-paneled closets. The only furnishings were a wooden bench, a full-length mirror, and a valet chair draped with a blue, pinstriped jacket that matched the trousers worn by Jonas Prince. Another open door led to a small bathroom.

One of the closet doors was open, and Louis started his search there. It held a worn gray cardigan sweater, a wrinkled raincoat, a pair of chinos, and a plaid shirt. The sweater gave off a strong, earthy smell—like it had been stored in an old cedar closet. There was a pair of worn, brown Hush Puppies on the floor of the closet.

Louis guessed that Jonas Prince had probably come to the church dressed in these street clothes and changed into his suit and dress shoes before putting on his robe for the Wednesday evening service.

Louis opened the second closet. It held more robes, a rainbow of colors. On the inside of the door was a rack, draped with six stoles and several gold-tasseled cords. Each stole had a different embroidered pattern, one with a crown of thorns and a chalice, another with a star of Bethlehem, a third with two gold bands and white candles.

Louis understood now—Jonas Prince had a collection of stoles for every occasion from Easter and Christmas to a wedding ceremony.

He looked down. The floor was white tile. He dropped to his knees and lowered his head to the floor, looking for black scuffmarks. Even if Jonas

Prince had been too feeble to put up much of a fight, his survival instincts would have made him kick as the breath was squeezed from his body.

And kick the reverend had.

There were several dark marks on the white tile.

Louis looked up at the sign on the door. PRIVATE. This was where the reverend had been strangled. A room everyone knew he would go to, yet a place few people were allowed to enter. But Anthony Prince had probably been in here countless times, maybe helping his father dress for services. And Jonas would have had no reason to not welcome his son in.

Anthony claimed he had left the church right after the service, gone to dinner, then went right home.

Louis rose, remembering what Emily had said. Four minutes was a long time to look someone in the eye as you strangle him.

But maybe four minutes was all the time Anthony had needed.

CHAPTER FIFTEEN

The crime scene techs had just began to crawl through Jonas Prince's dressing room, when Steele came up to Louis's side at the door.

"A state car is waiting for you," Steele said.

"Where am I going?" Louis said.

"The Chop House to verify Prince's alibi." Steele watched the techs for a moment then walked away.

Not one word, Louis thought, no thanks, no praise for finding the room where the murder was likely committed and saving the CSU guys a lot of wasted time and effort.

Louis bypassed the sanctuary as he made his way back outside. A deputy handed off the keys to the Explorer parked in the circular drive and Louis got in. It was near noon when Louis pulled up in front of the Chop House in downtown Grand Rapids. The restaurant occupied the ground floor of a refurbished red brick building, its double bronze doors shielded by a black awning. The big front window, swaged by drapes, looked dark. There were no cars in the adjacent parking lot, and the sign on the door told Louis that the place was open five to eleven p.m.

He went to the front window and peered inside. He could see people moving around and he tapped on the glass. A young man in a white shirt, black vest, and slacks looked up and came forward slowly. Louis held up his badge up to the glass.

A click of a lock, one of the bronze doors swung open and the man let him inside.

"Is your boss here?" Louis asked.

"Yes, sir. I'll get him."

The kid hustled away and Louis moved deeper into the restaurant. The lights were up, but he imagined that, at dinnertime, a gold glow gave a luxurious sheen to the apricot-colored sheers, the dark-paneled walls and the gleaming wood bar. The far wall was lined with Picasso knock-offs and he counted no less than four wine racks tucked in the corner. A faint but not unpleasant smell of musty hay and cedar told him there was a cigar lounge nearby.

A man appeared from a backroom and came toward Louis. "I'm Miles Beauchamp," he said. "How may I help you, officer?"

"I need to ask you about a customer you may have had last night," Louis said. "Were you here?"

"Yes. From six until closing at eleven."

"Do you know Reverend Anthony Prince?"

"Of course. We all know him. He's been coming in for at least five years."

"Was he in last night?"

Beauchamp nodded, his eyes filling with questions. "He comes in for dinner every Wednesday night."

Louis opened his binder and started taking notes. "Do you recall when he arrived and when he left?"

"He came in around eight, and he left sometime after ten. I greeted him at his table, as I always do, and told him I would see him later in the cigar lounge." He paused. "But come to think of it, he didn't go into the lounge like he usually does."

"How did he seem?" Louis asked.

"What do you mean?"

"What was his mood? Upset? Preoccupied? Anything out of the ordinary?"

Beauchamp paused, thinking. "Well, he seemed quiet. He didn't finish his meal, and I asked him if there was something wrong with his steak, but he said he was fine. And he asked me to bring him a fourth drink."

"What does he drink?"

"Hendricks martini." Beauchamp leaned closer, a small smile on his lips. "Just between you and me, I always thought that a bit strange, a minister who drinks gin. But I suppose even a man of God needs to wash away his troubles now and then." The smile faded. "But I've never seen him order more than three."

Louis nodded. "Was he alone?"

"He's always alone."

"Always?" Louis asked. "In five years, you never saw him with anyone? Not his wife or maybe his father?"

"No, his wife never comes in," Beauchamp said. "I met his father once, maybe three years back, when Mr. Prince brought his father here for a birthday dinner." He paused, frowning slightly. "I remember the older gentleman made a point of telling me that he liked his regular restaurant much more."

"Did he say which restaurant?"

Beauchamp raised his chin slightly. "Yes, that place out on Reeds Lake. Rosie's, I think it's called."

Louis wrote the name in his book.

"Can I ask why you're asking about the reverend?" Beauchamp asked.

Word of the elder Prince's death had not yet made the streets and Louis didn't want this man's statement colored with emotions or assumptions.

"I can't really say at this time," Louis said. "Could I please see a copy of his bill?"

"Certainly."

When Beauchamp left, Louis walked to the doors of cigar lounge, peeked inside, then stopped at the maître d's stand to check out the menu. Steak au poivre, beef Wellington, Australian lamb chops. And not a price to be seen.

101

Beauchamp returned and handed Louis a check. Anthony Prince had ordered a bone-in strip steak, extra rare with a side of sautéed spinach. Stapled to the back was a small cash register receipt time-stamped to show Prince had paid his bill in cash at ten-twelve.

Louis dug in his pocket for a business card. "Thank you, Mr. Beauchamp. If you remember anything else unusual about last night, I'd appreciate a call."

Louis went to the door. It was locked, and as he was looking around for a latch, the young man reappeared. He unlocked the door and held it open. As Louis started to step outside, the waiter touched his arm.

"You were asking about Reverend Prince?"

"Yes. Do you know him?"

The man looked back toward the dining room, then turned back to Louis. "Know him and hate him," he said. "We all hate him. He's like anal about his routine. The same table, the same martini, the same food, the same lousy twelve percent tip. But if his steak isn't bleeding out or we forget and put two olives in his drink, he stiffs us for the whole dinner."

Bitter service people. Great sources of information.

"Were you working last night?"

"Yeah. I've worked the Wednesday through Saturday shift for years."

"Did you notice anything different about Reverend Prince last night?"

The waiter hesitated, his eyes moving again toward the dining room. "I don't know if I should say."

"Just between you and me," Louis said.

The waiter nodded toward the glass doors. "Well, you know it was cold and rainy last night," he said. "Around the time Reverend Prince was getting his coat on, it started really coming down. I started to ask him if he wanted to borrow an umbrella or have someone get his car from the lot—we don't have a valet—but before I could, he went outside on his own."

"And?"

"He stepped out from under the awning and just stood here in the rain, like he was taking a freakin' shower or something."

"For how long?"

"At least a minute," the waiter said. "I finally had to get to work and when I looked back, he was gone."

Louis looked to the sidewalk, picturing what the waiter had described. Anthony Prince had said he spent his Wednesday nights alone to meditate, but standing in a freezing rain was a strange way to do it.

Louis handed the server his business card and told him to call if he remembered anything else about Anthony Prince. When he climbed in the Explorer, he looked back at the restaurant. Through the window, he could see the server talking to another employee, showing him Louis's business card. It wouldn't be long before Jonas Prince's murder hit the news and the media would be crawling all over this place.

And all over Anthony Prince's home.

He had to get out there before the cameras did.

CHAPTER SIXTEEN

It was a gated community of just thirty homes called Tammarron North. Big brick mini-mansions set on half-acre lots with circular driveways sporting BMW's and Escalades, sloping lush lawns and manicured shrubbery that reminded Louis of the sculpted bush animals at Disney World.

Anthony Prince's home sat at the end of a cul-de-sac. It was a sprawling pseudo-chateau of pale-gray brick with a three-car garage and a tri-panel front door of frosted glass.

Louis rang a doorbell that tolled through the house like church bells. A few seconds later, the door opened.

Louis expected to be met by a housekeeper, but the woman who stood in front of him looked nothing like a maid. She was tall and willowy, wearing a plain, soft-pink, shift-like dress. Her wavy, dark hair was long but neatly pulled back from her moon-shaped face. Her eyes—just about the color of his Persian blue Explorer—stared at him nervously, but warmly.

"Mrs. Prince?"

"You're the policeman my husband called me about."

"Yes, ma'am. May I come in?"

Violet Prince moved back and held the door open while he stepped inside the foyer. He waited until she closed the door and looked at him. She didn't seem to be wearing much make-up—with her flawless, lightly-freckled skin she didn't need to—but her eyes were red-rimmed like she had been crying.

"I'm sorry for your loss," he said.

"Thank you," she said softly.

"Is there somewhere we can talk?"

"May I get you something to drink first?" she asked. "I have coffee. Or maybe lemonade? I just made it."

"No, thank you."

Her face melted in disappointment, then she gestured to the hall. "All right then, please come with me."

The large living room was carpeted with thick, beige pile and furnished with a pale-blue sofa and matching chairs that looked like they had never been desecrated by any human rear end. There were glass end tables, an empty glass coffee table, and a tall glass étagère, which held a collection of pastel figurines that Louis recognized as Lladro, the same ones his foster-mother Frances collected. Frances had only a couple animals, including a bunny Louis had given her for her birthday years ago. Violet's huge collection seemed to be all humans—children in bonnets, a farm boy pushing a wheelbarrow, tiny ballerinas, two little boys in a wooden washtub, praying cherubs, and a trio of Mary, Joseph, and baby Jesus.

The far wall was given over to a huge picture window, framed by knife-pleat, beige sheers that looked out over a small lake. In front of the window was a glass console on which sat a crystal vase of tall irises so deep-blue and perfect that Louis was sure they weren't real.

Everything in this room had a slightly unreal feel—no family pictures, no clutter, no sound, no smells. The room felt like someone's *idea* of what a beautiful home should be.

"You have a lovely home," Louis said.

"Yes, I suppose," Violet said, her eyes drifting about the room and finally coming back to him. "Thank you."

It was a big house, Louis thought, which meant housekeepers, who were always good sources of domestic intrigue. "It must be hard on you," he said, "having to divide your time between your church duties and keeping such a big house. You must have good help."

"Help? Oh, you mean like servants?" She smiled wanly. "We don't have any servants. Anthony doesn't believe in paying for things you can do for yourself." Her smile faded. "I manage fine on my own, with God's help, of course."

Louis noticed a dark shape set off in a far corner that looked at odds with the light feeling of the living room. He moved closer and saw it was an old organ, made of cherry wood, carved with intricate scrollwork. The half-circle, double-tier keys were yellowed with age. It was only about four feet wide, but its upper wood casing—filled with burnished brass pipes and topped with a cross—rose a good foot over Louis's head.

It was the same organ that was in the picture of Jonas and his wife, Reeta, in the hallway back at the church.

"Is this an antique?" Louis asked.

Violet Prince moved quickly to the organ and stood next to the carved wood bench, nervously brushing dust from the glossy surface.

"I don't really know how old it is," she said. "It used to be in Jonas's church down in Vandalia."

"Where's Vandalia?"

"It's a small town about an hour south of here." Violet looked off toward the window, and for a moment Louis thought she was staring at something outside. But it was still foggy, and her eyes were unfocused, like she had gone some place far away in her mind. He had to get her back.

"Do you play?"

She was slow to turn back to him, and then her face colored slightly. "Yes, but only for myself. I'm not good enough to play for anyone."

Louis thought of the huge organ back at the cathedral that seemed to hover over the cavernous sanctuary like a giant, menacing flying saucer, and it occurred to him again how far the Prince family had come in just one generation.

"Your mother-in-law . . ." he began.

"Reeta," Violet said. "I didn't know her. She passed away before I met Jonas."

"I saw a photograph of her, sitting at this very organ," Louis said.

"Yes, the organ has been in Jonas's family since before I met him." Again, she slid a hand over the cherry wood, and as she did, her eyes brimmed. The way she had said Jonas's name, there was a tenderness there that, to Louis's ear, was absent when she said her husband's name.

"Were you close to your father-in-law?" he asked.

She looked up at him as if it was an odd question, though Louis knew it wasn't. She nodded briskly and dipped her head, but not before Louis saw a tear fall.

"I lost my own father when I was just sixteen," she said softly. "Jonas . . . always treated me like his own daughter."

It was quiet—a strange, smothering quiet—unbroken by the little, normal heartbeats of a house like a ticking clock or humming heat vent.

"Mrs. Prince," Louis said, "I know this is a hard time for you—"

"Yes, yes, it is," she said quickly, brushing at her face. She moved away from the organ, toward the picture window. She was crying softly. She pulled a Kleenex from a pocket and gently blew her nose. Louis waited until she turned to face him.

"I'm sorry," she said. "I . . . this all happened so fast, and I have so many things to do. Anthony told me to start making the funeral arrangements, and I don't know where to start." Her eyes drifted to the big picture window. A fog was pressing against the glass, making the lake beyond fade, then disappear.

"I don't even know what kind of flowers Jonas might like," she said. She touched one of the irises. "'He flourishes like a flower of the field. For the wind passes over it, and it is gone.'"

The last words had come out in a whisper.

"Excuse me?" Louis said.

She looked back at him. "Oh, I'm sorry. It's a verse from Psalms. I was reading the Bible just before you came. I was looking for something to help me make sense of this all, because the Lord always gives us the right words when we can't find them ourselves."

It was obvious Violet Prince was in a fragile state, but Louis had to get this back on track. "Mrs. Prince," he said, "I have to ask you some questions."

"Yes, of course you do." She moved to the sofa. "Please, sit down."

Louis sat down in one of the chairs and took out his binder and pen. "What time did your husband get home last night?" he asked.

It was a direct-assault question, aimed at throwing a spouse off-guard and sending them into a defensive crouch, but Violet Prince sat ramrod straight and didn't blink.

"It was right around ten-thirty," she said.

"You were awake?"

"Yes," she said. "I am on a strict schedule. On Wednesdays, Anthony always goes to dinner downtown. I eat dinner alone at seven, then clean up. I bathe at nine and then read my Bible. Anthony came home at ten-thirty."

"People can lose track of time. Why do you remember the time so well?"

"I am sure because I looked at the clock because I have to take my medication at ten-thirty."

Louis jotted this down as he did a quick review in his head. The service at the Beacon Light Cathedral had ended around seven-thirty. Anthony arrived at the Chop House around eight, the restaurant owner said. The restaurant was only a fifteen-minute drive from the church. According to the time stamp on the check, Anthony paid at ten-twelve. The drive from the restaurant to his home was about twenty minutes, which put Anthony pulling into his driveway right around when Violet said he did.

This pointed to Anthony having what looked like an airtight alibi—except for that ten-minute window just after the service ended.

As for the body being moved, Anthony could have done that anytime during the night, sneaking out to return to the church after he was certain his wife was asleep.

Louis decided to change course. "When did you last see your father-in-law?" he asked.

"Last Sunday night, after service."

"Why don't you go to Wednesday services?"

"I never go to service on Wednesdays," she said. "Anthony is usually at the church all day on Wednesday because he has meetings just before the service."

"Who does he meet with?"

"Board members of charities, the church council," she said. "There is so much business to be discussed. We are a very large congregation."

"Did you know that your husband and your father-in-law disagreed about expanding the TV coverage?" Louis asked.

She hesitated then nodded. "Yes, they did. But except for Fresh Start, I don't get involved in the business side."

"Fresh Start?"

"It's a family resettlement program, part of a large effort run by our churches here. I helped Jonas get our program started. We've been helping families here in Grand Rapids for more than twenty years now."

There was a note of pride in her voice, the first sign of strength Louis had seen in this wan woman.

"I have to ask you," Louis said. "Did you ever hear your husband and father-in-law argue about the TV coverage?"

Violet didn't move, but a faint cloud passed over her face. "Once," she said softly. "It was after a Sunday morning service and I was waiting in the receptionist area outside Anthony's office. I heard Jonas speaking loudly about the eye of the needle."

"The eye of the needle?"

"Jonas was quoting from Luke. 'It is easier for a camel to go through the eye of a needle than for a rich person to enter the kingdom of God,'" Violet said.

She let out a long breath. "That was the only time I had ever heard Jonas raise his voice. But I know that, in the end, my husband would have given in to whatever Jonas wanted. My husband deeply respects his father." She paused, her eyes tearing. "I'm sorry. Respected him, I meant."

"Did they disagree about anything else?"

"No, Anthony trusted his father's judgment in nearly everything."

"*Nearly* everything?"

She pursed her lips, a rise of color in her cheeks.

"Please," he pressed.

"Anthony and I . . . ." She paused. "The Lord has not blessed us with children, and Jonas wanted us to adopt. He hoped for a lasting legacy to the church, a third-generation minister to carry on his work. But Anthony didn't want to do that."

"Why not?" Louis asked. "Adoption is a very Christian thing to do."

"Yes, it is," Violet said.

She pressed her lips together and just stared at him. It was clear this hurt her. He resisted the urge to look at all those perfect porcelain children lined up on the glass shelves.

"Do you know anyone who might have wanted to harm your father-in-law?" he asked.

She was quiet for a long time, then she said softly, "That is something I have been thinking about all day. As I said, I have been searching for some sense in all this senselessness, trying to understand who could have done this."

Again, she became quiet.

"Mrs. Prince," Louis said, "anything you can give me would be helpful."

"My husband told you about that man in Detroit?"

"Yes. Walter Bushman. Anyone besides him?"

"I hesitate to cast aspersions, but there is Clinton Rose."

"And he is?"

Violet's face flushed with color again, embarrassment this time. "Clinton is a homosexual," she said.

"Why would he have problems with your father-in-law?" Louis asked.

"He was a deacon in the church, until last month. He decided to reveal what he was to everyone. They asked him to leave the church."

"Because he was gay?"

Violet stared at him, and he knew she felt he was judging her and the church. He was, but he tried to soften it.

"Your church is not tolerant of things like that?" Louis asked.

"The church's official position is that homosexuality isn't compatible with Christianity," she said softly.

"So your father-in-law made this man leave?"

She nodded. "Jonas believed homosexuals were sinners and should not hold a position of eminence in his church."

"How did Mr. Rose react?"

"I understand that he cried. Then he told my father-in-law that he would open his own church."

"That doesn't sound like a violent man," Louis said.

Violet smoothed her dress. He could tell that she was uncomfortable. "Jonas said that they were living double lives, one with God and one with the devil."

"I think the devil visits all of us from time to time, Mrs. Prince."

Now Violet was staring at him, those rich, blue eyes boring so hard into him that he wondered for a second if she could see inside him, down to that place where his own demons slept.

Slept until they roared to life and chased him down dark beaches.

What the hell had made him think of that?

Violet rose slowly, pushing back a long lank of hair that had fallen over one shoulder. "I don't mean to be rude, officer, but are we finished? I have so much to do."

Of course she did. Anthony Prince would be able to distract himself with the byzantine dealings of keeping a cathedral alive, but it would be left to Violet Prince to deal with the dead. He remembered that's the way it had been when his mother lay sick and dying back in Mississippi—the churchwomen closed circle to pray at her bedside, prepare the service after she passed, cook the food, and sing the hymns. And afterward, it was the women—always the women—who pulled the weeds from the graves.

He capped his pen and rose. "Thank you for your time, Mrs. Prince."

She walked him to the door and held it open until he stepped back to the porch. He started to close his binder but then stopped, looking down at one thing he had printed in caps.

111

TAKES MEDS AT TEN THIRTY.

He turned to face Violet. "One last question. What do you take medication for?"

Violet shrunk back slightly, lowering her eyes.

"Don't be embarrassed, Mrs. Prince. Please."

She met his gaze. "I take Restoril."

He knew that name. He recognized it from one of the old cases Steele had forced him to study, a case about a man who had murdered his wife and children. His defense was that he had been sleepwalking because he had stopped taking his Restoril.

"Do you sleepwalk?" Louis asked.

"Yes," Violet said. "I had been doing it for quite some time before Anthony finally figured out why, on some mornings, things in the kitchen were in such disarray. The medication is the only way I can sleep soundly through the night."

That explained how Anthony could have returned to the church to move his father's body. Violet would never have known he was gone.

"It's raining again," Violet said absently, looking out, past his Explorer, at the long, empty driveway. Not one other house could be seen from her door.

She seemed to drift away for a moment, and Louis wanted to say something, anything that might relieve this sad woman's mood. His own church experience was so spare, and not one Bible verse had sunk in. His own words would have to do.

"Again, I'm sorry for your loss, Mrs. Prince," he said.

When those blue eyes refocused on his face, there was something there that told him she wanted to say something, or maybe just didn't want him to leave.

"It was nice to have someone to talk to," she said softly. "You're a very kind man."

CHAPTER SEVENTEEN

He had just gotten back in the Explorer when Camille called on the car phone. Steele wanted him to head down to Detroit today to interview the atheist Walter Bushman.

A church janitor had leaked the news about Jonas Prince's death, and now Steele and the team were doing damage control before the six o'clock news blew the lid off everything. Things had gotten hotter when Cam discovered that, instead of Bushman being on the air during his usual eight to eleven p.m. time slot the previous night, the radio station had run an emergency "The Best of Bushman" tape.

"The captain said, and I quote, 'Tell Kincaid to interview Bushman today before he decides to start talking to someone higher,'" Camille said.

Louis knew Steele was referring to God, and meant it as a joke. Dirtbags had a way of finding Jesus when things got too rough, but Louis doubted Walter Bushman was the type. He was, by all accounts, a man of deep conviction, even if his conviction was in nothing. In Bushman's case, talking to a higher authority probably meant lawyering up.

"I just left Mrs. Prince. I'll report in after I see Bushman," Louis told Camille and signed off.

He headed the Explorer east on I-96, breaking the speed limit to stay ahead of a bank of roiling, black storm clouds. The storm followed him past the flat, fallow fields below Lansing, through the gentle hills of Huron Recreation Area, and into the amorphous western suburbs around Detroit. It was raining by the time he reached the city limits.

He slowed, checking the directions Camille had given him. He hadn't been back to Detroit in years, and he couldn't remember the last time he had actually set foot in the downtown itself. He had heard a lot about the attempts to bring the city back from the brink, big talk about redevelopment and E-Zone grants that had pumped millions into the city.

But except for a few rehabbed Victorians, and an old factory with a sign touting LOFTS FOR SALE, the outer-ring neighborhoods looked much as he remembered—block after block of weedy empty lots, collapsed caverns of abandoned boarding houses, wild pheasants roosting in the rafters of burned-out mansions, and bullet-ridden stop signs standing sentry on corners where nobody came anymore.

He headed into the gray canyon of the downtown core. The radio station was housed in the Guardian Building on Griswold, not far from the Detroit River. He parked the Explorer in a lot, and sat there for a moment, looking up at the Guardian Building.

Thirty-some stories of rust-red brick and limestone, with a couple of Aztec—no, Indian figures—carved into the stone façade. Way up top, he could make out a needle-like spire and an American flag that was big enough to be seen from Canada. He looked around at the other nearby buildings. He'd forgotten how rich Detroit was in Gothic and Renaissance architecture, how distinctively jagged the city's skyline was. Each building had its own character—intricate marble work, swanky gilded entrances, gargoyles and stone lion heads. Blight had eaten the fringe neighborhoods to the point that they resembled an apocalyptic movie set. But downtown, here amid these beautiful old buildings, Detroit was still breathing. Gasping maybe, but breathing.

Louis entered the Guardian Building's lobby. A soaring, domed ceiling of orange and brown mosaic tile gave the place the feeling of a Spanish cathedral, but the paint scaffolds and a large OFFICES FOR LEASE sign near the security desk told Louis the building was in bad need of tenants. There was a large banner hanging from a balcony railing touting the downtown revival from a civic group called Motor City On The Move. The slogan was big and bold: DETROIT IS ALIVE!

Louis found Bushman's name on the wall directory and rode the creaky elevator to the twentieth floor.

Unlike the lobby, Bushman's office was utilitarian, done in cheap paneling and faux-suede chairs. The brass letters WROR hung on the wall with the slogan underneath: The Station that Roars.

The receptionist gave him a bored look-over when he showed his badge, then she picked up the phone. "There's a cop here to see you, Walt." She hung up and pointed her pen left. "Third door back."

The door was ajar and Louis went inside. It was a corner office with big windows that didn't offer much of a view given the downpour. The office smelled of cigarette smoke, despite the hum of an air purifier next to the hulking old wooden desk. The desk was heaped with papers, magazines, and newspapers, except for one clear area in the middle that held an overflowing ash tray, a plate of bare rib bones, and an empty LaBatt bottle.

At first, Louis thought no one was in the office, but then the huge black leather chair turned and there he was—a walrus of a man with unruly brown hair and a fleshy, gray face that poured like wet concrete into the collar of a black T-shirt emblazoned with Albert Einstein's face.

"You got a badge?" Walter Bushman said.

Louis flipped open his wallet to let Bushman see his badge. Bushman's eyes flicked from the badge back to Louis's face.

"Never had a statie in my office before," Bushman said. "This must actually be important. Did you guys finally figure out who's sending me death threats?"

Louis wasn't surprised the man got threats. "Sorry, that's not my case."

"Then why are you here?"

"Where were you last night between six p.m. and midnight or so?"

"You need someone to write you better dialogue."

"Just answer the question, please."

Bushman stared hard at him. Then he made himself busy moving his rib plate and beer bottle aside, clearing a small spot on the desk so he could fold his hands.

"Is this about that woman at the Stonehouse bar?"

Louis also wasn't surprised the man had a problem at a bar. "No," he said. "It's about Jonas Prince."

Bushman arched an eyebrow. "That old fart? Why are you asking me about him?"

Maybe the news had trickled out back in Grand Rapids but it hadn't made it to Detroit yet. Still, Bushman would probably hear it himself within the hour.

"He's dead," Louis said. "Murdered in his church."

Bushman's eyes narrowed. He picked up a pack of Kools, shook out a cigarette and lit it. He took three long pulls, letting each out in a slow stream of smoke. Finally, he smiled.

Louis couldn't resist. "Why the smile?"

"Just picturing old Jonas wandering around out there in the dark, waiting for his God to welcome him to the ever-after."

"Where were you last night?" Louis asked.

"I'm a suspect?"

"You and a few others. Where were you?"

"I was on the air."

"No you weren't. The station played a tape."

Bushman grunted. "Right, you would've checked." He took another draw on the cigarette.

"One last time, Mr. Bushman. Where—"

"I wasn't feeling so hot. I have bad asthma. It gets worse when it rains. I was home in bed."

"You want to take another minute to think about that?"

Bushman started to say something then shut his mouth, just staring hard at Louis. Then he smiled again. Not the smile of pleasure that had been triggered by the news of Jonas Prince's death, but the dry smile of a man who knows he's about to be checkmated if he takes his hand off his knight.

"Right. That isn't a very good alibi, is it," he said. "I was with two women. All night. I suppose you need their names so you can invade their privacy, too?"

"You know I do."

Bushman opened a drawer and started rummaging around. He gave up, slammed it shut and opened another, cursing under his breath. It gave Louis time to look around the office.

The rain had stopped and the big windows now offered a view. To the left, Louis had a glimpse of the gray-green ribbon of the Detroit River. To the right, the beacon atop the radio tower of the beautiful old Penobscot Building pulsed red like a slow beating heart in the gray sky.

Louis went to the opposite wall. It was dominated by a poster of Bushman below the lettering: TEN YEARS OF FREE-THINKING FREE RADIO! Next to it hung a large calendar with the month's daily programming topics marked in color-coded pen, from blue for Monday's "Where Did Cain Get His Wife?" through orange for Wednesday's "Reasoning With the Religious" to flame-red for Friday's "The End Is Near!" There were also a couple of tin-hat conspiracy topics: "The GOP's Secret Plan to Destroy Detroit!" And "Was Hinckley a CIA Mind-Control Plant?"

Another wall held a collection of haphazardly hung pictures of Bushman posing with people Louis didn't recognize. In the center of the portraits was a large gold-plated emblem—an atomic swirl with an A in the center. Under it were the words American Atheists.

"Here."

Louis looked back at Bushman. The man was holding out a business card. Louis came forward and took it. Bushman's information was on the front with the atheist symbol. On the back he had scribbled a phone number.

"It's an escort service," Bushman said. "I don't suppose there is any hope you'll be discreet."

"If you're telling me the truth, no one will ever hear their names."

"I appreciate that. Can you tell me exactly what happened to Jonas?" Bushman asked.

"Sorry, no."

"Well, then we're done here, aren't we? Goodbye, detective."

Louis tucked the card in his binder. He would call the escorts, but he already suspected Bushman's alibi would hold up. The radio jock was far from charming, but he didn't come off as violent. And with his weight and apparent bad health, he probably couldn't move fast enough to take down Jonas Prince let alone carry or drag him out to the altar. And Bushman was lazy, too lazy to throw his ribs away or empty his ashtray. Lazy men didn't use strangulation as a way to kill. It was too much work.

But there *was* something to be gained here, Louis knew. Background information on Jonas Prince and the other players in his life. Often, the stories and gossip from friends and enemies got filed away deep into the murder book and were never needed again to make the case. But once in a while, somebody would drop a crumb of information that later would later break the case wide open.

"I understand you and Jonas Prince had a pretty public feud going on a few months ago."

Bushman leaned forward to snuff out his cigarette then melted back into the leather chair. "Who called it a feud? That malingering son of his?"

Louis nodded.

"I'll say this," Bushman said. "Jonas was a salesman peddling salvation, but at least he believed in his product. Anthony Prince is a huckster. Elmer Gantry without the great hair, a TV snake oil salesman. Lose twenty pounds while sitting on your ass eating Cheetos, just send twenty-nine-ninety-five for the Fat-Zapper. Extend your penis five inches in five easy payments with the Bone-a-Meter. Send a hundred bucks to the Beacon Light Cathedral and God himself will be at the door in a gold-braid uniform to show you inside."

"So why wage a war with Jonas then?" Louis asked.

"Challenging Jonas was better publicity for my movement," Bushman said. "He was the face of the church. Nobody cares if you kill the lieutenant. They do take note when you kill the king."

"Not a smart metaphor, Mr. Bushman."

Bushman waved a hand. "You know what I mean. Anyway, all I wanted was a debate, an intelligent discussion in a public forum."

"Anthony Prince said you harassed his father."

"I issued a challenge," Bushman said. "It only got ugly after Anthony hired someone to follow my daughter and get photos of her with her partner.

She's a lesbian. I guess he thought my followers would actually care about something like that. They don't, but I did."

"What did you do?" Louis asked.

"I hired someone to follow Anthony," Bushman said.

Now this could be one of those crumbs.

"When was this?"

"A couple months ago. It was only for one week and I didn't get much for my money, except to find out the man likes his gin. I went to Anthony's father and told him I would use the drinking to knock his son off the morals train if he didn't rein Anthony in. We agreed to a truce."

"What about the blistering sermon Jonas gave about you?"

"It got me almost sixty grand in donations. I loved it."

Louis thought about the PI Bushman hired to shadow Anthony. He himself was only a few months past scratching out a living doing the same thing. As a PI, he had tried to keep himself above following adulterers and disability scammers. But the truth was, he had sat in the dark outside a few restaurants himself, waiting for the right moment to snap some incriminating photos. Right now, the badge clipped to his belt felt damn good.

"I'd like to see the file your investigator put together," Louis said.

"I told you, there's nothing in it. Anthony's as regular as a German cuckoo clock. After reading the first couple of daily reports, I told the guy to finish out the week and that was it. I didn't see any point of paying for more than one week."

"I'd still like a look at it."

Bushman shrugged. "I got it at home somewhere. I'll try to dig it out for you."

Louis pulled out a business card and laid it on the desk. "Call me as soon as you find it."

Bushman picked up the card, gave it a quick look, then put it in his shirt pocket. "Can I ask you a question, detective?"

"Sure."

"Why are you a cop?"

"Excuse me?"

PJ PARRISH

"Why would a black man choose to be part of the oppression that goes on every day? Do you know how many citizens of color are beaten every day by the police? How many black men die in custody?"

"Save it for your broadcast, Mr. Bushman."

"Oh, I see. You're one of them—an assimilator. A minority who adopts the ways of the majority in order to survive. Tell me, do you also believe in God?"

"That's none of your business."

"I will assume you do, because how could you not? It's in your blood, a remnant of slavery where the only hope of salvation came from the belief that the next life would be better than the one we have now."

Louis knew Bushman was baiting him and he knew he should just leave, but he didn't. He was remembering a book he had, still packed up in his boxes back at his new apartment. It was a paperback collection of poems by Langston Hughes, purchased for a sophomore lit class, but he had carried it around with him since college, cracking it open to random pages on the nights when TV or drink wasn't distraction enough. There was a poem in it—was it was called "Goodbye Jesus"?—but he couldn't remember any of the lines right now.

"No comeback, detective?" Bushman asked.

"What's wrong with believing that something better is to come?" Louis asked.

"The problem is not believing something better's coming. It's believing that it will come by way of some all-powerful entity who will float down from the sky."

Bushman shook his head slowly. "Let me tell you something," he said. "There is no one out there who can save us from anything. No God, no Allah, no Buddha, no George Burns. When you pray, you're just talking to the wind."

Louis rose. "Goodbye, Mr. Bushman."

He left the office and took the elevator back to the lobby. A security guard was at the front desk now, head bent over a newspaper. Louis looked at the sign over his head.

120

DETROIT IS ALIVE!

Maybe Detroit was alive, Louis thought, but on the twentieth floor of this building, God—and any kind of positive human spirit—was certainly dead.

Suddenly, the lines from the Hughes poem were there in his head, something about the Bible being a good ghosted-up story in its day . . . *but it's dead now. The popes and the preachers've made too much money from it.*

Louis pushed out the door and stepped into a gray mist. He felt light-headed and drew in a deep breath of air, glad for something fresh after the fusty smell of Bushman's office. His stomach rumbled and he looked around for somewhere to grab a sandwich. There was a little café, tucked between two office buildings, its front windows foggy with steam.

He started toward it, hungry enough to settle for whatever the dive was offering. But before he even stepped off the curb, he was struck with a memory of sitting next to his foster father, Phillip, at a counter, commiserating over the Tigers' loss of an opening-day game. Suddenly he knew exactly what he was hungry for.

The place was somewhere close by, he knew. Working on instinct, he started up Griswold, looking for the triangle-shaped intersection and that old newsstand where Phillip got his magazines, his nose alert for the smell of frying beef.

Then there it was, as big and gaudy as a huge American flag—the red white and blue façade of American Coney Island. He hurried to it, but when he reached the door, he was stopped cold by a voice in his head.

We are Lafayette people, Louis. It's in the blood.

Louis's eyes swung right to the drab gray and burgundy sign of the restaurant next door—Lafayette Coney Island. Through the steamed windows he could see men in stained white aprons manning the pots of chili and hot dog grills. He went to the second restaurant and stepped inside.

The warmth hit his face and, for a moment, he stood stock-still, because although he hadn't been in the place since he was a kid, everything was exactly as he remembered it. A long narrow diner with tiles the color of nicotine-stained teeth. Buzzing florescent lights that bounced off stainless steel coffee urns the size of small missile silos. And that smell—frying meat, onions, grease and warmth, warmth, so much warmth.

Louis slid onto a red vinyl stool at the Formica counter next to a thin old guy in a Tigers ball cap. His mind was playing tricks on him. Maybe it was because he was so tired, or maybe it was just being in this place again. Whatever the reason, the old man—with his concave cheeks, hooked nose, and cigarette smell—reminded him so very much of Phillip.

"Whatcha have?"

Louis looked up at the counter man. There was only one answer. "Two coneys, extra onions and an order of cheese fries, please."

"You got it."

Less than a minute later, the counter man deposited the coneys and fries in front of Louis and, for a moment, all he could do was stare. There was no food like it on the planet—hot dogs swathed in steam-limp buns, drowned in a brown morass of meat and chili sauce, topped with chopped onions and neon-yellow mustard.

Coneys. That's what Detroiters called them. Not Coney Dogs or Coney Islands or hot dogs or Saugies. And never "Michigans," the dumb name New Yorkers and Canadians hung on them. Just coneys.

Louis wolfed the first one down, then ate the second more slowly, his thoughts drifting away from Walter Bushman, Jonas Prince and this case, and back to Phillip. He hadn't called his foster parents since returning to Michigan. There had been no time, he had told himself, but that was just an excuse. How hard was it to pick up the damn phone? Phillip would never bust his chops over it because he understood the way Louis was, that reaching out to anyone was hard and had gotten less hard only in the last year or so when Joe and Lily had come into his life, unclenching his heart. He had reconnected with his lover and his daughter. Why was he waiting to do the same with the man who had raised him?

Before and after.

That's how he had come to think of his life lately. The before part was when he was eight, before he had come to Phillip and Frances Lawrence's home in Plymouth.

The before was a mostly a blank, like his brain had only taken snapshots of his boyhood in Mississippi. His mother Lila—not the memory of the alcoholic dying in her bed, but the framed photograph of the pretty young woman that sat on his bookshelf now. No pictures of his half-sister Yolanda and his half-brother, just shadows now. And stuck in a box somewhere in the bottom of a drawer back at his apartment, one faded Polaroid of the white man—his face hidden by a hat brim—who had fathered him and run away.

Fathered. Father.

Jordan Kincaid was a ghost. But Phillip Lawrence?

Phillip had given him the *after.* Dozens of foster boys had passed through the Lawrence house. Louis had seen their pictures on the wall of Frances's foyer, that gallery of good boys—Boy Scouts, high school grads, Kmart Christmas portraits. Louis was in there with the others, but it was a just one blurry snapshot taken at Edgewater Park, and he was wedged between two white boys, sullen and small. Once, just after Louis graduated from college, he and Phillip were down in the knotty pine basement and, after a couple brandies, Louis had worked up the guts to ask Phillip why he didn't merit his own portrait on the wall like the others.

Because you're not like the others, Louis. You're like a son to me.

Louis looked up, catching his blurred reflection in the big, aluminum coffee urn.

Walter Bushman was wrong. Not everyone could save themselves. Sometimes, someone else had to be there to help. How that person came to you, well, who knew what was behind that?

"You need anything else?"

Louis looked up at the counter man. "Just the check, please."

CHAPTER EIGHTEEN

When he got back in the Explorer, Louis pulled Bushman's business card from his pocket, picked up the cell phone, and dialed the escort service number.

A woman answered. "Midnight Lace Models, this is Sylvia. How can I help you?"

After he gave his name and identified himself as a detective with the Michigan State Police, there was a long pause before the woman spoke again. "Yes, officer?"

The purr was gone from her voice. She had some experience talking to cops.

"I need to talk to whoever is in charge, please," he said.

"That would be me. I am the owner of Midnight Lace."

Louis had a vision of a housewife in a caftan and curlers, sitting out in a suburban tri-level, answering the phone. He doubted Midnight Lace even had a real office. These outfits rarely did.

"I'm calling about one of your clients," he began, adding that he needed to verify Bushman's whereabouts last night. Sylvia countered with a few quick parries about wanting proof of Louis's position and that she wasn't going to give out personal information about clients, but finally Louis interrupted.

"Sylvia," he said. "Listen to me. I don't care what Walter Bushman was doing last night or what kind of place you really run there. I just need to verify he was doing it with your escorts."

A long pause. "Walt told you to call?"

"That's what I said."

"I'm going to put you on hold."

She was gone before he could object. He sat there, taking in the gray downtown buildings and listening to honking horns. He was well past tired now and moving fast toward exhaustion.

"Officer?" The purr was back in her voice.

"Detective."

"Detective . . . Mr. Bushman said it was okay to talk to you. Yes, he was with two of our ladies last night."

"I need proof."

"Mr. Bushman said you might. I can fax you his Visa receipt. And Amber and Shannon are at work right now but will be happy to talk to you tomorrow at your leisure."

The receipt didn't prove where Bushman had spent the night and the word of two hookers wasn't golden. But at least it was something to take back to Steele for now. He gave Sylvia the task force fax number and told her to include the women's phone numbers.

"Thank you, Sylvia, you've been very helpful," he said.

"Call us anytime, Detective. You have our number."

He hit the button to end the call then sat there, staring at the phone. It gave him an odd sense of power knowing he could get anyone anywhere at the punch of a button. His thoughts drifted to Joe. He hadn't talked to her since his first night in his new apartment. And yet, as he stared at the strange device in his hand, he had the thought that—although he was only a phone call away and Echo Bay was a mere four-hour drive—for some reason, he felt farther from her now than he did when he was in Florida.

He picked up the phone and was about to call her when it rang. He stabbed at the button. "Detective Kincaid."

"This is Camille, Louis. I've been trying to reach you. I left you three messages on the phone."

He didn't want to tell her he hadn't figured out yet how to retrieve messages from the cell. "I'm sorry. I just got back into the car."

"I'm calling to get a status report."

Louis quickly summarized his interview with Bushman and his follow-up with the escort service.

"Captain Steele wants the team assembled at the church tomorrow at nine a.m.," Camille said. "He said grab a room down there, get some rest, and head home tomorrow."

"Got it."

"One more thing, Louis. You had a call today from a Reverend Grascoeur."

Louis sat up straighter. The minister of the Church of the Northern Lights up in the U.P. "What did he say?"

"Just that he got your message and needed to talk to you." Camille paused. "Do you have a pen? I'll give you his number."

Louis grabbed a pen and scribbled the number on his palm. He thanked Camille, hung up, and dialed the new number.

"Pierre Grascoeur here. Life is short and I'm getting long in the tooth, so let's make this quick."

The name came out with a French accent but all the rest had the distinctive Yooper lilt. Louis thought of the rainbow-painted log cabin church up in Copper Harbor and a picture formed in his head of Reverend Grascoeur as Jerry Garcia in a monk's robe and sandals.

"This is Louis Kincaid, state police, returning your call, sir. Thank you for—"

"State police! Yes, yes . . . well! I'm sorry for being smart there. It's been a long day. Thank you for calling back. I didn't think anyone actually would."

"Why not, sir?"

"It's been . . . well, it's been such a long time since . . ." the voice trailed off.

"Reverend Grascoeur, did your sister tell you why I was trying to get in touch with you?"

"Yes. This is about the two boys."

"Right, sir. I was told you might have presided over their memorial service and—"

"No, no . . ."

Louis slumped slightly in the seat. Shit. Another dead end.

"I was supposed to do it," Grascoeur went on, "but the sheriff told me it wasn't necessary."

"Sheriff Halko?"

"Yes, he told me . . ."

The line went silent and for a second Louis thought they had been disconnected.

"Detective, I can't do this," Grascoeur said.

"Reverend, this is important. If you—"

"Yes, I know. It is important. Which is why I can't do this over the phone. Can you come up here?"

"I can't get back to Copper Harbor, sir."

"No, no, no . . . I'm downstate, here in Saginaw."

Saginaw. That was only about a ninety-minute drive north from Detroit. Louis ran a hand over his face. The coneys and cheese fries were fighting a fierce battle in his gut. But no way was Steele going to let him go back to the U.P. any time soon for a detour back to the boys-in-the-box case. He couldn't let this chance go by.

"Where do you want to meet?" Louis asked.

"How about the Savoy Bar and Grill? You know where it's at?"

"No, sir," Louis said. "But I'll find it."

• • • • • • • • •

The art deco neon sign for the Savoy Bar and Grill stood out like a beacon in the misty night. The interior looked like someone had crossed a

127

speakeasy with a diner—one long room with a towering tin ceiling, scarred wood floor, and an old wood-rail staircase near the entrance leading up into the shadows.

There were only a handful of customers and—as Louis stood just inside the door, looking for anyone who matched the picture of Rev. Grascoeur in his mind—a hand waved from a booth in the back.

Louis went toward the booth. The man sitting at the table wiped his face with a paper napkin, stood up, and extended his hand. "Detective Kincaid, I'm Reverend Grascoeur," he said.

His handshake was strong, his face even stronger—craggy and heavily lined, with a prominent, thin nose and piercing, deep-set, dark eyes. He was bald except for a fringe of white hair. He was wearing a white dress shirt, sleeves rolled, and a gray, striped tie was bunched on the booth seat next to him. Sheriff Nurmi had said Grascoeur had been in Copper Harbor for a long time, and Louis estimated the reverend was probably in his mid-seventies, but he wore the years well, looking more like a small-town doctor than the aging weed-wilted hippie Louis had been expecting.

"Sit down, please," Grascoeur said, gesturing. "I hope you don't mind but I went ahead and ordered. I've been working all day and this is the first moment I had to eat."

Grascoeur's plate of half-finished liver and onions made Louis's stomach churn. "I already ate, thanks," he said.

"Yes, well," Grascoeur seemed suddenly nervous, staring hard, and Louis had the feeling he was being sized up. Louis was used to it, especially after his trip to the Upper Peninsula where black faces were rare.

"I'm glad we could meet," Grascoeur said finally. "I don't get downstate very often but I had business here in Saginaw. I'm on the board of the Castle Museum here. Do you know it?"

"No, sir. I'm not from here."

The reverend nodded. "It's dedicated to the preservation of French-Canadian heritage here in Michigan. My family, they have been here since the 1800s."

"So you've lived up in the Keweenaw Peninsula all your life then?" Louis asked.

"I was born in Escanaba, yes, but the turns of life took me away for quite a while. I didn't come home until 1975." He paused. "That I am down-state at this time and you are here, I take it as a sign."

A waitress appeared and Louis asked for just a glass of water. "Reverend Grascoeur," Louis said, after she left, "why couldn't you talk to me over the phone?"

"I had to see who I was dealing with first," he said.

"What do you mean?"

"I had to see who was taking an interest in this after all these years." He paused. "I had to know it was somebody who was going to follow through, someone with *sisu*."

"Sitz-what?"

"It's a Yooper term. It means tenacity, like a pit bull. It's spelled S-I-S-U."

SISU . . . that's what had been on the front of Monica Nurmi's sweat-shirt and he has mistaken it for a college name.

"I take it then you've gone to the authorities before?" Louis asked.

Grascoeur hesitated. "I did once. I talked to Sheriff Halko but he didn't seem to care much about two unidentified boys. Then the years went by and I tried to forget about it. Then my sister told me you called."

Louis took out his binder and a pen. "Do you have information about the boys?"

"The boys," Grascoeur said softly. His eyes drifted away, but Louis was certain he wasn't seeing anything in the bar. "They were so very small," he said.

Louis sat forward. "You knew them?"

The reverend drifted back. "Knew? No, no one knew them. I just saw their bones. Once, just once, laid out on a table in the sheriff's office. I had heard about it in town—I had just returned to the Eagle River area back then—that children's bones had been found in the mine, so I went to the sheriff's office. I don't know why really. It was too late for last rites, of course, but I thought someone should pray for their souls."

"Last rites? That's a Catholic ritual," Louis said.

Grascoeur hesitated. "I was a Catholic back then."

That was interesting. A priest turned new-age prophet. Louis thought about asking why he had left the church but decided it was probably more than he needed to know about this man right now.

"Do you know what happened to the bones?" Louis asked.

Grascoeur shook his head slowly. "Several weeks went by and when no one came forward to claim them, the folks in town decided to hold a memorial service and bury the boys in Evergreen Cemetery. But two days before I was supposed to do the service, Sheriff Halko called me and said someone had claimed the remains and taken them away."

Louis sat back in the booth, his fatigue deepening. So there it was then, the answer to the mystery. It had been there in the back of Louis's mind since the moment he had opened that foot locker back in Jennifer Halko's barn. Most likely, Halko had taken the bones to sell in his macabre souvenir business, and God only knew where the remains had ended up. Maybe there was something left to trace back in Jennifer's farmhouse—a ledger of Halko's business dealings, a receipt maybe. But Steele would never let him go back to the U.P. anytime soon, especially with Jonas Prince barely cold in the morgue back in Grand Rapids.

Louis closed his binder. "Thank you for your time," he said.

"So you're going to keep looking for the boys, for their remains, I mean?"

The reverend's eyes felt like they were piercing right into Louis's deepest parts. For a moment, Louis considered telling him about Halko's hobby. But wasn't it better to let the old man believe his prayers had been for some good?

"I'll do what I can," Louis said. "But you have to understand, old cases like this are really hard to solve. Evidence gets lost, witnesses die, people forget things."

Louis rose, pocketing his pen. He stuck out his hand. "Thanks for your time, Reverend."

Grascoeur took it, but he didn't shake it. He held it, like he didn't want to let go. Louis slowly slipped back down into the booth.

"Do you have something else you want to tell me, Reverend?"

Grascoeur was quiet. Louis watched the shifting shadows of emotions slide across the reverend's face until finally only one was left: agony.

"Are you Catholic?" Grascoeur asked.

Louis shook his head.

"Do you know what the Seal of the Confessional is?"

"Something about not revealing anything when someone confesses?"

Grascoeur nodded slowly. "Let no priest betray the sinner." The waitress reappeared, set a water glass by Louis's elbow. Grascoeur watched her leave then looked back at Louis.

"It happened four months after the bones were found," he said softly. "By then, the bones were gone, winter came, and folks in town had pretty much forgotten about the incident. It was a bad winter that year and everyone just pulled way down into themselves the way we do up there. We were in the middle of a three-week sub-zero blizzard. I still held mass, but by that third Sunday, I was talking only to myself. The wind was raging so hard, I don't think even He heard me."

Louis almost asked who "he" was, but then understood.

"We lost power the night of that third Sunday," Grascoeur went on. "I sent my housekeeper and assistant home and I stayed in the church office alone that night because it had a wood stove. That's where I was, huddled there in a blanket with a fifth of brandy, when I heard a noise out in the sanctuary."

Grascoeur picked up his water glass and took a long drink before he started again.

"It was a man," he said. "He said he wanted to make his confession."

Louis leaned forward. "Who was he?"

"I don't know. You don't ask the sinner his name."

"What did he say?"

That expression was back, a dark shadow of pain passing over the old man's face. He shut his eyes and shook his head slowly.

"He said he killed the two boys. He said he put them in a box and put the box in the mine."

"What did you do?"

Grascoeur opened his eyes. There were tears in them. "What did I do? I listened to him. Then I told him he needed to go to the police and turn himself in."

"What did he say to that?"

"He said he was afraid.

"Afraid of what?"

Grascoeur's brow was knit, as if he were concentrating hard. "He said he was afraid of the Father hating him forever."

"What did you tell him?"

"I told him the Lord does not hate. The Lord forgives."

Louis leaned back in the booth. He had a suspect, yes, but one as insubstantial as a ghost. He wanted to ask Grascoeur why he hadn't gone to the police that night, but he didn't. Because he could read Grascoeur's face, read that the old man was asking himself the same exact same thing. How many times had he asked himself over the years?

"What did you do next?" Louis prodded.

"I repeated that he needed to go to the police, then I gave him his penance, and told him to give thanks to the Lord for He is good, and His mercy endures forever."

"Then what?" Louis pressed.

"Then he was gone."

"Gone? What do you mean gone?"

"I don't know. By the time I emerged from the confessional booth, the front door was wide open and the snow was blowing in." Grascoeur let out a long breath. "He was just gone."

The old man bowed his head, and for a second Louis thought he was praying. Louis let the moment lengthen but then he couldn't stand it any longer.

"What did he look like?"

Grascoeur looked up at him. "Look like? I don't know. I didn't get a good look at him. I had only the one lantern I took with me into the church that night."

"Anything would be helpful."Grascoeur was quiet for a long time, the lines on his face seeming to deepen.

"Was he young?" Louis asked.

"I don't know. I didn't get that impression. His voice was deep but . . . very quiet and fearful. It was almost like a boy was inside the man trying to speak."

Louis stifled a sigh.

"He wasn't Catholic," Grascoeur said after another long silence.

"How do you know?"

"Someone coming to the confessional always says right away, 'Forgive me, father, for I have sinned. It has been whatever-days since my last confession.' He didn't say that."

"Do you remember exactly the first thing he said?"

Grascoeur paused, then nodded. "He said, 'I need to tell someone what I did to them.'" His dark eyes searched Louis's face. "I didn't remember that until just this moment. Do you think that matters?"

"Everything matters, sir. Can you recall any physical details about the man?"

Grascoeur shook his head. "He was wearing a heavy coat and a wool hat. I think he had a beard. It was very dark. As I said, all I had was one lantern that I had set down outside the confessional. I never really saw his face."

Louis took a drink of water, thinking about Grascoeur's distinctive lilt. "Did he have an accent?"

"Accent?" Grascoeur frowned. "Oh, you mean our Yooper accent." He nodded slowly. "Yes, yes he did. A very strong one."

That meant the man was a local. "Where exactly was your church?" Louis asked.

"Just south of Copper Harbor. It's closed now. After I left, well, the diocese in Marquette felt there wasn't enough of a congregation left to keep it financially viable. I guess they always thought we were something of an outpost up there."

Louis had been thinking that he could ask the old priest for a list—even a mental one—of who had been in his congregation eleven years ago. How many murdering sinners could there be in one town? But that was out now.

"Is there anything else you can remember? Did you go outside after him? Maybe see a vehicle?"

"I didn't go outside afterward. But I remember he smelled of wet wool and I remember there was a big puddle in the confessional after he left. He probably walked to me."

If nothing else, Louis now had a geographical profile for his suspect's residence. He was already calculating just how far a man would walk in a snowstorm to confess his sins when the reverend spoke again.

"*Deponatur sacerdos qui peccata penitentis publicare præsumit,*" Grascoeur whispered.

"I'm sorry, sir, what did you say?"

"Let the priest who dares to make known the sins of his penitent be deposed."

Louis remembered a talk he had with a fellow cop in the locker room back when he was a rookie on the Ann Arbor force. The cop told him that a priest he had interviewed would not give up the name of a man who had confessed to stabbing his wife. The cop was Catholic, and Louis remembered how angry and confused the man had been.

"We all find ways to carry our guilt," Grascoeur said. "Jesus Christ is there to take it away for us, but sometimes He leaves just enough so we don't forget."

His eyes filled with tears. "I'm sorry," he said. "I should have done something more. I am so very sorry."

CHAPTER NINETEEN

It wasn't much of a motel, but they accepted his state police credit card and gave him a room as far away from the railroad tracks as possible. By ten p.m. Louis was settled into a lumpy bed, exhaustion fogging his brain.

Louis took a minute to call Joe and they shared a few words about their jobs. She was more interested in how he was adjusting to having rules and a boss than she was in Reverend Prince's murder, but that was okay. He liked telling her how he felt. He told her he loved her and hung up. He had almost drifted into a light sleep before he remembered he needed to check in with Nina at his apartment house. She was watching Issy. And from the sound of her voice, she was getting quite attached to the old cat. That was okay, too. Cats—and Nina for that matter—pretended they didn't they need anybody, but they did.

He stripped down to his boxers, turned up the heat, and switched on the TV. The eleven o'clock news was on, the anchor recapping a segment called Around the Mitten. A small plane crash in Alpena killed two. A four-car accident blocked traffic along I-96 for three hours. A prostitute was found dead in a suitcase on a farm outside of Ionia. A cop had been shot and wounded in Detroit.

Finally, he killed the TV. The darkness settled in around him and, within minutes, he was asleep.

The dream started almost immediately.

At first it was just a feeling, the same deep-chest crush he had felt in the Eagle River Inn, the closed-in feeling that had compelled him to get out of his room and run down the cold beach.

But this time he could see where he was. He was running up some stairs. And he could hear something, footsteps thundering behind him on a wood floor. Then the dream shifted and he was floating high above, watching two boys run, and he was rooting them on, his own voice coming out small and feeble.

Run, run faster!

The dream raced on, like a speeded-up film. He tried to reach down for the boys, but they didn't see his hand and they kept running until suddenly a door slammed and darkness came. He was no longer watching the boys, he was in the darkness with them.

A burst of light.

Come out of there!

No! No!

Something warm pushed against him and a boy's face came into focus, close. So close Louis could see his tears, hear his gasps, feel the tremble of his fingers.

Then the boy was gone, dragged away by giant hands that sparked with prisms of light. Louis shrank back into the darkness, listening to the clapping of the giant hands and the other boy's whimpering.

It'll be okay. Stay there. Just stay there.

Then it was quiet, and the light changed to a pale pink and he could see a boy turning in slow circles to follow the movement of the pink light. The smell of simmering greens filled his nose, making him both nauseous and hungry. Then a pale old man appeared at a rainy window, a minister draped in a purple silk robe and wearing a red and green knit wool hat with tassels. The old man held a book of poetry by Langston Hughes that he pushed through a liquid glass window.

Do you want to know?

The minister spoke but his lips didn't move.

Do you want to know?

The boy in the pink light started to cry. The minister melted away, morphing into a dragon-like monster with yellowed claws and black wires coming out of his head.

Louis bolted awake. He tumbled to the floor as his legs got tangled in the sheet. Gasping for breath, he stayed on his knees in the darkness.

What the hell was happening?

He never dreamed like this, not this vividly and not about his work or monsters or missing children.

He sat back against the bed, fighting the urge to get out of the motel room and run off the adrenaline. He could hear the steady pelt of rain against the window and looked at his watch. It was two a.m.

He shut his eyes and tried to replay the dream in his head before it faded away. It seemed important to remember it, as disturbing as it had been. He concentrated and a few more details came into focus. The hallway had ugly, yellow wallpaper. The other boy was wearing a striped T-shirt. The smell of the simmering greens was surely a memory of his childhood in Mississippi. The minister was faceless, but he had to be a manifestation of Jonas Prince and Grascoeur.

The dream was fading. There was nothing left now but that awful tightness in his chest.

Get a grip, Kincaid.

He opened his eyes, pushed to his feet, and went to the bathroom. He turned on the tap and splashed his face with cold water. When he looked up, he caught his reflection in the cracked mirror. His eyes were wide, the pupils black pinpricks.

Do you want to know? Do you want to know?

Suddenly it made sense. He *knew.*

The shard-images in the dream passed before his eyes, flashes of light from a prism, blurry and fast. And even though nothing was in focus, now he understood.

The creature with the giant hands and flashy rings, it was not a symbol of the killer who had left two boys in a candle box. It was a real man.

Moe . . .

That was his name. He was real. And that hallway with the yellow wallpaper was real. It was a real place in a real house, a big decrepit house in Detroit. A house where the man named Moe took in foster kids in exchange for state money.

And the boy . . .

Louis shut his eyes. It came slowly, so very slowly, like something pulled from some place deep inside him. Not from his memory, but from his heart.

Sammy.

Louis leaned on the bathroom counter, breathing hard against the tightness in his chest.

God. My God.

And that other boy, the second boy who had escaped the monster by staying hidden in the closet, he knew that boy, too.

It was him.

Louis moved back to the bedroom but had no desire to get back into bed. He threw open the drapes, grabbed the chair and sat down at the window. For a long time, he just stared out at the rain-blurred car lights.

After a while, he leaned forward and reached around his ribs, feeling for the only small, round burn scar of the six on his back that he could reach. When he found it, he traced the tiny rope of raised skin once with the tip of his finger, then drew his hand away.

He closed his eyes, remembering what Steele had said to him the first day the team had gathered around the conference table.

Bienvenue chez vous.

Welcome home, Louis. Welcome home.

CHAPTER TWENTY

It was nine-twenty-two when Louis got to the church the next morning, and Cam, Tooki, Emily, and Junia were seated around the conference table, case folders spread open in front of them. Steele stood at the head of the table and made an exaggerated gesture of glancing at his watch as Louis slid into the only empty chair.

Louis pulled out his binder, and flipped past his notes from his interview with Grascoeur to focus on his interviews with Anthony Prince and Walter Bushman. When he looked up, he noticed the changes to the murder board behind Steele. A large schematic of the Beacon Light Cathedral had been added, with colored pushpins designating primary and secondary crime scenes. There were new photographs, including several angles of Jonas Prince's corpse, the dressing room, and headshots of the suspects this far—Bushman, Anthony, and a man Louis assumed was the expelled gay guy whose name he could not recall at the moment.

Steele's voice drew his attention back. "Junia, continue."

Junia began a summary of the preliminary forensics, which confirmed that Jonas was killed in the dressing room by manual strangulation, with no evidence of defense wounds. A church employee said that Jonas had worn a purple robe for that evening's service and not the blue robe and gold stole that Jonas had been found wearing in death.

Steele interrupted her. "Cam, I want you to find out if there is anything special about this blue robe and gold stole."

"Will do, boss."

"Junia, go on please," Steele said.

Church employees also confirmed that the door to Jonas Prince's dressing room was always locked and only Jonas had a key, but so far no key had been found. The dressing room was also not a regular stop on the cleaning crew's route, as Jonas never wanted anyone in there unattended. They cleaned and vacuumed once a week, on Wednesday mornings, with the Reverend there to monitor.

Louis looked down at his notes, and closed his eyes, fighting exhaustion. Even after a morning shower and the ninety-minute drive down from Saginaw, adrenaline still coursed through him, like a low-grade fire just under his skin.

Emily was talking now, offering a profile of the killer as organized, methodical, and comfortable in the church environment.

"You have a working profile of Jonas?" Steele asked.

"He was very private but well liked and considered kind," Emily said. "He was known to give parishioners money from his own pocket, but he was conservative in his social views, to the point of banishing those who did not adhere to his high moral standards." She glanced at her notes. "His favorite sermon topic was forgiveness and he often said that the church was not a country club, it was a hospital where souls were healed."

"And his son, Anthony?" Steele asked.

"His distress seems genuine and he is mildly disoriented, which is normal for family members of murder victims," she said. "He has, I believe, an inflated sense of ego that he reinforces by surrounding himself with symbols of his achievements."

"Not unusual for a man living in the shadow of an icon," Steele said.

"But I also believe he is deeply insecure," she said. "This manifests itself in several forms of OCD, primarily the need to arrange things and control what is happening around him. And the more a person tries to control the external psychological and physical stimuli surrounding him, the more things are raging out of control internally."

"OCD," Steele said, tapping his pencil. "Isn't there a type of compulsion where you fear having sinful thoughts?"

Emily nodded. "I'd need a much longer interview to go there. I have to say that if he killed his father, it wasn't to take over the church. The man clearly understands he does not have his father's charisma."

Steele turned to Tooki. "How about the family finances?"

Tooki spoke without looking up from his computer screen. "The church is incorporated and grosses about one million a year in donations, and another two million from its television broadcasts. All of Jonas Prince's assets were owned and managed by the church and all but about ten percent remains with the church in the event of Jonas's death."

"What about Anthony's finances?" Steele asked.

"His assets—his home in Grand Rapids and two cars—are titled in his name only. He earns an executive manager's salary of two-hundred-and-fifty thousand a year. I am still working on his investments and expenditures. His bank has not yet computerized."

Tooki looked up, squinting. "His wife, Violet, has a trust, left to her by her father. Anthony administers it, but I haven't been able to find out much about it yet."

"Cam, how did your interviews go?" Steele asked.

While Cam rattled on about the janitorial staff and the homosexual Jonas had banished from the congregation, Louis's mind drifted back to the wilderness of the Keweenaw Peninsula and the guilt-ridden, faceless man who sought out absolution in the middle of a blizzard. He was re-reading his notes from Grascoeur when Steele said his name.

"Louis?"

He looked up.

"I asked, what was your impression of Walter Bushman?"

Louis closed his binder. "He liked Jonas Prince, but he had no kind words for Anthony. Anthony tried to blackmail him a few months back and Bushman got Jonas to back him off. Plus he has an alibi. He was with two hookers."

Cam slammed his folder shut. The gesture drew Steele's attention and, for a moment, no one moved. Then Steele turned his attention back to the table.

"You'll each get a set of crime scene photos this afternoon," Steele said. "I need your witness statements and summaries by three p.m. There's a copy machine in the back room. Make copies for each of us. I want you to share everything. I'll see you all at four."

Steele started away toward the loft. Cam had disappeared, his chair still swinging back and forth. Tooki retreated to his desk computer. Emily was at her desk, feeding paper into her typewriter. Louis watched her peck with two fingers for a minute, then he stood up and went over to her.

"All your time in the FBI and you never learned to type any better than that?"

She didn't smile.

He sat down. Her desk was littered with pink and green Post-It notes and folders of varying colors. He could see a bright-yellow file folder, labeled "CMU suicides" in the bottom rung of a stacked in-box.

"How you doing?" he asked.

Emily shrugged and leaned back in her chair. He noticed her gaze drifted to the CMU file.

"Did you make any progress on your test case?" he asked.

"Didn't have much time," she said. "But so far, it's pretty much what you'd expect. The families say no way would their kids take their own lives."

"Maybe they're right," Louis said. "They should know their kids better than anyone."

Emily's eyes slid to Louis. "No parent really knows their kids. And most don't want to. It's too much work, too much of an emotional investment. It's easier to look the other way and hope that when you look back, your kid will have somehow emerged from the darkness of adolescence as a normal human being."

Emily drew a deep breath, but the bitterness he had heard in her voice shadowed her eyes, making them a deep sea green.

"What about you?" Emily asked. "You look like hell."

"Not sleeping."

"How come?"

He hesitated. He liked Emily, but she was a psychologist and they liked to pick the lockboxes of the brain.

"Talk to me," Emily said.

"I'm dreaming about my childhood," Louis said quietly. "And a boy I haven't thought about in over twenty years."

Emily said nothing, but her eyes were intense on his.

"Aren't you going to tell me that my subconscious is struggling with some sort of unresolved issue and I should tackle it head on?" Louis asked.

"Actually, no," she said. "I don't believe in dream interpretation. It's just your brain on overdrive."

"I don't think so," Louis said. "This is different."

"Then go with your gut. You're dreaming about someone you haven't thought about in years. Something triggered that and I suspect you know what that is."

"I do."

"Then you probably also know what to do next."

Louis shook his head. "I'm not sure now is the right time to look him up."

"When will the right time be then?" Emily asked.

Damn her. He never should've brought this up.

"Thanks," he said, standing.

"Anytime."

He started back to his own desk then paused halfway across the nave. He glanced up at the loft then headed over to Tooki. When Louis pulled up a chair, Tooki looked up from his computer.

"You need something, Louis?" he asked.

"Yeah, maybe. Can you access state files on that thing?" Louis asked and nodded at the computer.

"Criminal records? Sure."

"No, child services."

Tooki leaned back in his chair. "What are you looking for?"

"I need to find a foster child who went through the system in the late sixties."

"What does this have to do with Jonas Prince?"

"Nothing." It wasn't fair or even legal to ask Tooki to use the state computer for a personal objective so he lied. "It has to do with my boys-in-the-box case."

Tooki leaned into his computer and started typing. Louis watched as he filled the screen with search terms. A generic-looking form appeared with the words Michigan DHS at the top. Tooki tabbed down and looked back at Louis.

"Name?"

"Sammy."

"Last name."

"I don't know. Can you add race and age and get anything?"

"Maybe."

"Race black, age . . . try 1957 for the year of birth."

The screen went blank for a second then popped back up with a long list of names, dates, and cities in Michigan. Louis started to scan the names to see if anything clicked.

"What if we add the city as Detroit?" Louis asked.

"Won't do any good, Louis," Tooki said. "Look at the dates here. The oldest one on this list is 1988. That's as far back as these records go. They aren't even close to being fully computerized yet."

"Dammit."

"It looks like you'll have to do a manual search," Tooki said. "The files are probably in some warehouse in Detroit but you'll be in there for months if all you have is a first name."

"I get it," Louis said.

Tooki tapped a few buttons and the screen changed. "Here's their fax number for records requests. Do you want me to print it out?"

Louis's first thought was that even an official request on state police letterhead wouldn't do any good without Sammy's last name, but then he realized he had all the information he needed on another boy inside that house—himself. If he could get his own file, maybe Sammy's name would be in there.

"Yeah, thanks," Louis said.

The printer next to Tooki's desk kicked out a piece of paper. Louis grabbed it and stood up.

Tookie touched his arm. "Hey, you said at the table that Anthony Prince tried to blackmail that radio jock. Over what?"

"Bushman's daughter is a lesbian," Louis said. "Apparently Anthony Prince thought that Bushman's listeners would care about that. They didn't."

Tooki nodded slowly, then turned back to his computer. "Lots of people do, though," he said softly.

There was a resignation in Tooki's voice, and Louis couldn't help but wonder if Tooki was gay, then he noticed the accordion file on the edge of Tooki's desk. He had selected the Palmer Park wolf pack murders as his test case. If Louis remembered right, Palmer Park was once a gay haven in Detroit. He knew that rising crime in the 1980s had forced the gay community to relocate but he didn't know where.

"The wolf pack murders," Louis said. "Those involve gay guys?"

Tooki hesitated then nodded. "Four of them."

"You have any leads?"

"The Detroit police department let me look at the file but they refused our help. One detective told me they know who did it but they don't have enough evidence to make an arrest."

A man came to Louis's mind—pink-faced, pampered, and genteel—a gay man who worked as a "walker" in Palm Beach, serving as a sexually-safe escort for the dowagers on the charity circuit. Bullied and abused more times than he would ever admit, he was one of the most interesting and bravest men Louis had ever met. He had given Louis the silk Brioni bow tie that was now resting with the other mementoes on Louis's book shelf.

"If you need any help, let me know," Louis said.

"It's a dead case."

"It's never dead, Tooki. Not as long as you keep it there on your desk."

Louis went back to his desk, his mind turning back to the boys in the box. He knew it had to wait. Jonas Prince was now their top priority, but as he typed up his foster file request to child services, the idea that the boys would remain lost started to gnaw at him.

A few minutes later, he sent off the request for his child services file. As he stood at the fax machine, his gaze drifted to the loft. Crime techs would be scouring the church and Jonas Prince's house for days. And it would take weeks for the forensics to come back. Maybe Steele would let him return to Keweenaw for a few days.

He headed up the stairs, stopping at the top to knock softly on the wall so he didn't intrude.

"Come in, Louis."

Steele's nook had changed a little. The once-bare bookshelves were now filled with what looked like law enforcement textbooks and a few legal journals. A rug lay in front of his desk, a gold and blue plush pile customized with the Michigan State Police emblem. A small sofa and file cabinet had been added in the corner. Louis could just make out the label on the top file drawer—PERSONNEL. Steele was standing in front of the leaded glass window, holding an open folder. "Yes?"

"I'd like to return to Eagle River," Louis said. "I have a suspect on my boys-in-the-box case."

Steele set the folder down on the desk. The back lighting from the window was so murky that Louis couldn't clearly see his face.

"Why were you in Saginaw last night?" Steele asked.

Louis was surprised by the question. First because he wondered how Steele knew, and second, why did it matter?

"I was playing a hunch," Louis said. "I met with a witness from Keweenaw. He's a priest—or *was* a priest and he—"

"When you veer off course, I need to know," Steele said. "When you're traveling and I tell you to grab a room in Detroit, I expect you to do it. And we don't play hunches here. We follow the evidence and stay focused."

Louis was pissed, feeling if he were being treated like a patrolman. But he hid it. Or hoped he did.

"So tell me about this priest."

Louis let out a breath. "Four months after the bones were found, a man came to his church in the middle of a snowstorm and confessed to killing the boys. The suspect left before the priest could convince him to turn himself in."

"Who is this suspect?"

"I don't have a name yet. Just a description."

"Good enough for a sketch?"

"No, but you know what it's like up there. Lots of people have lived there all their all their lives. They're isolated and insular. Someone knows something, even if they don't know they know it."

"You're not going back to Keweenaw right now."

"But it will be weeks before forensics comes back. I only need a few days up north."

"I said no. This case is more important."

"More important to who?"

"To the team," Steele said sharply. "I shouldn't have to tell you how hot the spotlight is on us. We're expected to perform and to perform quickly and well. I know you understand that."

Louis looked down, to the bold, gold-and-blue shield under his feet. *Keep your mouth shut, Kincaid. You need this job.*

"This is what I understand," Louis said, looking up. "You're under intense pressure and you've put a lot on the line forming this team. But we both know a detective can't prioritize victims based on who they were. When that starts happening, it cheapens what we do."

Steele came out from behind his desk and stopped two feet from Louis, so close Louis could see a shaving nick on his chin. Louis flashed back to the last time Steele had gotten in his face, six years ago back in Loon Lake. Steele had shouted at him, calling him incompetent, in front of the whole police force.

Louis didn't move, silent.

Then, to Louis's surprise, Steele suddenly softened and, as quick as it came, the anger was gone.

"I know what you are saying," Steele said. He paused, and for a moment Louis thought he was about to be dismissed, but then Steele let out a breath.

"The nameless, the faceless—they pull at us, I know that," Steele said. "But we have to answer to the living, not the dead."

The phone rang, its trill echoing in the loft. After four rings, Steele picked up the receiver.

"Yes," Steele said. "Give me the name and address again."

Steele grabbed a pen and scribbled something on his notepad. When he hung up, he held the page out to Louis.

"We have a witness who says he saw someone lurking around Jonas Prince's house the same day he was killed," Steele said. "When he read about Prince in the newspaper this morning, he called the police. I want you and Cam to head back to Grand Rapids, talk to the man, and get him with a sketch artist."

Steele sat down at his desk and opened a folder. Louis waited, hoping Steele would reconsider his request to head back to Keweenaw but his boss was just sitting there, reading.

"Sir, you know they still haven't found them," Louis said.

Steele looked up. "I'm sorry?"

"The boys," Louis said. "They still haven't found my boys."

Steele stared at him, not with anger or even impatience. It was a different look, something almost paternal. And when Steele spoke, his voice was so soft Louis almost didn't hear him.

"They're not your boys, Louis. Remember that."

CHAPTER TWENTY-ONE

The traffic heading west to Grand Rapids was heavy, but Cam drove with impatience and a lead foot that had his Explorer weaving through the semis and Louis grabbing for the armrest.

"Damn it, Cam, slow down."

Cam didn't look at him but he did ease the SUV back under eighty. Louis let go of the armrest and watched the farmlands rush by. During the meeting back at the church, Cam had suddenly fallen silent and the easy-going jokester who Louis had come to know in their short time working together had been replaced by a sullen zombie who looked like he hadn't slept in days.

"You okay?" Louis asked. "You seem tense."

Cam threw him a none-of-your-business glance. "In-tense," he said softly. "I'm intense, that's all."

Louis didn't press it. He figured he didn't look much better himself. Three days with little sleep, no decent food, and memories floating up he didn't want to deal with.

And Emily wasn't much better. She had been oddly cool when he had sought her out about Sammy. Something was bothering her.

The Explorer made a sudden swerve. Louis looked over to see Cam flip down the visor to snatch a pack of Kools. He used his knees to steer as he lit up. Louis tensed, ready to grab the wheel, but Cam managed to keep

PJ PARRISH

it steady until he had a hand back on the wheel. They drove on for a couple more miles, acrid smoke and a hard silence filling the Explorer.

"Fresh air, please," Louis said.

"Oh, sorry," Cam said, rolling down the window. "Been a while since I had a passenger."

Louis knew a little about Cam from Emily's research—service in the Marines, five years Chicago PD, and a one-time stunt man—but there was one important thing he didn't know.

"How'd Steele find you?" Louis asked.

"We met working a kidnapping about six years ago," Cam said. "Michigan victim, Chicago drop site. I was the money man."

"You must've made an impression on Steele," Louis said.

Cam shrugged. "I was only picked because I spoke Russian and the kidnappers were right off the boat from Moscow. We arranged the payoff to take place in Jackson Park. Know where that is?"

"Nope."

"It's a park full of lagoons," Cam said. "Anyway, right in the middle of the exchange, the victim manages to escape from the trunk of the car and takes off running. One bad guy starts shooting at me, the other runs after the vic. My backup was five minutes out."

"What'd you do?"

"I shot the guy shooting at me and took off after the other shooter. I caught him about a half-mile away, and took him down. Then I realized the victim was in the lagoon, flailing around, in some kind of panic attack. It's fucking December but I jumped in after her."

Louis was quiet. He would have done the same.

"It was only afterwards," Cam said, "that I realized I had done all of that with one bullet in my vest and three more in my body."

Suddenly the idea of Cam being Stallone's stunt man didn't seem so far-fetched. "Impressive," Louis said.

"Yeah, I guess Steele thought the same thing. What about you? How'd you grab the captain's attention?"

Louis looked away, at the cornfields. *I killed a fellow cop to save a juvenile delinquent.*

Cam waited a few moments. "Okay, some other time then. This is our exit anyway."

Louis looked at the sign as they curled around an exit ramp. IONIA STATE REC AREA.

"Why are we stopping here?" Louis asked.

"A quick detour," Cam said. They passed empty fairgrounds and turned onto Main Street. The downtown was a neat mix of restored Victorian storefronts, and Louis counted four churches before Cam turned again, this time into a complex of red brick buildings. Cam parked the Explorer and turned off the engine.

"You going to tell me what's going on?" Louis asked.

"The body's still here," Cam said, nodding toward one of the buildings.

Louis looked at the sign on the building—IONIA COUNTY HEALTH DEPARTMENT.

Ionia? Why did that ring a bell? Then he remembered—on the news last night, a story about a prostitute found in Ionia. All he could remember was something about a suitcase in a cornfield. But then he understood. Cam had picked the case on the dead hookers that first day they met.

"Come on, let's go," Cam said, reaching for his door.

Louis grabbed his sleeve. "Cam, wait. Does Steele know we're stopping here?"

"No."

"He just backed me off my cold case," Louis said. "He made it clear Jonas Prince is our top priority. I don't—"

"The only person who's going to tell Steele about this detour is you, partner," Cam said. "You in or out?"

Louis pushed open his door and followed Cam into the complex's lobby, holding back as Cam showed his ID to the receptionist. She made a call, then gave them directions to head down a hall to the "medical annex." Inside the yellow-tile room, a small, dark man in green scrubs with a nametag that read ACERO met them. He took one look at Cam's badge and frowned.

"State police?" he asked. "Why are you guys here? This is an Ionia County case."

"Let's just say we're following up a lead," Cam said.

Acero hesitated. "I'm not supposed to let just anyone view the body."

Cam gestured toward Louis. "He's family."

Acero's eyes moved over Louis. "Doesn't look like family."

"Second cousin," Louis said.

"Uh-huh," Acero said. "Well, you guys got the gold badges, so I guess that's what I'll put in the log. Follow me."

Acero led them down a hall. "You're lucky she's still here," he said. "Tomorrow they'll be taking her to Lansing."

"Why Lansing?" Louis asked.

"That's where our medical examiner is," Acero said. "Sometimes she comes here, but sometimes we ship the body to her."

"So she hasn't been autopsied yet?" Cam asked.

"No, so don't mess around with the body," Acero said.

Aero led them into the storage room and opened one of two metal body drawers. When he pulled out the body, they both moved closer. Louis first thought was that Acero had pulled out the wrong corpse. This was a boy of about thirteen or fourteen—maybe five-foot-two, narrow-hipped, thin chested, and delicately muscled. His hair was close-cropped and black.

Louis looked up at Cam and it was clear he was thinking the same thing. Cam gently pulled down the drape, revealing the genitals.

Female.

Louis focused again on the chest and now he could see the soft shape of very small breasts. And the face—round, small nose, eyes closed, maybe Asian, but it was hard to tell because it was bruised and puffy.

Acero left, the door echoing in the room. It was so quiet Louis could hear the soft wheeze of Cam's breathing, and then the crackle of his leather jacket as he pulled the drape back up to the girl's waist.

Louis glanced down at the hands. One was still bagged, but the other was exposed, revealing black fingerprint ink on the fingers. The fact that the TV report last night had identified her meant that she probably had a record somewhere.

"She was strangled," Cam said.

Louis looked at the woman's throat. There was a reddish-purple ligature mark, like a grisly necklace, that suggested she had been strangled by some kind of clothing, maybe a scarf, tie, or soft belt. Also along her neck, he could see fingernail scratches, probably left as she clawed to free herself.

Cam carefully pulled back one of her eyelids, revealing the petechial hemorrhages, the telltale tiny blood clots that formed in the eyelids during asphyxiation.

"Look at this," Cam said, prodding open the victim's bloody lips. "She almost bit her tongue clean through."

Louis's gaze went back to the neck. He wasn't sure, but it looked like there were old, healing bruises beneath the new ones, as if she had been strangled before. Which suggested a sexual ritual, maybe erotic asphyxiation. There were other older bruises on her body, and her left wrist was distorted as if it had once been broken and never reset.

"This girl had a rough life," Louis said.

"Yup."

Louis picked up the clipboard hanging from the table. The preliminary report listed only name, presumed cause of death as strangulation, and estimated time of death as between eleven p.m. and three a.m. two days ago.

"Her name is Tuyen Lang," Louis said.

Cam pressed his lips together and looked up toward the florescent lights. "Angel," he said. "Tuyen, that's Vietnamese for Angel."

Louis was about to ask him how he knew but then remembered that Cam had been not just a Marine, but also a member of the "Marine Security Guard." They were the men who had been in Saigon when it fell in 1975.

"Cam," Louis said, "we need to get going."

Cam nodded. He turned quickly and headed out to the hallway. Louis took a moment to check out with Acero in the lobby and by the time he got outside, Cam was standing by the Explorer, pulling his pack of Kools from his jacket. Cam's hand shook slightly as he lit the cigarette.

"How about letting me drive for a while," Louis said.

Cam tossed Louis the keys. Louis caught them against his chest and got in the Explorer. Cam slid into the passenger seat.

Louis started the engine, pulled out of the lot, and started south out of town. Soon they were back on I-96, heading west toward Grand Rapids.

Cam said nothing, just sat there, his cigarette dangling between his fingers. Louis was about to tell him to watch his ash when Cam took a final long drag and flicked the butt out the cracked window.

"I don't think this one's related to my others," he said.

My others. It was there in Cam's voice, that same possessiveness Louis felt toward the boys in the box.

"What makes you think that?" he asked.

Cam rubbed his face. "The four women back in 1988, they were all found around Detroit, left in Dumpsters. They were strangled with rough ropes and there was piquerism."

Louis nodded. Piquerism was a signature of sexual attacks where the body has "pick" marks—usually on the breasts, groin, or buttocks—from being repeatedly stabbed. The girl in Ionia had only bad bruising.

"Plus, eleven years is a long time between victims," Louis said.

Cam nodded. "Yeah, yeah, I know that. I was just hoping . . ."

His voice trailed off and he turned away, looking out the window.

Louis thought about telling Cam about his conversation with Steele in the loft about the boys in the box but decided the fewer people who knew about his own dead case detours the better off he was.

"Why did they have to be hookers?" Cam muttered.

"Well, you know what they say," Louis said. "We don't get to pick our victims."

"But in this instance we *did* pick our victims," Cam said. "I should've known better."

Louis watched the road. He was curious about Cam's obsession with four dead women he had never met and his long-shot hope to tie Tuyen

Lang to his other victims. But he wasn't sure he wanted to dig any deeper. The Explorer already felt stuffy with a swell of personal shit itching to get free, and Louis did not want to lift the lid on Cam's box of demons.

Cam did it for him.

"My mother was a prostitute," he said.

Louis stared straight ahead. The red taillights of the car ahead of him blurred a little as he tried to think of something to say.

"She was murdered by a John," Cam added. "He died in jail."

Still, Louis said nothing.

"She was a good mom," Cam said quietly. "I was sick a lot with this blood thing and we had a lot of bills, which is why she did what she did, I guess. I didn't find out about her work or exactly how she died until I overheard some talk at the funeral."

"How old were you?" Louis asked.

"Ten."

"Tough break."

Cam shifted in his seat and lit up another cigarette. "That's probably more than you wanted to know but I had to tell someone. I wanted you to know why my case is important to me."

"I understand. Does Steele?"

"Hell, I don't know. Why would he know something like that? Why would he care?"

It was a good question. It made sense that Steele needed to know the basics of their private lives, like not having any family ties. But beyond that? Why did Steele need to know what had been buried so deep inside each member of his team?

He was about to bring it up to Cam but then decided to keep it to himself, at least for now. He'd have to find out more about the other team members to make sure this wasn't some weird coincidence. And he'd have to do it on the quiet. The last thing he needed was to give Steele any reason to take away his badge.

CHAPTER TWENTY-TWO

East Grand Rapids, the town where Jonas Prince had lived, seemed like one of those places travel photographers sought out to capture the lost dream of Main Street America. Rows of white brick colonials, ivory-globed lampposts, colonnades of robust maple trees set along pothole-free streets. The town's anchor was Wealthy Street, a three-block strip of boutiques, sidewalk cafes, and beauty salons. A short walk away was the civic center, a streamlined brick building that sat on the shores of Reeds Lake. It was there they found the East Grand Rapids Police Department.

The clean, tiled lobby was empty except for the stern face of the current chief, Peter J. Gallagher, looking down at Louis from his portrait on the wall. A woman appeared at the reception window. She had a pole-vaulter's build, and wore a crisp blue uniform adorned with a chest full of service ribbons. She gave Louis an easy smile when he showed his badge.

"Nice to meet you, detectives. I'm Lieutenant Lou Ann Spence. I have your witness secured in room one. Follow me, please."

She led them down a hallway and stopped in front of a window. Inside the interview room, their witness, Victor Weems, sat at a table. He had the catcher's-mitt face of a man who made his living outdoors so it was hard to tell how old he was—maybe forty, Louis guessed. Dressed in old jeans and a faded, plaid flannel shirt, Weems sat ramrod straight, his eyes pin-balling across the fluorescents and walls and up to the window.

"Here's his statement," Spence said, handing Louis a paper. "Your captain asked us not to press him on specifics until you got here."

"What's his background?" Louis asked.

"He's on parole, convicted of assault on a police officer three years ago."

Weems's statement was handwritten. *Saw a man peeping in the windows of the reverend's house about seven a.m. Wednesday. White guy, dark hair. He saw me looking at him and ran off.*

"Did you ask him why he didn't contact the police that day?" Louis asked.

"Yes," Spence said. "He said he just doesn't like talking to cops, but when he saw the newspaper article he thought maybe he could help."

Cam looked at Weems through the glass. "I got this," he said.

When they went in, Weems's eyes shot up, ricocheting between them. Weems scooted his chair back when Cam sat down at the table.

"No one's going to hurt you, man," Cam said. "We don't give a shit what you did before. We only care about what you saw."

Weems looked up at Louis, who was standing near the door, then back at Cam. "I put everything I saw down in my statement," he said. "I don't remember anything else. I swear I don't."

"Let me see your hands," Cam said.

"Why?"

"Please, just show me your hands."

Weems did, slowly.

When Cam gently took ahold of Weems's wrists, he tried to pull away but Cam didn't release him.

"Relax," Cam said. "I'm not going to hurt you. I'm going to do what I call a sensory recall interview. I want you to close your eyes."

Louis wondered where the hell Cam was going with this but decided to stay quiet.

"I don't remember stuff too good," Weems said, still trying to pull free of Cam's grip.

"Listen to me," Cam said. "Think of your brain as a very powerful tape recorder. Your human brain consists of about a billion neurons. Each neuron forms connections to other neurons, adding up to more than a trillion connections. You have a gazillion memories in that head because the brain never throws anything away. We just need to dig it up."

Weems seemed to relax a little. "All right, I don't get it. But I'll try." Weems closed his eyes.

Cam's voice was lullaby-soft. "Now, I want you to put yourself back at the reverend's house at the moment just before you saw the stranger."

"Okay."

"Think back to that moment. Where are you standing?"

"I don't know."

"Look down at your feet."

Weems lowered his head, his eyes still closed. "I'm on the driveway of the house we're building next door. Maybe sixty feet from the rev's house."

"Who else is there?"

"No one. I'm the first to get to the site."

"Look around the street, do you see any other vehicles?"

Weems's brow furrowed and, for twenty or so seconds, the room was silent.

"A white pickup down the block," Weems said quietly. "It's parked in the street, not in a driveway. I think it belongs to a guy who works with us but . . ."

"You said you were the first to get there."

"Yeah, right. So I guess it didn't."

"Had you seen this truck before?" Cam asked.

"No. I never saw it on site before."

"Is the truck old or new?"

"Old. Beat to shit. Full of rust."

"Is there anything in the bed of the truck?"

Weems thought for a moment. "Yeah . . . yeah, there is. A tree stump."

"Can you see a license plate?" Cam asked.

Weems squeezed his eyes together. "No, no plate. But I can see some letters on the tailgate . . . like, you know, how they put F-O-R-D there?"

"So, it's a Ford?"

"No, no man, it's one of those foreign things . . . wait, I can get it . . . soo-sow or suzoo."

"Isuzu?" Cam asked.

"Yeah, that's it. Isuzu."

"Good," Cam said. "Okay, move up in time a few minutes. What are you doing now?"

"I'm putting up the scaffolding for the stucco guys. That's my job. I always get there early and set up the equipment."

"What else is happening? What makes you look toward the reverend's house?"

"I hear a dog barking."

"Could you see the dog?"

Weems sat up straighter but kept his eyes closed. "No, it's coming from the house on the other side of the rev's place and the dog sounds all upset. When I look over at the rev's house, all I see are these big evergreens that run along the side of the house. But I can see that they're moving, and I think that's weird since there isn't a lick of wind. Then I see a man. He's in the evergreens, looking in the rev's side windows, cupping his hands against the glass."

"What is the man wearing?"

"I can't see any colors."

"Why not?"

"He kinda blends in with the evergreens."

"So he's wearing . . . ?"

"Green jacket, maybe a hunting jacket or camo?" Weems said.

"How old is he?"

"I don't know."

"Watch him for a moment, watch how he moves his body. What's your gut impression of his age?"

159

"Forty something? He's being careful, creeping around the house, but he doesn't seem jittery."

"How does he seem?"

"Curious," Weems said.

"Good. That's good," Cam said. He glanced up at Louis again and Louis gave him a nod to keep going. Louis wondered where Cam had learned this technique. It made Louis think again about the odd skills of the five people Steele had gathered for his team.

"What happens next?" Cam asked Weems.

"I accidently drop a connector joint on the concrete and he looks over at me," Weems said, eyes still shut.

"Can you see his face?"

Weems was quiet for a long time.

"Can you see his face?" Cam asked again.

"Yeah, now I can . . . he's a white guy . . . brown hair, ragged to the collar. He kinda freezes then disappears around the back of the house, toward the lakeside. Oh, and I think maybe there was something was wrong with his leg . . . he moved funny."

"Very good," Cam said. "What do you do next?"

"I finish putting up the scaffolding."

"How long did this take?"

"About a half-hour."

"In your mind, look down the street. Is the white pickup still there?"

Weems opened his eyes. He looked different now, relaxed and beaming with pride. "No, it was gone."

Cam released Weem's wrists and sat back. He looked up at Louis. "Anything you want to ask?"

"Do you think you could provide a sketch of the man?" Louis asked Weems.

"Yes, sir. I think I can. Might not be too good but I can give you something."

"Thank you, Mr. Weems," Louis said.

"You need to catch this guy," Weems said as Cam stood up.

"Why do you say that?" Louis asked.

Weems shrugged. "I'm not a religious man, but us guys, we all liked the rev He would come out and visit with us, sometimes bringing us water and wanting us to take his prayer cards and come to his church. He seemed like a real decent guy."

"We'll do our best to catch him," Louis said. "Thanks for your cooperation. Sit tight for a few minutes."

Lieutenant Spence was standing out in the hall when they went out. She had been watching the interview through the window. "I can have an artist here in thirty minutes," she said.

"We'll wait," Cam said. "Can we get some coffee or something?"

"Sure."

She started to walk away but Louis called her back. "How far is the reverend's house from here?"

"Five, ten minute walk. Why?"

"I'd like to see it."

"Your own state guys already processed the house," she said.

Louis had seen the report from the troopers Steele had sent the same morning Prince's body had been found at the church. They had found nothing disturbed in the house, nothing was out of the ordinary. But they hadn't known then about the man lurking outside staring into the windows.

"Prince's house keys are back in Lansing," Cam said. "Steele had all his personal stuff found at the church sent back to evidence."

"I can get you a key," Spence said. "Reverend Prince was part of our House Watch program. Residents register their homes and give us a key. I'll go get it."

Spence left and Louis turned to Cam. "You mind staying here for the artist?"

"Hell no, you go do your thing."

Louis looked back through the glass at Weems. He was sitting there, picking at his dirty fingernails. "That was good work in there," he said.

Cam smiled. "Yeah, I seem to have a way with felons."

"Do you really believe what you told him, that the brain never discards a memory?"

Cam shrugged. "I believe our brains store a whole lot of shit we'd just as soon forget. I think some memories scab over, like a kind of protection, especially if it's from when we were kids. Unless something happens to tear the scab off, it just sits there. But who really knows, right?"

CHAPTER TWENTY-THREE

Jonas Prince had lived in his house on Reeds Lake for twenty-six years. The city of East Grand Rapids had grown "fancified" as Lieutenant Spence told Louis when she handed over the keys, but the reverend hadn't changed much about his little house. Tooki had said that after Anthony and Violet moved to their new house, Jonas lived alone except for the twice-weekly ministrations of a housekeeper.

The walk to Jonas Prince's house took Louis through a neighborhood of old-growth trees guarding homes with porch swings, picket fences, and swing sets in the side yards. An old guy walking a golden retriever eyed him as he passed, and Louis suspected that when the guy got home he'd be on the horn to the East Grand Rapids Police Department to report a strange black man casing his next break-in.

The homes got newer and larger the closer Louis got to the lake. When he made his final turn onto Frederick Drive, the first house he saw was a white monstrosity with a three-car garage tucked behind an iron gate, not much different than the mini-mansions in Anthony's neighborhood. The other new houses on the street all seemed far too grand for their modest-sized lots.

Near the end of the short street, Louis stopped in front of the Prince home. It was set far back from the street, a small, white Cape Cod cottage— its narrow driveway bordered by a rose garden, the bushes bare and the white trellises in need of painting.

Louis glanced left to the half-finished, Roman-columned monstrosity next door, the house where Weems had been working. He looked toward the west side of the Prince cottage. It was just as Weems had said—if anyone had been lurking in the evergreens, Weems would have had a decent look at him.

Louis went to the west side of the cottage. There were two windows about chest high, almost hidden by the evergreens. Louis got as close as he could without walking on the dirt right below the windows. If there was a boot print to be gotten by a forensics team here, he didn't want to foul things up. There was also a good chance Steele's techs might be able to raise a print from the glass or sill.

Louis retraced his steps to the front porch, unlocked the door and went in.

He paused in the foyer. He could pick a mix of scents—furniture polish, the normal mustiness of an old house, and an odd earthy, cedar smell, the same smell that had clung to Jonas's sweater in the dressing room back at the church.

He had a view into the small living room with a glimpse of the dining room beyond. Old pine floors covered with worn braid rugs, sofa and chairs slipcovered in faded blue chintz, pale blue walls adorned with framed seascapes—he recognized the Sleeping Bear Dunes up near Joe's town—and a white brick fireplace flanked with built-in bookshelves. It was a neat, understated room, but with no TV, newspapers, or even a book out of place, it looked like no one ever really used it.

Louis flipped through Junia's interview of Prince's employees looking for the name of Prince's housekeeper. There it was—Delia Arnold, who had worked for Prince for eighteen years, came twice a week, and had last been here Monday, two days before Jonas was found dead in the church. Her interview was unremarkable, Junia noting that the housekeeper was distraught and tearful.

He went to the fireplace to get a closer look at the three framed photographs on the mantle. They showed Jonas's wife at various ages, and it struck him that the youngest version of Reeta Prince resembled Violet.

164

He wondered what deep psychological meaning Emily Farentino would find in that.

Louis continued toward the back of the cottage, passing through a dining room and emerging into the kitchen. It still had its original 1940s white tile and white painted cabinets, and the appliances all looked to hail from the sixties, except for a small countertop microwave and a Mr. Coffee, its carafe half full. There were two dishes stacked in the sink, crusted over with egg residue and half-eaten toast.

A gray Formica dinette sat under the window. On the placemat was a saucer that matched the dishes in the sink, but no cup. Next to it was a copy of the *Grand Rapids Press*, one section folded over to reveal the crossword. It was half-finished, in green ink from the Bic pen next to the saucer. The top of the pen was chewed away.

Sunlight cast a long spill on the linoleum floor. It was coming from the kitchen's other door and Louis went toward it.

The sun was streaming in from a bank of large windows that offered a stunning view of the back yard's lawn that sloped down to Reeds Lake. Louis guessed the room had once served as a sun porch, but had been transformed into Jonas Prince's study.

There was a sagging yellow-print sofa with a toss of blankets and pillows and an old Zenith console TV. The only other furnishings were a bookcase, a file cabinet, and a large plain metal desk. That same cedar smell hung in the air here, stronger than it had been in the living room.

Louis went over to the desk. There was no computer and everything here was handwritten, in notebooks and on legal pads. He remembered a note from Tooki's financial report saying that Jonas Prince had no credit cards, paying his bills by check from the First Community Bank.

On one wall was a montage of framed certificates of appreciation from schools, politicians and charities—The Lord's Pantry food bank, the Butterworth Hospital Hospice and the Fresh Start program. There was one framed photograph and Louis stepped closer for a better look. It was old and blurry and showed what looked to be a soldier wearing a white uniform and fur hat—a bandolier with a holstered gun slung over his chest—standing in a snowy forest.

No mistake, the soldier was a young Jonas Prince. But where in the world had the photo been taken?

He turned to the bookcase. It held an eclectic array of titles—*The Confessions of St. Augustine, Dark Night of the Soul, The Importance of Living* by Lin Yutang, C.S. Lewis's *The Screwtape*, Norman Vincent Peale's *You Can If You Think You Can*, and many others that seemed to be religious in nature. There were at least ten different Bibles that Louis could discern. Most of the books sprouted scrap-paper bookmarks. Louis looked through a couple of the bookmarked pages but they all seemed to refer to religious texts.

Louis turned to the desk. It was untidy, in the way of a man who had been bedeviled by unfinished work. There was the cup from the saucer in the kitchen, half filled with cold coffee. Three green Bic pens, all with their tops chewed.

In the corner was a thin wooden box, the top engraved with a filigreed seal and the words PUROS REYNOSO. It was filled with fat cigars in cellophane. The smell of cedar and rain-soaked earth was so pungent he had to shut the box.

He turned his attention to a rattan basket, but it contained only bills, letters, a schedule of church social events, and an invitation to attend a global faith convention in some place named Turku.

Louis noticed a balled-up piece of paper on the floor, picked it up, and unfolded it, putting on his glasses to read. The top line in green ink read WED. SERMON—PRIDE AND HUMILITY, with notes and Bible verses.

The only other thing on the desk was a blue loose-leaf notebook. It was the kind any school kid would carry—except for the labels on the color-coded tabs: SALVATION, GRATITUDE, SUFFERING, SOCIAL ISSUES, and at least ten other sermon topics. There was a piece of paper sticking out the top and Louis opened to the bookmarked page.

It was a lined page like the crumbled one, filled with Prince's small, un-slanted handwriting in green ink. Louis leaned down to read it.

NEW SERMON FOR WED.

The Fruit of Forgiveness

Verses to use?

Gen 4:7 - If you do what is right, will you not be accepted? But if you do not do what is right, sin is crouching at your door; it desires to have you, but you must rule over it.

Luke 15:18 - Father, I have sinned against heaven and before you.

Gen 25:24 - The Lord said to her, "Two nations are in your body. Two tribes that are now inside you will be separated. One nation will be stronger than the other."

1 John 4:21 - And this commandment we have from him, that he who loves God should love his brother also.

The handwriting on this page looked different than that on the other pages, less careful, more scribbled, and with a harder hand that made the ink almost imprint into the paper. Louis straightened and took off his glasses. Apparently, Jonas had changed his Wednesday sermon topic. He looked over the room again, at the sagging sofa with its crumbled blanket and thin pillow, at the desk with its mess of unfinished work.

A life interrupted, as if everything on Prince's last day on earth had been frozen in time. The half-finished morning crossword. The coffee cup brought back here to the study. The last-minute switch to a new sermon.

The Fruit of Forgiveness . . .

What had compelled Prince to change it?

The cigar stink was getting to him. He left the study and made his way to the back of the house, opening a door on a bedroom with blue chenille-covered double bed, a chest of drawers, and a small desk. It was the room with the blue curtains that he had seen outside, with the window that the lurker had peered into. The room looked pristine, untouched, devoid of anything personal.

Except for the study, the rest of the house had that same feeling. Louis had seen the homes of men who lived alone before, and there was always a strange sadness to them, like the daily machinery of life went on, but the sweet, softening touches that came from being surrounded by a family were missing.

He went on to the master bedroom. A double bed with a maple headboard, its sheets in a tangle, the right side of the bed more concave than the left. The nightstand held a single lamp, an old rotary phone, a glass of water, and a small Bible.

A search of the dresser revealed only men's clothing, as did the small closet, all imbued with the cedar smell.

The only thing left to go through was a hope chest at the foot of the bed. Louis opened the lid. On top were a couple of blankets and a souvenir pillow from Sault Ste. Marie. He set them aside.

Underneath was a small, white satin jewelry box which held a tiny gold ring, a red-and-gold brooch, a photo of an old clapboard house set in pine trees, and a yellowed lace handkerchief. Louis turned his attention to a cigar box, an older version of the one he had found in the study. Inside were some old papers but nothing that looked interesting, except for one old certificate illustrated with angels, Jesus, and printed in a language Louis guessed was German or Dutch. He could read only the date 1920 and the name of the person at the top of the certificate—Sedrik Prinsilä.

Prinsilä . . . Prince. Apparently, Jonas had Anglicized his family name at some point, not an uncommon practice in western Michigan, which had a large immigrant population. Maybe Sedrik was Anthony's paternal grandfather.

Under the papers was an old prayer card. The front showed an angel hovering over a black-robed priest, identified as Sanctus Joannes Bosco. Louis remembered that Weems said Jonas passed out prayer cards to the workers.

The only other item in the cigar box was a thin piece of paper. Louis unfolded it. It was handwritten and seemed to be a receipt from a man named Thomas Revel for a donation to the church of an organ valued at $600. At the bottom, someone had written "Donated as consideration for the services offered to the Revel family." It was dated 1961.

There was only one thing left in the cigar box. It was a small black-and-white photograph, scarred with fold lines and yellow with age. It showed two boys, maybe four and six, staring deadpan at the camera. They were dressed alike in heavy wool coats, standing in front of a small, white church. Louis turned it over. Written on the back in faded ink were the words *My boys.*

Louis sat back on his heels, staring at the two faces. This seemed to be the only photograph in the entire house of the Prince children. Why was it tucked away in an old chest?

A noise somewhere in the front of the house. The creak of footsteps on the wood floorboards.

Louis rose, still holding the photograph. "Cam? I'm back here, in the bedroom," he called out.

No answer. No sound at all. The footsteps had stopped.

"Cam?"

Louis started to the door then froze.

The woman standing in the doorway was small and dark-skinned, wearing a plaid coat and holding out a can of mace. It was aimed straight at his face.

"Don't you move," the woman said.

Louis slowly raised his hands. "Take it easy, ma'am, I'm just—"

"Shut your mouth and move away from that bed," the woman said. "Get over there by that dresser."

Louis hesitated then moved toward the corner. The woman sidled in, her eyes darting to the phone on the nightstand. "Now don't make me use this, you hear? I'm going to call the police."

Then it hit Louis. Delia Arnold. This was the housekeeper. Of course she had her own key.

"Mrs. Arnold," he began slowly.

Her eyes narrowed. "How you know my name?"

"Mrs. Arnold, I'm a detective," Louis said calmly, his eyes trained on her finger on the mace button. He had been maced once, back in the academy as part of his training. He had seen giant men dropped to their knees with one spray, screaming and wheezing.

"Mrs. Arnold, my name is Louis Kincaid. I am an investigator with the state police."

"You expect me to believe that?"

"Yesterday, you were interviewed by one of my team members. Her name was Junia Cruz, a kinda large woman who wears a red cape. You remember her?"

Delia Arnold hesitated then nodded.

"Okay," Louis said. "I'm going to bring my left hand down and move my jacket aside so you can see my badge on my belt, okay?"

Delia Arnold brought up her other hand to steady the mace but gave another tight nod.

Very slowly, Louis lowered his hand and exposed his badge. The housekeeper stared hard at badge for a long moment, then she lowered the mace. Louis let out a long breath, but decided to stay where he was.

"What are you doing in the reverend's home?" Delia asked. "The police already came and went yesterday."

"I know. I'm here to follow up on some things," Louis said. "I'm sorry if I scared you."

"Sorry if I scared you," Delia said, holding up the mace. "I woulda used this, you know."

"I don't doubt that."

Delia put the mace in her purse. She suddenly looked very tired and her eyes went toward the unmade bed. Louis had the feeling she needed to sit down but he knew she wouldn't, not in this room, not on Jonas Prince's bed.

"Why don't we go sit down, maybe in the reverend's study," Louis said. "I'd like to ask you some questions if you're up to it."

Delia nodded and they headed back to the front of the house. As Louis followed her, he realized he was still holding the old photo of the Prince boys and he slipped it into his pocket.

In the study, Delia stopped short, staring at the sofa. She set her purse down and began to fold the blanket. "Poor soul," she whispered.

"Ma'am?"

She turned to Louis. "This isn't like him, to sleep out here. He's got a really bad back and this old sofa is no place for a man like him to be."

She stopped and her face fell. She had realized she was talking about Prince in the present tense, as so many grieving people did, just like Violet had done. Almost twenty years serving Jonas Prince . . . Louis had no doubt Delia Arnold cared for him deeply.

Delia stacked the blanket and pillow on the sofa. Then she looked to the messy desk, and Louis had the feeling she was thinking exactly what he himself had—a life interrupted, a morning frozen in time.

"Mrs. Arnold, can you tell me a little bit about the reverend's routine?" Louis asked.

She looked to him. "What do you mean?"

"Well, for starters, he apparently changed his Wednesday sermon at the last minute. Did he often do that?"

She frowned. "No, he worked hard on his sermons and always had them done days early." She smiled sadly. "He used to read them to me, you know, to try them out. He read me his one for this week when I was here Monday. It was on the sin of pride." She paused. "Course, I don't go to the reverend's church. I go to Messiah Missionary Baptist over on Henry Avenue. But the good word's the same wherever you go, you know. The Lord don't care how fancy His house is."

Louis had a sudden flashback, again to that hot-house of a wooden church in Mississippi. "No ma'am, He doesn't care," he said.

Delia looked around the study again. "I guess I should go get my things," she said softly. She looked up at Louis. "Is that okay? The police wouldn't let me in yesterday."

"Of course," Louis said.

She picked up her purse, started away then went back and got the dirty coffee cup. Louis followed her to the kitchen, where she set the cup in the sink. He had the feeling she wanted—*needed*—to clean things up, but instead she went to a broom closet and pulled out an apron, some rubber gloves, a gray cardigan sweater, a big, pink plastic tote, and an umbrella. Before she closed the door, Louis caught sight of a photo pinned to the inside of the door. It was of two little girls in white dresses.

"Your daughters?" Louis asked, nodding toward it.

"Granddaughters," Delia said. She carefully unpinned the photo. "I need to take this to Theo. He hasn't seen his girls in eight months and they've grown so."

"Is Theo your son?" Louis asked.

She nodded slowly, not looking at him.

"Where is he?"

When Delia's eyes came back to him, they were questioning for a moment, like she was looking at him but seeing someone else. "He's in prison, down in Jackson," she said.

"Sorry," Louis said.

"No need to be," Delia said. "He made a wrong turn, and he knows it. I'm watching over his babies until he gets out. Family is family. Even if they do wrong, you still have to love them."

She was looking at the photo of her granddaughters again, running one finger lightly over the surface.

"I found this picture of the boys in a chest in the bedroom," Louis said, holding out the old photo. "Why are there no other pictures of the family anywhere in the house?"

She glanced at the photo then cocked her head and gave him a hard stare, like she was trying to decide how personal she could get. "Mrs. Prince died before the reverend moved here," she said. "And his youngest, he died real young. Maybe the reverend just couldn't bear seeing what he had lost."

Delia started to the table and began to clean up. Louis pulled out his wallet and slipped the photo inside, thinking it might be useful to have it in the case file.

"How'd you come to work for Jonas Prince?" Louis asked.

Delia looked over at him from the sink. "I got a call from a lady at the church saying Mr. Anthony was looking for a housekeeper for his father. I went to the church, you know, for an interview, but it was Miss Violet who talked to me. She said that she used to come over here but her husband didn't want her to do that anymore. She said the reverend needed caring for."

Violet had told him that Anthony didn't want her to have servants of her own. And he didn't want Violet to take care of Jonas. He wondered if it was an attempt to isolate Violet. Men did that, narrowing their wives' worlds to maintain control.

"When I first came here, this house had an awful feel in it," Delia said. "The reverend hadn't even bothered to change some of the burned out lightbulbs and the freezer was chockfull of old frozen casseroles and lasagnas that the parish folks brought but he never touched."

She paused for a long time, looking around the kitchen. "I got him eating right, cleaned things up, helped him organize his study so he could work," she went on.

"Did Violet ever come over?" Louis asked.

"Yes, maybe once a month or so. Not to check up on me. She wasn't like that. I think she just liked my company. I liked hers, too, but she stopped coming about a year back. I don't know why. Is Violet . . . is Mrs. Prince okay?"

"Yes," Louis said. "Just very sad right now."

Delia nodded slowly, and started to put the rest of her belongings in the plastic tote.

"Mrs. Arnold, how would you describe Reverend Prince's relationship with Anthony?" Louis asked.

"You mean were they close?"

"Yeah."

Delia hesitated. "Mr. Anthony is . . . he's not given to displays."

"Meaning?"

"He's slow to show his feelings, his affections."

"Did Anthony visit his father here often?"

Delia shook her head. "Not that I saw. He and Mrs. Prince would come pick him up on Christmas and on his birthday. They tried to get him to go out to restaurants, but the reverend told me once he didn't feel right in the places Anthony liked, that he was happy eating his walleye at Rose's."

She paused. "I don't think Mr. Anthony is bad. It's just some folk's hearts are harder to open. Or at least that's what the reverend always says." She let out a small sigh. "Said . . . that's what he always said."

Louis was silent, watching Delia work through her grief.

"I heard talk," Delia said softly, "from a friend of mine whose brother works at the church. He said the reverend was strangled. Is that true?"

Louis didn't doubt that word had already leaked out from the employees. "I can't talk about the details," Louis said. "I'm sorry."

"Such a gentle man should not die such a horrible death," Delia said softly.

"Do you have any thoughts on who might have had reason to kill him?"

Delia shook her head. "No, sir."

Though he hesitated to ask, he knew had to. "Do you think Anthony could have killed him?"

Delia's eyes widened. "Good Lord, no. He could never do such a thing, because I know just by knowing the reverend all these years that Mr. Anthony was raised to be a good son. Why, he's man of God himself."

Delia stared at him, indignation hardening her eyes. He knew she couldn't fathom what he was saying, and he let it go.

"Thank you for your time, Mrs. Arnold. I'll help you carry your things out."

"No need," Delia said. "I can get them. Make sure you lock up when you leave. The reverend wouldn't want some burglar getting in here and disturbing his things."

"Yes, ma'am."

Delia made her way out and Louis stood there for a moment, thinking. The visit to Jonas Prince's home had yielded no helpful evidence and no special vibes. He returned to the study for a last look. A discarded sermon and the sudden impulse to create a new message for his congregation. A message on forgiveness.

His eyes drifted to the blanket folded on the sofa.

Insomnia.

Dreams bedeviled, as Delia would say.

That he did understand. What had been keeping Jonas Prince awake at night? And who was it that needed forgiveness?

And he knew—call it the *woo-woo* vibes or plain old cop instincts— that when he found the answer to that question, he would have his killer.

CHAPTER TWENTY-FOUR

When Louis got to St. Michael's at seven the next morning, he was the first one in. He went quickly to the thermostat, turning it up to eighty. Back at his desk, he typed up a summary of the interview with Weems and his analysis of his walk-through at Jonas Prince's home. He had hesitated to include his opinion about Jonas's insomnia the night before his murder and his emotional estrangement from Anthony. But in the end, he included everything he saw and thought, *woo-woo* vibes and all.

He was about to distribute copies to every desk when Tooki came in. He was bundled in a down parka and when he pulled off his wool hat, his black hair sprouted to life with static electricity.

"Morning," Louis said, dropping a report on Tooki's desk.

"Ada Ka-da-vous-lay," Tooki gasped.

Louis looked at him, wondering if he heard right.

Tooki smiled. "In Tamil, it means 'oh my freaking God,' kinda. Days like this I wish I was back in India."

"What's the average temperature there?"

"Ninety-three."

"In the summer or winter?"

"Both."

The door opened again, washing the nave with blast of cold air that scattered papers off the conference table. Cam hustled in, followed by Steele.

"Briefing in five minutes," Steele said over his shoulder as he started toward the loft.

Louis looked at his watch and then at the door. Where the hell was Emily? Then the door opened and she slipped in. She shuffled toward her desk, lugging her oversized briefcase like it was filled with rocks. She shook off her coat and pulled off a wool cap. Her bronze curls were still wet from her morning shower and she looked paler than normal, with circles under her eyes.

Louis thought about asking her if she was okay, but there wasn't time now. He resumed distributing his reports, but when he got to Junia's desk, he paused. The desktop was bare. He slid open the middle drawer. It was empty, except for a few a paperclips. Same with the drawers.

Shit. Junia was gone.

The unit was less than a month old and had already lost a member. It took time, sometimes years, for a team to really gel, and turnover interrupted that process. What was the brass going to think of a captain who couldn't keep a handpicked forensic expert longer than a few weeks?

Steele was coming back down the stairs. "Chairs, please," he said.

Louis set a copy of his report in front of Steele as he passed him. He took his seat at the conference table next to Emily, who didn't look up from her notes.

Steele moved immediately to the case without small talk, speaking in a monotone. He was talking forensics, a topic that would have belonged to Junia, Louis noted.

"Preliminary forensics have confirmed Prince was indeed killed in the dressing room. We have kick marks and saliva on the floor. There were no marks anywhere else in the cathedral so we can assume the killer carried Prince to the altar from the dressing room but we still have not located what appears to be the only key to this room."

Steele looked to Cam. "Have you found anything out about that blue robe?"

"Yeah," Cam said. "According to his secretary, that robe was his oldest, something he had before he got to Grand Rapids. He saved it only

177

for special occasions. Last time she recalls him wearing it was the funeral of one of the church elders a couple years back."

"And the stole?" Steele asked.

"Just as old," Cam said. "He always wore them together. I've left messages for Anthony to get some more info, but seems he's always tied up."

Steele gave a tight nod. "Tell us about this witness, Weems."

Cam recapped the interview, adding that a statewide BOLO had been issued for a middle-aged white man driving an older white Isuzu truck. He passed out copies of the sketch Weems had given the police artist.

"You want this sketch in the papers, boss?" Cam asked.

"Not yet," Steele said. "I don't want the subject to know someone saw him. If he thinks his visit to the reverend's house went unnoticed, he'll be more likely to stay around and maybe make a mistake."

Louis eyed the sketch. It looked like a million other forty-something white guys—rumpled, shaggy, shown wearing a dark sweatshirt.

Steele pushed a stack of papers across the table to Tooki. "These are from the tip line," he said. "I need you to categorize them and get them into the computer so we can analyze them."

Tookie took the papers without a word.

Steele turned to Emily. "Farentino, background on the Prince family."

Emily sat up straighter and pushed the curls off her face. "The first reference I found to Jonas Prince is in the 1962 census records for Cass County, Michigan. He and Anthony are recorded as living in Vandalia, a small town south of Grand Rapids. Jonas was hired by the Vandalia Community Church of God after the death of their pastor James Tripp." She looked up. "Tripp was Violet's father."

"Interesting," Steele said. "Go on."

"James Tripp was a widower and Violet was only sixteen when he died," Emily went on. "The Tripp's house was owned by the church so Violet had nowhere to go. Jonas took her in."

Louis thought of what Violet had told him, that Jonas was like a father to her.

"Three years later, the census shows all three living in Jonas's home in East Grand Rapids," Emily said. "By then Jonas is pastor of the Beacon Light Methodist Church and Anthony and Violet are married. Soon after, the church incorporates as the Beacon Light Cathedral, though it was much smaller then."

"Church to cathedral in just six years," Steele said.

Emily nodded. "Tooki helped me track down financial records that show a clear pattern of Anthony pushing his father into fast expansion in all areas—donor building funds, radio and TV broadcasts, buying up real estate, hiring public relations people and graphic designers to do the programs and newsletters, and public relations."

Emily paused, frowning, as if she lost her place in her notes. For a long moment, the only sound was the faint wheeze of wind in the organ pipes. Louis let out a breath when she finally went on.

"Anthony studied the demographics," she said. "He recognized that East Grand Rapids was gentrifying, becoming a hot spot for young families with big bucks. He began a very aggressive recruitment campaign to grow the congregation. Some of the other churches called it poaching."

"How many members does the church have now?" Cam asked.

"Over three thousand," Tooki said.

Cam whistled softly.

"You hit a certain size and you become self-generating," Emily said. "You attract people by your sheer size. People know that the church is that big place they saw on TV. There is a sense of something going on and people love that, want to be part of it. And size itself begets more size."

"Jonas was against this expansion, right?" Louis asked.

Emily hesitated. "Yes and no. Everyone I talked to said Anthony had to push hard for everything he wanted. Jonas was, by all accounts, a modest man and suspicious of any technology or anything new. Anthony always managed to sway him by convincing him that this was God's way of getting the gospel to more people."

Emily looked down at her notes. "Anthony's secretary told me she heard Jonas and Anthony only argue about one thing. Anthony was big on appearances, you know, expensive suits, capped teeth, styled hair. He wanted his father to wear a suit and tie to preach in, told him he should be more like Jim Bakker. Jonas put his foot down and insisted on his wearing his robes. He told Anthony he had no respect for tradition. Anthony gave up."

Steele nodded. "Good work."

"I'm trying to find more about the family before they settled in Vandalia, but so far I'm striking out."

"Try the name Prinsilä," Louis said. "I found it on an old certificate in Jonas's house. It might be the old family name."

Louis spelled it for her and Emily wrote it in her notebook.

Steele nodded in satisfaction. "Okay, Farentino keep digging into the family history." He looked at Louis. "Did that radio jock ever get back to you on the surveillance his PI did?"

"Not yet."

"Lean on him," Steele said. "Go back to Detroit if you have to."

"Yes, sir."

Steele stood and went to the large bulletin board on the altar. It was plastered with crime scene photos and diagrams, along with head shots of Jonas and the suspects they had unearthed. Steele took down the photos of the gay deacon and Bushman and tacked up the Weems sketch next to Anthony Prince. He didn't need to say anything. It was clear they now had only two primary suspects.

Steele faced his team. "Anyone have any questions?"

"Where's Junia, sir?" Tooki asked.

Steele hesitated. "We had a disagreement we couldn't reconcile. Anything else?"

When no one said anything, Steele came back to the table, picked up his folders and walked briskly across the nave. Halfway up the stairs to the loft, he paused, and for several seconds stood still, hand on the rail.

"It was her choice," he said, looking back at them. "All of you need to understand that. It was her choice."

Louis waited until Steele disappeared then turned back to look for Emily. She had just emerged from the coffee room, cradling a mug. She sat down at her desk, paused, then folded her arms and laid her head down. Neither Tooki nor Cam seemed to notice her. Louis went over to her desk.

"You all right?" he asked.

She raised her head, and it took a moment for her eyes to focus on him. She opened the middle drawer of her desk, took out a pair of blue-framed glasses and put them on.

"What happened to your contacts?" Louis asked.

"My eyes hurt too much this morning to put them in."

She began to sort through some papers. Louis slipped into a chair. "Emily, what's wrong?" he asked.

She kept arranging the papers then finally gave up and stacked them in a corner. "I'm adjusting to a new medication," she said softly.

"Medication? Are you sick?"

"No, not the way you mean anyway. I've gone back on my anti-depressants and my doctor is trying a new one. Zoloft."

He sat back, not a clue as to what to say.

"You're looking at me weird," Emily said.

"I'm sorry," Louis said. "I'm just surprised. You always seemed so—"

"Normal?"

He smiled. "No, so confident and in control."

"Well, thank you," she said. "But I'm not. No one is really. I've been on and off anti-depressants most of my life, but I was able to get off them six years ago. I was doing great but with all the changes in my life this year, I guess I should have known it would catch up with me."

"Is it this job?" he asked. "Are you sorry you left the FBI?"

"No, God, no. It's something else."

He waited for her to offer more. Behind him he could hear the *tap-tap* of a keyboard and the whirr of the copy machine.

"Talk to me," he whispered.

Emily sighed and extended her left forearm to him, pushing up her sweater. At first he didn't know what he was supposed to see but then he did—a tiny white scar across her wrist.

"Oh Jesus," he said softly. "How old were you?"

"Sixteen," she said. "It wasn't a serious attempt, really, and I haven't even thought about ever doing it again, but it changed everything. It cost me everything."

"How?"

She closed her eyes for a second. "I was struggling in school. My boyfriend had just broken up with me and my best friend moved away. I thought maybe . . . somehow, someway, cutting myself would make things better."

He touched her hand and she gently drew it away and tugged the sweater back down over her wrist.

"Anyway, a friend took me to the emergency room," she said. "They called my parents to come get me. On the way there . . . they were broadsided by a truck. They were killed on impact."

A chill crawled across his skin. For a teenage girl, this was guilt at its worst, the kind of guilt that defined an entire life.

"So that's it," she said, before he could say anything. "I still see a therapist every so often, take my pills and try to live as they would have wanted me to. Most days, I'm good."

He still didn't have any words and his face must have shown his discomfort because Emily leaned close.

"I'm good, okay?" she said. "Just let it drop, please. I don't need this getting around."

Louis saw her eyes flick up toward the loft then quickly settle back on his face. "You think Steele knows?" he asked.

"I was off meds by the time I started with the FBI. And I'm paying for them myself, not going through our insurance plan." She shook her head. "He never would have hired me if he had known."

"Lots of cops see shrinks," Louis said. "I had to once, after a shooting."

"That's standard procedure." She shook her head again, more vigorously. "Steele hand-picked us, Louis. You think he'd tolerate any cracks in his precious team?"

Louis was quiet, but his mind was churning. Something was bothering him, like he was looking at pieces of a puzzle and not seeing how they fit together.

Cracks . . .

His foster father Phillip was in his thoughts suddenly, and something Phillip had told him one day when they were talking about Phillip's experiences in Korea, how the military changed men, how some men just lost it.

We called them cracked jugs, Louis. They're okay except for a tiny crack that you can't see. You keep filling them up, pouring in more water, and everything's fine. Then, one day, without warning, the crack gives way.

Louis looked over at Junia's empty desk. When he turned back to Emily, she had resumed sorting through her papers.

"Emily, did Junia mention anything to you about wanting to quit?" he asked.

She set her file aside, glanced up at the loft then lowered her voice. "No, but something weird happened yesterday when you and Cam were in Grand Rapids."

"What?"

"I noticed Junia over by the bulletin board. She was holding a file, but she was just standing there, like in a daze, staring at something. Then suddenly she went charging up to the loft. Steele was up there and they were trying to keep it down but I heard her say something to him like, 'Don't screw with my head.' He kept telling her to calm down and suddenly I hear papers flying."

"She threw the file folder at him?"

"I don't know. All I know is that a few seconds later she's out the front door. I was here all day yesterday and she never came back. She must've come back late last night to clean out her desk."

He wanted to talk more, but Emily's phone rang and she picked it up. Louis sat there, his eyes going from Junia's empty desk up to the bulletin board. What had Junia been looking at that had set her off?

He rose and walked to the altar. He took a quick look at the items tacked to the front of the bulletin board, but it was just the same material on the Prince case that they had all been looking at for weeks now.

Louis stepped around the back of the bulletin board.

Nobody had bothered to take it down. It was all still there, just as it had been that first day they had all set foot in the church. Five photographs, each with a simple description beneath.

The Dumpster Hookers.

CMU Death Ring.

Palmer Park Wolf Pack Murders.

The Bay City Black Widow.

The Boys in the Box.

For a second, he just stared at the photos. But then the pieces came together and it hit him hard, like a fist to the chest.

Cam had chosen the hookers. His dead mother was a hooker. Emily was stuck with the CMU students' suicide pact. Palmer Park involved gay bashing. Louis didn't know if Tooki was gay, but he was pretty sure a nerdy guy like him had experienced his share of bullying.

And Junia? He didn't know much about her, except that she wore expensive clothes and her immigrant father was a self-made millionaire.

But he knew Steele.

Knew first-hand how mercurial, even how cruel Steele could be. Seven years ago, after the sniper case in Loon Lake, a furious Steele, looking to blame someone for the crash-and-burn of the state's intervention, had used his high position in the state police to destroy Louis's career—and almost his life—in Michigan.

Louis stared at the photograph of the small skeletons. The Boys in the Box. An ice-cold case of child abuse, there to be selected by an investigator with his own raw boyhood scars.

Louis closed his fist, his heart quickening.

It wasn't just the idea that they each had gravitated toward cases that interested them. That happened all the time. This . . . this was orchestrated, like some grand scheme. Five hand-picked but damaged investigators matched with five specific unsolved cases.

But why the hell would Steele concoct such a scenario? Was it a test of their emotional stamina? A drama to be played out for Steele's private amusement? An arrogant game of mind fuck?

"Louis."

The voice came from above. Louis stepped out from behind the bulletin board and looked up to see Steele leaning over the loft's railing. Louis knew Steele couldn't see the back of the bulletin board from above, but he had to know Louis had been looking at it.

Louis cleared his throat. "Yes, sir?"

"You driving down to Detroit soon?" Steele asked.

"Heading out in a few minutes."

"Good."

Steele disappeared back into the dusk of the loft. Louis went back to his desk to get his briefcase and jacket. As he neared Emily he considered telling her about his theory about the cold cases, but decided not to. He wasn't sure exactly what Steele was trying to do or what he hoped to gain. And he didn't know if he should burden Emily with this shit about Steele until she found her footing with her medication. He couldn't share with Cam, either. Playing games with mothers—especially murdered ones—was not something Cam would take well.

Who could he tell? Who could help him figure out what do?

He stared at the phone on his desk. With a glance back at Emily, he picked up the receiver and dialed the sheriff's office in Echo Bay. He was surprised when Joe herself answered.

"Hi," he said quietly.

Her voice lifted with surprise. "Well, hello stranger."

"Listen," he said. "I need to see you. Is there any way you can come down for a few days?"

"I thought you were coming up on your first days off?" Joe asked.

"So far, Steele's not offered any days off and it looks like we'll be working straight through until something breaks."

Joe laughed softly. "Welcome back to the real world."

Louis leaned on his desk and closed his eyes. He had told her dozens of times that he loved her. But it was still hard to tell her he needed her, needed her to just listen.

"Louis?"

"I'm here."

"I have two meetings tonight and breakfast tomorrow with the mayor of Traverse City," she said. "Maybe I can get away next week. How's that?"

"Sure," he said.

There was a long silence. "Are you okay?"

"I'm good," he said. "I have to go. Goodbye, Joe."

He hung up and picked up his briefcase. He looked over at Emily. She was bent low over her desk, intent on reading something, but she was twisting a lock of her hair, a gesture he had seen her do often back in Florida when the horrors of the case they had worked together were heavy on her mind. He looked around the room, his eyes settling finally on Junia's empty desk.

He had no idea why she snapped so suddenly and walked away from a job others might kill for. And he would probably never know. But he did know one thing. He was not walking out like Junia had.

Louis looked up at the choir loft.

If this was a test, he would pass it.

And if it was a game, he would win it.

CHAPTER TWENTY-FIVE

Louis had left Bushman's office a message that he would stop by to get the PI surveillance report, and he had expected Bushman would either leave it for him with the security guard or not show at all, intending to hold out for a warrant.

But Bushman was waiting for him in the lobby. He wore a purple John Lennon "Imagine No Religion" T-shirt and had an unlit cigarette stuck over one ear, a neon-green file folder in his hand. Except for a sleepy guard at the reception desk, the lobby was deserted, and it took Louis a moment to remember it was Saturday. Downtown Detroit had a way of emptying fast once the work week was over.

"You're late, detective," Bushman said as Louis approached.

"Five minutes," Louis said. "Is that the file?"

"Yeah," Bushman said. "It's all yours."

Louis held out his hand.

"You could express some appreciation," Bushman said.

"For what?"

"For me not making you guys jump through a shitload full of legal hoops to get this."

Louis wanted to grab the folder and hit the road. All the way down from Lansing, he'd thought about Steele and cracked jugs and the five cold cases on the bulletin board. He didn't need any crap from this blowhard.

"Just give me the file. It's been a long morning."

Bushman thrust the neon-green folder out. Louis snatched it and started to turn away.

"You know," Bushman called after him, "that kind of attitude is exactly why law-abiding folks in this city don't like you guys. You cops are so full of yourselves you taste your own shit when you burp."

Louis stopped and drew a breath before he turned. He stepped back to Bushman. The radio jock's face was florid in the streaky light and his breaths, heavy with cigarette smoke and phlegm, rasped softly in the quiet marble lobby.

"Yeah, okay, thanks," Louis said. "You saved me a lot of time. Good enough?"

Bushman nodded. "I got something else for you."

"What?" Louis asked.

"I got a strange phone call yesterday afternoon to my talk show," Bushman said. "I believe you might be interested in it."

"Why?"

"I think it might have to do with Jonas's murder."

Now Bushman had his attention. "Okay. Talk."

"So, I'm on the air," Bushman said. "It was an open mic show, where people call in and talk about whatever they want. Those shows attract a lot of weirdos. You wouldn't believe the nut jobs I get. People think—"

"Get to the point," Louis said. "Please."

"Okay, okay," Bushman said. "So, my screener takes a call and, like always, he asks her what she wants to talk about. She says she wants to ask me what happens to an atheist's guilt."

"Excuse me?"

"Well, you know how it goes," Bushman said. "Christians commit sin and they ask Jesus for forgiveness and voilà, their conscience is clean. This woman wanted to know how do people who have no savior alleviate *their* guilt? Like, who do non-believers pawn our sins off on?"

"All right, I get you. Go on."

"So, my screener says okay, sounds good, and he puts her on hold while we finish the calls before her," Bushman said. "But when he goes back to her and tells her she's up next, she's suddenly all freaked out, saying she can't talk anymore. When he asks her why, she throws a damn Bible verse at him and hangs up."

"I'm still not seeing the connection," Louis said.

"Then let me finish, will you?" Bushman said. "So later, my screener mentions this to me and I get curious and look up the verse." Bushman reached in his jeans pocket and pulled out a paper. "It was Psalm 146:3. Here, take a look."

Louis took the paper and turned it toward the light so he could read it. Bushman had printed it in bold black letters.

Put not your trust in princes,
nor in the son of man,
in whom there is no help.

"Did you get the phone number of the caller?" Louis asked.

Bushman shook his head. "Only for the ones we put on the air. But my screener always asks people where they are calling from, and this woman said Grand Rapids. Now tell me you don't think that's kind of weird. Thirty-six hours after Jonas buys the farm, some woman from Grand Rapids calls me about princes and gets too freaked out to stay on the line?"

Louis folded the paper. The prince reference was probably just a coincidence. And Bushman's suspicions were colored not just by his animosity toward Anthony Prince, but also by his tin-hat conspiracy tendencies.

"The verse might just mean she thinks there is no salvation out there, in man or God," Louis said.

"Then why not stay on the phone and talk about that?" Bushman asked. "I'm telling you, most of my callers are obsessed with spouting their opinions. They wait an hour or more to get on the air. They do not hang up."

Louis tucked the paper in the neon green folder. "Was there anything specific about her your screener noticed that might help identify her? Anything about her voice that stood out?"

"No. I told you everything he remembered."

"Do you record your calls?" Louis asked.

"Not the pre-screens. Just the ones that get on the air."

Louis nodded. The Beacon Light Cathedral had to have hundreds of female parishioners and employees who might suspect something but were afraid to come forward against such an influential family. Then there was Delia, Jonas's housekeeper.

And there was Violet Prince. But Louis couldn't fully buy into the idea that a wife—especially one of such deep faith and devotion—would betray her husband by calling one of his most ferocious enemies and blurting out a Bible verse. If she had something substantial, why not just call the police?

"Okay," Louis said. "Thanks. This is probably nothing, but if she calls again, can you make sure you take her call?"

"Already planned on that."

"And I would still appreciate it if you didn't share this with anyone. Are we good on that?"

Bushman thought for a moment, then he nodded. "Sure. I can do that."

Louis held out a hand. "Thank you."

Bushman slowly accepted the handshake, seemingly surprised Louis had offered it.

"Just promise me that if Anthony Prince did this, you'll find a way to nail that bastard," Bushman said.

Louis smiled as he turned away. "From your lips to God's ears, Mr. Bushman."

Bushman called after him, his husky voice amplified by the cavernous marble walls. "I think you're on your own with this one, detective."

Louis hurried down the steps and stepped outside, figuring Bushman was right. Homicide investigators were always on their own, even those who believed in the possibility of divine intervention. Because they all knew leads and clues didn't fall from the sky. You had to hunt them down yourself.

He looked down at the thin neon-green file. It looked like something a grade-schooler would carry around, and he was already thinking about what a lousy job that PI had probably done. How much could be learned from one week's surveillance done two months ago that had given Bushman nothing better than gin martinis to fire at Anthony?

Louis's stomach rumbled with hunger and he turned, intending to head over to Layfette Coney Island. But his eye caught something—a glimpse of a giant, green statue across the street in front of a tall municipal building.

For a few seconds, he just stared at it, struck with the feeling that he had seen it before, but he couldn't place the time. It could have been any number of trips downtown as a child, just another Detroit landmark seen from the window of Phillip's car on the way to a ball game. But he didn't think so.

Louis crossed the street and walked toward it. Behind the statue was the City-County Building, a concrete monolith of municipal offices, meeting rooms and courtrooms. He couldn't remember ever being inside for any law enforcement purpose.

But the statue . . .

It was thirty feet high, a massive patina-green bronze that depicted a man in a loincloth who was sitting cross-legged, arms extended. In one hand he held a gold star-burst sun and, in the other, a small gold sculpture of a man, woman, and baby.

Don't climb on the statue, Louis. Get down from there.

The voice was only a whisper, like a soft exhale from the past, but felt so real that Louis turned to see if someone had come behind him. But there was no one.

There was a plaque at the statue's base with the statue's name—The Spirit of Detroit—and words from the sculptor:

The artist expresses the concept that God, through the spirit of man, is manifested in the family, the noblest human relationship.

Louis's eyes swung up to the building. This was the place that housed the Department of Child Services. He had assumed his records were at the old Wayne County Building a few blocks away, but his foster care records had to be here.

191

He looked again at the massive statue with its outstretched arms. Ironic that it celebrated both the family and the sadly-flawed system that too often and too quickly broke it up.

His eyes swung to the dark front doors of the building. None of the offices would be open on a Saturday. No point in trying to get his file today.

Thunder rolled in the distance, somewhere over Canada, and the sky was darkening, fog curling around the spire atop the Guardian Building. He hurried to the parking lot, intent on getting back on the road to Grand Rapids before the rain started. He'd take I-96 straight out of the city. It would be easy driving once he passed . . .

Louis slowed, a map of the city forming in his head—a yellow splotch of color, carved up by that familiar pattern of roads that splayed out from the hub of the city like spokes on a wheel.

He knew suddenly where he needed to go. He wasn't sure of the exact address, but he knew once he got close he could find it.

CHAPTER TWENTY-SIX

G rand River. That was the name of the street he was heading down now, but there was nothing grand about it. Four lanes of asphalt that spurted out from the heart of downtown Detroit like some great life-giving artery. But Grand River was lined with shuttered storefronts, weed-choked lots, drugstores with bars on the windows, and concrete-block taverns with no names above their doors.

Louis had few memories of the time he had spent here as a foster kid. It had been for a few months and he had been just seven. What memories he did have weren't good, and one came back to him now. It started with the smell of smoke, drifting in through an open window. Then he could see images flickering on an old TV set, images of orange flames. He didn't re- ally understand then what was going on just seven miles away, that Detroit was burning and black boys not much older than he was were rioting in the streets. All he knew then was it made him feel very frightened, because as hellish as his existence was inside the house on Strathmoor, at least he knew what to expect. But what was going on outside, the fires and screams and beatings in the streets, that made him feel like there was no place safe anywhere in the world.

He turned left on Lyndon, looking for something familiar, anything to help him get his bearings. He passed an old brick building, Coyle Middle School, slowing when he spotted the athletic field. The baseball diamond was empty but it triggered a memory—a boy's high-pitched voice yelling "Loogy! Loogy!"

Loogy . . . it meant something, he was sure. Maybe a nickname that someone called him? But nothing else was coming.

He drove on and was about to give up when there it was—the street sign for Strathmoor. He hung a right into a neighborhood of small brick homes and old trees that sagged over the cracked asphalt. The odd juxtaposition of the homes was disconcerting—a boarded-up vacant hovel with the message GAS TURNED OFF spray-painted on the plywood, sandwiched between two well-kept houses with neat lawns and Hot Wheels lying in the driveway. He couldn't remember the address, and he was seeing the house now with his kid-brain, as it had looked back then—an ugly red thing with a pitched roof that pierced the sky like a knife, and a strange positioning of a door and two windows that when seen at night had reminded him of a Halloween pumpkin.

He pulled to a stop at the curb, and leaned over to stare out the passenger window.

This was it. Smaller, of course, because all the places you lived in as a kid were bigger in memory than in reality. It was more sad than evil in the gray light. But this was the place where he and Sammy had lived.

There were no boards on the windows, but it didn't look occupied. For one moment, he considered going into the backyard and finding a window to pry open. But sitting here in his state car, feeling the soft weight of his badge wallet in his jeans pocket, he knew he couldn't do it. Things were different now. He was different now.

He was about to pull away when he noticed the FOR SALE sign half-hidden in the high grass of the yard. He grabbed the cellular phone and dialed the realtor's number.

Four rings and the beginning of a message then a woman's voice cut in. "Jane Talley, Coldwell Banker. How can I help you?"

"Ah, yes. I'm sitting outside your house for sale on Strathmoor," Louis said. "I'm very interested in seeing it."

A long pause and the sound of papers shuffling. "Strathmoor . . . yes, I have it right here. Well, it's a three-two with a full basement and—"

"Can I see it today?" he interrupted.

"Now?"

"Yes. I'm only in town for a couple hours."

"Well, I'm at the office now, mister . . ."

"Kincaid. Louis Kincaid."

"Mr. Kincaid. Yes, well, Mr. Kincaid . . ."

She was going to kiss him off. He had to get in the house.

"I'm representing an investment group. Detroit redevelopment." He remembered the sign on Bushman's office building. "Motor City on the Move."

"Oh! Yes, I know about that. Okay, look. I can't get there for a half hour or so." She went silent and he was thinking about just telling her he was a cop when she continued.

"Look, I'm not supposed to do this because I'd be liable for any damage you do, but the place is in rough shape anyway." She paused. "I can give you the code for the lock box."

She rattled off a four-digit code, told him she would try to hurry, and hung up. Louis set the phone back in its cradle and looked back at the house.

Why was he hesitating?

"Screw this," he whispered and pushed open his door.

The lock-box was hanging on the door knob. He punched in the code, released the key inside, and unlocked the door.

He paused in the small foyer to put the key in his pocket as he surveyed the living room. The place was empty and cold, the wood floors scarred, the fireplace dark with soot, and the walls dotted with rectangles on the faded blue wallpaper, imprints from the picture frames that once hung there.

Pictures? Had there been anything remotely ornamental hanging on these walls? He couldn't remember anything like that.

It was quiet, the drizzle a steady *tick-tick-tick* against the windows. From somewhere outside, Louis could hear the *boom-thucka-boom* of a car's speakers blaring music. The sound grew, built to a crescendo, then tapered off. His heart kept time to the dull beat as it died away down the street.

When he looked toward the corner, he could see a TV in his mind, pulsating orange with fire, and Moe slumped in a chair murmuring at the TV. Something about burning it all down . . .

Another memory came to him, what he had thought that first day he had set foot in Moe's house, that he would be okay here because Moe was black like him and he would *know.*

Louis walked slowly through the living room and the dining room with its sconces dangling by wires from the walls. He found his way to the kitchen, dark in the rainy dusk. Curling green linoleum, pale-green countertops, ivy-print wallpaper, yellowed with the years and nicotine.

Another memory. He and Sammy sitting at the table, giggling as they used their spoons to catapult peas at each other.

One moment. One precious good moment.

A noise, somewhere near the front door. A creak of a door. Footsteps on old wood.

"Mr. Kincaid? Yoo-hoo! Anybody here? Mr. Kincaid?"

He went back to the living room. A pudgy woman in a raincoat was standing in the foyer. She spun when she saw him emerge from the shadows, and it was there in her face before she could hide it, that look that told him she was the kind of woman who voted Democrat when the curtain was closed but at night would always cross the street to avoid a black man.

"My goodness, you startled me!" She hesitated, glanced back at the open front door then thrust out her hand. "Jane Talley," she said.

He went to her, shook her hand then took a step back to distance himself from her perfume.

She looked beyond him toward the living room, then pasted a weak smile back on her face when she turned back to him. "So! Have you looked around?"

"Some."

She dug a paper from her tote bag. "Here's the sheet," she said, holding out the paper.

Louis scanned it quickly then folded it in half. Another car was coming down the street, and he could hear its rumbling music, a dirge for an old house in a dying neighborhood.

The real estate woman was babbling, something about no one living in the house for years even though it had been a pretty house in its day before Detroit started going to pot and the mayor who didn't know his butt from a hole in the ground was letting everything go and no matter what anyone said the new casinos down on the river and in Greek Town were *not* going to bring people back downtown but this was 1991 after all and who *didn't* want to live out in suburbs where at least you could walk the streets at night and your kids didn't have to go through metal detectors at school . . .

Louis's head started to pound, something that felt like the beginnings of a headache but not quite. He shut his eyes.

"Mr. Kincaid?"

He opened his eyes. The real estate woman had backed up, standing closer to the open front door. He considered that she probably hadn't connected him to the bubble-light state cruiser sitting out at the curb, and he thought about flashing his badge. But why did he owe this woman the reassurance that he wasn't a thug or rapist? The pounding in his head was growing worse.

He rubbed his temple as he looked at the woman, and suddenly he wasn't seeing her as a white woman scared of being alone with a black man. He was seeing her as a real estate agent who had probably been advised to never be alone with any man of any color in an empty old house.

"I'd like to look around some more," he said. "If you need to leave, I can put the key back when I am done."

She looked relieved. "I'd appreciate that. I am actually late for another showing." She nodded to the paper in his hand. "That's my card stapled to the top. Call me and we'll talk. The owner is very motivated."

She hurried out into the drizzle, and Louis watched her until she was in her car then closed the front door. He tried a light switch but nothing came on.

His eyes went to the staircase, and he peered into the darkness above. That was where he had to go, he knew.

The stairs groaned under his weight and when he got to the second floor, he had to stop and orient himself, trying to remember where the bedroom was that he had shared with Sammy. He peered into the nearest room, but it triggered nothing in his memory, so he continued down the hallway. He passed a grimy bathroom with a pedestal sink dripping water into a rusty basin. At a closed door, he paused before jerking it open. But it was just a closet. The pounding in his head got worse for a second, but then subsided.

This isn't it. This isn't the place.

Another bedroom and another blank. Then he was at the end of the hallway, facing a final door. He opened it.

The room was small, painted a bright orange with sixties-style flower decals on the walls. But he could still see the room as it once was—pale-blue walls marred with small handprints and crayon scribbles, the small wood dresser with the broken bottom drawer and, over by the window, the bunk beds where he and Sammy had slept.

Louis went to the middle of the room. The pounding in his head was stronger now, as if he had finally found the gravitational center to some faraway and long-forgotten universe.

Images drifted in and out of his thoughts, glimpsed but then gone, like those weird, floating string-things he got in his vision when he was tired.

He closed his eyes, trying to bring something, anything, into focus. He could smell something, the faint tang of urine from the other nameless boys who had slept here and wet the bed. He could hear voices, a hard loud one yelling at them to be quiet, and a soft one whispering in the dark from the bunk above.

Louis? Louis? You asleep, Louis?

No.

I'm scared.

Be quiet, Sammy.

I'm scared. Louis, can I come down there with you? Louis?

No, stay up there. Be quiet. You gotta be quiet or he'll come in here again.

But Sammy wasn't quiet. He was crying. Louis could hear him clearly now, hear Sammy's sniffles in the dark above him.

Louis opened his eyes. The only sound in the empty room was the rain on the window and the awful rushing in his head. He turned slowly in a tight circle.

There it was, there in the corner. The closet.

And there it was in his head, a memory so sharp and clear that he felt it like a slap in the face.

Run. Run! Faster. Faster!

Come on! Come on!

He was running up the stairs and Sammy was behind him. There were footsteps behind them on the stairs—heavy, unsteady footsteps.

Get in the closet! Quick!

That is where they hid when things got really bad, when Moe came after them stinking of sweat and whiskey.

Louis went to the closet. He hesitated, hand on the knob, but then opened it. It was small and narrow, lined with scarred cedar. Louis touched the glass door knob inside, remembering how he had looped a piece of rope around it so he could hold it closed from inside. He stared into the small space, his gut twisting into a hard knot. Something bad had happened here. Why couldn't he remember? Seven . . . he had been only seven years old then, but if this was the center of his nightmares, surely the memory had to be somewhere inside him still. Why couldn't he remember what had happened?

He needed to remember. He *had* to know.

Weems . . .

The worker in Grand Rapids. Louis was thinking about how Cam had coaxed out his memories of what he had seen outside Jonas Prince's house.

Louis stared into the closet. He knew what he had to do. He stepped into the closet and crouched down. Then he slowly pulled the door shut.

Darkness.

No, not all darkness. There was a slit of gray light at the bottom of the door. Just like there had been that cold November night twenty-three years ago. Louis stared hard at the sliver of light, but even as it began to blur, his memory began to sharpen. Stabs of sensation at first—the rough feel of the rope in his fingers. The swirl of cold air—Sammy's breath warm against his cheek. The whisper of Sammy's voice as he prayed.

And the memory of what he had thought in that moment, that no one was going to hear it, not man or God.

It was cold in the closet, just like it had been that day, but Louis was sweating. He shut his eyes, still gripping the glass door knob, wanting to get out but knowing he had to stay right where he was. Because . . .

The creak of the floorboards outside the closet.

Then the burn of the rope on his palms as Moe ripped the door open and Sammy's screams as he was pulled out of the closet.

Louis's eyes shot open and he focused on the slit of light under the door. What had happened next? It was like he was looking at a mirror. No, not a mirror, just broken pieces of one lying on a floor.

Mirror . . .

Louis let go of the glass knob. The door swung open a few inches and now, for the first time, Louis saw the full-length mirror on the inside of the closet door.

And suddenly he saw it. He saw everything in the mirror, just as he had that night. He had crouched in this closet and watched what happened outside in the reflection of this mirror because he was too afraid to watch it for real, and too afraid to leave the closet. He watched in the mirror as Moe tossed Sammy against the bunk beds like he was rag doll. Watched Moe kick him and beat him. Watched Sammy curl into a ball as the blood pooled on the floor. Watched as Sammy went limp and silent. Watched as Sammy . . .

Louis flung the door open and fell out of the closet, gasping for air. He stumbled to his feet and bolted out of the room. He half-fell down the stairs, yanked open the front door and stumbled out onto the porch. He braced himself against the railing, feeling sick.

With a trembling hand, he got the key from his pocket and put it back in the lock box. He went down the steps and paused on the sidewalk.

It was raining, and he raised his face to let it wash over him. He pulled a deep breath of cold air into his lungs, then another. Finally, when he felt steadier, he straightened and looked back at the house.

The sting of tears came to his eyes, and he wiped a shaking hand over his face.

Other memories were there now. He could remember how big the men in blue looked, how they filled up the living room. He could remember the warmth of the blanket someone put over his shoulders.

More fragments. The tuna fish smell of the white woman in the plaid coat who took his hand and led him outside to a car. The blue and red lights washing over the faces of the neighbors who had come outside to stare. And one more thing so awful and clear that he couldn't believe now he had ever forgotten it.

Moe . . . sitting in the backseat of the police car. Moe turning to look back at him one last time through the back window.

Louis was staring down the street now, still seeing that face. But there was another face he wasn't seeing in all this.

Sammy.

Sammy wasn't there.

The rain was turning icy cold. Louis went to his cruiser and got in. The sleet had caused the windshield to freeze over, giving the black bare trees a wavy, surreal look. Louis sat perfectly still, hands gripping the wheel, his breath pluming in the cold womb of the car.

There were still gaps in his memory, but at least now he understood the truth.

He had stayed in that closet and hadn't done anything to help Sammy. Sammy had died, but he had lived.

Louis laid his head against the steering wheel and closed his eyes.

Over the years he had managed to bury much of his childhood, stuffing it so deep inside him that it had shriveled and calcified, becoming little more than a rock-hard tumor he had been unable to cut out, so he had simply learned to live with it.

But this . . .

What did he do with a truth like this?

He started the engine and turned on the wipers. For a few seconds, he kept his foot on the brake, as if there was something else keeping him here, something more for him to do. Then he hit the accelerator, spitting up ice behind the tires as he pulled away.

CHAPTER TWENTY-SEVEN

St. Michael's was empty, filled with a slow-moving light show of grays and silvers that slipped across the walls and desktops like a restless spirit looking for a place to settle.

Louis closed his eyes.

It was just past seven in the evening, and he had only been back in the church for a half-hour. During the drive back from Detroit, he had tried to blot out the thoughts left over from the house on Strathmoor by turning the car radio up loud, but all he caught was talk radio and old rock and roll from the seventies. So finally, he settled on silence. And the company of a ghost named Sammy.

A soft tapping started up in the loft. Louis figured it had to be Steele. It wasn't rare for him to be here long after everyone else had left for the day. Louis rubbed his eyes and picked up the top folder from the stack on his desk. It was Tooki's updated financial records on the Prince family. Louis opened it, but it was just a blur. He was too tired to think. He'd take it and Bushman's PI report home to read.

He rose, stuffed the files in his briefcase and put on his windbreaker. As he passed the main computer in the middle of the nave, he paused. Someone had left it on, and it was open to the state criminal database.

Louis looked up at the loft. He set his briefcase down, sat down at the computer, and tabbed the curser over to the open field for subject's name. He couldn't remember Moe's last name. Hell, he wasn't sure Moe was his real first name or if it wasn't short for Morrie or Murray. But he typed it in anyway, along with the Strathmoor address, and the year he was removed from the house. He hit search for records.

A message flashed: No Results.

It should have been here, if Moe had been arrested. But Tooki had said not all the records were in the system yet. And the child services offices wouldn't open until Monday morning. Louis glanced at the phone, thinking about calling Phillip. His foster father might know Moe's last name, or have it in some old paperwork, but Louis didn't want Phillip to know he was digging into what happened on Strathmoor, even though they had talked of it once, briefly, a few years ago.

The episode still hung heavy in Louis's memory. Louis had provoked his foster father with some stupid remark about Phillip ignoring Louis's blackness. The moment had culminated in Phillip tossing a couple of old photos of Louis's scarred back on the kitchen table and telling Louis he had never cared what color he was. To Phillip, Louis was a just a child in need.

"What are you looking for?"

Louis spun around in the chair. Steele was standing at the bottom of the spiral staircase, his tie loose, a raincoat draped over his arm.

Louis closed the database and the screen went black.

"Nothing."

Steele came closer, stopping close enough to take a long look at the blank computer screen.

"Did you get that PI report from Bushman?" Steele asked.

"Yes."

"You had a chance to go over it yet?"

That slow simmer of anger he sometimes felt for this man started up the back of Louis's neck and he knew where it was coming from—those five cases tacked to the back of the bulletin board, that walk through the Strathmoor house, and the idea that, for some reason, this asshole had set him up to relive all of it.

Louis drew a slow breath. "Not yet. I plan to go over it tonight."

Steele shifted his coat to the other arm. "You might get a better grip on it if you go to Grand Rapids tomorrow and physically walk through it, paragraph by paragraph." Steele paused a beat. "Put yourself in the shoes of the private investigator, so to speak."

Was that condescension in Steele's voice? A subtle reminder of the exile Steele had rescued him from?

Steele was heading toward the door, pulling on his raincoat.

Don't say it. Don't say a word.

But he did. And he said it loud enough to make sure Steele heard him across the echoing nave.

"That should be pretty easy for me, right?"

Steele stopped and turned to face Louis. "With all due respect, Louis, yes. It *should* be easy for you. You were a PI for five years."

Louis wasn't sure how to respond, not sure he even wanted to have this conversation at this moment. What did it matter now?

Steele seemed to want to say something else, but he just turned and pulled the front door open. A wash of cold air swept into the church.

Louis stood up. "Six years," he said, loudly.

Steele stopped again and turned back to Louis. "Pardon me?"

"Six years," Louis said. "Six years and three months."

Steele stared at him, no emotion on his face.

"You stole those years from me," Louis said. "You stole my *career* from me. And you didn't even do it because you thought I was a dirty cop or had screwed up so bad I wasn't redeemable."

Louis drew a hard breath. "You did it because you lost control of a case and cops got killed and you needed someone to blame."

Steele was silent for a moment, then said, "If that's how you feel, why did you agree to work on my team?"

Louis reached into his pocket, pulled out his badge and held it up. "Because *this* is more important to me than you are."

Silence. Louis waited, his heart and head pounding.

Steele gave him a tight nod. "Good," he said. "Make sure you keep it that way. Goodnight, Louis."

PARRISH

It wasn't much of a dinner. Fried pickles and a cheeseburger at Dagwood's. And two shots of brandy to wash it down. Louis had switched to beer finally, sitting at the far end of the bar. Cops did that, sat in the rear, their backs to the wall so they could see trouble coming. But he didn't see much trouble here.

There was a pudgy man sitting four stools away, probably an auto mechanic, given the man's nicked-up, oil-stained hands. He was nursing his beer and kept looking at his watch, like he had to be somewhere. Or not be somewhere. A beefy guy was chalking his pool cue, hustling a drunk in an off-the-rack suit but expensive wing-tips. A dime-store lawyer, maybe, looking for a win, any kind of win.

Louis closed his eyes.

Who does this kind of shit? Who profiles strangers in a bar? You got nothing better to waste your brain cells on, Kincaid?

"You okay, sweetie?"

Louis looked up. The bartender stood in front of him. Big hair, big curves, and big eyes the color of good brandy.

"Have a bad day?" she asked.

"Who in here didn't?" he asked.

He reached into his pocket for his money but got his badge wallet instead. He fumbled it and it fell to the floor. When he moved off the barstool to get it, he stumbled.

"You all right?" the bartender asked.

Louis stuck the badge in his jacket pocket and steadied himself on the bar. "Yeah. I'm calling it a night."

"You want a cab?"

"I'm walking, thanks. Goodnight."

The night was cold, the wind-rustled trees still shaking off water from the day-long rain. He dug his hands into his pockets and walked as fast as he dared given his state. His head was pounding, and he was angry at himself for drinking too much. Worse, he was embarrassed, an emotion he didn't feel very often. He had dropped his badge in a bar and he dropped it because he was drunk. The bartender didn't see what it was, but it didn't matter. It was sloppy. And he couldn't help think that there was something more sinister behind the drop, like it was a Freudian slip of some kind.

By the time he reached his house, he was shivering. He quietly let himself in and took a look into the parlor, where Nina was usually splayed out watching MTV. There she was, asleep on the sofa, with Issy curled on her stomach.

He started toward the cat, intending to take her upstairs, but then Issy looked up, her gold eyes scornful.

Well, what did he expect? Even cats found someone else to sleep with when they were ignored.

He made his way up the stairs, unlocked his door and went in. The apartment was dark except for one light on in the bedroom, and he trudged toward it, shucking off his wet windbreaker to the floor.

At the door, he stopped cold. For one beer-fueled moment, he couldn't fathom what he was seeing—a sheet-wrapped body on his bed. His hand went automatically to the holster at his belt.

But then the body moved and one arm fell free from the sheet. Louis let out a long breath and walked slowly toward his bed. For a second, all he could do was stand and stare because there, asleep on his bed, was the most beautiful thing he had ever seen.

Joe was wearing one of his white T-shirts, and her face was partially covered by her light brown hair. He sat down on the edge of the bed, knowing it wouldn't wake her because nothing ever did. In all the nights they had slept together, he had learned that—while he would jump awake at the scrap of a branch on the window—she would sleep through the howl of the worst winter wind.

He sat still, just staring down at her.

Her eyes fluttered open. "Well, it's about time," she whispered. "I've been waiting here for hours."

"And now you'll have to leave," he said.

"Oh? And why is that?"

"I'm not allowed to have girls in the room after eleven."

Joe drew to a sitting position, raking back her hair with long fingers. "I'm not a girl. I'm a woman."

His eyes dipped to her breasts. "Yes, you are," he said. He pulled her close, crushing her against him, so close her could feel every rib in her body. It was a long time before she finally pushed gently away.

"What are you doing here?" he asked.

"You sounded like you needed me. I have two days."

"I'm so glad you came," he whispered.

She kissed his cheek, then his lips, and finally drew back so she could see his face.

"How'd you get past Nina?" he asked.

She frowned then smiled. "Ah, your gatekeeper. I told her we're working together. She didn't believe me. I had to show her my badge."

He cupped her face and kissed her again, a deep kiss that he hoped didn't feel desperate. When he felt her melt into him, he slipped his hands under the T-shirt, hoping his hands weren't too cold against her skin, hoping he hadn't had too much to drink.

It didn't matter. Joe took charge, and he let her. She unhooked his holster and set the Glock on the dresser next to his badge wallet. She slowly undressed him, and then led him down into the bed. The sheets were cold. Her mouth was so very warm. After they made love, he lay there, watching the shadows move across the ceiling, listening to Joe's even breathing. He was exhausted and emptied of every bad thought, image and memory. The mirrored closet was gone. Sammy was gone. For the moment, at least, for the moment

CHAPTER TWENTY-EIGHT

A bell was tolling somewhere, but Louis couldn't see a church anywhere nearby—though he knew Grand Rapids had more than its share of them. He counted nine chimes and, on the tenth, he saw Joe emerge from the Biggby coffee shop carrying two take-out cups.

"Sugar?" he asked, taking one cup.

"Four, already stirred in."

He smiled as he popped off the lid. Partly, it came from the lingering memory of making love last night. But mostly, it was because she remembered how he liked his coffee. As he sipped it, he stole a glance at her, specifically at her hair, pulled back in a ponytail, still damp from her morning shower.

It amazed him how quickly she could get dressed. When he told her this morning that he needed to go to Grand Rapids and retrace the steps of the PI Buchman had hired to dog Anthony, she had jumped out of bed. Fifteen minutes later, she was showered, dressed, and ready to go.

It was sunny but no more than forty degrees. Joe was wearing black jeans and her old, black leather jacket, open to a man's tuxedo shirt. She took a drink of her coffee then slipped on sunglasses. "So, what's the plan?"

"I want to retrace the PI's steps." Louis opened the thin neon-green file Bushman had given him.

"Is that all there is?" Joe asked.

Louis nodded. "Check out how he signs off his daily reports every night."

Joe glanced down and then looked back at Louis. "'End of report. Yours Truly, Johnny Dollar?'"

"Johnny Dollar was a PI from the old radio days," Louis said. "That's how he signed off every program. He was famous for cheating his clients on the expense accounts."

"I doubt Bushman got the joke," Joe said.

"Yeah, but his PI actually did a pretty good job. His time logs are to the minute, he notes exact locations, and even describes the weather. But his surveillance only lasted for one week, from six a.m. Thursday, February 7 through midnight, Wednesday February 13."

"That was two months ago," Joe said. "What good is this to you now?

"Maybe nothing, but I have a hunch about something. According to the PI's report, Anthony left his house every morning at eight forty-five to go the cathedral, the time never varying by more than a minute. Every day at noon, his lunch was delivered from Luigi's, and his black Lincoln Town Car never left the church parking lot all day. Until he left to go home, always at six-thirty on the dot. And every night, for six nights, the PI recorded: 'Second story lights out at the Prince residence at eleven thirty. Yours Truly, Johnny Dollar.'"

"Okay, you have a tight pattern," Joe said.

"He's obsessive compulsive."

"What was his timeline on the night his father was murdered?"

"Anthony said he left the church at seven thirty after the evening service to go to dinner." Louis pointed across the street to the Chop House. "I talked to the owner, who told me he comes in *every* Wednesday night, orders the same dinner and gin martinis and leaves at the same time. The owner verified his arrival and I saw the time stamp when he paid his bill. He left here at ten fifteen p.m. and says he went home."

"Can anyone verify he went home?"

"His wife. But wives can lie. Plus, she takes a medication that knocks her out."

"So what are you thinking here?"

"I think he killed his father right after the service and locked up that room, came here for dinner then went home. I think, he was consumed with guilt and, with his wife out on sleeping pills, he left the house in the middle of the night to go back and reposition the body in a gesture of respect or something."

Joe took a drink of coffee as she considered this. "Okay, I think I get it now why we're here. Because Anthony is such a creature of habit, you're looking for some deviation in the PI report for that Wednesday two months from what Anthony did last week. If he did something different two months ago, maybe he did something different the night his father was killed. And if you can find it, you can break his alibi."

"Long shot, but yeah, that's what I'm hoping."

Joe nodded to the green file. "Can I take a look?"

While Joe read the PI's file, Louis sipped his coffee, watching her. It hit him in that moment that she had jumped out of bed so fast this morning because the cop in her, the cop who had worked her way up in the Miami PD homicide squad, was hungry for meat. She had a sheriff's badge, and she talked about how she loved her life, her dog, her cabin up in the woods. But she was here, and a part of him wondered if it wasn't because of more than just him. She missed the rush of a homicide investigation.

"Louis, look at this," she said, holding out the file. "The PI says that on Wednesday night two months, Anthony left the restaurant at 10:02 but he didn't get home until midnight."

"Yeah, I know. That's what got me thinking about this whole variation in the routine thing. Two months ago, he varied from his routine on one night. What did he do for those two hours?"

She looked up at the street. "According to this report, he went for a walk."

Louis remembered what the Chop House waiter had told him, that on the night Anthony left, he had stood outside in the cold rain for a while. The waiter had assumed Anthony had then gone to his car. What if he had walked somewhere, just as he had on that Wednesday night two months ago?

Louis looked up and down Monroe Avenue, then tossed his coffee cup in the trash. "Let's see what's around some of these corners."

Joe read from the report as they walked. The PI had recorded every move Anthony made, following him from the church at seven thirty until he pulled into the parking lot of the Chop House at 7:42. He exited the restaurant from the front door at 10:02, but did not return to his car. Instead, he walked north on Monroe Street, then turned west onto Lyon Street.

Lyon was a long block of plain gray structures. On their left was a granite building with a blue-awning entrance. On the right was a squat building with CIVIC AUDITORIUM carved into the façade and a four-story parking garage.

Joe stopped suddenly. She looked up, pushing her sunglasses up on her head.

"What's wrong?" Louis asked.

"This is where Anthony disappeared," Joe said.

"What do you mean?"

"The PI says he lost sight of Anthony here on this corner, Louis," she said. "All he records is 'Subject gone. Temperature now thirty-one, weather deteriorating. No vehicular traffic. Observed party of ten departing from Amway'."

"Amway? The cleaning stuff people?"

Joe didn't answer, walking back toward the blue awning. She pointed to a brass plaque near a double door. "They also own hotels," she said. "This is the back entrance of the Amway Grand Plaza."

Louis looked down the block. It dead-ended into a concrete plaza with five flagpoles. Beyond that, the Grand River glimmered, gray-green, in the sun.

"Anthony had to have gone into the hotel," he said.

"Gee, what would a man do in a hotel for two hours before he went home to the wife who's zonked out on pills?" Joe said with a smile.

"*Cherchez la femme*," Louis said.

They went in, finding their way to the lobby. It was a marble and mahogany-paneled two-story palace with a soaring ceiling and a Versailles-worthy chandelier. The lobby was quiet on this Sunday morning—an old lady in a wing chair near the fountain reading *The New Yorker* and a young couple in parkas, just coming through the front doors, dragging their wheeled suitcases.

Louis beat the couple to the front desk. The young clerk's smiled faded when Louis showed his badge and explained why he was there.

"I don't think I'm allowed to divulge our guests' names," the clerk said.

"Actually, it's up to your discretion. But you'd be doing us a big favor," Louis said. "Why don't you call your boss?"

The clerk called a manager who ushered the young man aside and gave Louis a tight smile. "Who is it you're asking about, detective?" he asked.

"Anthony Prince."

The manager's fingers froze over his computer keyboard. "Oh, I can assure you he's never been a guest here."

"Can you check anyway?" Louis asked.

The manager pecked at the keyboard, then smiled with satisfaction. "Anthony Prince was not a guest at our hotel on that night two months ago or on any other night."

Damn. But that didn't mean Anthony didn't meet a woman who was already registered here.

"I'd like to talk to your night desk employees," Louis said. "Can you give me some names?"

The manager looked like he had bad gas pains. "This is about the elder Reverend Prince, isn't it? I saw it on the news."

Louis couldn't answer the man's question but he could ask one. "Did you know Jonas Prince?"

"Not personally, but I know of him and his son," the manager said. "If either of them was ever a guest of this hotel, I would know it. Why, we were just talking about the crime yesterday in the lunch room and no one said a word about ever meeting either of them."

Louis handed the manager his card. "I'd like you to talk to your night shift anyway. Discreetly. Let me know if you learn anything different."

"I will, officer."

Louis walked to back to Joe. She was sitting in a wing chair and had the neon-green file open on her lap, flipping through the photographs the PI had taken.

"He said Anthony was never registered here," Louis said.

"You believe him?" Joe asked.

"Yeah. But Anthony could have met someone here."

Joe held out a photo. "Take a close look at this photo the PI took," Joe said.

Louis took the picture. It was fuzzy, taken about a half-block away with a night-vision camera, but clear enough to show the back entrance of the hotel. It showed a crowd of people in formal wear, clustered under the blue awning waiting to get into taxis and limos in line at the curb.

"That has to be the party the PI mentioned leaving the hotel," Joe said. "The PI lost Anthony at the back entrance, in that crowd. I think he got into one of those cabs."

"Let's get back to the car," Louis said.

They hurried back to the Explorer. Joe went to get more coffee while Louis called Camille. It wasn't possible to make out the names on the taxis in the PI's photos, so he gave Camille the time and date stamped on the PI's photo and asked her to check out any cab that picked up a single male fare at the back entrance of the Amway Grand Plaza.

By the time Joe returned to the Explorer with two more coffees, Camille had reported back.

"Great Lakes Taxi picked up one man at ten sixteen p.m. at the back hotel entrance."

"Where did he drop him off?" Joe asked.

"The corner of Wealthy Street and College Avenue."

Wealthy Street . . . it was the same road that wound through the neighborhood around Jonas Prince's lakefront cottage. But as they drove to the corner of Wealthy and College Avenue, Louis could see that the western end of Wealthy was very modest in contrast. It was a neighborhood of old rental apartments and small wood-frame bungalows.

He pulled to a stop at the corner where the taxi driver had said he left Anthony. Nothing remarkable. Just three corner-lot homes and an old, two-story red brick apartment building.

"I still think he was seeing a mistress," Louis said. "But without an address we'll have to canvass the whole neighborhood."

During the drive over, Joe had been silent, turning her attention to the Prince case file. She looked up and pointed to the red brick building. "He went in there, apartment 2-B."

"How do you know?"

She held up a set of stapled papers and he recognized the updated Prince financial report that Tooki had left for him yesterday. Louis hadn't had time yet to review it.

"It's one of two dozen addresses listed under the heading of something called the Fresh Start Program," Joe asked.

That name had been written on a manila folder in Anthony Prince's office and on a letter in Anthony's office back at the church. Violet had mentioned it, too.

"It's some sort of charity," Louis said. "Does that say who lives up there?"

"No," Joe said. "It's all leased by the church. No tenant names."

"Okay, then," Louis said, pushing out of the Explorer. "Let's go knock on the door."

Inside the foyer, they found metal mailboxes, but the label for 2B had no name. When they got to the top of the stairs, they froze.

There was a green sticker slapped across the edge of the door frame on apartment 2B. Louis moved close to read it.

These premises have been sealed by the Grand Rapids PD pursuant to section 456 administrative code. All persons are forbidden to enter unless authorized by the police department or public administrator.

"It's a crime scene," Joe said.

The seal was intact, which meant the apartment had not yet been released back to the tenant or the landlord. They couldn't set foot in this place, even if was unlocked.

"We need to find out what happened here," Louis said. "Let's get back to the car and call Grand Rapids PD."

Louis started to the stairs but stopped when he saw a man coming up, carrying cardboard boxes. When the man reached the landing, he paused. He was north of sixty, with a halo of white hair and blue marble eyes.

"Can I help you folks?"

"Detective Kincaid," Louis said, showing his badge. "State police. And you are?"

"Rudy Piccoli." He dropped the boxes and kicked them toward the door of 2B.

"Why are you here, Mr. Piccoli?"

The man's face wrinkled. "I'm the owner, here to clean out the apartment. I got permission this morning from Lieutenant Maxwell to unseal it. Man, don't you guys talk to each other?"

Louis didn't want the man asking any questions about why two more cops were here, especially two not connected to Grand Rapids. Piccoli might call this Lieutenant Maxwell and the Grand Rapids PD would show up to stake out their territory. Which meant he and Joe would be shut out. As long as the place was still sealed, Louis had no choice but to go through Grand Rapid PD. But if Rudy Piccoli was going to let them in . . .

Louis gestured to the door. "You're free to go in, sir."

The man used a key to rip the seal and unlocked the door. He went in, leaving the door open. Louis and Joe stopped at the threshold.

"An open door implies permission to enter," Joe said quietly.

"Yeah, but I'm not going to chance it working for Steele," Louis said. "Mr. Piccoli, can we come in, sir?"

"What? Now you need an invitation?"

"Yes, we do."

"Come on in then. Maybe you can help me clean up the mess you guys made."

The small living room was washed in pink sunlight from the drawn red curtains. Cheap furnishings—a worn white futon draped with a fringed, red-patterned throw, a plastic end table holding a brass lamp, its shade covered with a pink, silky scarf, a small rattan chest that served as a coffee table and held a vase of white plastic flowers and a chipped, ceramic incense burner in the shape of a Buddha. No television, stereo or radio that Louis could see. The walls were painted the dirty white of all rental units, and there was nothing to relieve their plainness except for two garish prints of peacocks, the kind of stuff you could find crammed onto the clearance shelves of Pier 1. Smudges of black fingerprint dust were everywhere.

"Plain sight, Louis," Joe whispered.

He glanced at her, mildly piqued she would feel the need to remind him that he didn't have a warrant to look beyond what was considered "left in plain sight." The fact that the place had been searched by the Grand Rapids cops meant nothing to the state. If they wanted to search drawers and closets, they needed their own warrant. Or permission from the owner.

Louis looked back to Rudy Piccoli, who was in the kitchen, standing at the open refrigerator.

"Mr. Piccoli?"

He came back to the living holding a white container of take-out food. "Yeah?"

"I need to be up front with you," Louis said. "We have nothing to do with the Grand Rapids PD. My partner and I were chasing a lead on another case and we tracked our suspect here."

Rudy Piccoli's eyes narrowed, like he felt he'd been conned.

"Can you tell me what happened here?" Louis asked. "Why the apartment was sealed?"

Piccoli's eyes ricocheted between Louis and Joe. "If I do, are you guys going to lock it up again for another week?"

"I can't promise we won't," Louis said. "But I really need to know what happened here."

Piccoli tossed the takeout container to the trash. "Jesus H. Christ," he muttered. "Try to do a good thing for the church and this is what I get. Lost rent and a mess to clean up."

"Mr. Piccoli, please," Louis said.

He came into the living room. "All I know is the cops came here last Friday morning with a warrant and told me to let them in. They said the woman who lived here got killed."

Louis heard the crinkle of Joe's leather jacket as she moved closer in behind him, and he knew she was thinking the same thing he was. If Anthony had come here two months ago, there was a good chance he might have returned the night of his father's murder, the same night someone else was killed here.

Piccoli was still talking. "So I called the lady at the church that I deal with for the rentals and told her that was it, I was ending their lease."

"Did the police say how the tenant was killed?" Louis asked.

Piccoli shook his head. "They didn't tell me nothing. But I overhead one of the cops say something about her getting murdered. Then I was told to leave."

"What was her name?" Louis asked.

Piccoli had gone to the door to pick up one of the cardboard boxes and didn't look back at Louis. "I don't usually pay much attention to tenant names because the church signs all the leases and sends rent checks. But I think the secretary lady called her Sue . . . or maybe Lynn or Sue Lynn or Linda Sue."

"Did you ever meet this woman?" Louis asked.

"Nope. She was only here six or seven months. The family before her was real nice. I met them and would've liked to have them stay longer but the church lady told me they went home to China. Didn't like it here in America, I guess."

"China?" Louis asked.

"China, Japan?" He waved his hands in the air. "I don't know. I just know they were refugees."

Louis looked around, his gaze moving over the room. It struck him that a single woman, a refugee, might want to surround herself with familiar symbols of her home culture. But with its cheap red drapes and sad attempts to disguise its shabbiness, the apartment seemed more like some young woman's notion of a place of seduction.

Louis couldn't see Anthony here, a man who needed to fold his hand towels and line up his pens. But then again, some guys got off on a whiff of seediness.

"Mr. Piccoli," Louis said. "You said you terminated the church's lease?"

"Yeah."

With no renter and no lease, Piccoli could give them permission to look anywhere they wanted.

"Can we do a full search, Mr. Piccoli?" Louis asked.

"Yeah, I guess," he called out.

"And could you wait a few minutes before packing stuff up?"

Piccoli's head appeared from the kitchen opening. "Good grief," he said. "I'm going down for a cig. Call me when you're done."

After he was gone, Joe looked to Louis. "I'll take the bedroom."

Joe wandered off and Louis did a quick search of the living room. The Grand Rapids police had been looking for evidence that this apartment was a murder scene, but he was looking for any evidence that Anthony Prince had been here.

But even if he found anything, this was still going to be Grand Rapids PD's case. And if Anthony Prince was tied to this, there was no way GRPD would relinquish control of a career-building case, not even to Steele's team. Louis had to know what he dealing with here before let anyone else in.

He moved to the kitchen and looked in the fridge. Juice, milk, yogurts, and more take-out containers from a place called Pho Anh Trang's. He opened the cupboards and saw a lot of canned chow mien, soy sauce, lime juice, sesame seed oil, and a bottle of Vang Đàlat wine. Nothing else.

He sighed. A bottle of Hendrick's gin would have been nice.

"Louis," Joe called. "Come here."

PJ   PARRISH

Joe had opened the drapes and the tiny bedroom was flush with sunshine. It was a drab canvas of beiges and browns, with a small bed and a boxy dresser with tarnished knobs.

Joe gestured to the bed, where she had laid out two pairs of faded jeans and a couple of wrinkled men's cotton shirts. "I think a guy was living here, too," she said.

Louis picked up the jeans and checked the size. They were definitely men's jeans, but small—size fourteen slim. It was how boy's jeans were sized, not the standard men's waist sizing.

"Maybe she wore them," he said.

Joe moved to the dresser and opened a drawer. "Think she wore these, too?"

She held up a pair of white briefs, small, with a wide elastic band and a fly. Men's underwear.

Louis tossed the jeans on the bed, disappointment swelling inside him. It was still possible this woman was Anthony Prince's mistress and that he had killed her. But the fact that she had a boyfriend, or that any male lived here, complicated the investigation. It gave the police a second viable suspect.

Joe started to the door. "I'm going to check out the bathroom," she said.

He turned to the dresser and started opening drawers. He found women's blue bikini panties, a couple pairs of plain white socks, some filmy pastel nightgowns, and in the bottom drawer, a soft tangle of women's scarves in bright colors and gaudy patterns. He was about to close the drawer when one piece of fabric caught his eye.

He pulled it out. It was a long and narrow like a scarf but was made of rough cotton in a black and white checkered pattern. It looked like kitchen dish towel. He peered at the small white tag on one end. It had some odd symbols on it, but it was the line at the bottom that he focused on—*Fabriqué en Vietnam.*

Linda Sue . . . Sue Lynn.

Su-Lin . . .

220

For a second, he didn't move because his mind was suddenly some-where else—in an autopsy room in Ionia. He looked around for Joe but she was nowhere to be seen, so he headed back to the living room. Piccoli was just coming in the open door, trailing a stink of cigarettes.

"Mr. Piccoli, the woman who lived here," Louis said. "You called her Sue Lynn. Could her name have been Tuyen Lang?"

"Huh?"

"Too-yin," Louis said, pronouncing the name as close as he could to the way Cam had said it. "Too-yin, not Sue Lynn."

"Sue? Too? Shit, I don't know," Piccoli said with a shrug. "I told you, I didn't pay much attention to their names because they all sound alike, you know?"

"Did anyone from the church ever say she was from Vietnam?"

Piccoli frowned. "Yeah, maybe. It's all Oriental to me."

Joe came up next to him. "What's wrong?"

"Her name was Tuyen Lang," he said.

"How do you know?"

Louis was remembering his first thought when he saw the body lying on the table, that he was looking at a boy not a girl.

"There was no male living here," Louis said softly to Joe. "Those men's clothes in the bedroom? They belonged to her."

Louis took Joe's arm and walked her toward the bedroom, out of earshot of Piccoli.

"I think that Anthony Prince likes boys, Joe," he said. "But he couldn't cross that line to children because that would be too big a sin for a man in his position. So he found a woman who looked like a boy." He remembered how Tuyen's hair had been chopped short. "Maybe he even had her dress up like a boy."

"How do you know this?"

"Because I saw her," Louis said. "In a morgue in Ionia."

Tuyen's face was there in his head now—her hair that looked like someone had chopped it off with an axe and her skin, mottled with old bruises. Two months ago, Anthony had evaded the PI and probably had come

221

here, to his boy-woman mistress. Had he also come here last Wednesday after murdering his father, and driven by rage or guilt or something else, killed this woman?

He realized he was still holding the black and white scarf, and he ran it through his hands now, testing its rough texture, thinking how it might match the ligature marks on Tuyen Lang's neck.

"Louis," Joe said. "Her murder is not your case."

"It is if I can pin it on Anthony," Louis said. He turned to Piccoli who had picked up a box and was starting back toward the kitchen.

"I'm sorry, Mr. Piccoli," he said. "We're going to be locking this place up again."

"Lord deliver me from cops and holy rollers," he said, waving a hand. "Do want you want. Just don't make a mess."

CHAPTER TWENTY-NINE

It took an hour for the state forensic team to show up at Tuyen's apartment. Louis led the search, directing the team to do a thorough dusting for fingerprints as he scoured the place again for any evidence that Anthony had been there. Joe retreated to the hallway, where she sat on the stairs reading the Prince case file. No one had to tell her that she had no jurisdiction to be involved in the apartment search.

On the drive back to Lansing, they had talked only about the case, and in the silences Louis could almost read her thoughts—that she had no authority here, no place on the team. Louis understood that. There had been other cases, other times, when his lack of a badge had kept him from going places and doing things that she could.

Four hours later, they pulled into the church parking lot in Lansing. Joe's eyes lingered on the name ST. MICHAEL'S CATHOLIC CHURCH on the lawn.

Inside, Louis counted five state troopers hanging out by the coffee machine. Emily was on the phone, gesturing angrily as she talked, and Tooki was hunched over his computer, tapping furiously. Things were heating up. The nave even felt warmer than usual.

Joe was taking it all in—the computers, evidence boxes, and the large murder board up on the altar. When her eyes came back to him, she smiled. "Pretty impressive," she said.

Louis heard a sound and looked up. Steele was standing at the railing of the loft watching them. When he disappeared, Louis turned to Joe.

"Joe, I'm sorry, but I have to—"

"Go," she said. "I need to call in. I'll wait here."

"Coffee's over by the confessional," he said.

She nodded, then picked up the nearest phone.

Louis hurried up the steps. Steele was alone at his desk, writing furiously on a legal pad. When he looked up, the light from the desk lamp washed over his face, bringing into high relief a stubble of whiskers and deep lines of fatigue around his mouth. His expression was as it was always was—somber and serious. But his eyes, nearly black in the low light, shimmered with a euphoric glaze, like a guy in the first seconds after snorting a line of cocaine.

Louis knew it wasn't from any drug. It was different kind of high, a kind of high only a few people would understand—the high of a good lead and the chase.

Steele spoke first. "We've confirmed the tenant in the apartment was Tuyen Lang. I don't have to tell you how big this is. But it seems you've started a turf war."

"Grand Rapids won't relinquish the case, right?"

"Right. They're pissed you even went in without calling them."

Louis knew they could continue to investigate, but without access to what Grand Rapids already had on Tuyen Lang's murder, it would be almost impossible to link her death to Anthony.

"Were you able to find anything to put Anthony Prince inside that apartment?" Steele asked.

Louis shook his head. "Not yet, but we were able to find some prints and fluids Grand Rapids didn't lift. If we can match them later to Anthony—"

"What's that?" Steele interrupted, gesturing toward Louis's hand.

Louis had brought an evidence bag. "It's a Vietnamese scarf," Louis said. "It's how I made the connection."

"Why'd you bring it back?" Steele asked.

"It might be what she was strangled with. Plus, I thought Cam might want to see it. It's only because of him that Tuyen Lang was even on our radar."

A glimmer of irritation crossed Steele's face, but he nodded. Earlier on the phone, when Louis told Steele about the visit to the Ionia morgue, Steele had been silent for a long time then quickly went on talking about securing the apartment. Louis suspected at some later date, Cam would get his ass chewed for the detour, despite the fact it had broken the Prince case wide open. Louis decided to defend him.

"Sir, about Cam, sometimes we have to go with our gut," Louis said. "Sometimes—"

The phone rang. Steele held up a hand to silence Louis and hit the button to put the phone call on speaker.

"Captain Steele here."

"Hello, this is Lieutenant Sid Newton. Ionia S.O."

Louis took a step closer to the desk. Steele was making an end run around GRPD to get the file.

"Thank you for returning my phone call so late on a Sunday night, lieutenant."

"Well, it's not every day a man gets a call from the state's Special Investigations Unit. How can I help you?"

"Before we get to business, let me ask you. How is your daughter?"

There was a brief silence. "Tara? She's good."

"She's graduating from the Michigan State Police Academy this spring, right?"

"Yes, she is. Tenth in her class," Newton said, his voice slow and questioning.

"I hear she'd like to join the K9 unit."

"Yes, sir. That's what she wants to put in for."

"I started my patrol career in K9," Steele said. "Great place to work. I still have a lot of good friends over there."

"Yes sir."

225

"Now, to business," Steele said. "You guys found a body over your way in a field last week, a young Asian girl named Tuyen Lang, stuffed in a suitcase."

"That's right."

"I'd like you to hand that case along to us."

Newton went quiet. When Steele looked up at Louis his eyes gleamed in the low light, eyes that all but shouted *I am in control.* And Newton's lengthening silence proved it.

"I don't know about that, captain," Newton said finally. "From what I hear, this poor girl was killed in her apartment and that would make it Grand Rapids's jurisdiction."

"We don't yet know for sure where she was killed," Steele said. "And until we do, jurisdiction remains with the agency that found the body."

"But I already gave it to GRPD," Newton said. "What do you want me to do? Just call them up and take it back?"

"Yes."

The phone went silent again, then came a few heavy, resigned breaths. "I'll look like a fool if I snatch a homicide case back from another department," Newton said softly.

"On the contrary," Steele said. "You'll be a hero."

Another long pause from Newton. Louis knew what Newton was thinking but wouldn't say—a hero to whom?

"Tara will make a fine K9 officer," Steele said. "Do we have a deal?"

"Yes."

Newton said goodbye and hung up.

Louis knew Steele had wanted him to hear the bribe, to impress him or teach him, maybe both. He remembered hearing that Steele once wanted to be attorney general. Steele had chosen to remain a cop but the politician in him was alive and well.

"Tell the others I'll be down in a minute," Steele said, picking up his suit jacket from the back of his chair.

"Yes, sir."

When Louis got downstairs Joe was standing at the murder board, looking at the photos, and she turned when she heard him coming.

"I have to go," she said.

"I don't know how long this will take," Louis said. "Wait for me at my place and we'll have a late dinner and—"

"No, I have to go home, to Echo Bay," Joe said.

"I thought you said you could stay until Tuesday?"

"I know. I thought so, too. But I've been called to testify tomorrow morning in a domestic abuse case. I know the woman involved. I have to be there. It's important."

So are we. That's the first thing that came to his mind, but he didn't say it because it was selfish. What did he expect? That Joe would be here waiting whenever he wanted? That her job was less important than his own?

"I called a cab," she said. "It's probably outside by now."

"I'll walk you out."

Outside, they paused on the church steps. Joe glanced at the taxi idling at the curb and when she looked back at Louis she let out a deep sigh.

"I'm sorry," she said.

"For what?"

"Leaving you right now."

"Joe, look, we both have—"

"No, it's not about the jobs," she said. "We can work that out. I know we can." She took a breath. "I think you need me here with you right now. I don't know why, but I feel it." She paused again, as if weighing every word that was in her head. It made Louis tense, like he felt something bad coming.

"Last night, you had a nightmare," she said.

He didn't remember it. But he could guess what it was about.

"I feel bad that we didn't talk. I feel bad that I have to go right now," she said.

"I'm okay," he said quickly. Too quickly, he knew.

The cabbie honked his horn. Joe waved in irritation toward him then looked back at Louis. She hesitated then brought up her hand and gently

227

laid her palm against his cheek. It was more devastating than a kiss. Louis shut his eyes.

She buried her head in his shoulder. "Call me," she whispered. And then she pulled away quickly and there was just cold air where she had been.

Louis watched her jog to the cab and get in. When the cab disappeared around the corner, he went back into the church.

Steele was standing at the head of the conference table and turned at the sound of the door banging shut. Louis could feel his eyes on him as he approached. Emily and Tooki, seated at the table, were watching him as well.

"Cam is running late," Steele said. "But we will get started anyway."

Louis retrieved his binder from his desk and sat down next to Emily.

Steele pulled a paper from his binder and laid it in the center of the table. "I got this faxed over from immigration about an hour ago. Here's our victim."

It was a date-stamped visa photo, taken three years ago when Tuyen first arrived in the U.S. The contrast between the bruised face Louis had seen in the morgue and the one in the photo was striking.

In the visa photo, Tuyen's face was rounder, her eyes brighter, as if reflecting hope for a new life. Her black hair flowed like silk to her slender shoulders, making her look fourteen or fifteen instead of her true age of twenty-two.

Louis pulled the photo closer. How did a girl go from this to being a hooker? The records check he had run on her earlier showed her single arrest for prostitution had come only six months after she entered the country when she was busted during a sweep on the city's west side. There was nothing for her after that, but she had entered the church's Fresh Start program a year later. Louis was positive that was all Anthony's doing, maybe first finding her on the street then stashing her at the apartment under the guise of the refugee program so he had easy access whenever he wanted.

"Did you tell Cam about Tuyen Lang?" Louis asked.

"No," Steele said. "I want him here with us when we tell him. Louis, bring everyone up to speed, please."

Louis opened his binder and started laying out the day's events, including the latest development that Tuyen had a car, a 1982 silver Civic, that hadn't been found.

A loud bang drew everyone's attention to the door. It was only as the man came closer that Louis realized it was Cam, wearing a tweedy brown sports coat, checkered tie and a brown wig.

Cam dumped his binder on the conference table, wiggled out of the jacket and yanked off the wig. "Sorry I'm late," he said. "I wanted to get back here and find out what the big break was."

"What's with the disguise?" Emily asked.

Cam peeled off his moustache. "The captain asked me to shadow Anthony today. I didn't want the guy to make me so I threw on my Wonder Bread wrapper. I blended right in at that church."

"You went to the evening service?" Emily asked.

"Sure did," Cam said. "Man, what a long freakin' sixty minutes."

"Did Anthony give the sermon?" Louis asked.

Cam didn't answer, didn't even seem to have heard him. He was looking at the visa photograph of Tuyen on the table. He picked it up, stared hard at it, then looked to Louis.

"Is this Angel?" Cam asked.

"Yeah."

Cam was standing there like a coiled spring. Louis knew Cam was making the connection but didn't want to believe it. "Did that fucker kill her?" Cam asked tightly.

Louis did a quick look around the table before he answered. "We think so, yeah," he said.

"She was his . . ." Cam didn't finish.

Louis nodded. "It's complicated, but we made the connection with this." He slid the bagged Vietnamese scarf across the table to Cam. The scarf was folded so the tag was visible.

Cam didn't pick it up, but he stood there staring at it, his fists clenched. Louis stole a glance at Steele. His expression was deadpan, watching and waiting. Waiting for what, though? For the cracks to widen?

229

The urge was powerful, to call Steele out on his ugly game, right here in front of everyone. But Louis knew he couldn't. It would jeopardize the case. He would wait. The right moment would come.

Louis touched Cam's arm. "Sit down," he said.

Cam pulled his arm away, yanked out a chair and sat down. He was still holding Tuyen's photograph, but he was looking up at the altar to the murder board where Anthony Prince's photograph hung in the center of all the others.

A few silent seconds ticked by.

"Cam," Steele said. "Did Anthony give the sermon today?"

Cam set the photograph on the table, face down, and drew a heavy breath. "Yeah," he said, "but I wouldn't call it a sermon."

"What do you mean?"

"It sounded like more of a eulogy for his father. But Anthony's right about one thing—he is definitely not a chip off the old block. He sounds like one of those noise machines that is supposed to put people to sleep."

Cam fell silent, pulling in long, slow breaths. Louis could tell he was trying hard to get a grip on himself, not fall apart in front of everyone. Finally, Cam sat up straighter and opened his binder.

"I figured what he talked about might be a good indication of his state of mind, so I made some notes."

"Good thinking," Steele said.

Cam scooted his chair closer and squinted down at his notes as he picked at the glue on his lip. "He started out talking about his father, how he walked with God in every aspect of his life and how his father's devotion to God came at the cost of unspeakable personal sacrifices."

"Did he elaborate on those sacrifices?" Emily asked.

"No," Cam said, turning the page. "Then he talked about how his father's legacy should live on through all of God's channels. I guess that meant he should still get that TV gig. But the weird thing was, at the end, he suddenly stopped talking and he just stood there for maybe half a minute like he'd lost his train of thought. Then he threw out a Bible verse and told us all to go home and pray."

"What was the verse?" Louis asked.

Cam looked at his notes. "Exodus 20:12. 'Honor your father and your mother, so that you may live long in the land the Lord your God is giving you.'"

"How did he behave afterwards? Anything odd?" Steele asked.

Cam shook his head. "Seemed okay. Shook hands, accepted hugs. I followed him to make sure he went home, then I headed back here."

Steele looked around the table. "Okay, it looks like Anthony's not onto us, and that buys us some time, but not much. What about prints from the apartment, Louis?"

"Our techs re-dusted the whole place," Louis said. "But I checked and Anthony's not in the system. He's never been printed so we have nothing for comparison."

"Do you think he'd volunteer them? Tooki asked.

Emily shook her head. "By offering anything, he'd have to relinquish some control and he'd never do that."

"And we don't have enough for a warrant," Steele said. "We need something to put him inside that apartment."

"He was inside Tuyen," Cam said tightly. "Did the autopsy turn up any semen?"

Steele hesitated. "We don't yet have the autopsy report, but I talked to the ME. There was no semen found in or on her body."

The nave was quiet. Cam was staring at Tuyen's photo again, Emily was scribbling something in her notebook, and Tooki was slowly flipping through some papers on a clipboard.

"Tooki, did you get anything new from the tip line?" Louis asked.

Tooki pushed his glasses up his nose and flipped back to the first page on his clipboard. "We have troopers following up on three white Isuzu trucks seen around the cathedral and a couple tips we've already discounted. But calls have dropped off considerably."

"Maybe we should release the sketch of the man seen outside Jonas's cottage," Emily said.

Steele was quiet, tapping his pen lightly on his pad.

"Sir," Louis said, "if nothing else, we need to rule that man out as a suspect in Jonas Prince's murder. If we nail Anthony, we don't want some defense attorney holding this guy out there as another suspect."

"Okay," Steele said. "Tooki, see if you can get the sketch in the morning paper."

It was quiet again, except for the low moan of the wind in the organ pipes.

Louis struggled to organize his thoughts, figuring out what their next move could be. It occurred to him that they were too hung up on the details of fingerprints, semen, sketches. But facts didn't always tell the story or give you the answers. What did they know for sure? That they had two murders, committed within hours of each other. One victim was a man of God, the other a girl of the streets. What was the big picture here? What connected them? And what connected them to Anthony Prince the night of the murder?

He looked at Cam, who was looking at the photograph of Tuyen again. Louis thought again about Steele's head games. Cam's mother. Emily's suicide attempt. Louis's childhood in foster care. Cracked jugs . . .

Who didn't have fault lines in their past?

Louis hesitated, a memory tugging at his brain, something buried in his notes. He opened his binder and flipped through the pages. He was looking for his interview with Walter Bushman.

There it was.

Put not your trust in princes, nor in the son of man, in whom there is no help.

"Sir, I think I might have something," Louis said.

Everyone looked up.

"I think Violet Prince knows something and may want to tell us."

Steele sat back in his chair. "What makes you say that?"

"When I interviewed Walter Bushman, he told me he got a phone call from a Grand Rapids woman who refused to identify herself, but she left a Bible verse with the call screener." He looked down at his notes. "Listen to this: 'Put not your trust in princes, nor in the son of man, in whom there is no help.'"

"Why do you think it came from her?"

Louis paused. "Let's call it a hunch."

"When did this call come in?"

"The Saturday after Jonas was murdered."

"But this woman caller never referenced the murder?" Steele asked.

"Not directly but—"

"Wait!"

Tooki had spoken, so much louder than his normal near-whisper that everyone stared at him. Tooki rifled through the pages on his clipboard then looked up. "A woman called our tip line yesterday and left the same verse. Here it is. Anonymous call, ten fifteen a.m. 'Put not your trust in princes, nor in the son of man, in whom there is no help.'"

"She's not going to turn him in. She's a minister's wife," Cam said.

"That doesn't mean she can't feel frustrated, sad, or angry," Emily said. "She might be doing it because she's had enough but doesn't feel she can confront him. Classic passive-aggressive." She looked at Louis. "You're the only one who's talked to her. Did you get that vibe from her?"

Louis nodded. "I got the sense that she's lonely. And that she knows more about her husband than she's willing to admit, maybe even to herself."

Violet's voice was in Louis's head. *When you have no words of your own, the Lord will provide.*

"Okay," Steele said, tossing his pen on the table. "This is what we're going to do." He looked around the table, his gaze stopping on Cam. "Tuyen Lang belongs to you. You'll have her case file by tomorrow and I want you to go through everything GRPD put together and then start digging on your own. Track her clothes, her groceries, anything that might have been purchased by Prince on his credit cards. Find a connection between them."

"Got it," Cam said.

"Tooki, Emily," Steele said. "I want you working on all the background you can get on Violet."

Louis knew where this was going. And where he was going—right back to Violet Prince.

"Louis, you already have a rapport with Violet Prince," Steele said. "I need you to find out what she knows. All right, that's it."

The others were moving toward their desks. Louis remained seated, thinking now that, while it was his idea to talk to Violet, and that it was a primo assignment, a part of him wasn't looking forward to it. A part of him felt it was . . . cruel.

"Louis."

Steele was staring at him. There was a softness in Steele's face, and Louis thought he might be getting ready to drop a compliment about the long day's good work.

"Anthony Prince's entire life is about to come crashing down around him," Steele said. "Once that happens, he may panic and turn violent. He might hurt someone else."

"I understand," Louis said.

"You have one shot at Violet," Steele. "Make it your best."

CHAPTER THIRTY

When Louis got to the church at seven thirty the next morning, Emily's report on Violet was there waiting for him on his desk. Emily was there, too, arms folded, head down on her own desk, fast asleep. Louis suspected she had been there all night working to get the report done.

He decided not to wake her and slipped out. He drove to the nearby Dunkin Donuts and ordered two sprinkle donuts and a large black coffee, intending to kill some time reading the file. If Anthony stuck to his usual routine, he wouldn't leave his house until eight forty-five a.m., and Louis wanted to make sure Violet was alone when he confronted her.

Confronted . . .

That wasn't the right word, of course. If he was going to flip her, he had to tread carefully because they had no proof that she was the one who had called Bushman and the tip line, and by all appearances she didn't seem like an aggrieved wife. But then, you never knew what dark currents flowed below the surface of a marriage or in the heart of a woman.

Louis opened the file and began to read.

Violet had been born in Vandalia, a small town an hour and half south of Grand Rapids. Her father James Tripp was the pastor of the Community Church of God, and her mother died when Violet was twelve. Emily hadn't found much on the Tripp family, other than Violet was a steady presence at her father's side in the church. One interesting fact struck him: Violet's great-great-grandfather had worked closely with the local Quakers who harbored slaves on the Underground Railroad, which ran through south-western Michigan to Canada from 1840 to 1850.

Violet's father had continued the family's civil rights crusade by writing columns in the local paper railing against the prejudice directed at the Mexican immigrants flooding into the state to work in the auto plants.

Emily had found a photograph from the Vandalia newspaper of James Tripp with Violet taken on the steps of a handsome white clapboard church. The caption read, "The Rev. Tripp aided by his daughter Violet, 15, has opened his church to the needy families of the brown man."

Louis stared hard at the young Violet in the photo. She was as tall as her father, standing ramrod straight with a confident smile on her face. Violet's vein of Christian charity ran long and deep—back to slaves, through the Mexican influx, and up to the refugee resettlement program Fresh Start.

What had happened to her? How had Violet gone from an activist in her church to a passive housewife?

He returned to the file. In 1962, Rev. Tripp died from cancer. Violet, then just seventeen, was legally homeless because the church owned the parsonage house she and her father had lived in. Two months later, when Jonas Prince was installed as the new minister of the Vandalia Community Church of God, he took Violet in, letting her stay in the parsonage home. Violet married Anthony a few years later, just before Jonas moved the family to Grand Rapids.

Emily had scribbled a note in the margin: *Re Trust Fund. Refer to Tooki report on Prince financial background.*

Louis turned to Tooki's report and flipped through the pages until he found Emily's red-inked bracketing of two paragraphs.

Violet's father had left her a trust fund of $50,000. It had come mostly from the sale of some acreage near the Vandalia church to an agricultural organization back in 1960. The fund, deposited in the G.W. Jones Exchange Bank in Cassopolis, grew to $75,000 and was untouched—until November, 1979 when one withdrawal was made for $25,000 in cash.

There were eight more cash withdrawals over the years, each for $6,000. The last withdrawal was about three and half years ago in December of 1987.

Here, Emily had written something in the margin: *Violet signed her trust fund over to Anthony one year after they married.*

Louis sat back in the booth. The withdrawals could have been for any reason. But given Violet's submissive obedience to Anthony, it was possible she didn't know about it. Was Anthony paying someone off? Had he gotten involved with a woman back in 1979, someone who tried to blackmail him? And did Tuyen also threaten to go public, or worse, did she tell Jonas? Did Jonas threaten to disown Anthony and Anthony murdered him? Did an enraged Anthony then murder Tuyen the same night?

He finished off his coffee and glanced at his watch. Just past eight-thirty. It was time to go see Violet.

Louis parked the Explorer behind some trees just outside the Tammarron North entrance. Anthony's black Lincoln rolled past at a quarter to nine. Louis waited until he was out of sight then drove to the house.

When he rang the doorbell, it was a long time before Violet opened the door. She was dressed in a blue robe, her hair uncombed and her face bare. She blinked rapidly, like it was difficult for her to focus on his face.

"Officer . . ." Her voice trailed off.

"Kincaid. Louis Kincaid. I'm sorry to bother you so early. May I come in?"

She looked past him, down the long, empty driveway, then nodded and held the door open. The house was cold inside, and there were no lights on anywhere.

Violet closed the door and ran a hand through her hair. "My medication leaves me a little fuzzy sometimes." She looked around the foyer and toward the far hallway. "Did you want to see my husband? I think he's already left."

"No, I'd like to talk to you," Louis said.

"Oh . . . well then," Violet said softly. She pulled the belt of her robe tighter. "Would you like some coffee?"

Louis's bladder was floating from the Dunkin' Donuts coffee, but he had to establish empathy with Violet. "I could use a cup," he said.

"So could I," she whispered as she started away down a hallway, her bare feet not making a sound on the white tile.

The white, French, country-style kitchen was large and brightly lit, with a breakfast bar and a dining nook overlooking the sloping backyard. Violet took two mugs from the cupboard and poured coffee from a machine on the counter. She turned back to the nook then stopped. Louis noticed she seemed to be staring at the table. There was a plate with the remains of toast and eggs, an empty juice glass, and a half-filled coffee mug. A newspaper lay open near the plate.

Violet set the mugs down, frowning. "I'm sorry. Things are such a mess. Let me clear—"

"Don't bother with that right now," Louis said. "We can just sit here at the bar."

He took off his jacket and draped it over the stool, sitting down before Violet could protest. She hesitated, still looking at the dirty dishes on the table, then came over to sit next to Louis, bringing him sugar and cream. Louis stirred in his sugar, trying to gauge if she was clear-headed enough to talk. If he moved too fast, she'd probably shut down and throw him out.

"How are you holding up, Mrs. Prince?" he asked.

"Okay," she said softly. "I'm very tired. I called the police yesterday. They told me they don't know when they can release his . . ." She let out a sigh. "I have to arrange for the funeral. When can I do that?"

"It should be soon. Maybe another day."

She fell quiet, drinking her coffee. Louis did the same and set his mug down. "You make very good coffee," he said with a smile.

She blinked. "Oh, Anthony makes it." Her gaze went again to the dirty dishes on the table. She was frowning, like she was having trouble thinking.

"Mrs. Prince," he began, "I have to ask you something important, something about your father-in-law's murder." He waited until her eyes refocused on him. "Did you call the police tip line?"

"What?"

"Did you call the police and leave a message about your father-in-law's murder?"

She was frozen, the mug inches from her lips. Her face had gone blank. But there was a small tell—a slight shaking of her hand holding the mug.

"The last time I came to visit, you told me that God gives you the words when you can't find your own." Louis had the verse memorized. "'Put not your trust in princes, nor in the son of man, in whom there is no help.'"

Still she didn't move.

"You also called Walter Bushman's radio station and left the same message, didn't you?"

She was staring at him, but it was like she was looking straight through him and searching for something else. Louis knew she wasn't going to answer. She would never admit it. But she hadn't denied it either.

"I know you lost your own father when you were a girl. I know you were close to Jonas. I know you loved him," Louis said. He had waited to use Jonas' first name, waited until this moment to make it personal.

She set the mug down and shut her eyes tight.

"It's okay to have suspicions, Violet," Louis said. "What does the verse mean?"

"David was trying to tell us that we are should not put our faith in the men of earth and forget the Great One above," she said. "Because the men of earth will disappoint us."

"Who disappointed you, Violet?"

She opened her eyes, those eyes as deep as a summer dusk sky and as sad as a dying iris.

"I'm his wife," she whispered.

She was leaving him no choice. He had to push her.

"Your father left you a trust fund," Louis said.

She frowned in confusion but nodded.

"Anthony has been taking money out of it for more than ten years. Did you know that?"

Her expression told him she didn't.

"There's very little left," Louis said.

Her eyes brimmed, and she withdrew slightly, like she suddenly didn't want Louis near her. He was losing her. He had to do it.

"There's something else, Violet," he said. "Anthony was seeing another woman."

She let out a strange mewing sound and looked away, swiveling on the stool, turning her body away from Louis so he couldn't see her face.

A minute ticked by, then she pushed off the stool, went to the sink and turned on the faucet. She splashed water on her face, dried it with a towel, then turned to face Louis.

"I knew," she said softly.

The wife always knows.

"He hasn't touched me in years," she said. Her cheeks reddened but she was able to keep her eyes on Louis's. "I just had to know where he went on Wednesday nights and I don't drive so I couldn't follow him. So, one Wednesday night about a month ago, I didn't take my pill and I stayed awake. He didn't come home until nearly four in the morning."

She paused, but Louis said nothing, sensing there was more.

"And when he got home," she said, "he spent more than an hour in the shower before he came to bed. That's not normal, is it?"

Louis knew she didn't really expect an answer and he didn't offer one. Violet was still standing by the sink, holding the towel, facing the window.

"Is she someone from our church?" Violet asked.

Louis hesitated. "No, she was a prostitute. Your husband was keeping her in one of the Fresh Start apartments."

She began to twist the towel between her hands. Louis wanted her to turn around so he could read her face because he wasn't sure how far he could go, how much this fragile woman could stand.

He knew she would find out the rest soon enough and maybe it would be better coming from him. If she fainted, had a breakdown or something, he could deal with it more easily, here in her own home.

"There's one more thing I have to tell you," he said. "We believe your husband killed her." He paused. "The same night he killed Jonas."

She kept twisting the towel, so hard and tight, the veins in her hands were standing out.

"Violet," he said calmly. "I need to know what you know. What made you call the tip line? What happened that made you suspicious?"

The twisting stopped. Violet set the towel on the counter and turned. "I have to go to the bathroom," she said. Her voice was flat, her expression stony.

"Wait," he said. "I can't let you go alone, I—"

"It's where I hid it," she said.

"Hid what?"

Violet left the kitchen and Louis followed her down a hallway leading toward the back of the house. They passed through a large bedroom with an unmade bed, and into the adjoining bath. Violet switched on the light, flooding the spotless white marble room.

He watched her as she opened a drawer of a built-in vanity and began taking things out, setting them on the counter. Finally, she stopped, stepped toward Louis, and held out her hand.

In her palm was a silver chain with a single key. Louis knew immediately what it was—the key to Jonas's dressing room at the church. The same key the killer used to lock the dressing room door after he strangled Jonas. And the same key the killer used to let himself back in so he could move the body to the altar in the middle of the night.

Louis spotted a Kleenex dispenser and pulled out a tissue. He spread the tissue in his own palm. "Drop it in here, Violet," he said.

She set it in the Kleenex and Louis folded it over and slipped it in his pocket.

"Where did you find this?" he asked.

"In the pocket of Anthony's pants," she said.

241

"When?"

"The morning after Jonas was killed. It was after Anthony left for work. I was gathering up his clothes for the cleaners, emptying his pockets like I always do, and that's when I found it."

Violet let out a deep breath that made her thin shoulders shiver. "I know it is the key to Jonas's dressing room," she said. "He told me once that it's the only one."

"Then you know what that means," Louis said.

She nodded, her eyes brimming.

In the bathroom's harsh light, Violet looked suddenly older. Wearier. A phone began to ring. Violet looked toward the bedroom.

"You should answer that," Louis said.

"I can't. It might be another reporter," she said, shaking her head.

Louis heard the beeping of his pager on his belt and the number on the display told him the ringing phone was probably for him. He hurried to the bedroom and grabbed the receiver from the nightstand phone.

"Kincaid."

"This is Camille, Louis. We just got a call from the trooper sitting surveillance at the cathedral parking lot. Anthony Prince hasn't shown up yet. The trooper wants to know if he should give him more time."

Louis glanced at his watch. It was nine-twenty-five. The man was never late. He was gone and he had a half-hour's head start. What had spooked him?

"Put out an ABP for his black Lincoln Town car," Louis said.

"Follow or apprehend?" Camille asked.

"Arrest him," Louis said. "Tell the captain I have the key to the dressing room and alert the team. I think he's on the run."

He hung up and turned. Violet was staring at him, her lower lip quivering.

"I need your help, Violet," Louis said. "I need you to look around and tell me if anything is missing? Clothes? A suitcase?"

She glanced around the bedroom, dazed and eventually moved toward a walk-in closet. "His suitcases are still here," she said." She hesitated. "Except for that Vuitton thing."

"What thing?"

"It's a leather duffel bag, like a gym bag, but Anthony never exercised. It's not here."

"Do you have a safe?"

She shook her head. "Is Anthony—"

"Do you keep any cash in the house?"

"About four hundred dollars. It's my household money Anthony gives me. I keep it in the kitchen."

"I need you to check to see if it's there, please."

He followed her back to the kitchen. Violet opened a drawer and pulled out an envelope.

"It's empty," she said. "The money's not here."

Louis grabbed his jacket off the barstool and put it on. He was eager to get back to the Beacon Light Cathedral where the team would be assembling. But he still needed to know what had spooked Anthony.

"Violet," he said.

She was still staring at the empty envelope.

"Violet, did you notice anything strange about Anthony this morning?"

Her eyes drifted to the dirty dishes on the table. "He didn't put his dishes in the dishwasher," she said flatly.

Louis had assumed it was her breakfast. "He ate alone?"

She nodded. "I wake up too late, so he always makes his own breakfast—two poached eggs, toast, orange juice, and coffee—and he always reads the newspaper before he goes to the church. And he always cleans up after himself."

He went to the table and looked down at the newspaper spread open by the plate. It was that morning's Grand Rapids Press, open to page six. At the top of the page was the police sketch of the man Weems had seen outside Jonas's cottage Wednesday morning.

Was this what had done it? Was this man the reason Anthony had panicked?

He pointed to the sketch in the newspaper. "Violet, do you recognize this man?"

She came forward, stared down at it then shook her head. She moved away slowly, picked up the juice glass and put it in the sink.

"Violet, stop, please," Louis said. "Don't touch anything."

"But I just want to clean—"

"No, you can't. We're going to have to search your house, take some pictures."

He could see something shift in her expression, like she was running everything through her brain, processing everything that had happened in the last week, the last month, the last years, when her husband had come home late, when her husband had taken her money, when her husband hadn't touched her.

"Is there anyone I can call for you?" Louis asked. "Is there somewhere you can go?"

She was slumped against the kitchen sink. Her blue robe had fallen open, revealing an edge of a lace nightgown, but she didn't seem to notice or care. She shook her head slowly.

"*Sisu*," she whispered.

For a second, he didn't realize what she had said. But then he recognized the word. It was the same one the Rev. Grascoeur had said in the bar in Saginaw.

Violet looked up at him. "I'm sorry. You don't know what that means, do you."

"Determination," Louis said.

"It's more than that," she said softly. "It's an old Finnish word Jonas used all the time. It means . . . different things, good and bad. Bad sisu is ruthless and vengeful. But good sisu . . . it means having courage. But not just any kind. The courage to do the unthinkable."

Had he imagined it, that hint of anger in her voice? No, it was there in her eyes, too—those amazing eyes that now burned with the color of a gas flame.

The pager buzzed on his belt again and he saw it was Camille. He had to get to the Explorer and call Steele.

"I have to go," Louis said.

Violet pulled the lapels of her robe together and led Louis out of the kitchen. They were in the living room, almost to the foyer, when she stopped suddenly. She was staring at something off in the corner.

"Violet? What is it?" Louis asked.

She pointed to the old organ. "It's open," she said.

Louis couldn't figure out what she was talking about but then he saw it—a small padlock hanging open on the organ's bench. He went to the bench and opened the top. It was empty.

"What did he keep in here?" he asked.

She had come up behind him and was staring at the bench. "He told me it was Jonas's old gun. I saw it once. Anthony told me he locked it up because he was worried about my sleepwalking."

Louis remembered the photograph in Jonas's study, the one of Jonas wearing the bandolier with the holstered gun. It was a World War II pistol, probably a Lugar, but just as deadly as a modern Glock.

"Violet, listen to me," Louis said. "I'm going to call for a police officer to sit outside your house."

"But why? Anthony would never—" Then she stopped.

Hurt me. That was what she was going to say. But Louis could read her thoughts there in her eyes, that she didn't know that for sure. She didn't know this man anymore. Or maybe she never had.

A single thought flashed through his brain in that moment. What would happen to this woman when this was all done?

He opened the door, letting in a rush of cold air, and looked back at Violet.

"I'll be okay," she said.

Louis wanted so much to believe that.

CHAPTER THIRTY-ONE

The four men stood under the portico of the Beacon Light Cathedral, their backs turned against the stiff breeze that pushed in from the north. They had come outside to get some fresh air and try to wrap their heads around the day's events, while they waited for Emily to arrive from Lansing.

They knew now that Anthony Prince had left his home at eight forty-five a.m. and had stopped by two different banks at 9:02 and 9:23 this morning. He withdrew a total of $10,000 in cash, the maximum he could get without paperwork and pre-approvals.

No one at the church knew anything about Anthony's life before Vandalia. No one had heard him speak of friends outside the congregation or ever mention anywhere he wanted to travel.

A rushed search of his home had failed to turn up Jonas's gun, now verified as a Luger pistol, and the assumption was that Anthony was now armed and dangerous. And, despite the state-wide APB, despite the conspicuous style of his Lincoln Town Car, and despite the deployment of seventy-five extra MSP patrol cars onto Michigan highways, Anthony Prince had vanished.

Louis reached into his jacket pocket and pulled out his copy of the sketch of the man seen outside Jonas's home. In discussions this morning, Steele had been cautious in making any connections, arguing that an already nervous Anthony could have seen the trooper's cruiser parked near the cathedral, or been tipped off by a leak from the disgruntled GRPD about

Tuyen's apartment. But Louis had disagreed, certain that the sight of this man's face had sparked Anthony's sudden departure.

"I think that's Emily coming," Cam said.

Louis stuck the sketch back in his pocket and looked down the road to see a blue Explorer crest the hill. Then his gaze moved around the three other men.

Tooki, shivering in a V-neck sweater, holding a clipboard and rifling the dozens of pages he had printed out from Anthony's office computer, still looking for that one shred of information that would tell them where he had gone. His bulky portable computer case sat his feet.

Cam, in his creased leather jacket, stood off to the side, chain-smoking Kools and impatiently shifting from one foot to another.

Steele stood a few feet away, hands deep into the pockets of his black overcoat, staring grimly toward the sprawling fields that surrounded the cathedral.

The blue Explorer wheeled to a stop near the portico. Emily bounded out of the driver's side and hurried toward the doors, carrying a manila folder.

"I'm sorry I'm so late," she said. "I was waiting on one last phone call. And I know this is all stuff we should've had before, but nothing's in the computers and—"

"Just tell us what you have," Steele said.

Emily opened the file and slapped down a hand to keep the papers from blowing away. "When I was researching Violet's history last night, I realized that we still didn't have much information on the Prince family. So, I started looking using the other family name Louis gave me the other day."

"Prinsilä," Louis said.

Emily nodded. "I spent most of last night and today on the phone, and I discovered we have a major problem in the family timeline."

"What kind of problem?" Steele asked.

"I found a record for a Joonas Prinsilä emigrating from Finland in 1940 and settling in Oulu, Wisconsin. I found a marriage certificate to Reeta, and birth certificates for the two boys, Antero in 1946 and Naatan in 1949."

"Any family left in Wisconsin?"

"None that I could find," Emily said. "But I talked to this woman at the Oulu town hall who remembered the family. She said Jonas was pastor of the church there and was well liked and respected. She said he was a quiet, conservative man, rigid in his faith. His wife was devoted to him, rarely seen in public on her own and the boys were clean and polite. But she said, despite the generosity of the community, Jonas choose to keep his family in almost abject poverty."

"What else?" Steele asked.

Emily turned a page in her notes, still talking fast. "Even though they were poor, Jonas still took in every stray around—kids, homeless men, and animals. Reeta gave food from her own home to those she felt were in greater need and spent days on end sitting with sick parishioners and visiting hospitals."

"Find anything specific to Anthony?" Steele asked.

Emily nodded. "When Anthony was about thirteen, Jonas pulled them out of public school to homeschool them. Seems he was really smart, always looking for ways to earn extra money with odd jobs. But then a few months later, some Christmas decorations caught fire and burned down the church. There was no money to rebuild, so the Prinsilä family packed up and moved away."

"To where?" Louis asked.

"That's the problem," Emily said, closing her folder. "No one knows. The next time I found any records was three years later, in 1962, when Jonas assumed the ministry of the Vandalia church, where Violet is from. Only, by then, they were calling themselves Jonas and Anthony Prince, not Joonas and Antero Prinsilä."

"So we have a three-year gap in their history," Steele said. "From early 1960 to late 1962."

Louis did a quick calculation in his head. If the younger brother Nathan Prince died at age twelve, that set the year of his accident in 1961, midway through the family's missing years.

Louis looked to Emily. "Did you pull a death certificate for the brother, Nathan?"

"I tried," she said. "Nothing on file in Wisconsin and I'm still waiting to hear back on Michigan, Minnesota and Canada."

"What are you thinking, Louis?" Steele asked.

"This might sound crazy," Louis said, "but what if the Princes deliberately tried to erase those years? What if they weren't just starting over, but running from something?"

"Like what?" Tooki asked.

"Like maybe Nathan's accident wasn't an accident," Louis said. "What if something horrible happened between the boys and Nathan ended up dead? Jonas, like most fathers, would protect his family and his ministry. So, he tells a few lies, moves away and changes his name. It would've been easy in 1961."

"And who in Vandalia would question what a minister told them about his background?" Cam offered.

Steele turned to Tooki. "Go plug that thing in. We need a death certificate on Naatan Prinsilä and we need it now."

Tooki grabbed his case and disappeared back into the church. Steele turned back to Emily, but before he could say anything, his radio squawked to life.

He grabbed it from his inside pocket. "Captain Steele. Go ahead, Camille."

"We found the Lincoln Town Car."

It was in a parking garage. And not just any garage, but one on the corner of Lyons and Monroe, in downtown Grand Rapids. Across the street from the back entrance of the Amway Grand Hotel and two blocks from the Chop House restaurant.

Louis stood quietly, thinking, as he watched a state trooper work a Slim Jim into the window panel to unlock the car door. The Town Car was parked on the third floor of the garage, backed into a space near the elevator and locked up tight. The attendant did not recall seeing anyone leaving on foot. There were no cameras at the entrance and exit.

Cam came up next to Louis and blew out a stream of cigarette smoke. "Why here?" he asked. "What's close to this place he could walk to?"

Louis looked to the opening between the garage floors, where he could see the tops of downtown buildings and patches of blue sky. They had already checked the Amway Hotel and the Chop House, even though the restaurant wasn't even open for business yet. No sign of Anthony. "I don't know," Louis said.

"Think he took a cab somewhere? Like O'Hare or Detroit airport?"

Louis shook his head as his eyes moved down a row of parked cars. "No, he would know we alerted the airlines."

"Well, we know Violet didn't help him set up an escape plan," Cam said. "And he doesn't seem to have any close friends. How'd he get away?"

Louis's gaze stopped on a non-descript silver sedan as he remembered that they still had not found Tuyen Lang's 1982 silver Honda Civic.

Louis turned back to Steele. "He took her car," he said.

Steele looked at him. "What?"

"He's in Tuyen's car," Louis said again, now talking to the whole team. "On the Wednesday night he killed her, we know he took a cab from this corner to her apartment. I think he then used her car to take her body to Ionia and dump it. Then he drove back here, parked her Civic in this garage and took his own car home. This morning, he switched back."

Steele rubbed his brow, as if he couldn't quite believe no one had thought of putting Anthony in Tuyen Lang's car before now. And they had wasted more than five hours looking for the wrong car.

As Steele yanked his radio from his coat to issue a new APB, Louis turned and walked away, down the line of parked cars. He was sure Anthony was long gone in Tuyen's Civic, but still he looked for silver Hondas, just in case he was wrong.

A pickup truck caught his attention, a small red one with the manufacturer's name stamped across the tailgate: ISUZU. It was not the truck seen outside Jonas's home—that had been white—but the sight of it still made him pause.

His eyes drifted to another pickup a few spaces down, an older model, sloppily repainted in yellow that covered the word DATSUN on the tailgate, making it almost invisible. But even from this distance of thirty feet, it was impossible to miss the huge red and white BUSH-QUAYLE '88 bumper sticker.

He looked back the Isuzu, a bad feeling settling in his gut as he recalled the interview with Weems. What had they missed? What had they not asked?

I can see some letters . . . like you know, how they put F-O-R-D on the tailgates?"

So, it's a Ford?

No, no man, it's one of those foreign things . . . wait, I can get it . . . Suzoo.

"I-suzu?"

"Yeah, I guess . . . that's it. Isuzu."

A foreign-made Isuzu was not the most popular truck in Michigan, yet they had not turned up one Isuzu truck owner with any connection to Jonas Prince, the church, or the East Grand Rapids neighborhood.

Could the reason be as simple as a witness misreading a truck's name?

"Hey Cam, come here for a second."

Cam tossed his cigarette and trotted over to Louis. "Yeah?"

"You know that memory thing you did with Weems, how you had him close his eyes and almost force an image to come forward?"

"Yeah."

Louis hesitated. He didn't want Cam to think he was questioning his interrogation methods. "I think," he said slowly, "I think maybe one of Weems's recollections came more from something you suggested rather than from a real memory."

Cam's brow wrinkled. "You saying I *told* him what to remember?"

"No, but I think sometimes we're so desperate for information, we start out trying to help the witness articulate what he saw and end up suggesting what he saw."

"What exactly are you talking about?"

"The Isuzu truck," Louis said. "He kept saying something like soo-sow, but you actually gave him the truck name."

Cam stared at him, hard.

Louis softened his voice. "What if it was something else he saw on that white truck?"

"Like what?"

"Like a bumper sticker."

Cam looked around at the cars. "That would have to be a big ass bumper sticker for Weems to see it a couple houses away."

"Then maybe it was a business name, painted on the tailgate," Louis said.

"Like what? Like Ow-Sow plumbing?"

"Maybe."

Cam frowned, thinking. "Are we looking for someone from that town in Wisconsin? *Oulu?*" he asked.

An Oulu, Wisconsin link made perfect sense. That's where the family was from and maybe that's where this mysterious man in the sketch was from as well, a shadowy figure from the Prince family past, someone who threatened them in some way and set off this chain of events.

But then a voice was in his ear, soft and dispirited, yet full of truth.

It's just a word Jonas taught me.

Sisu.

S-I-S-U.

The same letters he had seen on Monica's sweatshirt when he was in Eagle River. The same word Reverend Grascoeur had said.

And he knew. Damn it, he *knew*.

The word Weems had seen was not Isuzu or Oulu but a word that meant so much more, not only in its varied interpretations, but in its importance. Its importance to the stalwart and hardscrabble people, who a century ago adopted it as their own—the Yoopers. And when people were proud of something they displayed it everywhere—on sweatshirts, in their business names, and on bumper stickers.

Louis went back to Steele and with a hand on his arm, led him away from the other officers.

"I know where he's going," Louis said, when they were out of earshot.

"Where?"

"The U.P.," Louis said.

"Why would he do that?" Steele asked. "To cross into Canada?"

"No, he's going after the man in the sketch," Louis said. "I don't know why or what the connection is between them, but I'm sure now the sketch is what spooked Anthony and I think that man is from the U.P. and—"

"Slow down," Steele said.

Louis looked down, trying to sort out his thoughts so he could explain his theory to Steele in only a few words. But only one word came.

"Sisu," Louis said.

"Excuse me?"

"Sisu. It means—"

"I know what it means. Go on."

"I think that's what Weems saw on the white truck," Louis said. "A bumper sticker or a company name. They use it on lots of things up there."

"The U.P. is over sixteen thousand square miles," Steele said. "Any idea on exactly where he's going?"

"No."

Steele looked back toward the Lincoln Town Car. The techs had opened the doors and the trunk, but it was clear from the defeated look on their faces they had found nothing of interest.

"Sir," Louis said, "one of the reasons you hired me was my instincts. Trust me on this."

Steele's gaze came back to Louis. There were a hundred questions he could have—and *should* have—questions asked about how Louis had come to this conclusion and what evidence did he have to support a major and very expensive shift in resources from Grand Rapids to an area of Michigan some folks called The End of the Earth.

But he didn't ask one.

He gave Louis a tight nod. "Gather the team and meet me down on the street. We'll take a plane to St. Ignace and spread out from there in teams of two."

"Yes, sir."

Steele started to walk away, then turned back. "You're riding with me."

CHAPTER THIRTY-TWO

S ome drives seemed longer than others. Sometimes it was only because you were anxious to get to where you were going. But more often, it was because of other things, like the straightness of the road or the monotonous landscape of barren trees and brown brush.

And sometimes it was just the lousy company in the car.

Louis looked over at Steele in the passenger seat. Steele had files open on his lap, and a flashlight in his hand so he could read in the waning light of the oncoming dusk. He hadn't said a word for fifty miles.

The Cessna had landed in St. Ignace over two hours ago. Their team had been met by another team composed of two detectives and handful of state troopers on loan to Steele from their own regions. Steele held a short meeting on the tarmac and laid out the task at hand, which was to check out any businesses that had even a remote connection to the word SISU. They were also directed to stop vehicles with SISU bumper stickers or decals and log the drivers' names for later follow-up.

Emily and Cam were assigned to canvass the northeast section of the peninsula, near Sault Ste. Marie. The new members were to cover the vast middle and Louis and Steele were headed northwest.

Steele then distributed the procedures, search grids and bundles of flyers showing a photo of Anthony and the man from the Weems sketch. He also reminded everyone to be vigilant on their search for the silver Honda Civic that an armed Anthony was assumed to be driving.

Then he said one last thing. "Fast is good here, people. We have for-ty-eight hours to turn up a solid lead."

Louis had climbed in the Explorer with Steele knowing one thing—that the response to this expedition from the Lansing brass had been lukewarm at best. The small number of bodies allotted to it and the absurd deadline was a set-up for failure. It wasn't that they didn't want Anthony Prince caught. Everyone wanted him caught. But Louis had to wonder if there was someone upstairs that didn't want to see Steele's team get the glory for it.

Louis glanced again at Steele. Now he was making hurried notes on a legal pad, holding the penlight in his teeth.

Steele had to have sensed the same thing Louis did, maybe even had it said to him outright by one of the higher-ups. But the fact that Steele was still here, chasing down long-shot SISU leads, meant something. In fact, it meant a lot.

"You hungry?" Louis asked.

Steele looked up. "Where's our first stop?"

"Negaunee. Sisu Tire and Car Repair. Owned by a Calvin Gagnon."

"How far is it?"

"Another hour."

Steele looked at his watch. "We can wait. It'll be past eleven when we get there, and I want to talk to him tonight. Afterward, we can grab something to eat and get a room."

Louis turned his attention back to the road, thinking that, despite all Steele's years with the state, the man hadn't spent much time in the U.P. If he had, he would know that their chances of finding a restaurant open in Negaunee at midnight were less than zero.

He was going to make that point when the cell phone rang. Steele answered it and listened quietly for almost a mile. Then he hung up and let out a hard sigh.

"Any news?" Louis asked.

"We dispatched the firearm K-9s to Jonas's cottage," Steele said. "They found his old World War II Lugar in a box in one of the closets."

"So it wasn't the Lugar that Anthony took from the organ bench," Louis said. "Maybe it was a different gun."

Steele shook his head. "We sent dogs to Anthony's home. They didn't alert on the organ bench or anywhere else. If Anthony kept any gun in that bench for years, the dogs would've found a scent."

"Maybe not. If he never shot it."

"He has no firearms registered to him," Steele said, an edge to his voice. "And I don't think a man like Prince knew any gun dealers, do you?"

"So what else could Anthony have kept there he didn't want Violet to see?"

"Money?" Steele asked.

"No," Louis said. "He took all of Violet's house money and he had access to his banks."

"Maybe he kept something personal in the organ bench," Steele said. "Sex videos or photos, something to do with Tuyen Lang or young boys."

Louis shook his head. "No, I don't think he ever touched a real boy. And he wouldn't have brought any part of that life into his home with Violet. It would've been . . . I don't know, sacrilegious or something."

"Like leaving your murdered father in a locked dressing room instead of sending him off in style at the feet of Christ?"

"Exactly."

"Well, whatever he took from the bench, he probably put it in a Vuitton duffel," Steele said. "That's the only thing Violet found missing from their home."

"The only thing?" Louis asked.

"That and whatever was in that damn organ bench."

In Negaunee, Sisu Tire and Auto Repair was easy to find, and the owner, Calvin, easier yet to eliminate him as a suspect. He was an old man with a pot belly and white hair. He had no sons, no close friends downstate, and no company logo on his truck. And he didn't recognize either Anthony Prince's photograph or the sketch of the man who had lurked outside Jonas's cottage.

They came across a second possible suspect in the parking lot of a mo-tel, a thirty-something man with shaggy brown hair driving a white pickup with a large oval decal that read GOT SISU?

Louis had hoped that they had miraculously stumbled onto their sus-pect, but the guy turned out to be an off-duty forest ranger who had just gotten out the hospital.

After the ranger pulled away, Steele stood in the parking lot, his gaze drifting to the red, blinking neon on the roof of the motel. PINE TOP INN. VACANCY.

"I guess this is it," Steele said. "Unless you want to backtrack to Marquette."

"This is fine."

"I'll go check us in," Steele said.

Steele disappeared inside the office. Louis peered down the dark, empty street, looking for something that offered hope of food. He saw a Zephyr gas station sign a half-block down.

When Steele returned, he was holding a key with a giant green plastic tab. "The guy said he's still closed down for the season, but I talked him into opening one room," he said. "We're bunking together. Number six."

"I'm going to walk down to the gas station and get something to eat first. You want anything?"

"I'll walk with you."

Louis zipped his jacket and they walked in silence down the side of the main road.

Inside the store, Louis found four shriveled hot dogs rolling around on a warmer. He bought all of them, pocketed a handful of mustard and ketchup packets, and grabbed a six-pack of Strohs, two bags of chips, and some Ho Hos.

As he set everything on the counter, he saw a display of souvenirs—everything from Yooper keychains to copper bangle bracelets to window decals. And sure enough, they had one for SISU.

He picked it up, not sure why he wanted it. Maybe just something for his shelf back in the apartment or for the bunk room at St. Michaels. He also picked up some postcards and was sifting through them when Steele reappeared with a quart of milk.

"Why are you getting postcards?" Steele asked.

Louis looked over, surprised the man could take his mind off the case long enough to work up any curiosity about one of his officers' personal life. And it wasn't like he didn't already know everything about him. Except this, maybe.

Louis debated for a couple seconds before he answered.

"I send them to my daughter, Lily," he said. "It's how we stay in touch."

Steele stared at him and although he said nothing, the look on his face said it all—*How did I miss this?*

Steele pushed the groceries toward the clerk, paying for everything with a MSP credit card. He also left the clerk a handful of flyers and asked him to pass them around.

They walked back to the motel in silence, stepping inside just as thunder rumbled overhead. The room was small, cold, and mildewed, with knotty pine walls, two twin beds with camouflage spreads, and ugly duck decoy lamps on the nightstands.

"Looks like my uncle's hunting cabin," Steele said.

"You're a hunter?" Louis asked.

Steele set his overnight bag on the bed and hesitated, as if he had gone away somewhere for a moment. "Not since college," he said finally. "Would you get the case files from the truck?"

Louis returned to the Explorer for the bulky saddlebag-type briefcase Steele had dragged with him from Lansing. When he got back, Steele had taken off his coat and was seated at a table near the window. He dug right into the saddlebag, pulled out a stack of papers and started reading.

Louis set two hot dogs and a beer on the table.

Steele looked up. "I don't drink when I'm working a case."

Louis looked around, spotted the carton of milk, and set by Steele's elbow. He turned on the TV and plopped down on the other bed. After running through the channels a couple of times, he settled on an old Humphrey

Bogart movie—he thought it might be *In a Lonely Place* but wasn't posi-tive—while he ate the hot dogs and downed a beer.

He had just written "Dear Lily" on the first postcard when he started feeling guilty. It was well after midnight and Steele was still working.

"What are you doing, sir?" Louis asked.

"I'm going back over the interviews with the cathedral employees," Steele said, without looking up. "Anthony Prince worked with these folks for years. He had to tell them something personal at some time. No one is that closed off from other human beings. We might have missed something."

"Give me some," Louis said. "I'll help."

"No need," Steele said, turning a page.

Louis turned back to the TV, not sure if Steele was being considerate or condescending. He suspected it was the latter, and it pissed him off.

"Louis."

Louis looked over at him.

"Never let what is urgent take precedence over what is important," Steele said. "Finish your postcards. Those are important."

Steele went back to his reading. Louis watched him, his irritation gone, but his curiosity about the man piqued. He thought about what Emily had told him, that Steele liked to ski on volcanos, collected Victorian death masks, and seemed committed to only one thing in life—the job, which Louis knew from experience had included a stint in Internal Affairs. But what other experience did he have? Had he ever worked an active homicide?

His thoughts came to the mind game Steele was playing, the game with the cracked jugs that formed his team, setting them up to face head-on the damage done to them as children. What kind of man—what kind of leader—did something like that?

Louis watched Steele slowly turn the pages of the reports, his hot dog and milk sitting untouched at his elbow.

The kind of man, Louis knew, who had damage himself. Damage that he had not yet repaired. The kind of damage that still took its toll on cold, rainy nights when you would do just about anything to keep your brain busy so you didn't have to feel your heart ache.

What was the damage done to Steele?

The long day was a deep ache between Louis's shoulder blades. He set the beer aside, switched off the TV and his bedside lamp, and slumped down in the bed. He fell asleep, fully clothed, to the soft rustle of pages turning.

They were on the road the next morning by six, following a chain of leads that started with a gun shop owner who had a personalized GET SISU license plate and ended with a wasted hour talking to a woman who had claimed the man in the sketch was her son—her long-dead, atheist son.

Around noon, Steele took a cell phone call from someone he addressed as "Major DeForest." It seemed pretty terse, one-sided from Louis's vantage point, and after he hung up, Steele popped a Tic Tac into his mouth and spent the rest of the drive staring out the side window.

Just before one p.m., they pulled into Watersmeet, a scrap of a town set down in the low lands of the western end of the U.P. This was the next-to-last business on their list, a place called UP NORTH NURSERY. Their advertisements claimed: Our Plants Have Sisu!

The company had two white trucks, the slogan printed in large blue letters on the tailgates. The owner, Mike Carroll, was a beefy guy with a crew cut who met them in the gravel parking lot. He laughed when Steele explained why they were there.

"That truck doesn't run," Carroll said. "And the other, that's my truck. No one else drives it and I haven't been under the bridge for months."

Steele showed Carroll the photo of Anthony, but Carroll said he didn't recognize him. Steele then gave him the sketch.

Carroll stared it a long time. "This says this guy is wanted for questioning. What did he do?"

"We just want to talk to him," Louis said. "You know him?"

Carroll nodded slowly. "This a real lousy drawing, but I think maybe it might be Buddy Lampo."

"How do you know him?"

"We had some brews together. He used to live over the way with his folks, down Duck Lake Road. Beat up old place that sits empty now. But he hasn't been around for a while."

"How long is a while?" Steele asked.

"About five years now. His mother died maybe four years back. His dad died a year later and that's when Buddy left."

"Do you know where he moved to?" Louis asked.

"Nope, but I don't think he'd go far. He was a Yooper to the bone. Nice guy, though he was a little on the miserable side."

"Miserable, as in angry?" Steele asked.

Carroll shook his head. "Miserable as in sad, like there was something short-circuiting inside him that kept him from making a connection with other folks, ya know?"

"What did he do for a living?" Louis asked.

"I dunno exactly," Carroll said. "Sold a little firewood, painted some barns, mopped some floors. He got along."

Steele turned to Louis. "Go check him out."

Louis walked back to the Explorer, slid into the passenger seat and called Camille. He asked her to run the usual checks on both Buddy Lampo and Mike Carroll. While he waited for her response, he looked around the nursery. Broken fences corralled an orchard of skeletal trees. Spiky evergreens in pots were turning brown, like they were giving up. The slap-dash greenhouse listed in the wind, propped up on one side by high stacks of mulch and crushed rock.

Louis's first trip to the U.P. had been back in 1985, when he was chasing a cop killer. He had been here again a few weeks ago for the boys in the box. And both times he had come to see it as a hard-scrabble kind of place, where nothing came easy. But now, he saw it as a more primitive, even militant, kind of place. A place where only certain kinds of people could survive. People, he knew now, who had *sisu*.

"Louis?"

"Go ahead, Camille."

"The nursery owner is clean, no record," she said.

"And Lampo?"

"I have a DL for a Buddy Lampo, first issued in 1965 at the age of sixteen in Gogebic County, and still current. Last known address is 1458 Duck Lake Road, Watersmeet, Michigan."

Louis grabbed a pen from his pocket and opened his binder. "Vehicle registration?"

"Brown Chevy pickup, Michigan license plate Tom-Edward-Peter 6432."

"Does he have a record?" Louis asked.

"Negative," Camille said. "Just a couple of traffic tickets. You want me to fax you a hard copy photo?"

Louis hesitated, not sure where to tell her to fax it to. They had one more stop to make. "Not yet but keep digging around on him. Lampo's no longer living in Watersmeet and we need to know where he is."

"Will do."

"Thanks."

Louis started to hang up, then thought of one more thing. "Camille, wait. What were the tickets for?"

She took a moment. "Improper left turn in 1977 and driving with an unsecured load in 1986."

Unsecured load could be logs, fill dirt—or maybe it was furniture because he was moving. The timeline fit to when Carroll said Lampo left Watersmeet.

"Where was he when he got the second one?"

"Bumbletown, Michigan. It was issued by the Keweenaw County sheriff's office."

Sheriff Nurmi's county—friendly territory.

He thanked her, hung up and grabbed the map from between the seats. It took him a few seconds to find Bumbletown, a tiny speck of a place north of Houghton, smack in the middle of the Keweenaw Peninsula.

"Why do you have the map out?"

Louis turned to see Steele standing next to the open door of the Explorer. "We need to head north to Keweenaw," Louis said.

"Got an address for Lampo?"

"No, but I have a feeling that's where he moved to. He got a ticket up there in '86, five years ago for hauling an unsafe load."

Steele stared at him. "So . . ."

"So maybe he was hauling his stuff to a new home."

Steele glanced at his watch then looked toward the trees, thinking. They had one more business to check out, a bar and grill in Ironwood, an hour's drive west near the Wisconsin state line. Keweenaw County was two hours north. And the clock was ticking.

Louis pressed his case. "Listen, we can split up to save time," he said. "I'll call for a car and head to Keweenaw and you—"

"No," Steele said. "We stay together. And we're going north."

CHAPTER THIRTY-THREE

They were just past Calumet when it occurred to Louis that he should call Camille and tell her to send the fax of Lampo's license photo to Nurmi's office.

He reached for the cell phone.

"Who are you calling?" Steele asked.

"Sheriff Nurmi. I thought—"

"Hang up," Steele said.

"Sir, once we get past Houghton we might not get a signal and it will be after five when we get there."

"I said hang up."

Louis set the cell back in its cradle and turned on the wipers. "Sir, I believe it's professional courtesy to let another agency know that we're coming."

"Not in this case," Steele said. "And not in this place."

"Why?"

"I don't want Nurmi or anyone trying to play hero by either confronting Lampo or tipping him off. We don't need them closing ranks against us to protect one of their own."

The finality in Steele's voice told Louis the subject was closed. For the next two miles, the only sound was the *slap-thump-slap-thump* of the wipers on the windshield. Louis glanced over at Steele. He was staring out his side window at the endless blur of asphalt lined by brown-gray trees.

The Explorer was silent again for miles, until Louis spotted the sign that marked the turnoff to Eagle River.

"Sheriff Nurmi," Louis said. "He's a good man."

"Why do you feel compelled to tell me that?" Steele asked.

"What you said about somebody trying to be a hero. And I was remembering what you told me before I came up here last week for the boys-in-the-box case."

Steele nodded slowly. "That we can't let small town sheriffs get in our way."

When Steele said nothing else, Louis decided to let it go. He had no choice. Steele had come here on a slim lead and Louis's instincts. Now Louis had to trust that Steele wouldn't go bulling in here with Nurmi and blow any chance they had for cooperation.

At the police station, Louis slowed to let Steele enter first. The deputy at the radio console looked up as they entered.

Steele showed his badge. "We're here to see Sheriff Nurmi, please."

The cop's eyes widened slightly at the sight of the badge but before he could say anything, Monica stepped forward. She gave Louis a smile but offered nothing to Steele.

"Good to see you again, Detective Kincaid," she said.

"Same here, Monica. This is my boss, Captain Steele."

"Captain," Monica said, giving him a tight nod, but the question in her eyes was for Louis—what's he doing here?

Steele looked at Louis. He didn't say a word, but Louis sensed what the man was thinking, that he wanted him to take the lead.

"We'd like to talk to the sheriff," Louis said.

"Well, he's still here," she said. "I tried to get him to leave an hour ago but he's working on some bills. Come on back."

Nurmi didn't look up when Monica opened the door. His desk was littered with papers and he was punching at an old calculator.

"Reuben, you got visitors," Monica said.

Nurmi turned his chair and squinted at them, then broke a smile when he saw Louis. "Well, hell's bells. Look who's back."

Louis motioned to Steele, one step behind. "Sheriff, this is my boss, Captain Steele."

Steele's eyes locked for a moment on Nurmi's wheelchair then he came forward, hand extended. "Sheriff, good to meet you."

They shook hands. Nurmi's eyes filled with the same question that had been in Monica's eyes. "Take a chair," he said.

Louis took off his windbreaker and sat down. Steele decided to assume a rigid stance near the file cabinet. He seemed uncomfortable in this homey, cramped, and very hot office.

Nurmi looked at Monica, who was lingering at the door, obviously too curious to leave. "Monica, I was supposed to take the groceries over to Ted. You mind dropping them off? I'll be home soon as I can."

"Now Reuben, you—"

"I'll be home soon."

Monica pursed her lips, picked up the brown shopping bag from the floor beside the desk, and left, shutting the door behind her.

"Ted Jackson lives alone way out on Garden City Creek," Nurmi said. "He busted up his leg last month, so I've been checking in on him to make sure he's got what he needs." He was looking directly at Steele as he said this, maybe with a need to impress the state police captain the only way he could—with small town values.

"I started out working for my uncle in a small town," Steele said, "It goes with the job."

Louis knew Steele's uncle had been a sheriff in a rural county downstate. But there seemed to be no affection or pride for him in Steele's voice.

"So, you got something new on the boys in the box?" Nurmi asked.

Louis sat forward in his chair. "We're here on a different case, Sheriff. And we'd like your help."

"Anything I can do," Nurmi said. "What ya got?"

Louis laid out the basics about Jonas Prince's murder, their investigation on Anthony and the sketchy leads on Buddy Lampo that had brought them to Eagle River.

When Louis was done, Nurmi sat still for a moment, then stacked the papers on his desk and set them in a wooden in-box.

"Guess the big Eagle River marijuana raid will have to wait," Nurmi said.

"Pardon?" Louis said.

"I got a tip that a couple brothers out by Copper Falls were running a marijuana farm. I couldn't get a search warrant, but I could check their power bills. Nobody up here pays $900 a month to heat an empty barn, so I—"

"Sheriff," Steele said. "Time is critical here."

Nurmi glanced at Louis, but when he leaned back in his wheelchair, he was staring at Steele. "Okay then, let's talk about your case. Interesting theory you've come up with. But it seems to me that what you really got here is a house of cards."

Steele pushed off the wall. "Excuse me?"

"Your case, or at least your reason for coming up here, is built on a big stack of *ifs*," Nurmi said. "If that guy lurking outside Jonas's house wasn't Lampo, your house of cards folds. If that Weems guy didn't remember *sisu*, it folds. If your man Anthony wasn't spooked by the sketch in the newspaper, it folds. If your nursery man didn't really recognize Lampo, it folds. If Lampo was just moving tree stumps instead of his furniture, it folds."

Steele took a step closer to Nurmi's desk, not threatening, but it was an invasion of Nurmi's space. But Nurmi smiled, almost as if he knew he had to diffuse Steele.

"Look," Nurmi said. "I know you gentlemen are really smart. And I have to give it to you, it takes balls to come all the way up here on nothing but your gut feeling. Hell, I'd even call it *sisu*."

It was a compliment, but Louis wasn't sure Steele understood that.

"You got a photo of this guy?" Nurmi asked.

Louis reached into his briefcase and retrieved the sketch from the Weems interview. Nurmi pulled it across the desk, studied it then shook his head. "This all you got?"

"Call Camille," Steele said to Louis. "Have her fax Lampo's DL here."

Louis used the desk phone to call Camille and asked her to fax Lampo's driver license photo. When he asked her if she had been able to dig up any additional information on Lampo, she said she hadn't.

"The fax will be here in a minute," Louis said when he hung up. "But she's got nothing else. After Lampo moved from Watersmeet, it looks like he just dropped off the grid."

"And this is the perfect place to do that," Nurmi added.

Steele unbuttoned his coat and yanked at his tie, finally surrendering to the heat. The silence was broken by the whirr of the fax machine on the credenza behind Nurmi's desk. Nurmi turned and pulled out the paper. After he studied it, he handed it to Louis.

"I don't know him," Nurmi said.

Louis stared at the black and white image on Lampo's driver's license. It was surprisingly sharp. It showed a thin-faced man with a long nose, shaggy hair and close-set eyes. The man in the license photo had a beard, the man in Weems sketch did not. And even though he knew the DL photo was five years old, and beards could come and go, disappointment started to gather in a dark cloud in his head.

Then he saw it. The eyes, the damn eyes, as empty, gray and sad as this godforsaken place. The eyes in both the sketch and the photo were the same. And they were the same eyes, he realized, that he had looked into once before. But where? Damn it, where?

"I've seen him," Louis said.

Steele snatched the sketch from Louis's hand and stared at it. "Where? Up here?" he asked.

Louis nodded. "On my first trip, but I can't place where. But I know it was here in Keweenaw. I know it."

Steele thrust the sketch at Nurmi. "Look again, sheriff," he said. "And this time take a good look."

Nurmi didn't reach for the paper. His blue eyes had iced over, and Louis had the feeling that if he had been able to stand up, he would have punched Steele.

"You think I'd circle the wagons around a wanted man just because he's a local?" Nurmi asked.

That's exactly what Steele thought, Louis knew, but he'd never admit it.

"No," Steele said. "I just want you to be sure."

"I'm sure," Nurmi said.

Silence filled the office, the kind that makes a small place even smaller.

"Where's your copy machine, sheriff?" Steele asked.

"Across the hall."

Steele left the office, leaving the door open. A moment later, Louis heard the steady *click-clap* of the copy machine.

"Intense man, your boss," Nurmi said.

Louis nodded. "It's just this case," he said. "And like you said, we're working on a lot of *ifs*."

"Well, when your boss gets back with Lampo's picture, I'll distribute it to my men and start a county-wide canvass," Nurmi said. "Somebody up here will know where he lives."

Louis looked up at the mitten clock. It was just after five. What daylight they had would vanish by nine, but Louis didn't think that would stop Steele. He'd search all night if he had to. And up here, the night could be a very dark place.

Louis heard the squeak of a drawer opening and looked back at Nurmi. He was digging for something in his desk. Louis's gaze moved to the folders in the in-box, and a scrawl of writing on one of the tabs. UPPCO.

"What's UPPCO?" Louis asked.

"Our local power company."

"May I?" Louis asked, motioning toward the file.

"Sure. Take a look."

Inside the folder were dozens of old electric bills for the weed farmers.

"You said you couldn't get a warrant for a search of the farm," Louis said. "How'd you get these bills?"

"I play Euchre every Thursday with the company president," Nurmi said. "I told you, up here, when you take care of people in their time of need, they'll take care of you."

"Would your friend be open to providing us an electric bill address for Buddy Lampo?"

Nurmi smiled. "That's a helluva idea. Though I might have to bribe him with a bottle of scotch."

"On me."

Nurmi punched at an intercom button on his phone. "Lenny, get Hank Mooreland on the phone, would ya? And if he's not at his office, chase him down. I need him."

"Will do, sheriff."

Steele came back carrying a stack of copies. "You got a photo of Anthony Prince in your briefcase?" he asked Louis.

Louis nodded. "Yeah, why?"

"Get it for me."

Louis opened his briefcase and grabbed the headshot of Anthony he had shown around Grand Rapids. He handed it to Steele.

Steele set it on Nurmi's desk then added one of the copies he had just made. It was an enlargement of Lampo's driver's license image, bringing Lampo's face into stark focus.

"What do you see?" Steele asked.

Louis stared at the two pictures, silent.

Steele took two blank papers and positioned them to cover the upper and lower portions of each face, leaving only the two sets of eyes exposed.

Louis saw it immediately.

Anthony and Buddy Lampo. They had the same eyes. They could have been the same man. But since they weren't, there was only one explanation.

Louis looked to Steele. "Nathan Prince isn't dead. Buddy Lampo is Anthony's brother."

CHAPTER THIRTY-FOUR

There were a thousand questions in his head. Why had the family told everyone that Nathan Prince was dead? How did Nathan end up here, in the most remote spot in the state, while the rest of his family migrated downstate? Why was he living under the name Buddy Lampo?

Then Louis remembered something Emily had said outside the cathedral when she was recounting the Prinsilla family history.

We have a three-year gap in their history that spans their time in Wisconsin to their arrival in Vandalia.

"Captain, you remember those missing years from the Prince family records that Emily told us about?" Louis said. "They had to have spent that time here, in the Upper Peninsula. This is where Nathan became separated from his father and brother."

Steele was looking at the two photos and nodded. "It might explain why Anthony Prince would come way up here. Lampo's the only family he has left."

Louis couldn't get the one question out of his head—the *why*. "Nathan Prince would have only been twelve or thirteen when Jonas went downstate," he said. "Why would they just leave him here? Why would Jonas abandon one of sons and tell people he was dead?"

"We don't know what happened to Nathan thirty years ago," Steele said. "And at the moment, it's not important. What is important is what happened between these two men the night Jonas Prince was murdered and in the days after."

Louis nodded, realizing there had been an edge in his own voice.

Steele started. "Let's lay this out with the new information we have. We know Weems saw Lampo outside Jonas's house."

"Jonas was upset the night before he was killed and changed his sermon at the last minute," Louis said. "Maybe it was because he and Lampo talked."

"What was the new sermon about?" Nurmi asked.

"Forgiveness," Steele said quickly. "Louis, pick it up from there."

"This is what I think happened," Louis said. "Lampo confronted his father about something, something that upset Jonas. Then after the evening service, Jonas and Anthony met in the dressing room, probably to talk about his brother's visit. But it didn't go well. Jonas may have said something or was going to do something, and Anthony lost it. He killed him in a rage."

Louis paused. Four minutes, Emily had said, that's about how long it took to strangle someone.

"Then what happened?" Nurmi asked.

"Anthony went to dinner at his usual restaurant," Steele said. "Maybe because it was habit, maybe to establish an alibi. He later took out his guilt and rage out on his hooker. Once he had composed himself, he came back to the cathedral to stage the scene at the altar."

"It was more than staging," Louis said. "His OCD demanded he clean up his mess and his faith demanded an act of contrition. He accomplished both by laying his father out in full regalia at the base of the cross."

"Sounds more like blasphemy to me," Nurmi said.

Louis nodded but didn't offer a deeper explanation. To normal men, putting a murder victim on an altar probably would be sacrilegious. But Anthony was not a normal man. He was a vessel of fragile faith with conflicting compulsions that seemed to rattle around inside him like shards of broken glass.

A cracked jug.

Nurmi's intercom buzzed. "Hank Moreland on line one, sheriff."

Nurmi picked up his phone. Steele took out a handkerchief to wipe his face, but when he heard Nurmi mention Buddy Lampo's name, he walked over to Louis.

"Who's he talking to?" Steele asked.

"President of the local power company," Louis said. "He's trying to get a service address for Lampo."

Steele nodded. "Good thinking."

Nurmi hung up the phone. "Hank's in Calumet. It's going to take him about twenty minutes to get back to the office."

"Thank you," Louis said.

"While we're waiting," Nurmi said. "Can I ask you fellas another question?"

"Feel free," Steele said.

"If Buddy Lampo was at the reverend's home earlier in the day," Nurmi said, "what makes you think he wasn't the one at the cathedral later that night?"

Nurmi's implication was clear and almost insulting. Had they dismissed Lampo as the killer too soon?

Louis answered before Steele could. "We did consider him a suspect," he said. "But we had no ID and we couldn't put a stranger like him at the cathedral. And at the time there was no other link to Jonas, nothing that would have indicated he had knowledge of or access to the private areas of the church."

"But now you have that link," Nurmi said. "He was family. He was the man's son. Maybe he had been there before, maybe his brother let him in. Either way, you gentlemen might just have found yourselves the real killer."

Louis looked down at the two photos on the desk, rethinking every decision he had made in the last few weeks. Reason told him there was no way he could have seen this brother connection coming—the evidence had just not been there until this moment. But a different part of his brain was kicking hard at his ego.

Steele seemed unruffled. "All right," he said. "Let's flip everything. Lampo decides to go downstate to see a father we believed was estranged.

Maybe he needed money. Maybe he wanted to make amends. But his father blows him off. Maybe even lectures him on forgiveness. So Lampo stews about it for the next eight hours and after the service, slips into the church and takes his revenge."

Louis shook his head. "It doesn't work. We know Jonas's body was dressed and moved after midnight. Lampo wouldn't have been able to get back in the cathedral at that hour or back into the dressing room. Anthony had that key."

"What if they did it together?" Nurmi asked.

Louis and Steele both looked at Nurmi. The sheriff gave a shrug, like it made perfect sense to him.

"Maybe they all met in that dressing room to sort out some family drama," he said. "And the younger brother gets the short end of the deal, just like he got thirty years ago. He goes off on dad. Anthony panics and tells him to high-tail out of town and that he'll clean up the mess."

"No," Steele said. "A man like Anthony Prince would not risk his reputation and prison to protect someone he hasn't seen in years. Not even a brother."

"You must be an only child," Nurmi said.

Steele looked quickly at Nurmi. Louis didn't think Nurmi meant it as insult, but clearly Steele was taking it as one.

"He's right, captain," Louis said.

Steele looked at him. "How so?"

"We know what life was like for these kids," Louis said. "Living hand to mouth in small towns, a moral rock of a father, a mother who gave so much away to strangers. All these two kids had was each other and that creates a powerful kind of bond. One that's not easily broken."

Steele was quiet. The look on his face not sympathetic but thoughtful.

A deputy appeared at the door, carrying an evidence box and a pad of paper. "Sorry to interrupt," he said. "Sheriff, I need to you look this over. I gotta get it to the DA by six."

Louis stepped back to let him pass. The deputy set the box on the desk and started talking to Nurmi about an affidavit he was writing.

Louis picked up the photos of Lampo and Anthony to get them out of Nurmi's way and took a moment to examine them again. The resemblance was easy to see now, but Louis also noticed something else.

Differences. Subtle differences, created not by their DNA, but by what had life had done to them. Anthony Prince . . . pale and pampered. Buddy Lampo . . . bark-rough and bent by winter winds.

"Excuse me, Louis," Nurmi said. "I got to get something there behind you."

Louis looked up to see Nurmi trying to maneuver his wheelchair closer to the bookshelf. He wedged himself into the corner while Nurmi rifled through his cluttered shelves.

"Shoot," Nurmi said, looking down at a Fed Ex envelope in his hand. "I forgot about this. It came for you this morning, Louis. You must have put my name in the wrong blank on the form because they sent it to me by mistake."

Louis took the envelope. The return address was the forensic lab in Marquette. He glanced at Steele, who was standing at the window trying not to look impatient, then opened the envelope. There was one paper and a small manila envelope inside. Louis read the report, which detailed "Item submitted for examination."

FP1 1 One (1) package containing circular metal object diameter 25 mm

RESULTS OF ANALYSIS

It was the medal he had found in the mine. Louis opened the clasp on the small envelope and shook the medal out into his palm. Except for a few spots of tarnish, it was almost as shiny as a newly minted coin. The etching showed the head and shoulders of a benignly smiling man, flanked by two boys who seemed to be looking up at the man with adoration. Without his glasses, Louis couldn't read the small etched letters over the man's head. He turned back to the form and read the results: Acid cleaning and examination of the object reveals medallion, composition silver, age unknown. Front reveals three (3) human figures and words SAINT JOHN BOSCO PRAY FOR US.

Louis stared at the image. He had seen this Bosco person before, but he wasn't sure where. He had been in so many churches lately he couldn't even make a guess.

He turned over the medal. There was an inscription on the back, too tiny to read.

"Damn it," Louis said. He grabbed his reading glasses from his pocket and slipped them on. The inscription was faint, only five words.

To my good son Antero

Antero. Antero Prinsilla. Anthony Prince.

Suddenly, everything around him blurred and grew distant and it was just him and the medal and those five words carved into the silver.

Louis realized he wasn't breathing and he drew a deliberate breath, then another, before he looked across the office at Steele.

"Captain," he said. "A moment, please. Outside."

CHAPTER THIRTY-FIVE

As Louis led Steele outside, his brain was in overdrive, flashing back on everything that he had seen and heard on his first trip up here and struggling to connect all of it to what was happening now.

They stopped on the front lawn. Steele pulled his collar up against the drizzle. "Talk to me, Louis."

"He killed the boys. Anthony Prince killed my boys."

"What are you talking about?"

"The missing years in Emily's report, they were spent here," Louis said. "And they left here because of the boys in the box, because Anthony killed those boys. This proves it."

Louis held out the medal and Steele took it, examining it slowly. But when he looked up his face was blank.

And Louis knew why. "You didn't read my reports on the boys in the box, did you?"

Steele squared his shoulders. "No, I didn't. I set them aside. Your cold case was on hold and Jonas Prince took priority. We talked about this."

Louis turned away and walked a small circle. He wasn't even sure who he was mad at—Steele? Anthony Prince? Louis turned back to Steele, but he had disappeared. Louis finally spotted him, taking shelter from the rain under the aluminum awning that housed the county cruisers.

As Louis approached, Steele was looking at him the same way he had looked at Cam across the conference table, like a lab clinician studying the behavior of genetically altered rats.

"All right, tell me now," Steele said. "Tell me about this medal."

"The remains of the two boys were in an old candle box that had been left in an abandoned copper mine," Louis said. "When I went to the mine, I found that medal in the area where the box had been found. The box was discovered in 1979, but the medal couldn't have been there then or the forensics team would've found it. Someone had to have put it there later and I think it was Anthony."

Steele looked at the metal's image of the man and the boys. "The Prince family is Methodist, and their symbol is the Luther Rose. It isn't common for non-Catholics to wear or carry saint medals."

Louis remembered the two other times he had seen the Saint Bosco figure. "This medal meant something important to Jonas Prince. This same image is on a prayer card I found in his home and it's on the keychain to his dressing room."

Steele fell silent, turning the medal over in his hand.

"The medal was important to Anthony, too," Louis said.

Steele shook his head slowly. "I can maybe buy the idea that the medal meant something special to Jonas. He was a devout man. But Anthony Prince is not . . ." Steele paused. "He is not guided by the same forces. So why would he leave a Catholic medal in the cave? Especially one with his name on it?"

"I don't know," Louis said. "Maybe it was his way of immortalizing the act, just like the way he plasters his walls with plaques. Or maybe he was just upset because the bones were no longer in what he considered their proper place."

Steele handed the medal back to Louis. "Now we know why Lampo made that sudden trip down to Grand Rapids," he said.

"What do you mean?"

PJ PARRISH

"It can't be a coincidence that he drove nine hours to go see a father he hadn't seen in thirty years on the same day we reopened this case. He must have gotten wind of it."

"It's a small town," Louis said. "People—"

Steele silenced him with a hand. "Weems said he saw a man outside Jonas's house on Wednesday morning. For Buddy Lampo to be there at that time he had to leave here Tuesday night. The same Tuesday you arrived here. That only leaves a couple hours for him to hear something, and that tells me there was a leak." He looked to the station house. "And I'd bet the leak came from inside that building, maybe from Nurmi himself."

Louis shook his head. "I called the sheriff and told him I was coming. He had someone pull the case file and make copies. Deputies were in and out. When people see a state police car parked out front here, they get curious. I don't think it was a leak. It could have come from anybody."

"Who else did you talk to?" Steele asked.

Again, Louis did a mental review of everyone he had encountered on his first trip here. Faces floated into his head—the waitress who had served him his hamburger. The bartender at the Eagle River Inn who had poured his whiskey. The girl who had served him coffee the next morning. All of them had seen him working on the file or asked about the case. But the face he couldn't conjure up was Lampo's. He was sure he had seen him somewhere before, but he couldn't remember talking to him.

Cam's technique . . . the one he had used on Weems.

Louis closed his eyes and lowered his head.

"What are you doing?" Steele asked.

"Bear with me," Louis said.

He took himself back to when he pulled up to the front door of the station. The brisk wind and the smell of the coming snow. The Band-Aid on the chin of the deputy he passed as he walked into the outer office. The place was hot, over-heated. No one else was there except . . . Monica, wearing a pink sweatshirt with SISU printed on the front.

Louis kept going back in his memory. The firm, moist grip of Nurmi's hand as he greeted him. The cold mist on his face as he went back outside,

280

the jangle of the evidence room keys in hand, and then walking across the grass to the . . .

Louis looked up and opened his eyes. Right in front of him stood the old, pillared courthouse. There was no one outside today, but there had been someone there that day. A man holding a rake and wearing a ball cap. The man who had given him directions to the Eagle River Inn. The man who had asked . . .

You from downstate? What you looking for?

Louis remembered clearly what he had answered.

Just some evidence. And an old candle box.

It was a simple question. But his answer, and what came after, had set off a murderous chain of events.

Louis looked back at Steele. "It was me," he said.

"What?"

"I was the one who tipped Buddy Lampo off," Louis said. "I told you inside I had recognized Lampo from somewhere before. I met him over there at the courthouse. He had to let me in. And he asked me in passing what I was looking for. I told him I was looking for an old candle box."

Steele looked toward the station door and he was quiet.

It had been an accident, him running into Anthony's brother. No, it wasn't an accident. It was worse. Just a weird but deadly twist of fate. Wasn't it?

Louis heard a door close and turned. Nurmi had come down the ramp of the side door and was rolling across the parking lot toward them.

"How did Nurmi not recognize a man who works next door?" Steele said. "I still think he's holding out, maybe protecting someone."

There was no time to answer before Nurmi got to them.

"Hank got a hit at the UPPCO office," Nurmi said. "I got an address for Buddy Lampo."

"Where?" Louis asked.

"It's south of here, down near Conglomerate Falls," Nurmi said. "Cabins out there are few and far between and the roads not much more than trails."

281

Steele looked at his watch. "I'm going to get some backup rolling. We'll also request Blue Falcon air support be on stand-by."

Steele walked away. Nurmi's gaze followed him until he disappeared inside the station, then he looked back at Louis.

"Maybe you ought to give that bottle of scotch to your boss," Nurmi said. "Loosen him up a little."

"He doesn't drink when he's on a case."

"Maybe he should."

Louis said nothing, still thinking about Steele's last comment about the sheriff.

"So what was in that FedEx envelope from Marquette?"

Louis knew Steele wouldn't want Nurmi to be more involved in all this, but Nurmi was invested in the boys in the box case. He deserved to know what was going on.

Louis showed him the medal. "It's something I found in the mine where the candle box was."

Nurmi took the medal and examined it, concentrating on the inscription. It was a long moment before he looked up at Louis.

"Damn," he said. "There's two little boys on the front of this thing."

Louis nodded. "I remember now where I saw Lampo. He's the guy who let me in the courthouse the day I picked up the evidence. Sheriff, I have to ask you again. Do you know Buddy Lampo?"

Nurmi frowned and looked toward the courthouse. When he turned back, Louis scrutinized his face for some reaction or recognition, but Nurmi's expression was blank.

"I'm sorry," he said. "I still can't place him. They hire a lot of day workers over there, vets, homeless guys. I swear I never saw him."

Louis hesitated. "Okay. I believe you."

"But I bet your boss doesn't."

Nurmi gave the medal back to Louis and looked back toward the station. Steele was coming out, zipping up his windbreaker against the chill.

"Let's go," he said to Louis and headed toward the Explorer. Louis slipped the medal into the pocket of his jeans and hurried to catch up.

"Captain!"

Louis turned at the sound of Nurmi's voice. Steele had stopped as well.

"I'd like to ride along," Nurmi said.

Steele's eyes moved to the wheelchair. But Louis knew it wasn't the chair he was concerned about, it was the man himself.

"Sheriff, I think—" Steele began.

"You think I'd be in the way," Nurmi finished for him.

"This is a state operation," Steele said.

"You'll never find Lampo's place without some help."

Louis waited as the two men stared at each other.

"All right, let's go," Steele said. He headed to the Explorer.

"I'll go get my gear," Nurmi said to Louis, and rolled off toward the ramp.

Louis jogged to the Explorer and got in the driver's seat. He started the engine and pulled around the station, parking at the bottom of the ramp at the side door. He and Steele sat there, with the heat on high and the wipers on low.

"I asked him about Lampo working at the courthouse," Louis said. "He said there are lots of day workers. He swears he didn't recognize him."

"He stays in this only as long as he's useful," Steele said.

The tone in his voice told Louis the subject was closed. It was warm in the Explorer, but every muscle in Louis's body felt cold and tight. He dug the medal out of his jeans pocket, not sure why he wanted to look at it again.

"Do you know who Saint John Bosco is?" Steele asked.

"I'm sorry," Louis said. "What?"

"Saint Bosco," Steele said, nodding toward the medal. "Do you know who he is?"

"No."

"He's the patron saint of lost boys."

Louis looked out the dirty windshield toward the station's side door. "No disrespect, captain," he said, "but it seems to me that in this case, Saint Bosco wasn't very good at his job."

CHAPTER THIRTY-SIX

The road to Buddy Lampo's cabin was a cracked strip of asphalt that ran south out of Eagle River along the shoreline of the Keweenaw Peninsula. As Louis drove, he caught flashes of the metallic roiling waters of Lake Superior to his right, but then the road turned inland and there was nothing but walls of giant pines, their trunks shrouded in the fog.

Nurmi said he had a fair idea of where the cabin might be because he had hunted in the area before his accident. There were only a handful of houses, he added, most used as hunting cabins or occupied by hermit-types who stockpiled guns for Armageddon.

The Explorer led a small caravan of two county Jeeps and two state patrol cruisers. They were looking for Farmers Block Road, which would take them uphill to the cabin. There was nothing beyond the cabin, Nurmi said. The road ended at Split Mountain Gorge.

"There's the turn up ahead," Nurmi said.

Louis slowed and made the turn onto a dirt road. About a mile later, the road veered right.

"Wait, stop!" Nurmi said.

Louis stopped the Explorer.

Nurmi leaned forward from the back seat. "Go left here."

Louis peered through the dirty windshield. The fork to the left was a rutted one-lane mud track. "You sure?"

Nurmi hesitated. "Yeah, yeah, I'm sure."

Louis turned left, but they made it only about fifty yards before the Explorer tires caught deep mud and they came to a hard stop. So did the Jeep behind them.

Louis hit the wipers to clear the mud from the windshield and stared at the trail ahead. Maybe six feet wide and carved with deep ruts and puddles, it curved upward into the hulking pine trees, where it was devoured by the fog.

Steele grabbed the radio and instructed his two state troopers, driving low-riding cruisers, to secure the turn-off in case Lampo somehow managed to elude them and double back. That wasn't likely since this was only road to the gorge, Nurmi said, but he added that there could be trails known only to the locals. Steele instructed Nurmi's two Jeeps to stay with the Explorer.

Louis shifted into four-wheel drive and moved forward, mud pulling at the tires. As he picked up a little speed, the truck bounced and jolted.

"How far on this?" Louis asked Nurmi.

"Not sure. It's not like we can check mailboxes out here."

Louis leaned forward, trying to get better visibility through the muck covered windshield. He hadn't seen a house or any kind of building since they had left the main road out of Eagle River. He didn't even recall seeing any power lines along Farmers Block Road, and he was starting to get a hard pit in his stomach, thinking that this was a waste of time.

He glanced at Steele, seeing the same doubt in his face. Then Steele rolled his window down and stuck his head out, hawking the thick trees for any sign of human presence.

"Keweenaw seven to S.O. one."

"That's me," Nurmi said, grabbing his portable radio from his belt. "Go ahead, seven."

"Be advised we're bogged down here," the deputy said.

"Is Keweenaw six with you?" Nurmi asked.

"Right behind us. We're blocking him."

Louis looked in the rearview mirror. The county Jeep was angled sideways, quickly becoming a green and white blur in the spray of mud.

"Sir, do we stop?" Louis asked.

285

"No. We'll never get traction again." Steele swung around to talk to Nurmi. "Tell your officers we're going on and we'll wait for them at the top."

The road was narrowing, branches scraping against the truck, but it didn't seem to bother Steele—he was still hanging out the window. Louis watched the odometer as they rumbled higher up the hill and deeper into the forest. Half-a mile. Then a mile.

"You guys smell that?" Steele asked.

"It's smoke," Louis said.

When Steele dropped back into his seat, he looked like he'd been hit with a brown paint ball. "There's a dry place up there to stop, next to that downed birch," he said.

Louis eased the Explorer toward the bed of pine needles on what he hoped was solid ground. When he stopped, he rolled down his window. It was definitely chimney smoke. Steele grabbed the radio mic and identified himself to the regional command post in Houghton.

"Is Blue Falcon in the air?"

"Negative. They are delaying take-off until visibility improves. It's pea soup here."

Steele swore softly under his breath before he keyed the mic again. "Be advised, we are approximately three miles southwest from the Five Mile Road turnoff onto Farmer Block Road, on the left fork of a heavy-mud trail heading uphill. We need some off-road back-up headed to our location ASAP."

"Ten-four, captain."

Steele pushed open his door and got out. Louis followed, joining Steele at the open hatch at the rear of the Explorer. Steele grabbed two Kevlar vests and thrust one at Louis.

"We're going up to take a closer look," Steele said. "Get the binoculars and find out where Nurmi's guys are."

Louis secured his vest and went back to retrieve the binoculars from the compartment between the seats.

"What's the twenty of your guys?" he asked Nurmi.

"Still stuck," Nurmi said. "They got a tow truck coming that can get through muck. They'll be here."

"Okay, good. We're going up the hill."

"I guess I'm the lookout, eh?" Nurmi asked.

"I guess so. Are you good here?"

"I'm good," Nurmi said, patting the rifle lying across his knees. Louis had to admire him. He seemed incredibly calm for a crippled man about to be left out in the middle of nowhere with a killer on the loose.

"Hey, Louis," Nurmi said. "You watch your butt up there. Men around here have more guns than sense."

"I hear you," Louis said.

Louis closed the door and hustled to catch Steele, who was already fifteen feet up the road. They crept along the sloppy edge of the trail, hoping to stay camouflaged by the forest, but in the still smoky air, every snap of every stick sounded like the racking of a shotgun.

They followed the smell of the chimney smoke for twenty yards before a green cabin came into view. It was small, with a sagging planked porch that ran the length of the cabin. The door was closed. There was maybe eight feet of cleared ground between the cabin and the platoon of trees that circled it. Just enough room left for a stack of firewood and a rusted-out Trailmaker snowmobile. There was no white truck and no Honda Civic. And the ground was too rutted and messy to define any fresh tracks.

Louis brought the binoculars to his eyes and focused on the small front window. There was a dim light on inside. He watched for a long time, but he saw nothing moving beyond the dirty glass of the cabin windows.

"Looks empty," Louis said. "But I can't be sure."

"We're going in," Steele said.

Louis lowered the binoculars and looked at Steele. As a PI, he had gone in guns blazing plenty of times, but now things were different. Now he was bound by rules and procedures. It surprised him that Steele wasn't being more cautious.

"We're not waiting for back-up?" Louis asked.

Steele glanced up to the smoky, silent sky. "You see any coming?"

"No, sir."

Steele pushed to his feet and drew his gun. "Okay then. You want the front or the back?"

"I'll take the front."

"On my go," Steele said.

Steele moved back into the trees to work his way around to the rear of the cabin. Louis drew his Glock and stepped quietly through the brush, getting as close as he could before slipping from the cover of the trees to the porch.

He looked through the filthy window and could make out the outlines of furniture but no people. He dipped under the window to the door. It had a rusty deadbolt. He dreaded the idea of having to kick it in. It wasn't as easy as Hollywood made it look. When he turned the knob, he was surprised to find it was unlocked.

Steele appeared on the opposite end of the porch and flattened himself against the cabin.

"No back door," he whispered.

Louis pushed open the door so hard that it slammed against the wall.

"Police!" he shouted.

He slipped inside, gun drawn, sweeping the dimly-lit interior in one glance. A black pot-bellied stove. Sofa heaped with blankets. End table with one small lamp, beer bottles, and ashtrays. A dusty wood floor covered in newspapers, magazines, socks and fast food bags. A gun rack on the wall—four empty slots.

Steele flashed by on his left, moving quickly toward an open bathroom door. To his right, Louis had full view of a kitchenette—empty but with the counters heaped with dirty dishes and more beer bottles.

"Clear!" Steele yelled from behind him.

"Police!" Louis shouted again, moving toward the only other doorway, a back bedroom. "If you're in here, show yourself!"

The bedroom was tiny, maybe ten feet square, just enough room for a narrow bed and a small dresser. There was no door on the closet and Louis could see sweatshirts, flannel shirts, and a camouflage jacket hanging from the pole. A pile of blue jeans lay in a heap on the floor.

"Clear!" Louis shouted.

He turned to leave, then noticed the bed. It was neatly made up with a smooth white pillow and blue and white quilt. The diamonds in the quilt's pattern were in perfect alignment to the edge of the mattress, and the hem was positioned exactly parallel to the dusty floor. Louis focused in on the few other things in the room—a spotlessly-clean dresser and a swept floor. Except for the jeans at the bottom of the closet, the bedroom was neat and orderly, in sharp contrast to the mess of the rest of the cabin.

"Captain, come look at this," Louis called.

Steele appeared behind him. "What?"

"Look at this room compared to the rest of the place."

Steele entered the bedroom. "What are you thinking?"

"Anthony would do this. He was here."

"Maybe, but it's not enough," Steele said, walking away. "We need to find something solid. We don't even know for sure this is Lampo's place."

Louis started in the bedroom, rifling the dresser drawers and shuffling the clothes on the hangars, but except for the perfectly-made bed, nothing looked odd or out of place. No expensive shirts. No gin bottles. No Vuitton duffle.

He went back to the main room and sifted through the yellowed newspapers and old gun magazines. He tossed the sofa cushions and blankets then dropped to his knees to check under the sofa. Just dirt, coins, and a dead mouse.

Steele was searching the kitchen and Louis could tell by the loud rattle of pans and slamming of cupboard doors that he was getting frustrated.

Louis moved to the dinette table, an old aluminum thing with a scratched yellow Formica top. On top was a bottle of Miller beer and a paper plate with a half-eaten cheese sandwich next to a messy pile of papers.

Louis began to sift through the papers and finally got a hit—a receipt from an auto repair shop in Ahmeek with Buddy Lampo's name on it.

"Captain!" Louis called.

Steele looked out from the kitchen.

Louis held up the receipt. "It has Lampo's name on it."

Steele nodded tightly and wiped his sweating brow. The pot-bellied stove had made the cabin stifling.

Louis looked down at the beer bottle on the table. It was sweating, and when he touched the bottle it was cold. And the bread on the sandwich was soft.

"Sir, they must've had a view of the road below and saw us coming," Louis said. "They bailed."

"You mean Buddy Lampo bailed."

"No, I mean *they*. Both of them."

Steele was still holding the plastic trash can he had been digging through. He tossed it to the floor. "Buddy Lampo is not our fugitive," he said. "Anthony Prince is. And he's not here. And maybe he never was."

"We don't know that," Louis said. "Keep searching."

Steele yanked open a drawer, pulled out a shoebox and threw the lid aside. Louis watched as he angrily sorted through a mess of papers and pictures, scattering them to the floor. Louis was about to say something when Steele stopped. He was staring at a yellowed paper.

He looked up at the ceiling and let out a hard breath.

"What is it?" Louis asked.

Steele held out the paper and Louis took it. It was a baptismal certificate.

This is to certify that Buddy S. Lampo, infant son of George and Doris Lampo, was baptized in the name of our Lord, the Father and the Holy Ghost on June 22, 1955 in Watersmeet, Michigan . . .

Louis looked back at Steele. "Shit."

Steele reared back and kicked the trash can across the room.

Louis stared at the certificate, not wanting to believe what he was seeing. But the math didn't lie. The certificate was issued in 1955. Nathan Prince was living in Oulu in 1955 with his family.

Louis lowered the certificate and wiped his sweating face. They were wrong. Wrong about everything. Wrong about Nathan Prince living as Buddy Lampo. Wrong about Anthony having any reason to come here. And wrong to have chased this crazy theory, all on Louis's hunch.

"Nurmi was right," Steele said. "We had a fucking house of cards, a shit-pile of *ifs* and *maybes* that we convinced ourselves didn't stink."

"Sir," Louis said. "This certificate is just a new puzzle piece. It doesn't mean—"

"Work it backwards!" Steele snapped. "Anthony Prince never came up here to the U.P. because he had no *reason* to come here because Lampo is not his brother. And if Lampo is not his brother, then he's probably not the guy Weems—"

"All right!" Louis said. "I get it."

Steele raked his hair, walking now, almost pacing. "Two days," he said. "Two wasted days up here in this Godforsaken place chasing our asses. And we don't have a damn thing to show for it."

"With all due respect, captain," Louis said, "I think we've conducted a helluva investigation. Downstate and up here. We not only have an arrest warrant out for Anthony Prince, we solved two other cases. What the hell more do you want?"

"Don't you fucking get it?" Steele shouted.

"Get what?"

"Nobody cares! Nobody fucking cares about a dead hooker and couple of Johnny Does left in a candle box thirty years ago."

Louis stared at Steele. Nothing had changed. It was like they were right back in Loon Lake again, and Steele was the same ambitious bastard who saw the badge only as a mirror to reflect his own glory.

Fuck this man. Fuck this job.

"So we're back to that?" Louis asked. "Putting price tags on victims? Is that what this is about?"

Steele threw up a hand and turned away, but Louis wasn't going to let him off that easy. He didn't care what it cost him.

"I asked you a question, captain," Louis said.

291

Steele just stood there, drawing quick breaths, staring at nothing.

"Is that what this team is about? Louis demanded. "You just adding another line to your resume?"

Steele spun toward him, shouting. "No! It's not about me. It's about—"

"About what?"

Silence.

"About what, captain?" Louis yelled.

"It's about *her!*"

What? Had he heard him right?

"Her? Who's her?" Louis asked.

Steele was staring at him in a weird kind of disbelief, then he slowly turned away and moved toward the open front door, silhouetting himself in the silver ribbons of rain pouring off the roof.

"Who is her?" Louis asked again.

"Nobody," Steele said softly. "I . . . I misspoke. Let it go."

Louis looked down at the baptismal certificate in his hand then set it on the table. He had a decision to make. And he knew exactly what it might cost him—his home, his lover, his daughter and his badge. But he couldn't work for this man.

"I need some air," Louis said. "I'll meet you back down at the Explorer."

Steele closed the front door, then stepped in front of it, blocking Louis's way.

"Give me five minutes," he said.

Louis hesitated, then gave him a tight nod. "All right, talk."

It was clear from the pained look on Steele's face that any sort of confession was going to come hard.

"About a year ago," Steele said, "when I started hearing about other cities setting up cold case squads, I decided that the state needed to get on board with a team of its own and that I wanted to command it."

That didn't surprise Louis. The first cold case squad in Miami was making news by the mid-80s. The new one in Dallas, too.

"I put my plan together, secured some grants and political backing and presented it to the brass," Steele said. "But it turned out that I wasn't the only one with the idea. By the time it got to the final approval stage, I had competition."

Steele paused.

"To eliminate that competition, I used knowledge I had gained in the OPR to force my opposition to withdraw. It wasn't anything on his record, but things he knew I knew. You could say I blackmailed him."

The OPR—internal affairs for the MSP.

"Major Deforest," Louis said.

"Yes. They gave the unit to me on a probationary basis," Steele said, "But they put Deforest on a special teams oversight board. He's one of 'the living' I told you we now answer to."

"How did we go from cold cases to Jonas Prince?"

Steele raked back his hair. "The minute Grand Rapids PD saw the scene in the cathedral they knew they needed help. When I heard about it, I went over Deforest's head and asked for the case."

"Why?"

Steele rubbed his jaw. "We were an experiment, and a very expensive one. And I knew that Deforest, and others, were going undermine us every step of the way. I thought if we could notch our belts with a high-profile arrest right out of the gate, the team would be bulletproof."

Steele fell silent, exhaustion and humility shadowing his face. In a strange way, it humanized him. Enough so that Louis decided to spare him some anguish and finish his story for him.

"So they gave you a chance," Louis said. "But I'm guessing they also gave you a warning. If you screwed up the Prince case, there might not be any more, hot or cold. Am I right?"

"Yes," Steele said. "But you have to know this. This team was never about me or my career. It was always about the work that needed to be done."

Louis almost scoffed. "That rings pretty hollow coming from a man who just said no one cares about two little boys in a box."

Steele's eyes closed for a second. "I apologize for that," he said. "And I meant them—the desk jockeys and bureaucrats and politicians. And like it or not, it's not their job to care. It's ours. And I do care."

Louis was quiet. He still wondered who *her* was, but now was the not time to push for more. Steele had given him enough answers for now. In fact, he had given him more than just answers. He had revealed himself as a boss Louis could start to understand.

"What do we do now?" Louis asked.

Steele ran a hand through his hair again and looked absently around the cabin. Louis could see Steele was having trouble getting his cop brain turned back on. Louis understood. A suit of armor was a damn heavy thing to pick up and put back on after someone knocked it off.

"Sir?" Louis said.

Steele looked at him, then his eyes went to the certificate on the table next to Louis. It was a visible recovery, a straightening of the shoulders and a clarity in his eyes.

"What are we going to do now?" Louis asked again.

Steele opened the door and looked out for a long moment before he turned back to Louis. He didn't seem to have an answer. Or maybe he did but couldn't bring himself to say it.

"What does your gut tell you?" Louis asked.

Steele held Louis's eyes for a second and Louis was sure Steele was going to tell him again that the team didn't operate on instinct. But he didn't.

"My gut tells me that this Lampo guy still left here in a hurry, and we need to find out why."

"Well, we know he didn't go downhill."

Steele nodded. "That leaves us one direction. We're going up."

CHAPTER THIRTY-SEVEN

It was a bone-jarring, slip-sliding grind through thick pines. If there was any road left, Louis couldn't see it through the mud-caked windshield. He had to rely on Steele hanging out the window to guide him.

Finally, the ground flattened and the trees broke just enough to suggest they were still on a trail. When Louis steered the Explorer left around a bend, the fog lifted for a moment and he had his first good look of what was ahead.

He slammed on the brakes.

In front of them, maybe four feet ahead, was narrow bridge. Its sides were made of old, gray planks. The bottom was composed of the same rotted wood overlaid with mud and gravel. Through the dissipating fog, Louis could just make out the other end—maybe thirty feet across. What he couldn't see was what the bridge crossed.

The Explorer was quiet, then from the backseat came a sound of a huge exhale.

"Jesus," Nurmi said hoarsely.

"What is this?" Louis said.

"It's gotta be Split Mountain Gorge," Nurmi said. "Sweet Jesus . . ."

Louis felt his heart thumping in his chest. If fog hadn't broken when it did, they probably would have driven right across—and down.

"Back up, slowly," Steele said.

Louis looked in the rearview mirror but couldn't see any place to turn around. They were fenced in by the pines and brush. He put the Explorer in reverse, eased it back ten feet and slammed it in park.

They were all silent again. Louis realized he was gripping the steering wheel and let go, flexing his fingers.

"How deep is this gorge?" he asked.

"About a hundred feet," Nurmi said.

Louis looked over at Steele. He was eyeing the surrounding trees and brush. "Any place they could have turned off before here?" Steele asked over his shoulder to Nurmi.

"None," Nurmi said. "This used to be a railroad line that ran thirty miles across the peninsula. After they took the tracks out no one used it." He sat forward to stare out the windshield. "Doesn't look like that bridge will support a vehicle and I don't know these woods good enough to say if there's another way out on foot."

"Shit," Steele said under his breath.

"Let's get out and look around," Louis said.

Louis climbed out and shoved the door closed. It looked like they were as high up this mountain as they could go. The sky was bruised with grays and blues, except for a slash of red in the east, where a setting sun was peeking through.

Steele walked toward the railroad trestle. Louis followed, moving slowly and keeping his eye on the forest, looking for crushed brush, something that would tell him someone had driven off the trail into the cover of the trees. But given the terrain, any escape would more likely be on foot.

"Come look at this," Steele called out.

Steele stood at the entrance to the bridge, rigid against winds that ripped at his nylon jacket. Louis came up next to him.

The wind coming up over the gorge had dissipated the fog and across the long bridge, Louis could see another a mountain, higher and tufted with pines.

Louis took a few steps to the weathered wood railing and looked down. *Holy shit . . .*

Nurmi had said it was a hundred feet, but it looked more like five hundred. Steep and deep, the gorge looked as if it had been cut into the earth by a giant meat cleaver. At the very bottom, he could see a copper river that trickled through the V-shaped gorge like a stream of blood.

He peered down at the supports for the trestle. It was constructed of three mammoth steel towers, braced by rusty X crosses all the way to the bottom.

Louis heard thumping and looked back to see Steele stomping on the rotted plywood that had been haphazardly laid across the trestle. "You want to drive across this thing, you go alone. Sir."

Steele glanced at him, offering a wry smile. "I'm just wondering if Lampo was familiar enough with this trestle to know he *could* drive across."

It started to rain again. Driven by the wind, it felt like tiny pins against Louis's neck.

"If he did cross, he's on foot," Louis said. "Let's look at the map and see if we can send anyone up that way to intercept him."

They started back to the Explorer. They had less than an hour's daylight left, but they could set up road blocks throughout the peninsula and operate them through the night. But even as that thought moved through Louis's head, so did doubt. Maybe they *were* chasing air. And if they were, he couldn't help but think about his future here. And Steele's.

A rustle in the trees came to him on the wind.

Louis drew his Glock and spun around, scanning the trees and bushes. A squirrel scampered across a fallen trunk. Leaves skittered across the path, caught up in a wind eddy.

Then something else . . . a voice?

Shut shut shut . . .

Had he heard words, or was it just the freakish whistle of the wind in the iron towers under the trestle?

The sound came again.

Shut up . . .

Louis moved closer to the trestle and again looked into the trees, watching for movement, a speck of color, anything that seemed out of place.

"Run!"

No wind. Real words. Louis spun around.

Two men bolted from trees back near the entrance to the trestle. One in camouflage, the other in dark pants and a yellow dress shirt. Buddy Lampo—and Anthony Prince.

They stumbled toward the trestle in a clumsy kind of run, one pulling at the other.

"Captain!" Louis shouted.

Louis broke into a run. For a few seconds, he lost the men in a thicket but when he reached the trestle, everything was wide open and he could see them clearly. They had stopped halfway across the bridge and were huddled against the wood railing. Anthony had an arm around Buddy's neck, talking in his ear.

Louis started onto the trestle but stopped when he saw the revolver in Anthony's hand. Steele pulled up next to Louis, his Glock in his hand.

"Anthony Prince!" Steele shouted. "We're the police. Stop now and put down your weapon!"

Anthony's gun came up level. "Get away from us!" he yelled. "Leave us be!"

Anthony was waving the gun and Louis edged sideways, putting space between himself and Steele. He watched Anthony carefully, eyeing his revolver. There was nothing more dangerous than a nervous man waving a gun he did not know how to use.

"Drop your gun, Anthony!" Louis shouted. "You have nowhere to go. Let's end this peacefully."

Anthony shuffled back against the railing, dragging Buddy with him. Louis could see that Buddy's hands were empty, but he was wearing a bulky jacket that could conceal a gun.

"Prince! No one else has to die!" Steele shouted.

Anthony yanked Lampo against him, leveled the gun and started yelling into the wind, but he wasn't making demands—he was quoting scripture.

298

"The unbelieving, the abominable, and murderers, and whoremongers—"

"Don't use the Bible to justify what you're doing!" Steele shouted.

Anthony fell silent and looked over the railing, down into the gorge. Then abruptly, he started shouting again.

"All shall have their part in the lake which burneth with fire and brimstone!"

"You want the lake, you go ahead and jump!" Louis shouted. "But let him go."

"He's my brother!" Anthony shouted.

Louis heard Steele let out a hard breath behind him. They had been right.

Anthony said something in Buddy's ear and started climbing the railing, gripping Buddy toward him as a shield. Buddy was shaking his head, grasping at his brother's arm, but it didn't look like had much fight in him.

"Buddy!" Louis shouted.

Buddy put a shoe between the slats and started to follow his brother over the railing. Louis thought about rushing them, grabbing Buddy to pull him back, but Anthony was not yet out of view, his revolver still visible.

"Buddy, listen to me!" Louis shouted. "You don't need to follow him down!"

Buddy threw a leg over the railing and started a descent down the other side, never looking back. A few seconds later, he and Anthony disappeared below the trestle.

Louis ran to the railing and looked down. They hadn't jumped. They had managed to get down to a narrow catwalk suspended about ten feet below the bridge.

They stood huddled together against the wind, Anthony holding on to his brother and Buddy holding tight to the only thing he could grab—a thick iron girder. A hundred feet below them the river snaked through the rocks.

"Buddy! Look at me. I want to help you!" Louis shouted.

Finally, Buddy looked up, his hair flying around his head, his eyes tearing from the wind. It was an odd expression—a resigned kind of terror, the same look a man got as he was strapped into the electric chair.

"Buddy!" Louis yelled. "You don't have to do this! You owe him nothing!"

Anthony clutched his brother close, still talking frantically in ear. Louis could not hear what he was saying.

"Buddy, look at me. Don't listen to him!"

This time Anthony looked up, and when he did, Buddy shifted his body and Anthony's shoe slipped off the beam. He skidded off the catwalk and suddenly both of them were grappling frantically for the other. The gun dropped, clanking against the catwalk before falling away into the gorge.

"Help me!" Buddy screamed. "Help me!"

Buddy was gripping the girder with one hand and holding the back of Anthony's shirt with his other. Anthony dangled in the air, clinging to the catwalk, desperately trying to get a foot back up.

"God, please help me! Help me save him!"

Louis took off his jacket and ripped off his Kevlar vest to discard the extra weight.

Steele put a hand on his arm. "No."

"I'm going down there," Louis said. "Go get the rope from the Explorer. I'll need it to get back up."

If Steele said anything else, Louis didn't hear it. He climbed over the railing and started down the outside of the trestle. Once he got below the bridge, he could see what the brothers had used to lower themselves to the catwalk. There was a rusted cable scalloping the underside of the trestle. Hanging from that, he would have to drop the last four feet to the catwalk. And if he couldn't catch the girder when he hit, it was another hundred feet down.

"Help me!" Buddy screamed.

Louis grabbed the wet cable and lowered himself as far as he could. He took a breath and dropped to the catwalk, catching the girder. Once he got his balance, he turned toward Buddy.

Anthony was hanging off the edge of the catwalk, too weak to get his legs or elbows up on the ledge to give himself more support. Buddy's fingers were white-knuckled around his brother's wrist, but he didn't have the strength in only one arm to pull his brother back up. He had to keep his other hand around the girder or he would be dragged to the gorge below.

Louis sidestepped along the catwalk toward Buddy, trying to stay upright against the push of the wind and trying not to look down. As Louis neared Buddy, he could hear Anthony's voice—the words pouring out breathless and fast.

"The righteous see their ruin and rejoice. The innocent mock them . . ."

"He's slipping!" Buddy shouted. "I can't hold him."

Louis dropped to his knees, one hand around the girder, the other stretched down toward Anthony.

"If you return to the Almighty, you will be restored. If you remove wickedness from your tent—"

"Shut up and give me your hand!" Louis yelled.

Anthony looked up at him. His eyes held the glazed stare of a man who was already dead in every way but one.

"Give me your hand!" Louis shouted.

Anthony let go of the ledge and for a few seconds, he spun in the air like a kite, held only his brother's hand around his wrist.

"Antero!" Buddy screamed.

Anthony gave his brother a final look then jerked his wrist free. He dropped through the air with a surreal kind of calm. No screams, no flailing. Just a silent falling away through the wisps of fog below the trestle.

Louis gripped the edge of the trestle, unable to look away until he saw the body hit the rocks at the river's edge and tumble like a doll into the coppery water.

Buddy let out a wail. "No! No! No!"

Louis looked up, and tried to focus on Buddy, but he couldn't seem to move, couldn't seem to get a full breath. Then he saw Buddy lean forward and Louis rose and put a hand to Buddy's chest, bracing him against the girder. Buddy almost crumpled against Louis's palm.

"Oh my God, oh my God! I dropped him! I let him go!"

"Buddy, listen to me," Louis shouted. "There was nothing you could do."

Buddy was trembling, tears streaming down his dirty face. Louis could feel Buddy's heat, smell the beer on his breath. God, he hoped the man wasn't drunk.

"Listen to me," Louis said, shaking him. "I get it. You wanted to protect your brother, but Anthony wasn't what you thought he was. He changed. He was not the brother you knew."

Buddy shook his head and looked down into the gorge. "You don't get it! You can't know! It was just us. Always just us. That never changes!"

• • • • • • • • •

Louis tightened his grip on Buddy's coat. "I do know. I had someone I couldn't save. I know how much it hurts. It hurts bad, but you can't go down with him!"

Buddy wasn't listening, or maybe he couldn't even hear him over his own sobs. He was shivering, soaked to the bone. And so was Louis. His hands were so numb he could barely bend his fingers. He had to try something else to reach this man.

"Naatan!"

Buddy shut his eyes tight.

"Naatan, listen to me!"

Buddy opened his eyes, trying to focus on Louis's face.

"God would not want you to jump, Naatan," Louis said. "God would want you to go on. He wants you to forgive yourself. That's how it works, right?"

"God doesn't care!" Buddy sobbed. "He gave up on me and I gave up on Him a long time ago. Let me go, just let me go."

Louis kept a firm grip on Buddy's sleeve. He had to get Buddy off this bridge. He had to find a way to reach him.

302

He dug into his jeans pocket and retrieved the Saint Bosco medal. He thrust under Buddy's nose.

"Look at this!" Louis demanded. "Look at it."

Buddy pulled away, almost losing his balance.

"Look at it, Naatan!"

Finally, Buddy saw it and he froze, his eyes wide. "No, I can't talk about that," he said.

Louis shook him by the collar and kept the medal right in front of his face. "Listen to me. I know you left this medal for those two little boys. I know you cared about them."

Buddy shook his head wildly, batting blindly at Louis's hand. "No, it's done. No one can fix that. It's over!"

Louis yanked on Buddy's coat, bringing his face close. "People need to know how the boys died," Louis said. "I need you to help me with that."

Buddy closed his eyes. Louis pressed closer, trying to hold him up on his feet as he talked.

"They don't have graves," Louis said. "They don't even have names. And if you jump off this bridge, they never will."

When Buddy opened his eyes, Louis saw a bone-deep sadness, and with it, a glimmer of clarity.

"Buddy, please."

Buddy started to nod, slowly at first, then with more vigor. "All right," he whispered. "All right . . . all right."

Louis put the medal back in his pocket and placed a hand on Buddy's chest, bracing him against the girder before he looked up into the rain to the top of the trestle.

Captain!" Louis shouted.

Steele's face appeared above the railing.

"You got that rope?" Louis shouted. "We're coming up."

CHAPTER THIRTY-EIGHT

It had to be eighty degrees inside the Explorer but still Louis couldn't get warm. He felt a little off center and lightheaded. In his mind, he was still seeing Anthony falling away.

"You're shivering," Buddy said from the backseat. "You might have hypothermia."

Louis didn't answer him.

"You should see a doctor."

"I'm fine."

Buddy was quiet for a few seconds, then, "What's going on?"

Louis sat up and looked out the front window. Two state SUVs and two Keweenaw County Jeeps that had finally made it up the hill. Nurmi had been moved to one of the Jeeps and was directing his men to secure the scene. Headlights lit up the trestle, and it looked like the bridge was floating in the coming darkness.

The driver's side door opened, and Steele climbed inside. He closed the door, flipped on the dome light and handed Louis a Thermos.

"I stole it from one of Nurmi's deputies," Steele said. "Thought you might want something warm."

"Thanks." Louis unscrewed the top. His hand shook as he poured himself a cup. It was hot and to his surprise, spiked lightly with something.

"You need something for that hand?" Steele asked.

Louis looked down at his palm. It was smeared with rust and blood, the palm slashed with a deep cut. He remembered losing his grip on the rope when he was scaling the trestle and he had grabbed at a sharp piece of iron. He hadn't noticed it at the time, but now it was throbbing like hell.

"It can wait."

Steele got out of the Explorer, went to the rear hatch and returned with a first-aid kit.

"Clean it up before it gets infected," Steele said, dropping the kit in Louis's lap. "How about you, Lampo? You got any injuries?"

"No, sir."

"You warm enough?" Steele asked.

"Yes, sir. Thank you."

Steele pulled a clipboard from between the seats. "I need to confirm something. You are Nathan Prince, right?"

"Naatan Prinsilä," Buddy said.

"There's a baptismal certificate in your cabin for Buddy Lampo dated 1955, when your family was still in Wisconsin," Steele said. "Explain that."

Louis knew Steele was asking not only to confirm Buddy's ID, but to satisfy his own curiosity about the piece of paper that had sent him off the deep end and almost derailed their investigation.

"It's was for the real Buddy Lampo," Buddy said. "The family I went to live with had a son who died. They seemed to look at me like a replacement son, so somewhere along the line, I just took his name." Buddy leaned forward in his seat. "Can you tell me what's going out there?"

"Keweenaw County's going to secure and monitor the scene for us," Steele said. "Search and Rescue will be here at first light to recover the body."

"My brother is going to lay down there all night?" Buddy asked.

"He won't know the difference," Steele said. Then after a moment, he added, "It's the best we can do. Someone will be here all night to keep an eye on him."

Buddy fell silent. Louis thought about offering him some coffee, but after they had confiscated the .22 from his coat, Steele had handcuffed him. A search of the woods near Buddy's cabin had turned up his white pickup, with a big SISU bumper sticker. Inside were three guns and two empty gin bottles.

"It was me, wasn't it?" Louis asked Buddy. "It was me telling you about that candle box that set all this in motion, right?"

"Yes, sir," Buddy said softly. "When I knew you were reopening the thing with the boys, I . . . I just lost it. I knew I had to talk to my father."

"You went downstate to his cottage?" Louis asked.

"Yeah," Buddy said. "It took me forever to get up the nerve, but I finally knocked on the door and he let me in. At first he didn't want to listen, but I just kept talking and talking until finally I saw him start to understand."

"Understand what?" Louis asked.

"That we couldn't keep the boys secret anymore."

Louis turned in his seat but before he could ask about what had happened with the boys, Steele gave Louis a subtle shake of his head.

"Let's stay with Anthony right now," Steele said. Then to Buddy, "What did your father say?"

"He said he was going to fix it, that he was going to talk to Antero after that night's service," Buddy said. "He believed me. First time in my whole fucking life my father believed me. He even gave me a hug."

Buddy paused, his next words softer. "But like it always did, everything went to shit."

Steele was quiet, writing on his clipboard. Louis looked away, toward the trestle.

"Can I go back to my cabin?" Buddy asked.

"No, you're under arrest," Steele said.

"What for?" Buddy asked.

"Harboring a fugitive."

"I didn't know he was a fugitive," Buddy said.

"You had to know he killed your father," Steele asked.

"I didn't know for sure," Buddy said. "He never talked to me about that."

"Your long-lost brother shows up after your father's murdered and you don't talk about that?" Steele asked.

"He wasn't long-lost," Buddy said. "He wrote sometimes. Sent me money a couple times a year."

Steele sighed impatiently. "Answer my question, Lampo."

"All I know is Antero showed up late, sometime after eleven and said we needed to talk. I think he was drunk. I gave him my bedroom, but he was up for hours bumping around in there. He finally went to sleep."

Louis pulled a gauze bandage out of the first-aid kit. He knew Steele was fishing for a confession, something he could add to the file to help prove their case. Even though Anthony was dead, they still needed evidence beyond any reasonable doubt to officially mark the case closed. Exceptional clearance, it was called.

"What about this morning?" Steele asked.

Buddy took a moment to answer. "When I woke up on the couch, my brother was sitting in the chair across from me. He was holding a Bible and one of my guns."

Steele turned in his seat to look at Buddy. "Did he threaten you?"

Buddy shook his head. "My brother wouldn't hurt me."

"He killed your father and he killed a woman he was involved with. What makes you think he wouldn't kill you?"

No answer from Buddy. Louis finished bandaging his hand and started putting things back in the kit. But he was thinking about Buddy and wondering where his mind was right now. Having to consider the possibility that your beloved brother drove six hundred miles to kill you had to play hard in the heart. Especially when you realized you almost jumped off a bridge with him to prove your loyalty.

Steele didn't wait for an answer. "So what did you talk about all day?" he asked. "Did he have a plan? Did he say what he wanted from you? Why he was here?"

"He was confused," Buddy said. "He kept quoting scripture and drinking. One minute he was talking about going to Canada and the next he was planning his next sermon at the cathedral. I just figured when he sobered up, we could work things out."

"But he never confessed to you?" Steele asked.

"My brother was never big on owning up to stuff."

"Where was the gun all this time?"

"He kept it in his belt."

"Why did you run?" Steele asked.

"I was outside taking a smoke and I saw you coming up the hill," Buddy said. "So I went in and told Antero and he just went crazy. He grabbed the rest of my guns from the rack and said we had to leave. I told him there was nowhere to go, that the road ended up here, but he wasn't listening. He said God would show us the way."

"So you just went along with this?" Steele asked.

"He was my brother," Buddy said. "My big brother. And he was in trouble. I didn't know he was going to do what he did and once he told me to climb over, I guess I didn't know how to say no."

Louis sipped the coffee, glad Steele was fielding the questions. But the surge of adrenaline he had felt on the trestle was dissipating and his brain was starting to fire up. He had a question of his own, one last loose end to tie up. They needed to find Tuyen Lang's car, the silver Civic. It could hold evidence from the night Anthony transported her body to the field in Ionia. They needed to close her case, too. Not only for her, but for Cam.

"Where did you meet him?" Louis asked.

"Huh?"

"The car Anthony drove up here is not at your cabin," Louis said. "Where did you pick him up?"

"Down in Ahmeek. We met up in front of the house where we used to live."

Steele shifted the Explorer into drive. "You're going to take us there."

Steele took the trail down slowly, the muddy headlights offering only a murky white path through the trees. But when the Explorer reached the main road, Steele hit the overheads and sped through the darkness at eighty miles an hour.

Louis was quiet as they drove, sipping the laced coffee. It helped take the edge off. Helped free his mind of what he had done up there and what he had seen. He still wanted to know what happened to the boys, but now was not the time. Buddy was exhausted.

The radio kept crackling with messages from Houghton to Steele, two requests to call headquarters in Lansing and three to call Major Deforest. Steele acknowledged each one with a dry "Copy that" and replaced the mic. He made no effort to see if the cellular phone in the console had service.

"We're coming into Ahmeek," Steele said.

"Turn right at the second street," Buddy said. "It's the white house on the corner."

It was only ten fifteen, but the town was closed down for the night. Only a corner convenience store with a blinding Marathon light offered any signs of life.

Steele turned into a neighborhood so dark the bubble light on top of the Explorer washed the shingled houses and pickup trucks in swaths of red. At the end of the block, the silver Honda Civic appeared in the Explorer's headlights.

When they pulled nose-to-nose with the Civic, Louis grabbed a flashlight, a pair of latex gloves, and pushed out the passenger door. Steele started searching the car's interior, so Louis walked back to the rear.

"Pop the trunk," he called to Steele.

The trunk rose open. Louis turned on the flashlight and swept the beam around inside. The only things in the trunk were a spare tire, a jack and a Vuitton duffel. Louis propped the duffel on the bumper and unzipped it. It was empty.

Why had Anthony brought it with him? What had been in it? Had they missed something, something Anthony had hidden back at Buddy's cabin?

Louis started to toss the bag back in the trunk when the flashlight beam caught a tiny object rolling across the bottom of the duffle. He reached inside to retrieve it, then shined the flashlight beam on his hand.

It was a white stone about the size of a small marble. Louis rolled it over between his fingers.

It wasn't a stone. It was—

PJ PARRISH

And the words that Anthony had repeated over and over on the trestle where there in his head. *If you return . . . if you . . .*

He walked back to the Explorer and opened the door. "What was that verse Anthony was quoting just before he let go?"

Buddy shrugged. "I don't know."

"Think. It was something about returning to God and removing something."

Buddy raked his hair and sighed wearily. "If you return to the Almighty, you will be restored. If you remove wickedness from your tent . . . it's about coming back to God. I think it's Job 22."

Louis spun around and scanned the street. Just houses and empty lots and parked cars. Where was it? Where the hell was it?

He looked back at Buddy. "Is there a church around here?"

Buddy nodded and pointed. "Yeah, my father's old church. It's down there at the end of the block. But it's all shut down now."

Louis slammed the door and started down the street, first walking, then breaking into a trot. Behind him, he heard Steele call for him, but he didn't stop.

The spire of the church came into view first, caught in the rain-glittered glow of a nearby streetlight. Then the church, a small white building with two Gothic style windows.

As Louis neared, he could see that the old double wooden doors had been jimmied. He threw the doors open and went inside.

It was dark, only the smooth oak of the rear pews catching any light. Louis swept the flashlight beam over the walls, found the switch and slapped at it. A faint mellow light came on the far end of the church from a simple brass pendant lamp over the altar.

Louis started up the long aisle, his steps slowed by the sudden chill moving up his arms, the hard beat of his heart and what he knew he would find at the end of the aisle.

He stopped.

Bones.

310

White bones laid out on the wooden altar. The skulls were tipped to their sides, as if they were looking at each. The tiny hand bones were arranged meticulously, the tips almost touching. Every rib bone was set exactly the same distance apart, like the gold pens on Anthony Prince's desk.

If you return to the Almighty . . .

Louis's eyes burned with tears. Then he dropped to his knees. An urge to scream was inside him but he remained silent, sitting on his heels, staring at the small skeletons until he felt a hand on his shoulder.

"My God," Steele whispered.

Louis rose slowly. Steele crossed himself and bowed his head.

Louis walked to the back of the church, stopping near the open door where the air was fresh. He realized he still had the tiny bone from the duffle in his hand and he closed it in his fist and leaned against the wall.

Steele came up to him. "I'll call forensics and get a team in here," he said.

"Before you do that," Louis said, "bring Buddy in here. I want to talk to him."

CHAPTER THIRTY-NINE

Buddy came in the church without his handcuffs, rubbing his wrists. When the door closed behind him, he stood near the back row of pews and took a long look around.

The church probably hadn't changed at all since Buddy had been here as a child, Louis suspected, yet Buddy seemed uncomfortable. Buddy had said on the trestle that he had given up on God years ago. Maybe it wasn't just the childhood memories making him uneasy now.

Finally, Buddy's tired eyes came to Louis and he held something out to Louis. "That other officer said you might want this."

Louis accepted the small tape recorder. It was Steele's way of telling him that the boys' case needed to be officially closed, too.

"Why am I here?" Buddy asked.

"I want you to see something."

When Buddy reached the third row of pews, he froze. His face drained of color.

Louis was prepared for him to turn and run, but he didn't. For a long time, they both just stood there, Louis looking at Buddy and Buddy looking at the small skeletons.

"That's them?" Buddy asked finally.

"Yes."

"Why did you bring them here?"

"Anthony brought them here," Louis said.

Buddy wiped his nose with his sleeve and tried to look away, but his eyes kept coming back to the bones. "I don't understand. Where . . . I mean, how?"

Louis knew he had to take the time to explain it to him so Buddy understood the journey the boys' remains had taken and, more importantly, what a sick son of a bitch his brother was.

"When the candle box was found in 1979, there was a sheriff here named Halko," Louis said. "He was corrupt, liked to steal and sell murder souvenirs. But he was also smart. I think he managed to link your family to the boys but instead of doing a real investigation, he chose to blackmail your brother. He sold the remains to him."

Buddy looked confused. "Antero bought the boys' bones? And he kept them?"

A part of him didn't want to tell Buddy where the bones had been stored, but Louis decided that truth worked two ways—if he wanted honesty from Buddy, he had to be honest with him.

"He kept them in an organ bench in his home."

Buddy continued to stare at the bones, but his eyes clouded with something that Louis couldn't decipher. It wasn't disgust or even surprise. It was more as if Anthony's grisly storage container made perfect sense.

"We need to talk," Louis said.

He motioned toward the rear of the church and Buddy followed him back down the aisle. At the last row of pews, he slipped in to sit down. Louis sat down next to him, turned on the recorder and set it on the pew between them.

Buddy sat very still, hands folded, head down. Somewhere outside, a siren wailed and died.

"I'm sorry," Buddy said. "I don't know where to start,"

"Start in Oulu," Louis said.

Buddy looked up at him. "Oulu," he said softly. He let out a long breath. "The boys weren't with us in Oulu. Why start there?"

Louis wasn't sure why he wanted Buddy to start his story in Wisconsin. Maybe it was because he wanted to know not only what happened at the moment of the boys' murder, but what had happened in the weeks, months and years before. Because that's what murder was. Not a singular flash of lightning, but a slow gathering storm of slights, injustices and unhealed wounds.

It was the kind of stuff some cops never took the time to listen to, because in court everything was reduced to the damage left after the lightning struck—footprints, blood spatter, DNA, and gun casings. But understanding the storm's formation helped Louis understand people and understanding people helped him understand why they murdered.

Buddy cleared his throat. "My memories of Oulu are mostly just being dark and lonely. It was cold, and we used candles to keep the electric bill down. Antero and I slept together to stay warm."

"You were poor." Louis said.

Buddy nodded. "Yeah, but I don't think we knew that then. Nobody in Oulu had much. We were the only church for like fifty miles. My father started it after he came over from Finland. He served in the Winter War, you know, with Kalervo Kurkiala. Do you know who he was?"

"No."

"He was this famous Finnish minister and soldier who fought against the Russians and became some big guy in the German SS. My father used to say that of all the things Kurkiala taught him, the most important thing was that faith alone was not enough, that it had to be strengthened by discipline, the kind of discipline soldiers get."

"Was your mother from Finland?"

"No, she was American," Buddy said. "A farm girl from a family of twelve. She was the youngest, and when her family joined the church, she became the organist. They got married right before the war. One of my aunts said she married him because the only men who were left were cripples and ministers."

Buddy sat back against the pew and let out a long breath.

"But *I* know he loved her," he said. "I know it because every once in a while, if she passed near him, I'd see him touch her hand. And one night, I caught him watching her when she was playing the organ, all affectionate like. When he saw me looking at him, he told her to stop, and he left the room."

"Maybe he was embarrassed you saw his feelings."

"That's what I thought then, too," Buddy said. "But I figured out later that it didn't have anything to do with embarrassment. It had to do with distractions. No one in our house was allowed distractions."

"Distractions from what?" Louis asked.

"Serving God."

Louis was quiet, sitting forward with his elbows on his knees. Buddy was quiet, too, picking at the rough skin of his palms.

"It wasn't all bad," Buddy said. "We had stuff going on at church for kids and we listened to Moody radio at night. But when Antero and I got older, things started changing. My father locked up the radio so we couldn't hear Elvis and Chuck Berry. We weren't allowed to visit friends if their families had televisions. The only movie I saw was *The Ten Commandments* when I was five."

"Strict stuff," Louis said.

Buddy fell quiet again. He bowed his head and when he finally spoke, his voice was a bare whisper.

"There was this night with the bread," he said.

Louis wasn't sure he heard right. "Bread?"

Buddy nodded. "I know it's stupid to remember something like this but it's like it was just so typical of how things were. My mother had made two loaves of pettuleipä bread. It was supposed to be one loaf for this poor family and one for us. It was a treat, and we were all excited. But then father came in and told us that we needed to give the second loaf—*our loaf*—to the church for Eucharist. When we complained, he told us our generosity was enough to nourish us."

Buddy raked his hair.

"It was like everything we had, everything we earned, had to be re-turned, like having fucking nothing and being hungry all the time somehow made us more righteous. Antero used to say we were slaves to a master we never saw."

"Your brother wasn't so devout?"

"He was good at pretending," Buddy said. "He had a great memory for the passages and he always knew what to say. And he came up with all these charity ideas, like asking the local farmers for fruit to feed the old folks and collecting coats in the winter. But at night, when we were alone, he'd bitch about how ignorant the farmers were, and he'd tell nasty jokes about Jesus."

"And you?"

"I believed," Buddy said.

He slumped back in the pew, like he was so tired he couldn't sit up any longer.

"But believing was never enough," he went on. "I couldn't memorize anything, and I couldn't seem to sit still or stay clean. No matter how hard I tried, father said I should've dug deeper or prayed harder."

Again, Buddy paused. "But I could draw good," he said. "So I figured that maybe I could serve God by painting pictures. So I painted like ten pictures of Bible stories and showed them to Father. He told me he would hang them in the church, but he never did. One time when I was cleaning the church, I found them in the trash."

Buddy closed his eyes.

"When did the other children start coming to stay with you?" Louis asked.

Buddy opened his eyes. "That last summer we were in Oulu, right after my grandfather Sedrik died in Finland. They sent my father Sedrik's favorite robe. It was blue, a real silky royal blue, and it had a gold stole with the Saint Bosco emblem on it. They also sent this pouch full of Bosco medals and a long letter telling father it was now his mission to carry on the work of Saint Bosco, helping homeless boys."

Buddy was sweating, despite the cold breeze wafting in from the broken door.

"That's how it started," Buddy said, "the boys, I mean. It started with this kid in town. They were going to put him in juvie down in Wausau and my father convinced them to let him try to save him. Father brought a cot into our bedroom. A month later, we had like four more cots in there. One night, Antero and I went to father to complain. He told us that we should think of it like living in army barracks and that it would rid us of pettiness and vanity. We figured that came from Kurkiala, and we started hating him, too."

"What was your mother doing during this time?"

"Taking care of sick parishioners and making father more robes," Buddy said. "She'd scrounge old drapes and bedspreads and sew them into these beautiful robes. The congregation loved seeing father in them. But all Antero and I could think about was how much food one of those damn robes could've bought us."

"Who took care of the boys?"

"Antero and I did," Buddy said. "Father set up these retreats he called lock-ins where he would take all of us into the woods and we'd spend hours reading and talking about the Bible. But most of these kids were too stupid or screwed up to get with the program. I think my father got discouraged and just wanted to get back to his church, so he put Antero in charge of the lock-ins. He told Antero if he did a good job, he'd get a Bosco medal. So, Antero took over handing out the lessons, grading the papers and . . ."

Buddy paused and closed his eyes again.

"And what?" Louis asked.

"Giving out the discipline."

"What kind of discipline?"

"At first it was just things like sitting in the corner or drinking castor oil. But it didn't take Antero long to figure out he liked being the boss. By the end of August, he had made himself a cedar switch wrapped with electrical tape."

"And you?" Louis asked.

Buddy opened his eyes, blinking slowly.

"I . . . I hated the lock-ins," he said. "I hated seeing Antero whip those kids, but when I threatened to tell, he whooped on me. Then one night he told me he was sorry and that if I kept quiet, he'd help me earn one of the

317

Bosco medals. There was nothing I wanted more than one of those medals, so I went along."

"What about your father? Did he know what was going on?"

Buddy shook his head. "All he cared about was if the kids were clean and polite and could sing all four verses of *Faith of Our Fathers*. And at the end of summer, Antero got his medal. Just like father promised him."

"And you?"

Buddy's voice dropped to a whisper. "I didn't get a medal. Father told me I had failed because I had limitations Antero didn't have. He told me that was okay because 'God knoweth our frame and he remembereth that we are just dust.'"

Buddy leveled his eyes at Louis.

"Do you know what it feels like to have your father tell you that you're just a pile of dust?"

There was probably a part of the forty-two-year-old Buddy that understood that wasn't exactly what Jonas was trying to say, but Louis doubted Buddy was hearing that voice right now.

"Then came Christmas," Buddy said. "For the first time I could remember, the congregation got together and brought us over some presents. New stuff, not second-hand. I got a sketch pad and colored pencils and Antero got a red model car. But then Father drove us over to Ashland and made us give our stuff to the sick kids in the hospital. I cried all the way home and ended up doing basement penance for my selfishness."

"What did Anthony do?"

Buddy looked at Louis. "Nothing. But that night, he snuck out. He was gone a long time, and when he crawled back into bed, he told me that since God took something from him, he'd take something from God."

"What did he do?"

Buddy shook his head slowly. "He burned the church down."

"Did anyone find out?"

"The police said some Christmas boxes caught fire and they told my father they found a broken kerosene lamp, but they couldn't prove anything.

318

Father didn't even ask the other boys or Antero if he did it. He came right to me."

"And you took the blame?"

"No, I denied it," Buddy said. "But father didn't believe me. He stopped talking to me. He wouldn't even look at me. And then he started praying for me, right out loud in front of everyone else in the house. I wanted to die."

"How did you end up here?"

"After the fire, we had to start over in new place where they didn't know us. The parish here in Ameek needed a minister. They didn't pay father much, but they gave us a nice house and told us we could take what we needed from the church food bank. It was good for a while, because the other boys were gone, and it was only us again. A church lady started homeschooling Antero so he could get into Faithbridge in Racine. And I spent most my time in the woods, hunting and fishing. But then . . ."

Buddy fell silent and the seconds passed. Louis sat forward, and folded his hands, sensing that Buddy was about to enter a very dark place. The doors to those kinds of places opened slowly.

"Buddy?"

"Mother started getting sick," Buddy said. "At first father accepted some help from the congregation, but then he decided we couldn't take charity, that Antero and me had to take care of her."

"That's tough on a couple of teenage boys," Louis said.

Buddy gave a small shrug. "Then around Thanksgiving in 1961, Antero and I come home from church one night and there's two little boys in the house. Mother tells us their father couldn't take care of them and asked my father to take them in."

Finally, Louis could ask the question he'd been wanting to ask since he first opened the boys in the box file. It was a question only Buddy could answer.

"What were their names?"

"Toby and Eli. They were like four and six. Eli was the little one."

"Last name?"

"Revel. Toby and Eli Revel."

319

Revel . . . Louis had heard the name before. Somewhere in the case file? Someone he had met up here? No, it was on the receipt for the donation of an organ to the church, the receipt he had found in the hope chest back in Jonas Prince's cottage. *In exchange for some services . . .*

"Did the church get a new organ about this time?" Louis asked.

Buddy thought for a minute. "Yeah, we did," he said. "I think my father thought it would be some sort of miracle cure for my mother since she missed her music, and for a while it made her real happy. But a few weeks later, my mother was back in bed and Antero and I were . . ."

"Left to take care of Toby and Eli."

"Yeah."

"What happened?"

Buddy shook his head and said nothing. He was far away again, holding himself and rocking gently.

"Talk to me, Buddy," Louis said softly.

"They . . . they wouldn't behave," he said. "They knew it pissed Antero off, but they would get in his room and mess everything up. So Antero got a lock. But Toby, he was real smart. He got a screwdriver and unscrewed the latch and he found . . . he found . . ."

"Found what?"

"He found some rubbers . . . you know, condoms. And they filled them with water and threw them out the window. Antero beat the crap out of Toby for that. He'd smacked them before but this time he left bruises, and mother saw them. She made Antero promise he wouldn't hit them again."

"So how did you keep them quiet after that?"

"We tried locking them in their room," Buddy said. "But they'd bounce on the bed, so Antero locked them in their closet. But they broke the lock. So one day Antero came home with the candle box."

Louis stared at the pendant light until it began to blur. He could feel his heart beating, slow but punchy.

"Antero called it the coffin discipline," Buddy said. "He would strip them down to their underwear and make them lay in the box. And then Antero would sit on it. Sometimes, he would sit up there for hours in his bedroom, listening to them whimper while he read the Bible to them. He told me he was just listening to them to make sure they didn't suffocate or something, but I knew . . . I knew . . ."

Louis didn't make him finish the sentence. Anthony was about fifteen at the time, Louis knew, a boy who was learning what excited him sexually. And it suddenly hit Louis—that's why Anthony had kept the bones in the organ bench in his home.

For a minute, he thought he might be sick. But he shut his eyes and swallowed back his revulsion because he wanted to hear the rest of Buddy's story. He needed to hear it.

"Go on, Buddy, please," he said.

"A few days before Christmas," Buddy said, "the doctor told us my mother wasn't going to make it too much longer and I remember my father just kind of broke. He stayed home a lot, spent hours with her in her dark bedroom reading to her. On Christmas Eve, he carried her into the church so she could attend the midnight service."

Buddy wiped his face and sniffled.

"January tenth was my mother's birthday," Buddy said. "It was snowing and there was this God-awful wind blowing in off the lake. Antero spent all afternoon in the kitchen making mother kringles. Toby and Eli found the kringles, and in ten minutes they ate half the pan. And when Antero found out . . ."

Buddy put his hands on the pew in front of them and leaned his head on his knuckles. Louis was willing to give him a few seconds, but the silence lengthened.

"Buddy, you made me a promise," Louis said.

"I never seen him so mad," Buddy said. "They knew it, too, and they took off up the stairs and he chased them. Then I could hear Eli crying and I went upstairs to try to calm things down, but Antero had already stripped them and was shoving them into the candle box. But this time, Toby was fighting him hard. But it didn't do any good. Antero grabbed the lid and yelled at me and to hold it down while he nailed it shut."

Buddy stopped, breathing hard. His next words came out rushed.

"I just stood there. I didn't want to help him but then he yelled at me that if I didn't help I would be the next one to go in the box so . . . so I pushed the lid down and I could feel them pushing back and I knew it was wrong but I couldn't . . . Jesus . . . I put all my weight on the lid and just closed my eyes while Antero hammered it shut."

Louis was silent. His body felt like stone, hard and cold.

"God, they still wouldn't be quiet," Buddy said. "So Antero screams at me to grab my end and says we're taking the box outside. We carry it downstairs and drag it through the snow and put it in the shed. I thought that maybe after fifteen minutes we would go get them, but then my father came home."

Louis closed his eyes.

"He came home and he said he cancelled the evening service because everyone was going down to Calumet for a free showing of *King of Kings*. And then my mother says she wants to go. My father hated Hollywood, but he wasn't going to deny her nothing at this point and Antero said he wanted to go, too. So he told Father that Toby and Eli were next door making cookies and . . . and, God help us, we . . . put on coats and left."

Buddy was sobbing now, bent against the pew in front of him.

"I don't even remember the movie," Buddy said. "I just remember getting home and running out to the shed. I couldn't get the door open because of all the snow and when I finally got inside, I pried the lid off the box with a hammer and when I touched them they were cold."

Louis stood up and walked away from Buddy, stopping across the aisle. He tried to remind himself that Buddy wasn't the real monster here, that he had been only twelve when he held down that lid and that he had endured his own gathering storm of neglect, abuse, and bullying. But knowing all that didn't ease the sharp pain in his chest.

"That night in bed, Antero and I talked about it," Buddy said, a little calmer now. "We knew we'd have to tell father the next day. Antero was so sorry. He told me it would kill mother, and maybe father, too, if they knew what he had done. All father ever wanted was that his sons serve the Lord as he had. Antero said he could do that by going on to be as good a minister as father, and since I would never be a preacher anyway, I could serve God by helping him do that. So I did."

Louis looked back at Buddy. He had left something out, maybe the one thing he was more ashamed of than anything else.

"He offered to give you his Saint Bosco medal, didn't he?"

Buddy sniffled and wiped his face.

"Answer me, Buddy."

"Yes, and I took it. But after they found the candle box in 1979, I went back there and put it in the cave. I didn't deserve it. I never deserved it."

Louis walked back to Buddy and picked up the tape recorder. Buddy grabbed his wrist to stop him.

"I need to finish," Buddy said. "I want the ending to be on that tape."

Louis nodded, and Buddy let go of his wrist.

Buddy wiped roughly at his eyes. "A few weeks later, my mother died," he went on. "A month after that, my father packed us up and left town. Down in Watersmeet, he pulled up to this house and told me to get out, that I was going to live with these strangers, the Lampos. I begged him not to leave me . . . I stood there in the yard and begged him to keep me but he just turned his back and walked away."

Louis understood what Buddy was saying and knew that was the kind of moment that could break a boy in half. But right now, he couldn't muster an ounce of sympathy.

"Are you finished?" Louis asked.

"Yeah."

Louis reached down and turned the tape recorder off.

"Let's go," he said.

When Buddy didn't move, Louis slipped a hand under Buddy's arm and helped him to his feet. Buddy's dirty face was streaked with tears. When he got to the aisle, he turned and looked back toward the altar. For a long time.

Louis's first thought was to tell Buddy to get moving, that it was time to bring this miserable day to an end. But he didn't say that.

"Do you need a minute?" Louis asked.

Buddy shook his head. "I told you, I gave up on God a long time ago."

"Why?"

"Every day for the last thirty years, I asked God to forgive me for killing those boys. I even went and saw a priest once. But God never answered me. Nothing ever changed. The pain never went away. So I don't see no sense asking again. Do you?"

Louis had no opinion on that and gestured toward the door. "Let's go then."

Buddy shuffled toward the open door, never looking up. Steele was waiting on the porch and Louis passed Buddy off to him. But before he stepped outside, he looked back. Over the long strip of faded red carpet, at the smooth backs of the wooden pews, at the gold cross at the far end and finally down to the small bones that lay beneath it.

Then he couldn't help himself. He looked up. At the high, arching beams and at whatever was beyond. He felt a sudden urge to say something, but no words came.

Finally, he turned and followed Buddy out the door.

CHAPTER FORTY

It was funny where the mind went in the twilight moments just before it succumbed to sleep. With all the things Louis had to think about that night in his Marquette hotel room after Buddy's confession, it was the memory of an old photograph that had jolted him back awake.

When Louis had first seen the photo, at the bottom of an old cigar box in Jonas Prince's hope chest, he had assumed the boys in the photo were Anthony and Buddy standing outside a church, a church he now knew was the one in Ahmeek. But he realized now that by the time the Princes arrived in Ahmeek, the Prince kids were twelve and fifteen, and the boys in the photo were much younger.

Louis pushed back the covers and rubbed his face, trying to remember what he had done with the photograph.

He had intended to put it in the Prince case file, but he never had gotten around to it. He rose and went to the dresser, where his gun holster and wallet lay. He switched on the light, blinking, and grabbed his wallet.

The photograph was here, stuffed behind his insurance card. He pulled it out and turned it over.

My boys . . .

The handwriting was back-slanted and light. It wasn't Jonas Prince's careful, small style. Another man had written it—Thomas Revel, the man who had given Jonas a beautiful old organ in exchange for taking care of his two sons.

Toby and Eli.

Louis sank down on a chair, turning the photograph over so he could see the boys.Faces . . . they had faces now.

Louis rubbed a finger gently across the surface of the old photograph, then slipped it back in his wallet. He turned off the light and went back to bed, sliding between the cold sheets. It was a long time before sleep came. But when it did, it was deep and dreamless.

He spent the next three days in Keweenaw wrapping up some loose ends with the case, then headed south. On his way back to Lansing, he made two stops. First, at a crime lab to get enlargements made of the photograph in his wallet. And then at Kmart to buy a frame.

It was near four in the afternoon by the time he walked back into St. Michael's. The place was empty, but things looked different. The conference table was stacked with white evidence boxes that would be transported to the storage warehouse now that the Prince and Tuyen Lang cases were closed. Up on the altar, the Prince murder board was gone, flipped over to display the original cold cases they had been given on the first day.

Cam's Hookers.

Emily's suicides.

Tooki's gay bashings.

Each case now had new photos and timelines, which told Louis that his three remaining team members were already back at work on their cold cases. Louis's section of the board was empty.

"Well, if it isn't Spiderman."

Cam emerged from the back holding a coffee mug. Emily and Tooki tailed behind, Emily popping the tab on a Coke can.

"So tell us about the Great Train Trestle adventure," Cam said.

Louis wondered if the edge in Cam's voice was good-natured ribbing or a snippet of resentment at being dispatched to the other end of the U.P. to hunt down SISU sightings while Louis and the boss grabbed the headlines.

"You all would've done the same thing," Louis said. "And in retrospect, it was probably the stupidest thing I've ever done."

"Was there a SISU sticker on his truck?" Cam asked.

"Yes, there was."

Cam looked away. Louis knew Cam's pique would pass as he and the others built own successes. But right now, he played it easy.

"Do any of you know if we have a hammer and nails in here any-where?" Louis asked.

"In the utility room," Tooki said.

Louis went to the back and found the hammer and nails. When he returned to the nave, the others were working at their desks and didn't look up as Louis busied himself putting an enlargement of Toby and Eli Revel in the Kmart frame. He took the frame, hammer, and nails to the wall of old confessional booths. He drove a nail into the old wood paneling and hung up the picture.

He took a step back to appraise his work. A few moments later, Emily and Tooki wandered over, followed by Cam. The four of them stood looking at the framed photograph.

"So you're starting a victim wall?" Tooki asked.

"Yeah, sort of," Louis said. "Though that's kind of a morbid name for it."

"Call it the 10-24 wall," Emily said. "Radio code for assignment completed."

Louis nodded. "The 10-24 wall it is."

Tooki shook his head. "But no one will know what this is, why the picture is here."

Tooki was right. The wall needed something else to help define it and Louis knew where to get it. He hurried up the steps to Steele's loft and grabbed the wood plaque lying on the credenza.

When he returned, Cam gave a low whistle when he saw what Louis had. "I think the captain wanted that for his office," he said.

"It belongs here," Louis said, picking up another nail.

Louis positioned the plaque about six inches above the boys' photo and nailed it in.

"'The Truth Takes Time'," Emily said, reading the engraved words aloud.

"Are you going to put Jonas and Tuyen up there too?" Cam asked.

Louis hesitated. "We're a cold case unit," he said. "That's our focus. I think we should dedicate this wall to those victims."

Cam pursed his lips and stared at the picture of the boys.

"Are you good with that?" Louis pressed.

It took a moment, but he finally gave a tight nod and started back to his desk. Louis watched him, trying to think of something to say to make things better without calling attention to Cam's pettiness. He couldn't change what happened or how it happened. And he wasn't going to apologize for doing his job.

Emily touched his arm. "The captain played Buddy's confession tape for us. Are we charging him with anything?"

"No," Louis said. "He was twelve at the time. Can't take a forty-two-year-old guy into juvenile court."

"I suppose not. Did you find the boys' father?"

"Sheriff Nurmi turned up a death certificate for him dated late 1962. Thomas Revel died of emphysema, so it's likely he knew he was sick when he gave his sons to Jonas. The mother died years before that."

Emily looked back at the photograph. "Poor little guys had no one. Where are they going to be buried?"

"Sheriff Nurmi is taking care of them," Louis said. "They'll be having a service up in Eagle River when the lab releases the remains. I'll be flying back for that."

The bang of the front door opening made them look up. Steele had come in. The last time Louis had seen him he'd been mud-splattered and exhausted, getting on a prop plane headed back to Lansing to calm the bosses at headquarters. Today, he wore a navy blue three-piece suit, white shirt and royal blue tie. He carried a bundle of newspapers and his black briefcase.

"Sorry I'm late," Steele said. "I've been at headquarters all day. Good to see you back, Louis. Everything wrapped up in Keweenaw?"

"Yes, sir."

Cam turned around in his chair. "So how are we looking down at headquarters?"

Steele tossed the newspapers on the conference table. "I can't say they were impressed with our methods," he said. "But they were with the results. And they like good press coverage. The team is on solid ground. At least for now."

Louis walked over and sifted through the newspapers. They ran the gamut from the *Detroit Free Press* to the *Mackinac Town Crier,* with a pile of mid-sized papers in between. The case wasn't the big headline in every edition, but Anthony Prince's picture was on every front page. And often, so was Steele's.

"What's this?" Steele asked.

Louis looked up. Steele had moved to the confessional wall and was staring at the photo of Toby and Eli. Then he turned, waiting for an answer from someone.

"We call it the 10-24 wall," Tooki said.

It took Steele a moment then he nodded slowly. "You're all in favor of this?" he asked.

"Yeah, we are," Cam said.

Louis suspected that Steele might be mildly pissed about his officers—his minions—taking things into their own hands, and he was probably struggling with how to express his approval.

"Well, let's get back to work on filling this wall up," Steele said.

He went to the conference table, picked up a copy of the *Lansing State Journal* and started up the stairs to his loft. Halfway up the steps, he stopped and looked back over the nave.

"It's Friday," he said. "I want all of you to take the next four days off. I'll see you all Wednesday morning."

Steele disappeared up the stairs and a few seconds later, the lights went on and the piano music started.

For a long moment, the four of them just stared up at the loft then looked around at each other.

"Four days," Cam said. "Long enough to get laid and wasted but not long enough to get into real trouble."

He grabbed his leather jacket off a chair. Emily picked up her purse and yellow rain slicker. Tooki was just standing there, looking bewildered and Louis had the feeling he had nowhere to go and no one to see.

Emily must have sensed it, too, because she went to Tooki and touched his shoulder. "I'm starved. You want to come to Dagwood's with me?"

"Dagwood's?" Cam piped up. "Is that that dive over by the freeway?"

"It's not a dive. It has good burgers and chili," Emily said. She picked up Tooki's windbreaker and held it out. "Come on, you're coming with me."

Cam hadn't made a move to leave. He was standing there, staring at Emily, and when she didn't say anything he said, "I could use a burger and a brew."

Emily smiled. "Let's go."

Cam and Tooki started to the door and Emily turned to Louis. "You coming?"

Louis shook his head. "I don't know," he said. "I'm still coming down from all this. Not sure I'd be good company."

She hesitated then said, "Okay, I won't push. But we'll save you a chair."

They left, the heavy door banging shut behind them, and the nave was quiet again. Even the piano music from the loft had stopped. Louis went to his desk and began to straighten up some papers, but his mind was already halfway up the highway on the way to Echo Bay, and he was imagining the look on Joe's face when he showed up at her cabin door.

"Louis."

He turned and looked up. Steele was standing at the loft railing.

"Can you come up before you leave?" Steele said. "I need to talk to you."

CHAPTER FORTY-ONE

Steele was standing behind his desk. His posture was stiff, his expression unreadable, except for a solemnity in his eyes, as if he would rather not do whatever it was he was about to do.

There was a chair in front of the desk, but Louis didn't take it. The air of formality told Louis that whatever this was, it should probably be taken standing up.

"Let me start with this," Steele said. "I knew when I put this team together that we'd be working long hours in close quarters. For that reason, I wanted to know everything about my candidates I could possibly know."

Louis tightened. Had something popped up in his past he needed to explain?

"When the time came for me to start whittling my list of candidates down to my final five," Steele said, "I'll be honest, I almost set you aside, despite your glowing recommendation from Norm Rafsky."

"Why?"

"Because I couldn't figure you out," Steele said. "I read your law school admissions essay. I rehashed every move you made in Loon Lake. I studied every case you worked as a PI. But I still couldn't figure out what it was that compelled you to chuck law school and put on a uniform."

Steele picked up a thick, tattered manila folder and a large yellow envelope bound together with a fat rubber band.

"So I went for what we call deep background," Steele said. "I requested your child services file."

A prickle moved up Louis's arms. He felt violated, just as he had that day he realized that Steele was screwing with their heads by offering up cold cases with personal undercurrents.

Louis struggled to keep his tone civil when he spoke. "Did you get your answer?"

"I did," Steele said.

Steele held the file out and Louis accepted it. Maybe now was the time to confront Steele on his game, but suddenly it seemed pointless. He was none the worse for having worked the boys-in-the-box case. Except for the nightmares. And now he had in his hand the one thing that could answer the rest of his questions.

"I know you requested your file from Detroit," Steele said. "I apologize for not giving it to you when they notified me, but we were deep into the Prince case and I didn't want you distracted."

Louis understood that, but said nothing, not quite willing to give Steele any indication he was okay with any of this personal shit.

Steele started putting papers in his open briefcase. "I have another meeting," he said. "If you'd like to sit up here and take a look through that, you're welcome to. No one will bother you and it's a good place to reflect. Or as Tooki would say, balance your Chakras."

Louis fingered the ragged edges of the folder. Truth was, he *did* want to read it and he wanted to read it now. But he hesitated to do it here, in Steele's office.

"Louis."

Louis met his eyes.

"You were a brave boy," Steele said. "And you're a brave police officer. I am pleased to have you as a member of my team."

The compliment was so unexpected, Louis had to play it over in his head a second time and then find the simplest of a reply.

"Thank you, sir."

Steele picked up his briefcase and left the loft. Louis looked after him for a minute, then moved to the sofa and sat down. He pulled the rubber band off the folder, set the manila envelope aside and opened the file.

On the left, he saw health and school records, full of checkmarks and notes from teachers. He flipped through those first, figuring they would be pretty benign, things he could handle before he worked up to the harder stuff. Occasionally, he paused to read the handwritten notes made by teachers.

Child is bright but refuses to do the work.

Child excels at solitary projects but resists participating in groups.

Louis turned his attention to the other side of the folder, to the reports that detailed each foster home placement. The document on top marked his exit from the system, when he aged out at eighteen, in November of 1977.

He had been living ten years with Phillip and Frances Lawrence by then in Plymouth. He wanted to read these eventually, but right now, they were not the years was interested in.

He wanted to read about what came *before* Plymouth, starting with the removal from his home in Mississippi at age seven, all the way through to that night the police arrived at the house on Strathmoor. The last night he saw Sammy.

He found what he needed in the back of the file, his first placement after he left Mississippi. It was on the east side of Detroit, with a distant aunt of his mother's. That explained why he had been sent out of state, here to Michigan. Maybe she was the only relative who wanted him.

The caseworker's notes . . .

Child is a compulsive runaway.

Child is almost non-verbal and lacks social skills.

Foster mother feels overwhelmed. Wishes to return child to state custody.

There was a photo of him stapled to one of the reports—a skinny, brown-skinned kid with a halo of unruly hair and empty gray eyes. It reminded him of the photos UNICEF put up on late night TV to get donations for African children.

He turned the pages until he found his next home. In April, he had been placed with people who lived in the heart of Detroit, near Tiger Stadium. He had a vague memory of hanging out near the ballfield, hoping for out-of-the-park home runs, but nothing else.

The caseworker notes . . .

Child has run away six times in one month.

Child is losing weight. Has many unexplained accidents.

Request for placement with approved fosters Phillip and Frances Lawrence of Plymouth denied at this time due to the department's policy on not placing Negro children in white households.

Louis re-read the last sentence several times, struck by the use of a word he had never had to write on forms as he grew older. It bothered him that Phillip had never told him he had made a request to take Louis in months before he was actually sent there. If the state had approved the Lawrences' request in April, he never would have ended up at Moe's house on Strathmoor that summer.

His next home was with a family on Detroit's west side.

Child has run away nine times in 30 days.

Child frequently caught trespassing after dark at nearby Henry Ford high school track.

Louis had no memory of the home, but he did remember the mindless, leg-burning runs through the darkness along the high school track. The same kind of runs he had made in high school as a cross country athlete. And the same kind he had made that night on the shores of Lake Superior after his first nightmare.

Another photo. Same boy, same empty gray eyes. He set this picture aside, too, and turned another page.

Suddenly he was looking at Moe.

His heart kicked as he stared at the ugly, brown, pock-marked face, bracing himself for an onslaught of memories—images, sounds, smells. But none came. Instead, there was just a pain, a breathtaking, deep physical pain that felt like the plunge of a knife in his chest.

Breathe, he told himself, breathe.

How could this man still trigger this kind of emotion?

Breathe.

He read the report. The foster placement was made in July, 1967, a few weeks before the Detroit riots and four months before Louis's eighth birthday. There was one home visit made in late summer with only a few notes.

Child appears well adjusted. Runaway attempts have stopped.

That was because Moe tied them to their beds at night.

Child appears healthy and has put on weight.

That was because all Moe kept in the house was junk food for his cravings that came when he got high. Dinners of donuts, Twinkees, potato chips, and one night two bowls of raw, yellow cake batter that Sammy made.

Louis turned the page.

Detroit Police Incident Report November 16, 1967.

Officers were called to home of Massimo Schrader at 2:06 a.m. in response to a report of child battery. Upon arriving at the scene, officers were confronted at the door by one black male and denied entry. The black male, later identified as Massimo Schrader, resisted arrest and assaulted an officer. He was taken into custody at the scene. Upon searching the premises, officers found multiple containers of marijuana, two "bongs," misc. drug paraphilia and seven handguns, three of which were determined to be stolen. Two black male juveniles, age seven and ten, were removed from the scene. (See supplemental DPD report #2455) Both juveniles were transported to the hospital.

Louis turned the page, looking for that supplemental report that would give him details on Sammy and tell him if Sammy was dead or alive. But there were no more police reports, only a series of CPS interviews with Louis.

He read each one, but they were simply his account of the horrors of life with Moe and throughout them, he mentioned Sammy only by his first name. They were followed by three pages of Xerox photos that documented the burns and bruises on his body. He set them aside, face down.

The next page detailed his final placement, at the tri-level home in Plymouth, with Phillip and Frances.

While it remains against our long-standing policy of inter-racial placements, it has been determined this case presents dire circumstances and that it is in the best interest of this child at this time to be placed with the Lawrences.

Louis was disappointed that there was no further information, but now that he had the case file and that Detroit PD report number, maybe he could find out more. He also made a mental note to call Phillip. He'd never been very good at staying in touch, but today he felt an urgency to hear Phillip's voice. There was a lot to say to him and Frances. A lot.

Louis started to close the folder, then remembered the manila envelope. He picked it up and opened it. Inside was a trial six-page transcript, with two lines typed on the first page.

Wayne County 24th District Criminal Court
State of Michigan v. Mossimo J. Schrader

On the second page, Louis found transcribed testimony, the participants listed only as Witness and Adams. He assumed Adams was a lawyer and had to look to the top of the page to see whose testimony he was reading.

It was his own.

Moe went on trial and Louis had testified.

How could he not remember this?

He had a few memories of being in courtrooms, but they were just like blurry film clips in his head. He had always figured he was there for a routine hearing, or to meet new foster parents. Never a trial.

But he realized that *this* would tell him exactly what happened the night the cops came to Strathmoor. This would tell him what happened to Sammy.

The first section of his testimony was a recount of what went on in the house over that summer and into the winter. He scanned it quickly, eager to get to the night the police took Moe away.

Finally, he found it.

Adams: Louis, do you remember the night when the police officers came to your house?

Witness: Yes, sir.

Adams: Can you tell me what happened before the police officers got there?

Witness: Me and Sammy watched Gunsmoke.

Adams: What happened after Gunsmoke was over?

Witness: We was cleaning up the kitchen but me and Sammy was messing around and I dropped a plate and it got broke.

Adams: What happened after that?

Witness: Mr. Moe come and he started yelling. Sammy told him he dropped the plate cause he always took the blame for stuff and Mr. Moe grabbed him and started hitting. We busted loose and ran up to the bedroom.

Adams: Did Mr. Moe follow you upstairs?

Witness: He always chased us. When we run, he gets madder.

Adams: What happened upstairs?

Witness: Sammy push me in the closet like he do sometimes to keep me from getting beat and he tried to get under the bed but Mr. Moe catched him and started whooping on him.

Adams: How did Mr. Moe whoop on Sammy? With a closed fist, like this?

Witness: Yes, sir. Then he used the strap.

Adams: What strap? His belt?

Witness: No, sir. The big strap he use to tie us to the bed at night.

Adams: How many times did Mr. Moe hit Sammy?

Witness: (Shrugs.)

Adams: Ten times? Twenty times?

Witness: Maybe one hundred times.

Adams: Where were you while Mr. Moe was hitting Sammy?

Witness: I told you, I was in the closet.

Adams: Was the closet door closed?

Witness: Not all the way.

Adams: So you could see what was happening?

Witness: I could see in the mirror.

Adams: What mirror is that?

Witness: The mirror on the inside of the door. If the door be open a little, I can see what's going on in the bedroom. That's how I seen Sammy get hurt.

Adams: What happened after Mr. Moe stopped hitting Sammy?

Witness: He call me out of the closet and told me to get in bed. Then he buckle us both down and he left.

Adams: By buckle down, you mean tie you to the bed?

Witness: Yes, sir.

Adams: After Mr. Moe left, did you and Sammy talk?

Witness: Yes, sir. Sammy was crying. He was bleeding all over and he couldn't talk right. He couldn't get up to go to the bathroom and he peed the bed.

Adams: What else did Sammy say?

Witness: He told me he wanted to die. I told him no one should ever want to die but he said that dying had to be better than living with Mr. Moe. He said his momma was in Heaven and he wanted to go be with her.

Adams: What did you do?

Witness: Sometimes if Mr. Moe don't buckle me up right, I could get my foot out of the strap and get loose and that's what I did. So I got up and get my coat and I opened the window.

Adams: Where were you going to go?

Witness: I was going to go the Dairy Queen and get Sammy a doctor. I didn't want him dying.

Adams: So you went out the window in the dark. How did you get down to the ground from the second floor?

Witness: It was snowing I just slid down the roof and then I jumped.

Adams: Weren't you scared, Louis?

Witness: No, sir, I been going out windows a long time. I'm good at it.

Adams: Where did you go?

Witness: I runned to the Dairy Queen but it was closed up. So I started walking but I got so cold I was going to go home but then I seen a police car.

Adams: You approached the policemen?

Witness: Yes, sir. They take me home and they call other policemen and then they arrest Mr. Moe but I didn't see Sammy. They wouldn't let me go back upstairs.

Adams: Thank you, Louis. You can step down.

There were no more pages. He sat there, sudden and unexpected memories filling his head. He remembered sliding down that icy roof and landing in a snow drift. Remembered running in the dark until his feet were frozen. Remembered crawling into the back of a warm car and into the arms of a police officer.

And now there were memories of that day in court, too. The itchiness of a stiff, new shirt, the rows and rows of white faces looking at him, and the feeling of being big and important, sitting in a chair so tall his feet couldn't touch the floor.

But the memories felt distant, not as visceral as he would have thought, and he wondered if he hadn't just conjured them up while reading. But then he thought about what Cam had said that day when they were talking to Weems.

You have a gazillion memories in that head because the brain never throws anything away.

He had a feeling Cam was right about that. At least he hoped Cam was right. He wanted these memories to be real. He wanted them to be his.

Louis slipped the trial transcript back into the envelope and straightened the papers in the CPS file before he closed it. As he reached for the rubber band, he noticed something he hadn't seen when he sat down.

It was a small message slip stapled to the front of the folder. The bold, squared-off handwriting was familiar. It belonged to Steele.

Sammy Robinson

2102 Hubble

Detroit, Michigan

Sammy was alive.

A powerful wave of relief moved through Louis, but he as he stared at the address, he had to wonder about Steele. Why had he made the extra effort to track down Sammy? How had he even known Louis was thinking about him? Dreaming about him?

Louis looked over at Steele's empty desk.

Was Steele simply that perceptive, that good a profiler? Or worse, had Louis had a nightmare in the Pine Top Inn that night he shared a room with Steele? Hell, maybe one day he would ask him. But right now, he had what he needed.

Louis pulled the slip of the paper from the staple and put it in his shirt pocket. Then he banded everything else together and went downstairs to the nave. He locked his file in the bottom drawer of his desk and grabbed his jacket off the back of the chair.

As he pulled it on, he took a minute to look around. The only sound was the soft wheeze of the wind in the organ pipes. The only light was a rainbow of colors that crept across the walls, a reflection of the setting sun through the high stained-glass window.

At that moment, it was easy to feel as if he were in a place of sanctity and grace. But the bulletin board and evidence boxes—like the 10-24 wall—were reminders that what they did here was a lot closer to Hell than Heaven.

But there was nowhere else he wanted to be.

His eyes moved to clock on the wall.

Except maybe Dagwood's.

He hoped the others were still at the bar and he hoped Emily had saved him a chair. He wanted a cold beer and a basket of fried pickles and he wanted to spend time with his cop friends.

He hadn't done that for a very long time.

CHAPTER FORTY-TWO

Dagwood's was dark and disorderly. Louis stood just inside the door, peering into the gloom and smoke haze. Friday night and the place was packed. Flannel-backed workers from the GM Assembly Plant. Waffle House waitresses in wilted robin-blue uniforms. And dominating the front, a huge pack of frat boys celebrating a brother's coming of age with screams to "chug the jug!"

Louis's spirits sagged. The team wasn't here. He was about to leave when he saw a flash of copper hair in the farthest corner. It was Emily, standing up and waving him back.

The three of them were seated in the last booth, Emily and Tooki on one side and Cam sprawled over the opposite booth. On the table between them were five beer bottles and two empty shot glasses. Cam was nursing a Strohs, Emily a glass of red wine, and Tooki . . .

Louis wasn't sure what he was drinking. A tumbler of orange juice with a cherry speared by a paper umbrella.

"We were about to give up on you," Emily said.

"She wouldn't let us order food until you got here," Cam said. "Man, I could eat a friggin' cow."

Louis wanted to sit down but there wasn't enough room for both him and Cam in the booth. Emily let out a sigh and got up.

"Move over," she said, slapping Cam on the shoulder. Cam straightened, and she sat down. Louis slid in next to Tooki, who was tucked in the corner, transfixed by the Pistons-Hawks game playing on the TV over Cam's head.

"What took you so long?" Emily said.

"I had paperwork to review," Louis said. He had already decided that when he got up to Echo Bay, he was going to tell Joe about his file and his past. It was like a long-rusted-shut door had opened, and the awful black void he had always felt inside was now filling with light. But he wasn't sure he wanted to tell Emily or anyone else. It was still too raw.

And he still hadn't processed Steele's part in all this. Steele had known he was foster child, had known Louis would choose the boys-in-the-box case. Steele had known each of the team's pasts and had picked the scabs over their most tender places. The question was still there unanswered—why?

Louis scanned his colleagues' faces. Cam was flirting with the waitress as she took his order. Emily was playing with the stem of her wine glass, her gaze a million miles away. And Tooki had given up on the basketball game and was sitting ramrod straight in the booth with his eyes closed. The frat boys up front had started feeding the juke box and "U Can't Touch This" blared out over the bar noise.

The waitress took their orders—burgers all around with a side of fried pickles. After she left, Louis reached across, tapped Emily's hand and nodded toward Tooki, who still hadn't opened his eyes even to order food.

"Oh, he's fine," she said softly. "I cut him off after two drinks. He said he never touches alcohol, but tonight he wanted to celebrate closing the case."

"What's he drinking?" Louis asked.

"Harvey Wallbangers," Emily said.

"Girl's drink," Cam said and belched softly.

Emily shot him a silencing look. Tooki didn't open his eyes.

The frat boys up front were getting rowdier, one of them trying to sing along with the juke box. The factory guys yelled at them to take it down a notch.

"Any plans for your time off?" Louis asked, raising his voice over the din.

Cam set his bottle down. "I was thinking of flying out to Phoenix. Got a half-sister out there I haven't seen in a while."

Louis looked at Emily. "Play some golf, redecorate the beach house, get my hair straightened," she said with a twisted smile.

Louis knew she had no living family and doubted she had any close friends anywhere nearby. Tooki still had his eyes closed.

"You going up to Echo Bay?" Emily asked.

"First thing tomorrow morning," Louis said.

"Good for you," Emily said.

Emily looked away and took a drink of her wine. The table was quiet, and the music rushed back in. The song was R.E.M.'s "Losing My Religion." Louis couldn't help but smile.

"Why do you think Steele did it?" Cam asked suddenly.

"Gave us four days off?" Emily asked.

"No, gave us those damn cases."

Louis met Emily's eyes over the tops of the beer bottles. No one spoke for a full minute.

"Okay, I'm going to fucking just say this," Cam said. "My mother was a hooker. And I don't think it was any fucking coincidence that one of the cases I had to choose from was about a dead hooker."

Louis pulled in a slow breath and let it out. "I was a foster kid," he said. "I had a foster brother I thought had died. Like the boys in the box."

"Jesus," Cam said. He looked at Emily, waiting.

It was a long time before she answered. "I've had an experience with suicide in my family," she said.

Louis knew that was as close as she would get to her own truth, at least for now. They fell quiet again. R.E.M. was heading into the chorus now.

Every whisper of every waking hour, I'm choosing my confessions . . .

Tooki stirred, opening his eyes. "The Buddha says there are three things that cannot be long hidden," he said softly. "The sun, the moon, and the truth."

He took a sip of his drink. "I am gay," he said.

Louis glanced at Cam, praying that for once he could keep his mouth shut. Cam didn't say a word. His expression didn't even change. He just picked up his beer and drained it.

The waitress appeared with a tray filled with drinks and plastic baskets of food. The awkwardness of the previous moment was dispersed by the business of doling out napkins and the squirting out of catsup and mustard. Then the only sound was of eating and the satisfied grunts coming from Cam. Louis was hungry, but he ate slowly, thinking about Steele as the last lines of R.E.M.'s song rattled around in his head.

But that was just a dream, just a dream, just a dream, just a dream . . .

Cam pushed his empty plate away, grabbed his beer and slumped back in the booth. "I did some looking into Junia's background," he said.

"Junia? Why?" Emily asked.

"I always thought it was weird the way she just upped and quit," he said. "She was real excited about this job and it just didn't make sense that she'd get mad and leave."

Louis knew where Cam was going with this, but he wanted to see how much Cam had put together before he said anything.

"Remember that first day when Steele told us to pick the cases we wanted?" Cam went on. "Junia was the first one to get up and she picked the Bay City Black Widow case."

Emily nodded slowly. "The abused housewife who murdered her husband."

"Yup." Cam took a swig of beer. "I found out that about ten years ago, Junia went through a real nasty divorce and a few years later, she was the prime suspect in the murder of her ex-husband."

"I did an FBI search on her," Emily said. "*That* never came up."

"She went back to her maiden name right after," Cam said. "Junia put her husband through medical school, then the asshole left her for a younger woman. It was a small town and a lot of ugly shit got tossed out there, like the husband had abused Junia for years. Junia was cleared when they caught the real killer, but the damage was done."

"He beat her?" Tooki asked.

They all looked at him.

"My father beat my mother," Tooki said softly. "And me sometimes."

Tooki's voice was so soft, for a second or two, the moment froze. Then Emily spoke.

"Because you were gay?" she asked.

Tooki shrugged. "For that and other things. It's why I left India so young."

Cam shifted uncomfortably. "Well, Junia's husband never laid a hand on her. It was all playing with her head shit, I might come back, I might not, and then someone released a whole bunch of phone messages from him calling her fat and stupid."

Louis picked up his beer and took a long, slow drink. That was why Junia had quit the team so suddenly. It wasn't just that the Black Widow case cut too close to the bone. It was also that she thought Steele was screwing with her head.

"So I'm going to throw the question out there one more time," Cam said. "Why did Steele do it?"

"He wants us to face something in our past?" Tooki asked.

"But why?" Cam said. "Who does that? Why would he even care?"

Emily, who had been quiet, put her wine glass down. "He might be psychologically projecting."

"What's that?" Cam asked.

"It's a theory in psychology. In simple terms, you have a problem you can't accept so you project it on others. It can be as simple as, I'm not stealing, you are. I'm not paranoid, you are. Or in this case, I don't have a problem with my past, but you do. And as a commander, Steele had five people to project onto—us."

They all stared at her.

"It's just a theory," she added.

They were all quiet, lost in their thoughts. Louis realized the bar had gone quiet. The frat boys had left and only three guys lingered at the bar.

"Well, maybe we should project shit right back at the boss," Cam said. "Considering what he did to us, we have a right to know what his heavy baggage is. Any thoughts?"

"A guy over at the computer lab told me something a couple weeks ago," Tooki said. "He said the captain's uncle was a chief of police in some small town and was arrested and jailed for corruption."

Emily nodded. "Steele's father died when he was twelve and his uncle pretty much raised him. And if you find out your father figure is dirty, it might explain why you end up in internal affairs busting other cops. But you'd think he would've worked that issue out."

"Then maybe it has something to do with this team," Cam said. "Maybe he has something dirty on his own record and this team is his last chance to redeem himself."

Louis knew Cam was drunk and wanted to keep the conversation going just to throw some shit-rocks at the boss, but Cam had no idea how close he was. Whatever damage Steele had hidden deep inside himself had come very close to revealing itself that day up in Buddy's cabin.

I asked you a question, captain. Is that what we are about? Is this team just another line to your resume?

No! It's not about me. It's about—

About what, captain?

It's about her!

It wasn't nothing. And it wasn't that Steele had just misspoken, as he had said. It was real, and it was so powerful that it had shaped and bent Steele into what he now was. A man alone with his work, always on the hunt, but a man with a wound. One old and scarred over, but so deep that the man couldn't even bring himself to say her name.

"So what do we do now?" Tooki asked.

Louis felt Emily's eyes on him, as if she had read his thoughts about Steele and now was waiting for him to lead the team. But lead them where? On a mission to expose Steele's past? Given their talents, they could probably do it, especially now that Louis had a good idea of where to start. But to what end? So they could all know something personal about the boss?

The irony of it was too weird. Five years ago, Steele had destroyed Louis's law enforcement career. Now Louis had the chance to wreak a little revenge.

But after what Steele had said to him this afternoon, after Steele had given him the gift of his own past, Louis wasn't sure revenge was what he wanted.

"What do we do?" Tooki asked again.

Cam drained his beer and smacked it down on the table. "I know what I'm going to do," he said. "I want this job bad and I'm not going to let that fucker fuck with my head. I'm going to solve my hooker case and whatever more shit that fucker throws at me."

He rose unsteadily. "I think I have a plane to catch," he said. "You all get some sleep, get laid and get drunk." He gave Tooki a smile. "Or say a prayer to Buddha for all of us. See you in church on Wednesday."

He tossed some bills on the table and walked away. Emily started to pull some money out of her purse but Louis said, "I got this."

She slid out of the booth, putting on her slicker. "Come on, Tooki," she said. "We're going over to Saugatuck for the weekend."

"What's in Saugatuck?" Tooki asked.

Louis laughed. Emily threw him a look that Tooki didn't seem to catch. She had forgotten Tooki had only been in Michigan a short time and had not yet found those hidden gems of little towns that dotted that mitten's lake shore, each with their own unique cultures and offerings.

"I gotta pee," Tooki said. "I'll meet you outside."

Louis waited until he was out of earshot, then looked up at Emily.

"So you're not going to tell him Saugatuck is gay heaven?"

"I don't think it will take him long to figure it out," she said. "It'll be a nice trip. Antiques for me, whatever for him."

"Take good care of him."

"I will," she said as she walked away.

And then he was alone. Louis lingered long enough to finish his beer and eat the last of the fried pickles, then paid the bill and left, stepping out of Dagwood's into a cool night. For a couple minutes, he just stood there, drinking in the fresh air and watching the red taillights disappear down Kalamazoo Street.

One word was swirling in his head.

Her.

In some moments, she had a face. Angular, with hooded gray eyes and lips that whispered his name in the dark. Joe's face. But the other *her* was there, too. The one without a face, the one without a name. The one who would unlock the mystery of Mark Steele.

He would find her, he knew suddenly.

He had to.

Because the man who had destroyed him had also saved him. And Louis had to know why.

CHAPTER FORTY-THREE

There was nothing he wanted more than to get to Echo Bay, make love to Joe, share a good dinner and sit on a dune together to watch the sun set over Lake Michigan. But on Saturday morning, as he put his suitcase in the trunk of the Mustang, Louis found himself slowing down. Because he knew there was something else he had to do first—two things, in fact.

One was to go to Detroit and find Sammy. He knew now he had been stuck on the same pages for too long, rereading and reliving a brutal fragment of his life that he had never really faced, or even understood. And he wanted to move on.

The other thing was something he needed to know. And it was something only the computer at St. Michael's could tell him.

The church parking lot was empty when he pulled in. Louis let himself in, went to the computer and logged into the state records database. A few seconds later, he had the answer he needed.

Moe was dead.

In 1968, he had been sentenced to nine years in Jackson State Prison for felony child abuse and weapons charges. Three years in, he suffered a major stroke and died six months later. He was buried within the walls of the penitentiary in a grave marked only by a number.

Louis shut down the computer, left the office, and got in his Mustang to head to Detroit. He tuned into a classic rock station, but he didn't really listen to the music. His thoughts drifted back to Moe, and the anger stirred inside him. Moe was no longer a monster lurking outside the closet. He was just a pathetic, angry man who had died alone, confined to a bed in a prison infirmary, with shit bags taped to his belly.

Good, Louis thought. That was damn good.

He knew that he would have to let his anger go. But right now, he let it simmer. He had earned this anger and he wanted to keep it for a while.

By the time he reached the Detroit city limits, the sun was out in full force and Motown music had taken over the radio. The neat lawns and pretty tri-levels of the suburbs were replaced by weedy empty lots and crumbling Tudors. Knots of teenagers hung on corners, with nothing to do and nowhere to go.

He was on the northwest side, not far from the Strathmoor house, and he was starting to worry about how he would find Sammy, if he would be as broken as this neighborhood, maybe entangled in drugs or a gang or worse. If that happened, what would he do?

What are you doing, Kincaid? Why are you here?

When he realized he had no good answer that went beyond a selfish need to know, he thought about turning around and heading north. But the scenery changed again, and he found himself on a street of brick bungalows with neat lawns and tulips in bloom. A blue and white sign offered an explanation: NEW HORIZONS DEVELOPMENT PROJECT. SAVING OUR CITY ONE BLOCK AT A TIME.

He slowed the Mustang and followed the house numbers to 2102 Hubble. Sammy's home was yellow brick, with a small porch covered by a white aluminum awning. Louis pulled to the curb and got out, taking a deep breath before he walked to the door. He had no idea what he was going to say.

He knocked. When no one answered, he knocked again. Then a voice came from the house next door, a big man standing on his lawn, holding a rake.

"You looking for Sammy?" the man hollered.

Louis came down the porch steps and stood on the grass. "Yeah."

Louis saw suspicion cross the man's face and he knew the man was just being protective of his neighbor. In this city, you had to be. He retrieved his badge and held it up. "State Police. He's not in any trouble. I'm an old friend."

"He's probably down at the school," the man said. "That's where he is every Saturday."

"The school?"

"Coyle Junior High," the man said, "Two blocks down on the right."

Louis thanked him and returned to the Mustang. Like most old Detroit schools, Coyle was a monument to fifties-era education, two stories of red brick and limestone, with grated windows and a giant wooden sign in front that declared the Coyle Panthers the AA State Baseball Champions for 1990.

He spotted some kids on a baseball field, parked the Mustang and walked to the chain-link fence that enclosed the diamond. There was an open gate about twenty feet down, but he decided to stand at the fence and watch.

The diamond was just dirt, the outfield patchy grass stippled with dandelions, the low bleachers needed paint and the rusted backstop was bowed. But the boys—all about thirteen and all black—didn't seem to mind.

Louis saw only one adult, a tall, gangly guy with a tight helmet of black hair and nut-brown skin. He stood at home plate with a lanky boy, guiding the kid's hands up and down the bat as he mimicked forward thrusts, teaching him how to bunt.

Sammy . . .

A slow smile came to Louis's face.

Sammy was a coach, maybe a teacher, too. And that meant he hadn't let what happened in Strathmoor—and God knows where else—break him.

Louis felt a swell of pride, though he had no idea why. It wasn't like he had anything to do with it. And the memories were back, memories that came now with just a bit more clarity.

Quit swinging like you Willie Mays. You ain't got the power for that.

But I wanna hit homers, Sammy.

It ain't about you. It's all about the other guys out on them bases. They's counting on you to bring them home. You hearin' me, Loogy?

Loogy . . . he remembered now. It wasn't just a nickname for his name Louis. Sammy had tagged him with it because he was left-handed.

A stray baseball clanged against the fence and Louis looked over to see a kid running toward him. He was a runt, probably a little brother of a player. A dusty Detroit Tigers jersey hung like a nightgown on his scrawny body.

The kid picked up the ball and looked hard at Louis. "You need something, mister?" he asked.

"No. I'm good."

The kid popped the ball in and out of his glove and continued to stare, suspicion darkening his eyes. "Why you hawking us then?"

"I'm not hawking you."

"You got a kid out there?"

"No. I just like watching."

"Then you must be a perv or something, man."

"I'm not."

"Why you here then?"

"I just stopped by to make sure someone was okay."

"Who?"

Louis's gaze turned back to Sammy.

"Well, is he?" the kid asked. "Is he okay?"

"Yeah," Louis said. "I think he is."

"Aight, then," the kid said. "Stay easy, man."

The boy trotted off toward the diamond. Louis stayed where he was for maybe a minute longer, then decided it was time to go. There was no reason to introduce himself. It didn't feel like the right time or place. And he had his answers now. That's what this trip had really been about, satisfying a need to find a good ending to this thing that he had come to call his story.

As he walked to his car, he noticed the only other vehicle in the lot, a red Ford Bronco. He glanced back at the diamond, then took a slow walk around the SUV. There was a Coyle Junior High faculty parking permit in the back window, a pile of bats in the rear seat and a bumper sticker on the rear that read: No Grass Stains, No Glory. Had to be Sammy's car.

Louis hesitated, reconsidering. Was it right to just walk away and keep this moment of closure to himself?

He pulled a business card from his wallet and started to stick it under the wiper, but then stopped. He couldn't just leave the card. If Sammy didn't recognize Louis's name and saw only the state police logo, the card would end up in the trash and the poor guy would probably lose sleep wondering why some cops wanted to talk to him.

Louis pulled a pen from his back pocket but again hesitated, trying to think of something to write that didn't sound corny.

He turned the card back to the front and drew a line through his first name. Above it, he wrote one word: Loogy.

He slipped it under the driver's side wiper and walked back to the Mustang. If Sammy wanted to revisit those months on Strathmoor, he would call and somewhere between Lansing and Detroit, Louis and his foster brother would sit and have a beer and talk about whatever long-lost brothers talked about.

And if Sammy didn't call . . .

Well, he could live with that, too. He knew Sammy was okay and if Sammy had ever wondered about him, then he would now know that Louis was okay, too. And sometimes, most times maybe, that was enough.

CHAPTER FORTY-FOUR

He was just outside Ann Arbor when he began to lose the signal for the Motown station. *My Girl* wavered in and out, and finally Louis gave up. He spun the radio dial trying to find something else but all he got was classical, sports talk, and Barry Manilow yelping about Mandy.

He was about to turn the radio off when he heard a familiar bass voice.

"The problem here is not just believing in some fantasy penned 2000 years ago by stupid men in the most ignorant part of the world, guys who thought the earth was flat and wiped their butts with fig leaves . . ."

Good Grief. Of all the radio stations in Lower Michigan, Louis had happened upon the weekend broadcast of Walter Bushman.

He reached down to turn the radio off, but then Bushman said something that gave him pause.

"The problem is duplicity. That starts with D and that rhymes with P and that stands for Prince."

Louis had to see where this was going.

"Just like that fast-talking Professor Harold Hill, Anthony Prince was a shyster, a hustler who sold tickets to heaven while he secretly wallowed in his own swamp of depravity."

Bushman launched into a litany of crimes and sins Anthony Prince had been alleged to have committed. Steele had done what he could to keep details of the case quiet until there was an official statement, so Bushman was left to make things up. Anthony's hookers had grown to dozens over the years, the murder of the boys had ballooned into sexual abuse of entire choirs, and the strangulation of his father had been reduced to an act of simple greed.

The first exit sign for I-127 had just come into view when Bushman started in on Violet. Louis braced himself.

"And then there's the long-suffering wife," Bushman said. "I've always said I don't have problems with the true believers as long as they leave the rest of us alone. So I need to say that Violet Prince did nothing wrong. She's just another victim here. She's a good woman. Don't ask me how I know, I just do. This woman deserves our sympathy, not our scorn."

Violet's face came to him, pained and wan.

I'll be okay.

That was the last thing she had said to him before Louis left to hunt down Anthony. By now, Violet had probably read all the news stories, and worse, watched the idiots on TV blathering about her husband's hookers and her marriage, as they posed the worst of all questions—how could the wife not know?

The turn-off to I-127 was coming up, the road that would set him on the northward path to Echo Bay and to Joe.

Damn it.

He let his exit go by and kept heading west. Grand Rapids wasn't far out of his way. A quick stop to see Violet, and he'd be back on the road north.

Just outside Kalamazoo, he stopped at a convenience store. When he showed the clerk his badge and gestured to the phone, the clerk quickly handed it over. He dialed Violet's home, letting it ring ten or eleven times before he gave up. Maybe she was at the cathedral. She probably wanted no part of the operations, but he suspected she would feel a duty to step up and at least try to keep the place running while the church council scrambled to get things under control.

He called Anthony's office and his secretary answered.

"I'm sorry, detective," the woman said. "Mrs. Prince was here this morning meeting with lawyers and the council members. But after she gathered up her husband's personal things from his office, she just bolted out of here."

"Bolted?"

"Yes. I asked her if she was okay and she said something strange. She said she had to go back."

"Go back? To where?"

"I don't know. That's all she said."

"Did she take anything with her? Maybe something she found in Anthony's office?"

A long pause. "Just an old Bible. I thought that was kind of odd."

"Why?"

"Well, she didn't have anything with her when she came in and Mr. Prince didn't keep a Bible in his office."

"You're sure?"

"Yes, sir. I worked for Mr. Prince for eight years, and I never saw a Bible in his office."

"How long ago did she leave?" Louis asked.

"A couple of hours."

Louis hung up and went back outside to his car. Maybe Violet had gone home and simply retreated in grief to her bedroom, ignoring the phone. But he didn't think so. Somehow it didn't seem like something she would do right now. That big, empty house would be too full of Anthony and all the hurt. And the thing about the Bible bothered him.

He got in the Mustang and started the engine. But he just sat there, thinking.

She said she had to go back . . .

Louis pulled a Michigan map from the glove box and unfolded it. It took him a minute to find the town. It was a faint dot, maybe forty miles south of where he was. It would add another two hours to his trip, putting him up in Echo Bay past dinner time.

Louis stuffed the map back in the glove box, and headed the Mustang back out onto the freeway, heading south instead of north.

It was a long shot, but he had to go. He had to make sure she was all right.

There was no nice Rotary Club welcome billboard or even a green state-issue sign to tell him where he was—just a plain white water tower emblazoned with VANDALIA. There was also no downtown to speak of, just one blinking traffic light, a small municipal building, a gas station, and a bar. He pulled into the bar and went in. The waitress hadn't heard of the Community Church of God, but she said that she when she was kid she used to play at an abandoned place on Water Street, out by Christiana Creek.

"It was just a wreck," she said. "But it had pretty windows. Could have been a church once."

Louis backtracked and hung a right on Water Street. He passed a small park and a scattering of wood bungalows and trailers, but then there was nothing but trees and finally a sign that said DEAD END.

He pulled to a stop, cut the engine and got out. He could hear the ripple of water and started toward it. At one time, there might have been a road but now it was just a rutted path overgrown with weeds. He emerged into a clearing and stopped.

He should have been surprised, but he wasn't. He was standing in front of a church.

Or what was left of one.

It was small, made of old clapboard that was once white but now weathered to gray. The short steeple had caved in on itself but the two goth-ic windows on the side were intact, just visible beneath a web of dead ivy. There was an old blue Chevy parked in the high, dead grass.

Louis went up the sagging wooden steps. The door was ajar, a rusted padlock hanging loose. He pushed the door open.

The inside was dim and had a funky smell, a mix of standing water, mold, and maybe nests from the animals that had taken refuge inside. The narrow aisle led between dull wooden pews and up to a simple altar where a single broken pendant lamp hung over a wood pulpit.

Violet was standing behind the pulpit, head down.

Louis hesitated, wondering if she was praying, but then she looked up. Her surprise at seeing him was fleeting, a slight widening of her eyes before she gave him the barest of smiles.

"Officer Kincaid," she said softly. "Come in, please."

Louis started toward her and heard a sound to his left. He turned to see Delia Arnold sitting in the corner of the back pew. The housekeeper was bundled in a plaid coat, her pink tote sitting next to her. She gave Louis a slow nod then looked down. As Louis passed the pew he saw she was holding an open Bible.

He continued up to the altar, stopping at the steps. Violet was wearing a beige raincoat, her long hair held back by a blue scarf. Her face was bare of makeup but the cold in the church had colored her cheeks pink.

"What are you doing here?" Violet asked.

It felt weird talking to her as she stood behind the pulpit. Violet didn't seem uncomfortable at all. In fact, Louis thought, she looked more at ease than he had ever seen her.

"I just wanted to make sure you were okay," Louis said.

"How did you know where to find me?" she asked.

"Just a hunch."

She smiled slightly.

Louis's eyes went up to the plain rafters, down across the puddles on the altar and finally back to Violet's face. A shadow crossed her face but was quickly gone.

"This was your father's church," Louis said.

Violet nodded. She closed the Bible on the pulpit and came out from behind it and paused on the first step. She looked around the church. Louis wondered what she was seeing—the rot and ruin or what it had once been, when she had been just a girl, barely old enough when she was married off to Anthony.

"This is the first time I have been back," Violet said. "I didn't have the courage before now. Delia convinced me it was time, so she brought me here. I didn't think . . ."

Her voice trailed off as her eyes went up to the windows. The sun streaming through the dead ivy left veined shadows on the wood floor.

"I didn't think it would be this hard," she said.

"To see how bad the church looks?" Louis asked.

She shook her head. "No," she said softly. "I didn't think it would be so hard to forgive."

Violet had said it in such a soft whisper, Louis wasn't sure he had heard what she had said, but then he understood.

"Anthony?" he asked.

Violet nodded.

Louis wasn't sure what to say. No words were coming because, for the life of him, he couldn't fathom why this woman needed to absolve Anthony of all the hurt he had created. She had a right to feel betrayed. She had a right to her anger.

She looked down at the Bible she was holding. "This was Anthony's Bible when he was young," she said. "He told me he had lost it a long time ago, but I found it locked in a drawer in his desk."

She looked back at the pulpit. "Anthony was eighteen when he gave his first sermon," she said softly. "I remember it so clearly. He had begged Jonas to let him do it, and finally Jonas agreed. It was for the Ash Wednesday service, and Anthony worked so hard on the sermon, rewriting it and rehearsing it. It was about repentance and turning your life around."

She paused, still looking at the pulpit. "When he got up here to deliver it, he . . . he just sort of froze. I was sitting in the back with Jonas and it was awful to watch. Anthony was stammering and wiping his face. People were whispering."

Violet paused again, looking toward the back of the church. "I looked over at Jonas sitting next to me, and his face was red. Then he got up. I was so afraid he was going to go up there and make Anthony sit down. But he did something even worse."

Louis knew what was coming.

"Jonas got up and walked out," Violet said. "He just turned his back on Anthony and walked out."

Louis remembered what Buddy had said to him. *Do you know what it feels like to have your father tell you that you're just a pile of dust?*

"I am trying to understand," Violet said. "I'm trying very hard to understand what happened, so I can forgive him."

Her eyes glistened. "But all I can seem to feel is pain. I have this hollow feeling in my stomach and this tightness right here," she said, touching her chest.

What did he tell her? That she had been hurt and what she was feeling was anger and that she had a right to it? An urge passed through Louis, a sudden urge to pull this woman into his arms and hold her.

He reached down and took Violet's hand. It was warm. She didn't pull away. For a long time, they just stood, hands interlaced. After a moment, Violet pulled her hand from his and moved away.

"Anthony's brother," she said softly. "Is he okay?"

"I think so."

"Does he need any money?"

Louis hesitated. "I don't think money means much to him."

Violet was quiet. "Does he have anyone?"

"Family? No, he's alone."

"I'd like to contact him," Violet said. "Do you think that would be all right?"

"I think Buddy might like that."

She stood there, cradling the Bible as her eyes wandered around the ruined church. She focused finally on the windows. They were dirty but not one pane was broken.

"What are you going to do now?" Louis asked.

"People here need a church," she said.

Louis looked up at the rafters. "There's a lot of damage," he said.

When she looked back at him, her eyes were bright with tears. "It can be repaired," she said.

Louis knew Violet was going to be all right. After everything was sorted out, he suspected she would turn control of the cathedral over to the board and step away. Maybe far enough to find herself again. As for that pain in her heart, he knew exactly what that felt like and he knew it would always be there. A memory came to him in that moment, a pastor back in that hot Mississippi Baptist church, something about Peter asking Jesus how many times you had to forgive someone who hurt you.

He couldn't remember the answer.

Louis looked up at the window. The sun was slanting in through the dead ivy. It was getting late.

"I have to go," he said.

Violet took a step back and smiled. "Thank you," she said.

Louis went down the steps and started down the aisle. Delia gave him a smile this time as he neared.

"Officer Kincaid?"

He turned back to see what Violet wanted.

"Go with God," she said.

Louis hesitated then nodded. "I'll try," he said.

He turned and went out the door. Outside, he paused. He could hear the rippling sound of water. But there was no sign of Christiana Creek anywhere nearby that he could see. He brought up a hand and pressed it to his chest. The tightness was still there—it always would be—but he could feel his heart beating stronger over it.

A Bible verse came to him. Nothing he had ever heard in any church but something he had seen on the sign that first day outside Saint Michaels.

The old is gone. The new is here.

Louis raised his face to the sun. That was something he knew he could believe in.

MEET PJ PARRISH

www.pjparrish.com

PJ PARRISH is the New York Times bestselling author of ten Louis Kincaid and Joe Frye thrillers. The author is actually two sisters, Kristy Montee and Kelly Nichols. Their books have appeared on both the New York Times and USA Today best seller lists. The series has garnered 11 major crime-fiction awards, and an Edgar® nomination. Parrish has won two Shamus awards, one Anthony and one International Thriller award. Her books have been published throughout Europe and Asia.

Parrish's short stories have also appeared in many anthologies, including two published by Mystery Writers of America, edited by Harlan Coben and the late Stuart Kaminsky. Their stories have also appeared in Akashic Books acclaimed DETROIT NOIR, and in Ellery Queen Magazine. Most recently, they contributed an essay to a special edition of Edgar Allan Poe's works edited by Michael Connelly.

Before turning to writing full time, Kristy Montee was a newspaper editor and dance critic for the Sun-Sentinel in Fort Lauderdale. Nichols previously was a blackjack dealer and then a human resources specialist in the casino industry. Kristy lives in Tallahassee Fla., and Traverse City, Mich. Kelly resides in Traverse City. The sisters were writers as kids, albeit with different styles: Kelly's first attempt at fiction at age 11 was titled "The Kill." Kristy's at 13 was "The Cat Who Understood." Not much has changed: Kelly now tends to handle the gory stuff and Kristy the character development. But the collaboration is a smooth one, thanks to lots of ego suppression, good wine, and marathon phone calls via Skype.